Lock's Earthly Maintenance

Lock Ferguson vs. The Aliens
Book 2

A Novel by
Jack Cullen

LOCK'S EARTHLY MAINTENANCE
Lock Ferguson vs. The Aliens – Book 2
Copyright © 2024 by Jack Cullen

All rights reserved. No part of this book may be used or reproduced in any manner whatsoever, without written permission, except in the case of brief quotations embedded in articles and reviews. For more information, please contact publisher at Publisher@EvolvedPub.com.

FIRST EDITION SOFTCOVER
ISBN-13: 979-8-89025-003-2

Editor: Robb Grindstaff
Cover Artist: Kris Norris
Interior Designer: Lane Diamond

www.EvolvedPub.com
Evolved Publishing LLC
Butler, Wisconsin, USA

Lock's Earthly Maintenance is a work of fiction. All names, characters, places, and incidents are the product of the author's imagination, or are used fictitiously. Any resemblance to actual events or persons, living or dead, is entirely coincidental.

Printed in Book Antiqua font.

Books by Jack Cullen

LOCK FERGUSON vs. THE ALIENS
Book 1: *Lock's Galactic Mess*
Book 2: *Lock's Earthly Maintenance*
Book 3: *Lock's Celestial Blunder* [2025]

RECOLLECTIONS OF A RUNE KNIGHT
Book 1: *Runes of Steel*
Book 2: *Runes of Blood*
Book 3: *Runes of Deception*

WHAT OTHERS ARE SAYING ABOUT...

LOCK'S GALACTIC MESS

"Author Jack Cullen's writing is witty and filled with humor, making this sci-fi tale a thoroughly entertaining read that fans of the likes of *Firefly* and *Star Trek* are likely to enjoy... I can't recommend it highly enough." ~ *Readers' Favorite Book Reviews, K.C. Finn (5 STARS)*

~~~

"Alien invasions have never been funnier than Jack Cullen's laugh-out-loud sci-fi novel, *Lock's Galactic Mess*. ...an exciting adventure that is not to be missed. In fact, it should be next on your reading list!" ~ *Readers' Favorite Book Reviews, David Korson (5 STARS)*

~~~

"The chuckles I had from Jack Cullen's humor, especially in the characters' often geeky referencing to movies in popular culture, the hyperbole action scenes, and all-round great storytelling technique, made for an enjoyable and relaxing read." ~ *Readers' Favorite Book Reviews, Paul Zietsman (5 STARS)*

What Others are Saying about...

RECOLLECTIONS OF RUNE KNIGHT

RUNES OF STEEL:
"Awesome read! Love the characters. The pop culture references were witty. Several clever twists. I adore the characters as they develop right in front of your eyes. I do love magic, and this was a fantastic read. Definitely worth the read. Thoroughly enjoyed it!" ~ *Sophie Ro*

RUNES OF BLOOD:
"WOW! I read the first book, *Runes of Steel*, in three days because I could not put it down. It actually ignited my love for reading too. I read this book in one day. I could not put it down and again, like with the first one, I was able to watch it like a movie in my mind while reading. It has action, humor, drama, and suspense that keeps you excited to turn the page to find out what will happen next!

The characters are likable and even relatable on a deeper level. The main character, Mike Brennan, is one tough SOB who has the will most of us strive for. All supporting characters have their own charm that allows you to invest in them (even the bad guys)!

I am greatly looking forward to the next book in this series and hope everyone who reads this book (and all Jack's Books) feels the magic I was able to feel." ~ *Monique Gisele of the Homewrecker Podcast*

RUNES OF DECEPTION:
"Jack, you evil genius you, I'm literally hanging by my fingernails on the edge of this incredible cliff you built. I'm so ticked that I know it's going to be a year or two till the next book. The wait is going to be killer." ~ *Zachary Ross*

Dedication

To Jocelyn. I'm so proud of you.

Chapter 1 –
In the Hoosegow

"I can explain all this, really!"

The police detective stared at me from across the table for a good thirty seconds before flipping open a file and studying the contents. "Stanley Kirby, born in Camden, Maine. No priors, no military training."

She looked up at me. "You weigh, what? A buck forty, soaking wet."

"That's about right, Detective Rogers." In order to hide from the government, KayCee, the alien currently taking up residence inside my head had created a new identity for me. We had also used my powers to shape my body. I was now skinny with long luxurious hair. New fingerprints too. A far cry from the bald, muscular guy I was six months ago. Even further away from the bald, fat man I had been before that. I was reasonably safe from detection, but I didn't want to spend any more time inside the police station than I needed.

"Careful, Loughlin Ferguson. She's trying to trip you up. I've seen this in your crime shows."

I ignored KayCee's mental communication. After having the alien stuck in my head for half a year, I had gotten good at that. "Why am I being held? I'm the good guy here. They were trying to rob a convenience store and were beating up on the clerk. He's an old man."

"Well, let's watch the footage and see why." She picked up a clicker from the table and turned on the TV mounted to the wall of the interview room. The footage from the store's security camera showed the four robbers pulled the clerk over the counter and onto the floor where they started kicking him. That was when I entered the store. The recording showed me entering and then went all static.

"I—"

She held up a finger, silencing me. The footage suddenly resumed with me standing in the middle of the store. It looked like a tornado had hit, and all the would-be robbers were strewn about like a child's abandoned toys. She dropped the clicker on the table and leaned back. "How do you explain that? Tell me how an alleged bookstore clerk can do all that to four hardened criminals?"

"Ah... I study martial arts!" I regretted it as soon as I said it, but it was the first thing to pop into my mind.

"Which one?"

A feeling of panic overtook me, and my mind went blank. I scrambled to remember the name of a martial art. *Any* martial art. "Tai... Chi..."

> *"Loughlin Ferguson, that is perhaps not the best choice. My understanding is you have used that excuse before, and it was unsuccessful."*

"Tai Chi? The slow-motion thing old people practice in the park?"

"Yeah, except, um, I did it really fast."

There was a knock at the door. Detective Rogers gave me another annoyed glare and scooped my fictional file before stepping out.

I glanced up at the surveillance camera. The red light on it suddenly stopped blinking. "Thank you."

> *"You're welcome. I also disabled the hidden microphone as well."*

"You're the best. How about we eavesdrop on what's going on." I concentrated and my hearing suddenly went up to eleven and I could hear the detective arguing.

"You're trying to tell me that skinny runt is military? Bull!"

A male voice I hadn't heard before answered her. "I don't know what to tell you, Linda. There are two members of the Space Force in the lobby, and they have paperwork that gives them custody. It's not like we have anything to charge the guy. He stopped a robbery, for cripe's sake."

"That's not good." I stood up and scanned the room. "Time to get out of here. KayCee, any ideas?"

> *"If we go out the door we came in, we will be confronted by the officers, and you already expressed your reluctance to fight law enforcement."*

"I'm not beating up some cops trying to do their jobs. Rogers has good instincts. She knew there was something off about us. A super-weaponized janitor with an alien in his head was just a little too far out of her experience."

"I tapped into the surveillance feeds for the station. On the other side of the wall to our right is an empty office and its door leads to a different hallway. One which is currently empty."

"That has promise." While my body currently looked scrawny, it still possessed the abilities given to me by an insane alien war criminal. One of those abilities was advanced strength. I slowly pressed my hand against the wall, breaking the sheetrock and creating a hole. I peered into the opening. "Not a support wall, just sheet rock and two-by-fours. Good, I was afraid there would be concrete or steel in between. While I'm doing the great escape, why don't you give us a new look."

"Any preference?"

"Something unremarkable but very different then our current appearance." I ignored the tingling sensation that signified KayCee had triggered my body's morphing power. I took a couple of steps back and launched myself. My body crashed through the wall and before I could stop, I hit a fifties-era heavy wooden desk. My momentum caused me to flip over, landing on the floor in a sprawl. "Well, that was undignified."

I stood up and brushed off the sheetrock powder. The skin tone of my hands had become significantly darker. I glanced at a picture frame on the wall and studied my reflection. My long hair had been replaced by curly black hair cut close to my head. A bushy mustache had found a home under my nose. "KayCee, my features have taken on a rather Hispanic look."

"Yes. As requested, I gave you a very different appearance."

"This feels uncomfortably close to blackface."

"Perhaps we should discuss the social nuances of your society when we are not escaping from the police."

"Good point." I pulled off my jacket and turned it inside out. I had bought it because it was reversible. Instead of the black and tan tartan pattern, it now sported a moss green look. I zipped it up so the tartan wouldn't show. My jeans and sneakers were common enough that they wouldn't stand out. "Is the hallway clear?"

"Just a moment."

I moved over to the door, resting my hand on the knob.

"Go!"

I slipped into the hallway and started walking.

"Other way."

I did an about-face. "Now where?"

"*End of the hallway and take the stairs down one flight. Turn right and keep going until you see the lobby. I'm blanking the cameras as we go.*"

I followed her directions. I was halfway down the stairs when an alarm went off.

"*They have discovered we are gone.*"

"Yeah, I gathered that."

"*This is not good, Loughlin Ferguson. I had hoped for more time.*"

"As long as they don't lock down the building, it should work for us. They'll be trying to empty out the lobby. This is a municipal building—there are other offices here than just the police station. They'll want to make sure any innocents are clear."

"*Are you sure?*"

"Well, I'm basing this off of thousands of hours watching movies and TV shows so... no." A large stream of people entered the lobby the same time I did. Lines formed at checkpoints where officers compared what I assumed was a picture of me to the people trying to leave. I entered a line and when I finally approached, the officer in charge of my line quickly waved me through.

I stepped out onto the street and forced myself to walk away at a casual pace. I pulled an earpiece out of my pocket and stuck in my ear to give the appearance I was talking on the phone. "Well, we going to need to move again. Do you think it's safe to swing by the apartment and grab our stuff first?"

"*It should be safe. There was nothing connecting us to it. Your license shows a Maine address.*"

"Still, let's approach carefully. Check the area camera and whatnot."

"*Is there a reason we need to go back? We can just buy new things when we get to our new location.*"

"That's getting old. I'd like to actually keep some of the stuff we keep buying. Besides, someone is eventually going to notice you keep diverting funds out of the bank accounts of criminals and then we'll have mob guys and cartel people after us as well."

"*Only Tavish Ferguson would have had a chance of figuring it out.*"

I felt a pang of sadness at her mention of my cousin but bit back what I was about to say as a black van pulled up and stopped at the intersection I was headed to. "Uh-oh. I've seen that trick before! That's how they tried to get Kreb."

"What do you mean?"

I whirled around expecting to see secret agent government types standing behind me, ready to push me into the van. I was wrong.

"Hey, Lock!"

"Stella?" Standing in front of me and waving was Stella Johansen, my former roommate and still best friend. Someone who was supposed to be hiding out from the government on a tropical island.

"Loughlin Ferguson! Watch out!"

Before I could overcome the shock of seeing Stella, she placed the barrel of a futuristic gun against my head and pulled the trigger.

Chapter 2 –
The Offer

I woke up with a splitting headache. However, considering my so-called best friend just shot me in the head, just waking up was a win. I slowly opened my eyes, slamming them back shut as the light in the room triggered a new wave of pain. "I thought I didn't get hangovers anymore. What happened?"

"Stella Johansen used an energy weapon that disrupted our synaptic connection and rendered both of us unconscious. I came back to awareness just before you did."

"So, she wasn't trying to kill us then."

"I do not believe that was her objective."

"Still the worse roommate ever." I opened my eyes in increments, slowly adjusting to the light. We were on a cot in the corner of a room. The walls were made of steel, and the only visible door made bank vaults look puny. A polished steel mirror was mounted on the back of the door. In the corner opposite us was a security camera. A steel table was bolted to the center of the floor, flimsy plastic chair on either side. "This doesn't look good. Pretty sure this is how ALF went out."

"Actually, they made a wrap-up movie later on. But, yes, I understand your point."

The door opened, and a woman in her midsixties entered. She wore a business suit, and her steel gray hair was swept up in an *I mean business* bun. She placed a folder on the table and sat in the chair facing me. "Good day, Mister Ferguson. Would you and Protector KayserCeenarlos care to take a seat?"

"That does not bode well for us."

I got off the cot and moved to the plastic chair on my side of the table. Once seated, I had a bit of a déjà vu feeling. This wasn't all that different from being interrogated by Detective Rogers. Except I hadn't been worried the detective wanted to experiment on me. "And you be?"

"Angie Goodall. I'm an attorney with the Justice Department. Today I'll be also representing the White House and the United States Space Force. It was thought best to limit the amount of people who know your... circumstances."

"So, this is an interrogation?" I managed to keep my fear out of my voice.

"No, Mister Ferguson. It's a pitch."

"Excuse me?"

"Colonel Brennan's after-action report was very thorough, and we know you basically saved the world. Your country is not ungrateful, sir." Goodall folded her hands in front of her as she spoke. Her posture was so ramrod straight it made *my* back hurt.

"Then why kidnap me off the street? And where is Stella?"

"Master Sergeant Johansen is waiting nearby. It was thought best to have a third party explain things to you first, as you may be upset with how we made contact."

"Ya think?"

"As to why we made contact in the manner we did, you have not made it easy to speak with you. We suspect you believe we wish to capture the two of you for study. I assure you, that is not the case. Since you continued to avoid any normal attempt to contact you, we were forced to... get creative."

"Okay, fine. I'm here. What do you want to say."

"Careful, Loughlin Ferguson. We should not anger these people until we can assess the situation better."

"We wish to offer Protector KayserCeenarlos sanctuary in the United States. It is our understanding that she is stranded here. We would like to offer her a home. In return, we hope she would be willing to aid us in a few things."

"You want her starcraft."

Goodall's head inclined slightly in acknowledgment. "We understand that's a big ask. So, instead of making that part of the agreement, we want to develop a relationship first. Work together to protect our planet from dangers. Teach us about what awaits us out among the stars. Advance our knowledge in nonmilitary ways. Medicine for example. In return, we will provide her with a safe place to live and perhaps even find a way to reunite her with her people."

"Interesting. Do you think she is telling the truth."

"No. I'm calling BS." I leaned forward and sneered at the lawyer. "Why would the government wish to give away their golden goose?"

"In order to take our place among the stars, we will need allies," the lawyer told me. "Her people could be those allies. Such a partnership is worth much more than you realize."

"Then why do you want her starcraft?" I leaned back. One can only sneer so long.

"If the starcraft was in our possession, we would of course, reverse engineer it. It would even the playing field considerably. Don't you think?"

"What I think is that her people would be very upset that you plan on stealing their tech."

"Perhaps at first. But we think they'll get over it. After all, it's only fair. Her people *did* invade our sovereign space and have been stealing from our sun."

"Hmmm. She does have a point."

"Whose side are you on?"

Goodall frowned. "What do you mean? I told you who I represent."

"Not you." I tapped the side on my head. "Different conversation."

"Ah, yes. That leads me to an additional offer. How would KayCee... May I call her KayCee? Protector KayserCeenarlos is a bit of a mouthful."

"That would be acceptable."

"She said it's okay."

"Excellent." Goodall's frown changed to a smile. "How would KayCee like to have a physical body again."

That got both our attentions. With a few bumps and bruises along the way, KayCee and I had managed to get along. That being said, both of us sharing the same body was no picnic, KayCee was reduced to a passenger for the most part and I longed for the days where I could take a pee and not know she was staring out of my eyes. "How is that possible?"

"Before we get into that, do you have the control orb for the starcraft?"

"No." Technically that was true.

"What happened to it?"

"We lost it in space fighting Kreb. I don't know if it drifted off into space or burned up in reentry, but we don't have it." That part was a complete and blatant lie. "Let's get back to the KayCee having a body again thing."

"There are two options. The first is a member of the Space Force who was injured in the line of duty. She is in a coma and has no brain activity. She has no family, and she donated her body to science. She is only being kept alive by medical equipment and it's scheduled to be turned off."

"Absolutely not!"

"Why not? She donated her body to science. What could be more sciencey than aliens?" I asked. Goodall stayed silent, realizing I was talking to KayCee.

"Are you an organ donor?"

"Yes."

"Would you want someone operating your body after you are gone. Eating with your mouth, having sex with your – "

"Yeah, I get it," I interrupted her. "But it's different though. I just signed up for them to use my body parts to save lives. She signed up to have her body used for science. They do all sort of crazy things with those bodies. Some of them are even displayed in a museum exhibit."

"And how did you feel on seeing that?"

I looked up at Goodall who was waiting patiently and sighed. "Option One is a no-go. It's too disrespectful."

She nodded. I thought I saw a glimpse of approval in her eyes as she marked it down in her folder. "That leaves us with option two."

"Which is?"

"We recovered two bioforms in the Roswell crash back in 1947. Neither work, we don't know what happened to the aliens operating them. To be fair, it's more like one bioform. The second is practically just spare parts. We are willing to offer them to KayCee."

"That is a much better offer."

"What? How? What if one of your people died in them. How is that okay, but coma girl isn't?" I waved my hand. "I'm sorry." I regretted it as soon as I said it.

"A biosuit is just a device. It is as if I am driving your car after you died, as opposed to flaying your dead body and walking around in your skin."

"Okay that was graphic. But I get your point."

"I have discovered that is the route I have to take with you sometimes. Tell them I am willing to give them some

technological advancements in exchange for what they offer but I am not giving access to Quiet Contemplation or reveal anything that could hurt or betray my people. This will be contingent on what they have planned for you."

"Okay, we have a winner. Some sharing of advanced tech, but no access to her spacecraft," I told Goodall. "So, what about me. How do I fit into your plans?"

"Oh, that's simple. We want you to save the world... again."

Chapter 3 –
The Bargaining Stage

"*What?*" I practically jumped out of my chair. "What happened now?"

"We have reason to believe there is another alien race on earth, one that does not have our best interests at heart."

"Who?"

"I can't tell you that. It's classified."

"Then why... Oh, nice. You can't tell me until you've recruited me, right? Gave me just enough to spark my curiosity. Dangling out there like a carrot."

"Did it work?"

I stared at her for a full minute before finally sighing. "Fine, give me the pitch."

"We want you to enlist in the US Space Force."

"In what, a Combat Janitor Unit?"

Goodall gave me a small smile. "In a manner of speaking. We want you in a specialized unit that could use those new abilities of yours."

> *Loughlin Ferguson, we should hear them out. After all they have not strapped us down onto a gurney yet. Stella Johansen has joined them and neither of us believe she would truly betray us. Perhaps this offer is legitimate.*

It wasn't a horrible idea. I sometimes regretted not joining the military when Stella did. Being a janitor gives you a lot of time to wonder about the roads not taken. Plus, the idea that the government had our backs was appealing. Even if said government wanted to throw us into the thick of it. Still, if we were going to do this, I wanted the biggest bang for my buck. "No way."

"Excuse me?" Goodall tilted her head.

"I'm not enlisting."

"Why not? Your friend Stella did, and she got bumped up several spots."

"Which she deserved since she was drummed out on that stupid *don't ask, don't tell* nonsense way back when. But I want a commission, not an enlistment. I think colonel would be a good rank."

"Absolutely not!" she said flatly.

"Why shouldn't I? I have a bachelor's degree and while I'm past the age limit, I'm thinking I qualify for a waiver, all thinks considered."

Goodall, flipped through her folder. "It's an online degree."

"Don't be knocking online degrees. They've come a long way."

"Not back when you got yours. It says here, the *school,* and I use that word lightly, folded after the owner-slash-dean went to prison for tax fraud and embezzlement." She flipped the folder shut. "Your diploma isn't worth the paper it's printed on, but even if it was, it's in film studies..."

"So what? You guys made John Ford a commander in the Navy!"

"It was the Navy Reserve during World War II. He was already a famous movie director, and they wanted him to head up the Photographic Unit for the Office of Strategic Services. We don't want you to take pictures for us."

"You know he was part of D-day? Filmed the first wave to land on Omaha Beach?"

"I believe I heard that, yes." She looked a bit frazzled.

"Got a purple heart after getting shot in the arm."

"Can we please stop talking about John Ford?" Goodall pinched the bridge of her nose like she had suddenly developed a headache.

"You are a mean man."

I hid my grin. Being in the military was a hell of a lot better than being hunted by it, and the pay had to be way beyond what I made as a janitor. But that didn't mean I wasn't going to get the best deal I could out of it. "Look, you give direct commissions all the time for lawyers and doctors because they have special skills and training. Well, so do I."

"That's at a first lieutenant or captain rank."

"Fine, I'll take captain, considering that aside from my unique abilities that you seem to need desperately, I also saved the Earth and didn't even get a *good job* sticker to hang on my fridge."

Goodall abruptly stood up. "Give me a minute."

"Of course." I leaned back and put my feet up on the table after she left. "That means, they'll do it."

"You seem very sure."

"It's the same as buying a car. She's pretending to talk to an imaginary boss. She'll be back in a minute with the paperwork. I bet they had both enlistment and commissioned papers already filled out. All they need to do is put in the rank."

The door opened and Liam Brennan strode in. "Get your damn feet off my table!"

I nearly fell off the chair struggling to comply. When I had last seen him, he had been a lieutenant colonel in the Space Force. From the rank insignia on his uniform, he had been bumped up to full colonel since then.

"Congrats on the promotion," I said.

"Are you really trying to leverage the United States Space Force?" He stared down at me with a scowl.

I scrambled to my feet. "Hey, you guys are going to ask me to risk my life again. Aren't I entitled to ask for a few things?"

"I guess." He suddenly smiled, proving the scowl as a lie. "Good to see you again. How have you been?"

I shook the hand he offered. "You know, the usual. Hiding out, dodging you guys."

He gestured at me. "What's all this? You identifying as Hispanic now?"

"Last minute disguise when escaping the police."

"Don't you think it's... a little bit inappropriate?"

"That's what I said! It wasn't my idea. KayCee did it on the run."

"How long doesn't it take you to change back?"

"With KayCee pushing the buttons. Not long."

Give me a minute.

"That reminds me. I want to keep my beard," I told the colonel.

"No way. It's out of regs."

"Well, That's a deal-breaker then. I know you guys give beard waivers these days." I could feel my body shifting back to my real form. Well, my post-active powers form. Lock 2.0, so to speak.

"That's for medical and religious exemptions."

"It's part of my religion."

"Strange, I don't remember you being a Sikh."

"Lockism requires me to have a beard!"

"Really, you're resting this argument on a religion you made up as a joke?" He raised an eyebrow.

"Who's to say which religions are made up and which ones are real?"

"Me, that's who."

"Come on, Liam. I've had a beard my entire adult life. I'd be off balance without one."

"How quick does it take you to grow one."

"I dunno, couple of minutes." I glanced at the mirror bolted on the door. I had been an out of shape, overweight couch potato before KayCee activated the abilities a mad alien war criminal had given me. Lock 2.0 was still average height but built like an Olympic athletic. My comb-over was gone, replaced with a shaved scalp look and even my beard had taken on a longer, sleeker, more menacing look. While I could now grow a full head of hair, I only did it with disguises. With my real body, it felt fake, like I was wearing a wig or something.

"Then have it off duty," the big colonel told me. "But be clean shaven when in uniform."

"Split the difference. Beard when I'm in fatigues, no beard in class A's."

"Your mixing branch uniforms, not to mention decades. The Air Force stopped issuing fatigues in the '80s." He gestured to what he was wearing. "This is a combat utility uniform. And it's service dress uniform, not class A's."

"Whatever, you know what I meant. Come on, all the special operators have beards — I've seen pictures."

"That's in the field, and when appropriate."

"No joke, this is a deal-breaker. No beard, no Lock."

We locked eyes. "Off duty only. Otherwise, no commission."

I studied his face. There was zero giveaway. Not a guy I wanted to play poker with. I finally sighed. "Fine."

There was a knock and Goodall stepped in with some paperwork. As she laid them on the table in front of me, Stella slipped in behind her. My face must have given me away, because Brennan shook his head. "You two can hash your shit out later. There is something more important we have to do first."

"Like what?" I asked as I glared at Stella over his shoulder.

"Raise your right hand, you idiot."

"Oh! Right."

Chapter 4 –
The Return of Stella

After I was sworn in, Goodall swept up the documents. Ones, I had studied very carefully before signing, mind you. She handed me a copy and shook my hand. "Good luck, Captain. I'm sure we'll meet again."

Stella narrowed her eyes as Goodall left. "Captain? What's this about?"

"Don't you mean, what's this about, sir?"

Brennan shook his head. "Not until you graduate fork and knife school."

"You made him a captain?" bellowed Stella.

I ignored her and eyed Brennan suspiciously. "What the hell is *fork and knife school*?"

The colonel gave me a big smile, obviously enjoying my surprise. "You have to attend OTS-A, The Officer Training School Abbreviated. It's a requirement for a direct commission. You know that thing you just forced us to give you? Relax, it's only five weeks and just teaches you customs and standards."

"Wait, if you need me to save the world, why are you sending me to a five-week school on how to make my bed properly?"

"We don't have enough intel to act right now. Hopefully, we will when you return. We also need time to come up with a way to insert you." Brennan informed me. "There will be time for all that later. Johansen, take him to the dining hall for food, then show him his quarters."

"Yes, sir." That was shocking. I always knew Stella had been in the military, but this was far from the booze-swilling, wife-stealing, bar brawler that I had lived with for so many years. "Let's go, loser."

Ah, there she is.

"I'm sorry, what do you mean?" replied KayCee to my errant thought.

I managed to keep my thoughts separated from her for the most part, but every once in a while my internal narrative leaked over. It's why I preferred to answer her out loud. "Nothing."

Stella tilted her head, realizing who I was speaking to. "Hey, KayCee. How's things?"

"Neither one of us is talking to you right now. Just show us our room."

"Seriously?" She gestured out the door and I followed down a corridor with painted cement walls. Old photos of WWII planes were the only decorations. "You kept evading us. It was the only way to track you down. Do you think I liked zapping you?"

"Yes! Yes, I do!"

"Well, maybe a little bit." She grinned.

We passed a window. Looking out of it, I could see nothing but trees.

"Where are we anyway?"

"You're going to love this. Remember Ducharme Airfield?"

"No. Wait, maybe." It took me a minute, but I remembered there had been a World War II Army Air station called that. "We're in New Hampshire?"

"Yup. About thirty minutes from home."

"Oh, come on! I can finally leave that place and you guys brought me back?" Part of the programming the alien called Kreb had put in my head was to stay close to home. I had spent my entire life in a hundred-mile radius. "Hold on, I thought Ducharme was just a grass field and some dilapidated buildings. Wasn't it just used as a bombing range?"

"Pretty much, but it still belonged to the Air Force. A couple of years ago they turned it into satellite support and research and development. Once the Space Force was created, it got transferred over and became Ducharme Space Force Station. Officially the base is under Space Delta 1. In reality, it belongs to Delta Black."

"That's a bit confusing." I shook my head.

"You are now part of the secret alien investigation division of Space Force called Delta Black. But if anyone asks, you're part of Space Delta 1, got it?"

"Sure. Maybe this knife and fork school is a pretty good idea after all."

We walked into a dining hall. There were a few uniformed people, but it was mostly empty. We got in line, and both got enough food for three people. The cook gave us an odd look but didn't say anything. Both our bodies had been changed dramatically, but we still needed energy, and that meant more food than most people. Though I had learned to convert energy directly in a pinch, I still preferred eating as a way to refuel.

After we sat, Stella leaned over and punched me in the arm.

"Ow! What was that for?"

"You broke up with Jeopardy in a letter? What are you? Five?"

"It wasn't an easy choice. I was afraid if I went to you guys, the military would follow me to you. I thought it was safer if KayCee and I just kept moving."

She frowned at me. "You don't think Jeopardy and I should have had say in the matter?"

"I already knew what you would say, and I'd have dragged you down with me."

"News flash." She waved her fork around. "They got me first."

"How *did* they get you? I thought that nudie resort where you were hiding out was in a country that didn't have extradition?"

"It didn't. I was all set there, bartending at a tiki bar surrounded by naked women of the lesbian persuasion, my second favorite thing in the world."

"The first, being straight married women you can talk into bed."

"It's like you've known me my whole life." She grinned. "Then the government tricked me by exploiting my only weakness."

"Booze."

"No, my other, only weakness."

"Guns?"

She sighed. "My other, other, only weakness."

"More naked women?"

"Bingo!"

"You really need to look up the definition of *only*." I finished one of my plates and moved to the next. "So, what happened?"

"Picture it. There I am, working at the bar, and this golden tanned, dark blond goddess with blue eyes and a Markie Post hairstyle comes up, wearing nothing but a canvas messenger bag."

"You do love your *Night Court*."

"Right? So, I ask her what does she want and she says, 'You.'" Stella took a gulp of her drink, wiping her mouth with her sleeve. "And then she slaps down re-enlistment papers on the bar. '''And so does Uncle Sam!'"

I coughed up food from laughing and had to take a drink to clear my throat. "Oh God! That's funny. What then?"

"Well, after I stopped laughing, she explained that they were not hunting us, but they needed my skills to save the world and would I re-enlist with a nice bump in rank. She was able to persuade me over dinner."

"Wait, they pimped her out?"

"Absolutely not. She made it very clear it was just dinner, and it was." I just stared at Stella until she ducked her head to hide a smirk. "Well, I may have reconnected with her months later, after I was back in, but that had nothing to do with her recruitment mission."

"So, you get seduced, but I get electrocuted? That sounds fair."

"Quit whining. It's only electrocution if you die. Besides, it was Jeopardy's idea. She said you wouldn't come quietly. Or maybe it was that you deserved it. I forget."

"Hold on, they got her too?"

"She was hiding out at the resort when I got approached. Not having near the fun time that I was, I might add. Anyway, we discussed options and decided to give it a shot. Brennan vouching for it being a legit offer cinched it."

My fork stopped halfway to my mouth, "Wait, Jeopardy's here?"

"Right now, she's off on a mission, but yeah, she's assigned to the same base as us."

"Really?" I sat up a little straighter.

"She seeing someone now. Ya know, cause some idiot dumped her with a *Dear John* letter."

"Oh." At Stella's words, I quickly deflated.

"But she gave me something for you when she heard you were being brought in." Stella reached into a pocket and pulled out a folded envelope. My name was written on it in Jeopardy's handwriting. I tore it open and unfolded the paper inside.

FUCK YOU.

"Okay, that's fair, I guess." I really liked Jeopardy, but it had been six months since I sent her that letter. I had moved on.

"Keep telling yourself that, Loughlin Ferguson."

"Shut up."

Chapter 5 –
Alias Smith & Williams

Aside from being stuck in Alabama, the training was a breeze. Brennan had me go through it under the alias Harold Smith. I made a smart-ass comment about John being taken and when I got to the base, the first name had been changed to Dick. I was the only one in the class that got called by their first name, and it was said with a lot of relish. I was also the only one in the class who wasn't a doctor or a lawyer. When asked by classmates, I said I was a Goa'uld chaplain. Not a lot of Stargate fans because nobody got the joke, and by the time we graduated, everyone thought I was Muslim. And that was *after* I got rid of the beard. I was sure I was going to hear it from Brennan when I got back.

After graduation and a brief stop to pick something up, I was flying back commercial. The military has a million planes but for some reason I had to fly back in a budget airliner. At least I had a window seat.

I had fallen asleep with my headphones on and jerked awake when I heard my name. My real one.

"Loughlin Ferguson."

Now fully awake, I glanced at the woman to my right. Prince Valium had sent her into dreamland at the beginning of the flight and based on the line of drool running off her chin, she was still there. "What do you think? Is she faking?"

"Let's find out."

I felt a tingling as KayCee activated my powers. I could hear the women's heartbeat. It was slow enough that unless she was a yogi, she was out. In fact, it was so slow, I was a little concerned for her. "Okay, we can talk."

"About time."

"I know it hasn't been that easy to speak to you. Even trying to speak in code the few times I was able to make phone calls during training. Who knew I was going to have a roommate."

"It could have been worse."

"Yeah, that was actually a nice set up. I thought it was going to be an open bay barracks."

"Moving on, I had some success using the abilities you mimicked from Tavish to worm into some of the Space Force's systems."

"What did you find out?"

"It appears to be legitimate. They shipped two damaged bioforms from Area 51 to Ducharme Space Station last week. Question: should it not have to be in outer space in order to be called a space station?"

"I would think so, but that's the military for you. Anything else?"

"You and Stella Johansen are not showing up in any of the military files under your real names. They have you down as Dick Smith and she is listed as Barbie Williams."

"Barbie?" I chortled. "Brennan is totally behind that."

"Your official assignment is overseeing custodial services for the base."

"Bastard!" I stroked my chin, missing my beard. "He wouldn't be messing with us if it was a trap. Thoughts?"

"I do not believe that Colonel Brennan is being untruthful."

"Yeah, I think it's on the level, too. Have you found anything on what the mission is?" I smiled at a flight attendant who walked by.

"A little, and it was not easy to figure out. I had to look for what was not there."

"Let's speed this up. The plane's about to touch down. What did you learn?"

"They are worried about an alien infiltration of the government and certain corporations."

"Any truth to it?

"Still looking. If there is, the aliens are covering their tracks enough that I could not find them."

"KayCee, any chance this involves your people?"

"I do not believe it is my people. That is not how we do things."

"What about the other countries on your planet?"

"Unlikely. There is no reason for any of them to do so. Should I attempt to access the systems at Ducharme Station? Perhaps see what I can find in their files when we get back to there."

"I'd rather not commit treason on my first day. Let's show them a little faith and see where it takes us."

"Agreed."

The plane landed at Manchester airport. The one in New Hampshire, not the one in the land of tea and crumpets. We disembarked to find Stella waiting for us. Like me, she was wearing civilian clothes. "You are not my taxi driver."

"Yeah, yeah. How was pretty-boy school?"

"You missed a good time. There were pretty women there too." I headed toward the baggage, forcing her to catch up to me.

"The whole thing's a joke. You should have gone to basic. Done it for real. Not that this branch has a real basic training, but anything's better than that resort you went to." She grabbed my duffel bag off the conveyor belt and tossed it to me. I swung it over my shoulder and headed for the door.

She led me to a nondescript black SUV. I looked it over. "Well, this is boring. Where's your Jeep?"

"It's a work car. Get in, I have to take you to a briefing. The timetable just sped up."

It might have looked boring, but the SUV had some pep to it. She gunned it as soon as we were on the highway, and we were flying down the road. "Aren't you worried about getting pulled over?"

"No, it's registered as FBI and has a blue light package. I just flip them on and keep going."

"I shudder at the idea of you with so much power." I gripped the door handle a little tighter. The mile markers were beginning to look like a picket fence, to quote an old song. She got us there in no time and pulled up to the gate. The guard peered at us as she handed him two ID cards.

While he studied them, another guard went around our vehicle with some sort of electronic device while a third guard had a dog sniff around the SUV. "Heightened security?"

"No, this is normal." The guard handed her back the cards and she gunned it. With one hand on the wheel, she held out one of the cards to me. "Here, this is yours."

I took it and looked it over. It was what I assumed was a standard Space Force identification card. It had my actual name and rank on it, with a chip embedded with it. I'd just stuck it in my wallet as she pulled up to a nondescript building.

Five more security checks including a retinal scan and, believe it or not, drawing blood. Eventually we wound up in a conference room. It was just the two of us sitting at a table that could hold twenty people. There were monitors on each wall and some fancy-looking telephones and computers. "Is anyone else showing up?"

Before Stella could answer, the door opened, and Brennan walked in. Stella stood up and I followed a few seconds behind. He waved us back down and sat across from us. "How was your time at the training school?"

"Great until everyone started calling me Dick."

"See where smart-ass comments get you." He took a clicker and turned on a monitor. It showed a building made of steel and glass. "This is the headquarters of Murtaugh Solutions Unlimited, or MSU. It's located in Nevada. MSU is a contractor with the government for satellites and aerospace."

"Colonel," I interjected. "Anyone with a TV has heard of MSU. They're crushing it in the civilian space race, leaving all the bored billionaires in their dust."

Well, they're a key player in the Ironsides Project."

"Which is?" I asked.

"An important project." He clicked through a bunch of slides showing the testing grounds and runways.

"That I don't need to know about?"

"Not at this time, no. The problem is that we think they and several other corporations with government connects have been compromised."

"Russia or China?" I played dumb.

"Do you really think we would need you for them?" He put the clicker down on the table.

"So, you think alien? Not KayCee's people?"

"We don't know, but there have been several accidents there recently with people left in comas."

"And you don't think it's unsafe working conditions?"

"All were key people in the project. We are going to send you in undercover, to snoop around."

I frowned. "Wouldn't it make more sense to get an actual spy to do that?"

"We did."

My frown deepened. "Accident resulting in a coma?"

"Two agents and they both have zero brain scans."

"Oh shit!"

He gestured to Stella. "Senior Master Sergeant Johansen is already in place at the Nevada facility. We're going to insert you as well."

I leaned back in my chair. "I don't want to tell you your job, but wouldn't Jeopardy be a better fit for this? She could just slip in and start scanning people."

"We considered it, but she's on a vital mission of a different kind and I don't want to pull her unless I absolutely have to. Also, until we know how minds are being affected, I don't want to expose our resident telepath."

"What about the fact that I have KayCee riding around in my brain?"

"We've been over this. I do not reside in your brain. I am sort of everywhere inside you."

Brennan shook his head. "The plan is that KayCee won't be going with you at first. She'll stay here at the base. Well, that is, if we can get her into one of the bioforms. Once you've been in long enough and we don't think you're being watched, then we'll bring her in."

"Ah..." I ran a hand across where my beard used to be. "I sort of need KayCee."

"What?" Stella's face took on a puzzled look. "Why? I would have thought you'd have jumped at the idea of having some quiet time inside your head. I mean, when she talks, there has to be a weird echo effect thing with all that empty space inside your skull."

I nodded wisely at Brennan. "I see now why you sent Stella in. No brain to erase."

Brennan narrowed his eyebrows and we both fell silent. "Explain why you need KayCee."

"Kreb didn't just transform me into a superweapon. He set it up so he would be inside my head, controlling me. Because of that, my powers are easier to activate for her then when I do it myself."

Brennan was big, very big, and his chair creaked in protest as he shifted in it. "But you can use your abilities?"

"So-so." I waggled my hand. "You ever see that show from the '80s? Aliens give the guy the red suit that gives him superpowers?"

"Yeah, Greatest American something or other."

"Right, he couldn't use his powers well because he'd lost the suits handbook. Well, KayCee is my handbook."

"Huh! Sounds more like she's your combat systems officer," Brennan mused.

"I dunno, what's that?"

"They gave you captain bars?" Stella groaned.

I shrugged. "The point is. When she's riding shotgun, my powers are smooth and flawless."

Thank you.

"When it's just me, it's kind of hit or miss."

Brennan shook his head, a disgusted look on his face. "This is why I argued not to send you in this soon. We need time to train you and figure out what you can and can't do."

"Brass overruled you?"

"It happens." He sighed and handed me the folder in front of him. "We'll just have to make do. Here's your legend for the mission."

I flipped open the folder and leaned forward. "Oh, this *is* bullshit!"

Chapter 6 –
Familiar Roles

My eyes ran over the paperwork in front of me. "This is my real name and info!"

Brennan grinned. "It's perfect. You have fifty years of backstory and no connections to the military. Stella got a job there working security as herself and it makes sense that she would get her childhood friend a job there."

"As a damn janitor? No way. I just escaped that life. I'm not going back to mopping floors and cleaning toilets."

"You're not. You going to be an undercover Space Force officer posing as a maintenance man. The fact that you know the ins and outs of the job is just icing on the cake."

I flipped through the paperwork. "I'm not even hired. This says I'm scheduled for an interview."

"It's fine." Stella punched me in the arm. "I've been there for months. The person interviewing you is on my bowling team. She's already said that as long as you pass the drug and background tests, the job is yours."

"Why do I need to pass a drug test to empty trash cans?"

"Why do you care?" Brennan asked back with a suspicious look.

"No, no, nothing like that. I just... Never mind." I slumped in my seat.

"You know what's the best part?" Stella grinned.

"What?" I hated to ask.

"I've got a two-bedroom apartment there. You don't have to look for a place. We can be roommates again!"

"I hate my life," I muttered.

Brennan grabbed the clicker and moved to another image. It showed a guy in his late sixties, maybe early seventies, wearing a dirty lab coat. He had a few wild wisps of hair left on his head and a messy goatee. "This is Doctor Edward Kemp."

"More like Doctor Unkempt," I mumbled.

"Funny you should say that. The doctor's personal appearance changed dramatically after a weekend away. And he's associating with people in other areas of the project that he's never really done so before. These others also have had some shifts in personality. Kemp is the head of research for the MSU section of the project. He's who we want you to focus on first. Part of your job will be to clean his office. We need you to search it and report back anything unusual to Stella."

"Um, I'm not exactly trained for that you know. Aren't you afraid I'll miss something?"

"Terrified of it, actually. So, you'll be having some down and dirty training on that later today. The important thing is to just do the job for a week or so. Then start snooping around. Let them get you used to you first." He started clicking through other photos. "These others are secondary persons of interest. There's a packet with their info in your room for you to study."

"Let's say I find out they're all being controlled by a bunch of Kreb wannabes? Then what?"

"It will depend on the circumstances. But most likely we'll surveil them until we know who all of them are and then we'll move to capture them." His phone buzzed and he looked down at a text. "Damn, we're going to have to cut this short. Sergeant, bring them to the lab where the bioform is and see about getting KayCee transferred over."

"I have to say. I am excited about this. No disrespect to you, Loughlin Ferguson, but I would very much like to have my own body, even if it's only a bioform."

"No, I get it. I'm very happy for you." I tapped the side of my head, so Stella and the colonel knew who I was talking to.

Brennan stood up. "Captain, your training is scheduled in two hours, and you'll be flying out at 0500. Make sure you study your packet and turn it in in the morning. Under *no* circumstances does it leave the base."

"Understood." I scrambled to my feet, only a few seconds behind Stella. As he strode out of the room, I glanced at Stella. "He's all business these days, huh?"

"It's the environment. Everything on base, I mean station, is always stuffier. He's a lot looser in the field."

"I get that the Space Force is new and has a lot to prove, but they're really pushing the whole sci-fi pretty hard. I mean they stole the shirt thingy from Star Trek."

"It's called a delta and it's *we*."

"What's we?" I gave Stella a puzzled look.

"It's *we* now. Not *they*. You, me, and Jeopardy. We're all part of the Space Force now. Also..." She pointed to the Delta design prominently displayed on the back wall of the room. "If anything, Star Trek stole it from us. Space Force is descended from the Air Force which in turn is descended from the US Army Air Forces. The Army Air Forces started using the Delta back in 1942. The Air Force later assigned the Delta symbol to Space Command in 1961. Star Trek didn't come out until 1966."

"Huh. That's kind of cool." I studied the logo for a minute before turning to her. "But those dress uniforms..."

"Oh, yeah, they suck. Got no defense there." She motioned toward the door. "Let's get KayCee set up and you and I can hit the gym."

"The gym, why?" Not knowing where this lab was, I followed just slightly behind her.

She frowned. "What do you mean? To keep in shape. You're in the military now."

"We don't need to do that. That's the best part of having these powers."

"Ah, Loughlin Ferguson. I would remind you that while you were transformed into a superweapon, Stella Johansen was not."

"Yeah, but you put her in that medical pod and it superpowered her up. I mean look at her, she looks like she should be fighting supervillains. That's a far cry from the middle-aged, over..." I became aware of the murderous gaze my soon-to-be-again roommate was fixing me with. "Ah, that is... slightly, ever so slightly, overweight cougar that she was before."

"All the medical pod did was put her in the most optimum state her body could achieve. It is now up to her to maintain it."

Communicating with KayCee is weird and with intense conversations, I sometime zone out the world around me, which is why I was startled to find Stella's face only an inch away from mine. She forced her words out through gritted teeth. "Are you telling me you don't have to work out? Ever?"

Stella with a full mad on was like a force of nature. Her temper tantrums were legendary in our hometown and that was before she could bench press a pickup truck. "Sorry?"

"What about dieting?"

"I mean we both have to eat a lot more to fuel our bodies. You know that."

"I mean junk food. Can you eat anything you want?" As I spoke, it dawned on me that the meal she had when we ate at the dining hall had been disgustingly healthy. It had vegetables and everything. Bleh!

I slowly backed away from her. It didn't do any good. She just matched me step for step until I was up against the hallway wall. "Answer me, Lock."

"Well, I seem to be able to convert all types of food very efficiently. I can even directly power up with different types of energy, so it's a bit complicated."

"You can eat and drink anything you want without getting fat, can't you?"

"Yeah..." I closed my eyes. The was a woosh of wind by my face and I cracked an eye to see her stomping down the hall.

"That's not fair. This is bullshit." She was more yelling at fate than me, but I still followed her from a distance as we got to the lab.

Two guards flanked the door to the lab, and we had to show IDs and do biometric scans. I rolled my eyes. "What no blood samples this time?"

The guard on the left gave an evil smile and stepped away revealing a tilted pad on the wall that had an outline of a handprint on it.

"Seriously?"

"Don't be a baby. It's a pinprick." Stella snorted. He placed her hand on it and then pulled it away, showing her index finger had a little drop of blood welling from the hole the needle had created.

"Doesn't seem very sanitary," I grumbled and placed my hand on the pad. "Why is it the whole hand?"

"No idea." The guard frowned as an angry buzzer sound came from the pad. "Try it again please."

I did as I was told, and the buzzer sound went off again. The guard shook his head. "Step back please, sir."

He studied the pad. "I don't understand this. The test needle is bent."

"You know who he is, right?" Stella asked the guard.

"Yeah, but..." He looked like he was about to protest but just gave a heavy sigh instead. "Fine, just go in."

We entered the lab. An Asian woman in her thirties stood there.

My rewired brain informed me that her ancestors hailed from the Altai Mountains. She smiled.

"Hello, I'm Doctor Sora Lake. Are you and KayCee ready to do this?"

"I guess so." I looked around. Various machines lined the walls, but my eyes were drawn to the two tables in the center of the room. One had the remains of a bioform. The head, part of the torso and the left leg. The one on the other table appeared complete. There was one very striking difference from the one KayCee had used on her starcraft.

"Um, KayCee?"

"Yes, Loughlin Ferguson?"

"Why are these bioforms green instead of gray?"

Stella nodded. "I was wondering that myself."

"These are much older versions than the one that I used. Based on the color, these were military model's from Kreb's country."

"So, wait. You guys really were little green men?" I fought back a laugh.

"Yes, yes, very amusing. Please move me closer so I may inspect the intact one."

"Last year's model," I told Stella and moved up to the complete one. My vision sharpened as KayCee enhanced it. Doctor Lake moved with us, placing her hands in the pockets of her lab coat. "We believe this one will work for KayCee. However, generations of scientists have tinkered with it since it was discovered in the wreckage back in 1947. KayCee may want to go over it before trying it on."

"May I use your hands for a moment?"

"Go ahead." I released control of my body and KayCee took over. She tapped various sections of the bioform's skull and suddenly the top of it popped open. She fiddled with the mechanics on the inside, making a few adjustments.

"Yes, your people took this apart and put it back together. There are a few things off but overall, they did a very good job reassembling it. A few more tweaks and it should be ready to receive me."

She switched out a couple of parts, replacing them with parts from the more damaged bioform, and then buttoned it up.

"Are you ready Loughlin Ferguson?"

"Whenever you are."

A weird tingling feeling spread across my body and golden motes pushed out through my skin. The cloud of motes settled onto the bioform and merged into it. Without KayCee, there was a strange empty feeling in my head. As much as I looked forward to having my body to myself, I had gotten used to her being with me.

The bioform head turned and its black eyes blinked. "Unauthorized entry. Self-destruction protocol initiated. Detonation in five seconds."

Chapter 7 –
Just Me, Myself, and I

As Doctor Lake drew back in fear, I tapped KayCee's forehead with two fingers. "Knock it off, you're scaring the nice doctor lady."

The bioform sat up at the waist in a very unhuman motion. "My apologies, Doctor Sora Lake. I was indulging in a little humor."

"I see." Using her index finger, the doctor shifted her thick black glasses farther up her nose. "It is good to finally be able to speak with you, KayCee. I've read a lot about you and have looked forward to getting to know you."

"It is a pleasure to make your acquaintance, Doctor Lake." KayCee swung her legs around and stood up. "Hello, Loughlin Ferguson. It is good to see you outside of a mirror."

"How's it feel?" I asked her.

The little alien flexed her arms and legs. "The left knee is a bit stiff. I will have to adjust it. I am currently going over the stored logs. This was a spare unit in the lander that crashed. None of my kind had been using it at the time. It's a very antiquated model and does not have all the features of the bioform that Kreb stole from me."

"Yeah," Stella grinned. "Not near as good as the big booby Barbie librarian you wore when we first met you."

"Yes. I would definitely prefer to use the infiltration model for a variety of reasons, but Kreb destroyed that one as well."

"KayCee, would you mind staying for a while to perform some minor tests as well as answers some questions I have for you." Lake asked.

"Of course, Doctor Lake." KayCee turned to Stella and me, her movement betrayed a stiffness that her other bioforms didn't have. "You two do not need to stay and babysit unless you are interested in learning the mechanics of this form."

"And that's our cue to leave." Stella grabbed my arm and pulled me toward the door. "Any issues, Doc, give us a call."

"See you, KayCee," I yelled as I got dragged out the door. "Good luck."

I pulled my arm out of Stella's grip. "What's the rush?"

"You need to study your assignment package plus you have that training tonight." Stella jerked her head toward one of the hallways. "Let's go back to your room and get you squared away."

I looked back at the lab. "Nice lady. I'm surprised there weren't more scientists there."

"There's a whole team of them but the colonel didn't want to freak you and KayCee out, so he limited the initial interaction to just Doc Lake."

"Smart. Now, why are you so hot to trot for me to read up on this assignment. Is there a surprise party waiting for me back at the room?"

"Yup, room's full of strippers and booze." She headed toward my room at a quick pace.

"While that totally sounds like something you would do, what's the real reason?"

Her shoulders slumped. "You can't screw this mission up, Lock."

"Right, right. World's in danger. I'm sure there are plenty of experts waiting in the wings to swoop in if I make a galactic mess of it."

"There is, but that's not the point." She sighed. "Brennan fought to have all of us brought into the fold. There's a faction among the brass that would rather we were strapped onto gurneys inside an operating room, so they could see what makes us tick."

"Yeah, KayCee and I figured as much. I'm willing to let them poke and prod me a little bit. Within reason, mind you! I didn't avoid getting probed by aliens just to have my own government do it!"

"What's the sword hanging over the Greek guy?"

"The Sword of Damocles?"

"Yeah, I feel we're all under the Sword of Damocles, including Brennan. We have to show that we're team players and are of value."

The bitter tone in her voice stopped me from making a mouthy reply. Stella acts like everything just rolls off her. For her to tell me that, she had to be really concerned. The more I thought about it, the more I wondered if some of this was from her first stint in the military. She had been in the Army and loved it. But it was during the whole *don't ask/don't tell* nonsense and she got booted out after getting exposed as a lesbian. She played it off and made jokes, but the idea that your government didn't want you simply because of your orientation, the way you were born, had to have hurt deeply. She was back serving her country, and I was beginning to think she feared getting rejected again because she was now an augmented human.

Personally, I was more worried we were going to wind up as lab experiments. Which is why KayCee and I made sure we had some insurance and an outside man, just in case everything went sideways. If it did, we'd grab Stella and Jeopardy and split. Brennan would be welcome to join us, but I knew instinctively he would stay to face whatever came his way. It was heroic and patriotic and very much not me.

We arrived at my room. It was a decent size and had its own bathroom, but it was underground and had no windows. If I planned on being there long, I'd have complained. The room consisted of a bed, a dresser, a desk, and a fridge. A TV was mounted on the wall across from the bed. On the desk was the folder Brennan promised me.

I grabbed the folder and jumped on the bed, motioning Stella to the chair. "If you're that worried, then stay and help me with my homework."

Stella snorted. "That's a nice reversal. In high school it was the other way around."

"See, anything's possible. I flipped open the folder. It consisted of dossiers for six employees at MSU. Each one had the photo of the suspected employee paper clipped to the right top. "Where's your room?"

She pointed to the wall with the TV. "Other side of that wall, so keep it down when you watch dirty movies."

"Why? You never did."

"Yeah, but what I watch is hot, your stuff was strange and weird."

"Hetero porn is strange and weird? I'm surprised we all managed to get born. All our parents must have been perverts!"

"Yeah, yeah."

"Anyways, what do you have next door for snacks and booze."

She frowned. "How is getting drunk going to help you study?

"We'll make it a drinking game."

"You can't show up drunk to training!"

"I won't." I smiled. "I can sober up on command. Don't even get a hangover."

"Oh, you suck! That is so not fair!"

"I'll tell you what. If we can ever go back in time and change this. You can be the kid who gets abducted by an alien mad scientist who turns you into a superweapon."

"Cool! I'm holding you to that." She bounced out of the room and returned shortly with an arm full of snacks and a bottle of bourbon. "Move over."

I wiggled over to one side of the bed as she plopped down on the other side, strewing the snacks over us. I shook my head. "What about glasses?"

"What? You think you're the King of England? Oooh, I'm too good to drink straight from the bottle."

"What are you? Five?" I asked as she took a swing from the bottle and handed it to me. "Besides, you've had your mouth in some very strange places."

I caught her midswallow, and she had a coughing fit. "Fuck you!"

"Wrong equipment, remember?" I took a drink from the bottle. I preferred bourbon in the form of an old-fashioned, but what the hell.

Stella saw the stupid smile on my face. "What?"

"Nothing."

"No, what?"

It's just..." I waved my hand around. "I've missed all this."

"Yeah. Me too, buddy." She must have had something in her eyes because she started blinking rapidly. "Me too."

Chapter 8 –
An Unfortunate Name

I pulled my bottom-tier rental car up to the front gate of the MSU facilities, ready to hand over my new employee ID card. Stella had been right. The interview turned out to be a breeze. HR liked Stella and was more than happy to give her childhood buddy a job. Especially with my extensive knowledge and training in picking up spilled meals, emptying trash barrels, and unclogging drains. Though, to be honest, this job was more than that. Aside from the usual janitor stuff, this job required maintaining the grounds and buildings, mowing, painting, and things like simple repairs.

Stella leaned out of the guard gate wearing a security uniform. "ID, please."

"Oh, hey. I didn't realize you'd be doing this."

"Hey, Lock. Yeah, I have gate duty today. She flicked a thumb over her shoulder at the other guard in the booth. An older black guy who had the look of a retired cop. "This is Fred. Fred, this is Lock, the guy I was telling you about."

"Hey, Lock." Fred never looked up from his newspaper.

I hadn't known people still read those. "Hi, Fred. Nice to meet you."

"Anyways." Stella leaned over and gave my car a once-over. "Still need your ID."

"What? You got me this job!"

"Well, you said you got it. How do I know you didn't lie to me?"

"Seriously?"

"Fred, you ever seen this guy before?" Stella asked.

Fred turned a page, still not looking up. "Nope."

"See, neither of us have seen you here before."

"Oh, this is bullshit. I..." I jumped as a car horn went off. I looked in my rearview mirror to see a line of cars behind me. "It's Sunday! Why are all these people coming to work? I thought it was just security and maintenance crew on the weekends."

"A lot of people here work weekends when it's crunch time on a project and then bank the time for later," my roommate informed me. "Now, about that ID, sir."

"Fine, here!"

Stella inspected the card carefully. "Hmm. I'm not sure this is you. Fred, doesn't this look off to you?"

"Mighty suspicious, if you ask me." Fred's nose never wavered from the sports section.

"Oh, c'mon. I'm going to be late on my first day. Open, the gate already!"

She placed a hand on the taser she wore. "Calm down, sir. If you continue to make a ruckus, I'll have to tase you!"

"Be a shame." Fred turned a page. "Lot of paperwork when you do that. What's this, second time this week you had someone ride the lightning?"

"Third."

"I'm going to get in trouble if my boss gets to work before me."

"Oh, you're fine. She's three cars back. She's the one that honked."

"Stella!"

"Okay, okay. Boy, you're no fun anymore." She handed me the ID and hit the button that lifted the gate. "What did I tell you, Fred?"

"No sense of humor."

"Right." She waved me on.

I fought the urge to flip them off and drove through. I parked my car in my designated spot. I'd never had my own spot before. Of course, I've never had to walk so far from my car to my place of work either so that dulled the excitement a bit.

The Bluetooth in the rental car sparked to life just as I was about to turn the engine off. "Loughlin Ferguson."

I jumped so high I hit my head on the ceiling. "Jesus! A little warning."

"Sorry." KayCee's voice came from the car radio. "I am using the communications packet in my bioform to speak with you."

"Yeah, I kind of figured that out."

"I know the colonel said no communication devices until you are more situated there, but I left you something that should not be detectable. Please, check your sun visor."

I flipped the visor down. "I don't see anything."

"In the fabric." I felt around the visor. There was a small object in it. It felt like a sewing needle. Using my finger, I moved it around until I located the original entry hole and pushed it out. "You're expecting me to rip my clothes?"

"No. It is a communication spike. A receiver transmitter made up of microbots. Well, it can do other functions, but that is its primary use."

"Microbots are not a real thing. Don't you mean nanobots?"

"No, I do not. They are two different things."

"What's the difference?"

"Size. A micropenis, while tiny, is still bigger than a nanopenis."

"*You're* a nanopenis!" I shot back. "You've been on Earth too long. Stella's humor is corrupting you."

"I assure you, sex organ humor is universal."

"Not when you say it like that, it isn't. Okay, What's this thing do?"

"As I told you, it is a communication link. Insert it under your skin along the back of your jaw. Use your ability to link to electronics to make a connection with it. It will allow us to communicate. Just tap it and I'll get an alert and be able to communicate.

"Like Bluetooth?"

"Close enough."

I was not good with this particular skill, and it took me several tries to activate it. Searching with my mind, I was able to find it's signal and felt a connection being made. "Now what."

"Turn off your car radio and tap the link."

I did as I was told. "Hello?"

"Sorry, the number you have dialed is no longer in service."

"Very funny."

"I am here all night. Do not forget to tip your servers."

"Keep it up and we're not watching any more comedy shows."

"Very well."

"So, what else does it do."

"In my opinion, this is the best part. When we are merged, it will allow me to communicate to others as long as there is some sort of electronic speaker nearby."

"Holy shit! Really? No more having to translate?"

"I will even be able to make phone calls."

"Very cool. I'm guessing I know who made this."

"Yes, so do not let Stella Johansen and Colonel Brennan know until we are ready. How are you on the mission?"

"I haven't started yet."

"Not the Space Force mission! I mean our real mission. Have you found it yet?"

"No. I don't know where they're keeping it yet. I'm going to ask Stella soon. Just waiting for the right moment." I took the needle and pushed it through my skin and muscle until it ran parallel to my jaw. My healing ability quickly sealed up the minor puncture wound. "Wait a minute. What happened when I turn into liquid form?"

Instead of coming from the Bluetooth, KayCee's voice was back in my head.

"That is why it was made out of microbots. They are programmed to sense when you turn liquid and to break into their individual shapes to be carried along. Once you return to shape, They will move back to your jaw area and reform into the communication link. Just press on it if you need me."

"Cool!"

"Glad you like it, Loughlin Ferguson. Go have fun mopping floors."

"Har-har..." I trailed off as a distinct click made me realize I was speaking to myself. "Could have let me have the last word."

I got out and headed for the main building. This place took its security very seriously. I had gone through such a ridiculous amount of checkpoints to get the locker room, I had the theme music to *Get Smart* playing in my head. I found myself missing KayCee in a weird way. Shrugging it off, I put on my assigned overalls and went to meet my boss in the breakroom.

There were six janitors on the day shift, but our boss was a lady from admin. This turned out to not be a good thing as she didn't know the first thing about the job. Not that it stopped her from being a know-it-all.

"You are late, Mr. Ferguson!"

"Sorry, I got held up at the gate. Something about my ID."

"I am Karen Seeman. You may call me Ms. Seeman."

Did she just say...

"Ah, sure. You can call me Lock."

"I will not. Have a seat, Mr. Ferguson." She gestured to where the other janitors were sitting. "You are assigned as an apprentice maintenance worker until I determine you are capable to be on your own."

"It's okay, I worked as a janitor for years."

"Be that as it may, Mr. Ferguson. Here you are a maintenance worker and an apprentice at that." She pointed to the guy next to me. "You will be assigned to Mr. Garza for now."

Dismissing me from her mind, she turned and started admonishing one of the other janit... sorry... maintenance workers for not hanging his mop on the right peg. As she did so, I leaned on the guy next to me. "Is she for real?"

"Why do you think the position was open." He snorted. "Even with the pay and bennies, they can't keep people here very long because of her. She's related to some high mucky-muck, so they won't get rid of her. We still have three open spots that need to be filled."

"Is her name really Karen Semen?"

"Yeah, but not spelled the way you're probably thinking." He grinned and told me the correct spelling. I glanced back at her and whispered back to him. "That *is* an unfortunate name. No wonder she's so angry."

"Yup. I'm Manuel Garza by the way. Call me Manny." One of the features Kreb installed in my brain saw fit to tell me that Manny's accent was from Cabo Rojo in Puerto Rico.

"Hi, I'm Lock."

Karen made her way over to us. "Since you two like to talk during the daily briefing. You can have the bottom level of Building C."

Manny frowned. "I'm assigned to Building A. You want me to do the basement of Building C?"

"No, I want you to do the subbasement."

His frown deepened. "Why? No one goes down there!"

"It's being reopened for a new project and needs to be made shipshape. Wash all the floors and replace any lights that are out." She turned on her heel. "You all have your assignments. Dismissed."

People slowly got to their feet after she marched out. "Sorry, Manny, I didn't mean to get you into trouble."

"Wasn't you, Lock. She was looking for an excuse. She always comes down on the new people the first day. I knew it was going to be a shitty day since I was told I'd be showing you around." He rubbed the back of his head. "Still, that's a weird assignment."

"Why's that?"

"Unless they need something, no one pays attention to maintenance. So, everyone always talks around us, which means we get the scoop on anything new, and I haven't heard anything about them reopening that subfloor."

We took a golf cart to Building C, Manny pointing out various things as we drove. Unlike Karen, he was pretty easygoing. He pulled the golf cart around to the rear of the building. "We usually park in the back so all the hotshots can park out front."

Going through more checkpoints, we eventually made our way to the supply closet and filled two utility carts with standard cleaning supplies as well as a couple of heavy-duty vacuum cleaners. Manny also threw in a bunch of lightbulbs. "Ready to go to the bowls of hell?"

"It's bowels, not bowls."

"Are you sure? That doesn't make any sense."

"And bowls of hell does?"

"I guess not. Bowels of hell it is."

"Is it really that bad?"

"Not really. It's just creepy. When they were building this compound, they broke into a cave system down below. Well, really two large caverns. The subbasement in Building C actually connects to them and every once and a while you have the odd critter or two coming through." He started pushing his cart toward the elevator, so I followed.

Well, that sounds like something that should be followed up on!

"Why did they leave it connected instead of sealing it up?"

"The caves are at a constant temperature of fifty degrees. Add in a dehumidifier system and you have a great place to store things in a cool, dry place for very little cost."

"Except for the critters."

"Yeah, but it's scorpions and stuff, not like mice or rats." We entered the elevator, and Manny pulled a keyring off his belt, inserted a key in the control panel, and hit the very last button.

"And how are scorpions better then mice?"

"Mice chew on stuff, scorpions don't."

"On the other hand, mice don't sting."

"No, but they do bite and have fleas. No scorpion ever started no plague."

"Good point."

The elevator dinged and the doors opened. The hallway was dirty with papers and other office debris, and the lighting was out, the emergency lights flicking. "Well, this doesn't look like a scene out of Resident Evil at all!"

"See! I told you. Creepy!" He pulled a pair of flashlights out of his cart and handed me one. "I think they turned off the breakers when they closed this up. Let's split up and see if we can find the breaker box."

"Dude! Have you ever seen a scary movie? Never split up. That's just mutual suicide." I pulled a water bottle out of my cart and stuck in in my back pocket. Always paid to have water with me these days.

He just laughed and pointed me down a hall. As soon as I was out of sight, I turned off my flashlight and changed my vision to be able to see in the dark. It wasn't as smooth as when KayCee did it, but I was able to change them over.

I'm no James Bond or Liam Brennan, but this screamed trap to me. My first day on the job and I'm sent into the creep cave basement.

Speaking of caves. Where the hell were they? So far, all I saw was cement block walls. Standard basement stuff. I passed a few rooms that had storage bins but nothing looking like it should contain the Batmobile.

I stopped and backed up. At the rear of one of the rooms I had walked past was a large steel door. It was pitted with age and looked like the gate to hell.

Bingo! Now, do I beat feet and tell Stella, or do I check it out?

I pulled out my phone. No bars.

Damn! You know what? Screw it!

There was a keypad next to it to the giant door. Without KayCee, I had no way to figure out the passcode and there was no way I was battering this door down. Still...

Trap or no trap?

I tugged on the door. It swung open.

Definitely a trap. All the security around here and this is left unlocked.

I should have found Manny and got the hell out of there. But snooping around was literally my mission. I sighed and pulled the door open farther. It was the entrance to the caves. I stepped through and was hit with a blast of hot air.

Whew! I thought Manny said these caves were at a constant temperature of fifty degrees. This is closer to ninety!

The cave I was in was large. A metal ramp led down to the floor, which was about ten or twelve feet below the entrance. Floor to ceiling, it was about two stories high and must have been parallel to both the subbasement and the regular basement.

A wooden floor had been constructed on the bottom, piled with large crates. Wires running down the wall connected to large dehumidifiers, but they weren't on, and judging from what I was feeling, weren't needed.

At least it's a dry heat. Isn't that what they say around here?

Unlike the caves back home in the Granite State, these walls had a reddish hue. I gave a cursory glance at the crates. They were filled with computer parts of some kind. I moved to the back and found a normal-sized door made out of steel. This one was propped open.

On entering, I discovered a smaller cave about half the size of the first one. Instead of a wood floor, the crates were stacked on pallets. The ground was more sand than rock. I was about to open the crates for a peek inside when I saw something in the sand. I clicked the flashlight on for a better look.

What the hell?

On the ground was what appeared to be bicycle tracks with some sort of weird footprints on either side. I bent down for a closer look. The footprints were about twelve inches long with two points in the front and one on the back. I had no idea what type of footwear could make something like that. I snapped a pic with my phone and straightened up. I shone the flashlight around. There were similar tracks all over.

I made my way to the back, where I discovered the rear cave wall had another opening. There was no door, and the marks on the walls surrounding appeared to be new.

So, I guess the question is, did someone expand from this side or break in from that side?

There was a hiss and a clicking of rocks behind me.

Oh, that's right. I forgot it's a trap.

Readying a quip, I whirled around to face the Saturday morning nightmare of my childhood.

"Oh my God!"

Chapter 9 –
Damn You, Sid and Marty

Saturday Morning TV in the '70s was a magical time for kids of that era. I was no exception and would get up early to veg out in front of the TV until my folks woke up. There was one show that came out when I was around four. I had no business watching it at that age, but I was an only child, and most parents back then didn't pay attention to what their kids watched. This show featured a family that wound up in another dimension and the land they were lost in had some pretty scary creatures on it for a four-year-old, one of which had haunted my nightmares for years. Not that that ever stopped me from watching the show every weekend, mind you.

It hadn't been a bicycle tire that had made those tracks, it had been a tail. The pointed footprints had been made by clawed feet. Coming around the crates toward me were about six good imitations of the creature from my nightmares. They were a deeper green, skinnier, and didn't have any horns, but the head and eyes matched the TV show creatures dead on. Though they were more lizard than dinosaur, it was enough to trigger an irrational fear in me. I would like to point out that six-foot-tall bipedal lizard humanoids with hands that ended in three large claws were enough to scare the hell out of anybody all on their own. Their tails dragged on the ground as they walked toward me and sure enough, they uttered hissing sounds as they approached. They each wore some kind of leather-like harness holding tools and pouches but no clothes.

What is it with aliens and nudity?

They had me cut off from the way I came, and I really didn't want to see what was on the other side of the newly dug entrance. "Um, hi guys. I come in peace. How about you do too?"

They continued to approach. "You know every alien abduction convention I've been to always has some angry guy screaming that aliens are lizard-like. Have you met those people? Maybe we know someone in common."

Another difference from my childhood nightmares was these things were fast and much skinnier. Lucky for Normal Mode Lock, Combat Mode Lock decided to take over and I was swept into an artificial calm.

"Detra Treyga, worker caste. Danger minimum to moderate depending on numbers."

As I said that, one of them scurried up the side of the cave wall like a gecko. I was pretty sure he didn't want to sell me insurance. I leaped up and pulled him down, tossing him about ten feet away.

I *moved*, dropping into a speed no human could match and started pummeling them. These guys couldn't keep up with my speed either, but they were a lot tougher than mere earthlings. My hits momentarily stunned them, but they weren't dropping.

Following the sage advice of the late Patches O'Houlihan, seven-time ADAA Allstar, I started dodging, ducking, dipping, diving, and... dodging. It was enough that none of them could get their hands on me. Eventually, my strikes added up, and I was able to take two of them down. I was starting to feel confident I could wrap the fight up shortly.

Of course, that's when the gods of fate decided to kick me in the crotch. The fight had forced me into the newer cave tunnel and four more monsters came up from that side. These new things looked like the result of an interspecies orgy at a reptile zoo.

Their heads were like stubby versions of alligators, though they had the black, bug-like eyes of the others. Their torsos were covered in a turtle-like shell with two sets of arms protruding from it. Instead of a lower torso and legs, the bottom half of these creatures were that of a giant snake. Their scales were an iridescent black. They slithered toward me, rearing up to about twelve feet in height.

"Detra Tal, warrior caste. Advanced strength and speed. Well armored with venomous bite and stinger. Extremely dangerous."

Stinger?

Sure enough, each of their tails had a foot-long stinger at the end. And because all of that wasn't enough, each of their hands held a variety of slicing and bashing weapons.

"Nope! Nopety, nope!" I wildly looked around to find an escape route. The Treyga blocked my way out, and the other side of the tunnel was filled with the warriors from reptile hell.

"Wait a minute." There were cracks in the rocks making up the tunnel. I grabbed my bottle and gulped down some water. My body tingled as my powers transformed me into liquid, allowing me to seep through a large crack. Howls raged behind me.

One of these days I have to find out how I can hear without ears.

I slipped through cracks here and there, completely discombobulated. Eventually I poured out of the ceiling of another cave and fell to the ground. Sensing enough space around me, I changed back to normal. "And... I'm freaking naked again."

With the danger gone. I was out of combat mode. I looked around, discovering I was in a roughly ten-foot by eight-foot cave with a makeshift cot. Some sort of moss gave off a dim glow, enough to see by without altering my vision. An opening in one of the walls was covered by a dirty green army blanket. US was stamped on it in black. There was a brighter light coming from the other side of it, and I could hear a series of hissing.

I tapped the comm spike. "KayCee, you there?"

"Yes, but I am currently attempting to salvage parts from the second bioform. Is this something that could wait?

"I'm deep underground and there are several reptile alien races running and slithering around."

"There is only one known reptilian race. Are you sure you — "

"I know what I saw!"

"Interesting. Are you not the one who once said there was no lizardmen aliens."

"Well, it turns out I was wrong," I shot back in a sharp whisper. "Some of them look like Sleestaks.

"Ah, Those would be the Detra Treyga, the worker caste."

"Then there's another species that looks like they are part alligator, part turtle, part snake and all deadly."

"That would be the Detra Tal. They are the warrior caste of the same species."

"Well, they look very different. So, you know this race?"

"I know of them, and they should not be on Earth. What can I do to help?"

"I'm not sure. Can you pinpoint where I am and plot a way out for me?"

"It will take some time, but I should be able to do some underground scanning as long as your comm spike is down there to bounce a signal through. Be glad you are not back in New Hampshire. It would never be able to get through all the granite."

"In the meantime, I think there is a conversation going on in the next cave. Can you translate for me?"

"Possibly. But if I can, you should be able to do it on your own."

"Doubt it. I couldn't even pass high school Spanish."

"Usa tu cerebro."

"Cerebro? Was that something about the X-Men?"

"Loughlin Ferguson, Kreb would have installed some sort of translation ability. There is a limited number of known sentient races. Odds are, he gave you the abilities to understand them. Including this one."

"Huh, that makes sense, I guess." I crouched near the entrance and concentrated on the hissing. After a few seconds, I felt the tingling feeling I get when my powers kick in and the hissing gradually turned into two voices, one deep, the other elderly sounding. Or at least that's how my head made them sound.

"Your job is to maintain the pod. Leave the security to the Detra Tal." The deeper voice said.

"Hear me well, Paldan. My job is to make sure the Detra Terra is safe. If there is a danger to her, you need to help me move her. Have the humans discovered us?"

"It's one lost human. It's nothing to worry about. He'll make one of my caste a quick snack and that will be the end of it."

Snack? They eat humans? Oh God. V wasn't a miniseries; it was a documentary!

"You Detra Tal are too over confidant."

"And you Detra Bel are too fearful."

My comm spike came to life.

"Loughlin Ferguson. I found a way out, but you are not going to like it."

I sighed. "It's going through those two, isn't it?"

"Yes. It seems to be a lab of some sort. I am picking up all sorts of equipment."

"Of course, it is." I stood up. The old me's knees would have been screaming in protest but my new body had none of those problems. "So, I have to go in there and fight two aliens while naked. Great."

"You are once again unclothed? For all your protests, I am beginning to wonder if this is a type of fetish."

"It's not my fault most of my powers aren't conducive to wearing clothes."

"How does fighting a lizard person result in you losing your pants? Even Captain James T. Kirk managed to remain clothed fighting the Gorn, and this is a person who was continually losing his shirt."

"I didn't have a choice." I snapped. "There was no way out. I went liquid and escaped through a crack."

"I feel Stella Johansen would have made a joke regarding what you just said."

Why was it anyone who hung out with Stella wound up with the humor of an eight-year-old? Even the damn alien had been corrupted.

"Can we concentrate here?"

"Of course. How would you want to do this? Streak through the cave as if at one of your sporting events?"

"Hey! If the comm spike can travel with me, why can't clothes."

"It might be possible, but such a thing is beyond my knowledge."

"Fine, but we're revisiting this." I scratch my... I scratched an itch... "Can you affect the machines at all?"

"Perhaps. Let me send out a pulse."

I waited as KayCee did whatever she did to make that happen. The spike came back to life.

"I can, but I am not sure of the effect it will have."

"That's fine, I'm thinking some sort of organized chaos blitz so I can escape in the confusion."

"That might work. There are some communication devices in there with speakers. You should dampen your hearing and eyes."

"I think I can do that."

"Then we can hit them with a sensory overload."

"Won't reinforcements come when they hear it."

"No one else is nearby, I believe they are all out looking for you."

"Screw it. Let's do it."

I concentrated on doing what she asked. It was a bit of a struggle without KayCee in my head but eventually I was able to adjust both my hearing and eyes. "Ready."

"And... Go!"

Chapter 10 – Fight Song

I burst into the room. In the center was what looked like a medical pod. The walls were lined with different machines. The two lizard guys that were arguing stopped to stare at me. One was a Detra Tal. The other being was about five feet tall and looked like a Komodo dragon walking on its hind legs.

"Detra Bel, creator caste. Advanced intelligence. Venomous bite and claws. Not to be underestimated."

The Detra Bel had protective goggles over his big eyes and wore a protective apron. He was standing in front of a table covered with potion tubes and vials filled with various colored liquids.

The Detra Tal was positioned in front of a very shut and very locked metal door.

"Crap!"

Loud music kicked in as the Detra Tal and I launched ourselves at each other. All the lights on the machines, including the medical pod, started flickering. There was a hiss and a vapor started to release from the medical pod.

"Did you do that?" I asked.

"Apologies, Loughlin Ferguson, I am forced to randomly activate programs. Their systems are foreign to me."

The Detra Bel shrieked and rushed over to the pod. At least I think he shrieked, even with my hearing dampened, the music was deafening.

All six of the big warrior's hands sprouted blades and he came at me like he was reenacting a General Grievous scene. I *moved* and my shift in speed caught him off balance. I ducked under the first swings and licked a blade as it went by.

Yes, I know that sounds weird and gross but there was a reason for it. Having tasted the metal, my body transformed, shifting my skin into a malleable form of the metal.

Sparks flew as the edges of the creature's weapons hit my metallic skin. What I wasn't prepared for was the strength behind the blows. They hurt! I slid out of the way of his next swings as we passed by each other. A couple of his weapons resembled oversized cleavers. Battered and bruised, I really didn't want to get hit again.

I pulled at the door. It wouldn't budge. There was a weird-looking lock on it. I spun around and sure enough, there was a key hanging off the harness of the Detra Tal.

"Double crap!"

He stopped, and with a smile full of very pointed teeth, tucked the key into a pouch. "Looking for this, human?"

"As a matter of fact, I am," I shouted over the music.

He reared back in surprise at me answering him in his own language. Let's not quibble over the fact that I thought I was speaking English when I said it. I didn't waste the opportunity though and *moved*, leaping through the air, intent on ripping one of his weird dagger swords out of his grip.

It was my turn to be surprised when he not just matched my speed but surpassed it and plucked me out of the air with one hand, slamming me into a cave wall. I coughed as rock dust showered down on us. "Yeah, I felt that one."

He had me pinned to the wall, the one hand grasping me around the throat while the other five had the pointy and edge parts of his weapons up against my skin. "How do you speak our language?"

"I took... an... online course," I coughed out. "Learn how to... speak... iguana in five... easy lessons."

This was not the first time I was in this position. In fact, it was a pretty common one in high school. I reverted back to a basic maneuver, kicking out. While it was a particularly devastating attack against a teenage boy, I suspected that its effectiveness against an opponent whose dangly bits weren't... well, dangly... would normally be underwhelming.

However, the fact that the skin of my foot was currently made of some alien metal acted the same way as steel-toe boots and added a little extra kick to my... ah, kick. The creature grunted and visibly winced. I followed it up with a metal thumb to his left eye.

He gave a howl of pain and anger, a free hand rising to the injured eye. As he did, I used both hands to twist myself loose from the hand holding me. Thanks to my abilities, I'm strong, and I mean like superhero strong, but if the alien hadn't been blinded and in pain, I didn't think I could have broken his grip. I dodged the bladed weapons in his other two hands and as my feet hit the floor, I was already pawing in his pouch for the door key.

A scaled claw gripped my wrist just as I triumphantly yanked the key out of his pouch. The creature's skin was surprisingly warm. As I attempted to tear myself from his grip, he pulled, flipping me around and flinging me upside down into another wall. I slid to the floor and scrambled back to my feet. The warrior slithered toward me, blue liquid that I assumed was blood was streaming out of the darkened eyehole where I'd jabbed him.

He stopped just out of range and pulled a ray gun out of a pouch, pointing it at me.

"Uh-oh!" Kreb had shot me with a ray gun before. It had damn near killed me. If these aliens had comparable technology, I was screwed.

"Paldan!" the Detra Treyga yelled at the Detra Tal warrior while holding a flask of a boiling green liquid. When the big warrior turned, the Detra Treyga threw the contents of the flask into his face, solidly contacting with the undamaged eye. There was no howl this time, instead the Detra Tal gave a high-pitched shriek like a tea kettle. Whatever was in that flask caused the big warrior's face to start melting like he'd just looked in the Ark of the Covenant.

"Jesus!" I scooped up a curved sword he dropped and swung with both hands. While the blades may have had trouble getting through my metallic skin, it had no problem cutting through the creature's neck and neatly decapitating him. And by neatly, I mean how easy it was to slice through, because that was the only neat thing about it. Gouts of blue blood poured out of his neck wound like a mini water fountain, Gagging, I *moved*, stepping out of spatter range. "Kill the music."

"I am doing so now!"

"Johnson's Motor Car? Really?"

"It is a good song. Who does not like the Clancy Brothers?"

"At the pub, sure. During a battle, not so much. At least not that song. That being said, I kind of like the idea of fight music. We'll have to do that again."

As the song died, I turned to find the smaller alien pointing the ray gun at me. "Um, I'd appreciate it if you didn't shoot me. I've been shot before with those things, and I don't enjoy it."

"You survived being shot by a beam weapon?" The expression of disbelief must be universal because I clearly read it on his scaly face. "By whom?"

"A mad scientist named Kreb the Incorrigible. Just before me and my friends ended him."

"That was you? If true, you did the universe a favor that day. I have read the humans reports on him. He was truly a monster." He cocked his head in a very human gesture. "What race are you? You look human, but if you were able to slay Kreb, I must assume you are in disguise. You should know the humans prefer to wear garments to cover their strange sex organs. Going around unclothed will give you away."

"I'll... keep that in mind." I pointed to the gun. "So, what do you plan to do with that?"

"Do you have designs to hurt me or the Detra Terra?" Ray gun still on me, he pulled a small handheld device out of one of the pouches on his belt and tapped the keys on it.

"I don't know what that is, and I have no intentions of hurting anyone. I sort of stumbled into your caves and I'm just trying to get out. Why did you help me?"

"It is an internal matter. And you helped me first. Courtesy dictated I do the same." A hopeful look appeared on his face. "Do you perhaps have a starcraft?"

"Sorry, no."

"Pity." He placed the ray gun in a pouch and moved back to the medical pod. "I have contacted a colleague. If you help me get her to him, I will tell you how to get out of here."

I made a snap decision to trust him. If it turned out to be a trap, I'd just go liquid and flee. "I left some clothes near the entrance to the human building. Can we pick those up?"

He tapped the device several times and studied the screen on it. "Yes. My colleague will gather them before meeting us."

"Do you have a name?"

"Of course, I have a name. I am Bel Crat of the Seventh Pouch of Magti, First Science Adviser to the Detra Terra."

Pouch? Huh, I'd have thought they hatched from eggs. Unless that means something completely else.

"That's a lot. Can I just call you Bel Crat?"

"That is acceptable."

"Okay, Bel Crat. Who am I helping you with?"

He pressed a button on the control panel of the pod. The lid slowly rose up, revealing a third type of creature. This one was more like a cross between a snake and a human. It had a single set of arms with five fingers on each hand. Its torso was more human shaped and narrowed to a tail similar to the Detra Tal. It was covered in fine scales that were mostly a pastel blue. The inner arms and front side were light yellow. It had a cowl similar to that of a cobra and the face had smaller finer scales in yellow, and its eyes more resembled an earth snake than the black bulbs of the Detra Tal and Detra Treyga, but the shape of the face was humanlike and... feminine?

Her eyes opened, revealing thin, black vertical pupils on light green eyeballs. She studied my face for a second then the eyes drifted downward.

Damn it. I really got to find a way to keep pants on with I use my powers. Anyone making another strange sex organs comment is getting hit.

I stepped closer to the pod, using its side to block her view. Her eyes slowly closed, and her breathing deepened. "Is she okay?"

"It's the effects of the hibernation." He looked up for the control panel, panic in his voice. "Don't make eye contact with her. You didn't make eye contact with her, did you?"

"Um. Nooo?" I lied.

"Please lift her, but do not make eye contact."

I grabbed a protective apron off a table covered with beakers and flasks. "Why? Is she going to attack me if we do?" I asked as I wrapped the apron around my waist.

"No, it's much, much, worse than that."

I froze. "What do you mean?"

"It's too hard to explain. The biological and social hierarchies of our people is very different that yours, and I don't have the time it would take to make you understand."

"Dude, as weird as this is, you are somehow making it weirder." Turning my head away, I reached in and lifted her out of the pod. She was tall... er... longer, then I was, and Bel Crat had to loop her tail around my neck to prevent it from dragging on the floor. I repressed a shudder. I had enough trouble dealing with Bel Crat looking like my worst nightmare, and now I had a giant snake tail draped over me. I kept waiting for it to tighten around my neck, strangling me. "Now what?"

"Follow me and be careful of her. We must go before the Detra Tal know she is gone. Do not speak in the tunnels. The sound will carry." He headed out and I followed him, praying the apron wouldn't fall off as I carried the snake lady.

A dizzying amount of tunnels later we entered into a small side cave where another slees... Detra Treyga, waited with my clothes and a floating gurney. He stepped back in surprise. Ignoring him, I placed the snake lady on the gurney. It dipped for a second and returned to its original floating height.

"Cool." I grabbed my clothes away from the startled Detra Treyga and started pulling them on. "Some sort of anti-grav device holding it up?"

"It speaks our language?" Bel Crat's colleague asked in a panicked tone.

"Yes, we have formed a temporary alliance. He has fulfilled his end of the bargain. Lead him to the exit and return here, We do not have much time."

These things didn't have eyebrows, but if they did, the new one would have been arching one at me. He made a *come-on* motion with his arm and headed out of the cave.

I didn't move. "Before I go, tell me something, Bel Crat. Why are you and your people on Earth? Are you invading?"

"Invading? We're not invading, we're trapped here!" He pointed at his impatient companion. "Go with him now, before we are discovered."

"Okay, good luck. Hope we don't wind up on opposing sides." I gave a half wave and followed the other one out.

After another couple of tunnels, I stepped out of a hatch back into the subbasement of Building C. Apparently, they had more than one way in and out of the building. I turned to say goodbye to the Detra Treyga who showed me the way, but he was already scuttling away. I shut the hatch and the light on the keypad next to it changed from green to red.

Hope that means it's locked.

I tapped the comm spike. "You there?"

"Yes, I have been trying to listen in. But reception was spotty. There seems to be division in the ranks."

"Looks like it. Are any of them headed this way?"

"I do not know. Once you moved out of range, I lost the image of the tunnels."

"Damn. At least we have a map of their system. If we need to send troops in, they won't go in blind."

"Yes, that would have been a good idea."

"What do you mean, *would have*?"

"I did not think to save it. As soon as I lost the signal, I lost all data gathered."

"What? How is that even possible? Aren't there redundances?"

"In what? To use a human saying, I was doing it all by the seat of my figurative pants. This is all new territory for me. And it is not as if you had told me to."

"I didn't think I *had* to!" I stomped off to find Manny.

Chapter 11 –
Totally Over It

During my time in the tunnels, the subbasement had gone under change. The trash was gone, the floors swept and mopped, and the lights had been repaired. The difference was jarring. I grabbed my cart and went looking for Manny.

I found him near the elevators looking down the hallway. I braced myself, ready for him to tear me a new one. As far as he knew, I went AWOL while he had to clean the entire area himself. "Hey, sorry about that. I got really lost."

He didn't reply, instead he continued to look down the hallway. I stepped in front of him. "Hey, Manny."

His eyes were unfocused, and he started when I waved my hand in front of his face. "Hey, you okay?"

He blinked a couple of times and looked around. "Sorry, I got distracted. Hey, you did a great job. I didn't think we'd be able to get everything squared away today."

Oh, that's not good.

"No problem, buddy." I forced a grin on my face. "Team effort!"

We made our way out of the building to find it getting dark. I checked my watch and discovered it was quitting time. "Now what?"

There was a long pause before he answered me. "Karen will have gone home for the day, so we can check out without a lecture."

We made our way back to the main building and headed to the locker room to change. The other maintenance workers had already finished up and were streaming out when we left. One of them held the door for us. "Hey Manny, how was the new guy?"

"Top notch, Karl. He crushed it."

Karl frowned. "Don't crush it too much new guy. Don't wreck the curve."

"I know the game." I gave him a thumbs up. "I was a town janitor before this. Where do you think the term 'good enough for government work' came from?"

He laughed and fist-bumped me. "We do drinks on Tuesdays after work. Make sure to come out tomorrow."

"Why Tuesdays?"

"Karen is tied up in some weekly meeting every Wednesday morning. We get half the day to recover from the night before."

"Ah, sure." I nodded and headed to my locker. Even with Karen, this was already better than my last job. Too bad about the whole lizardman infestation thing.

As soon as I pulled my car out of the gate, my comm came to life.

"I am sorry, Loughlin Ferguson. It appears you have had a rough first day."

I shrugged. "I wouldn't say that. No puke, no feces smeared on the wall. All and all, not bad."

"Even with these new aliens trying to kill you?"

"Dead is dead. The smell of a selectmen's puke after a liquid lunch, however, is forever."

"I have never looked at death that way before. What is the status on discovering the location of the lander?"

"Seriously? When exactly did I have time to look for it."

"We need to find it. Without it we cannot return to my starcraft."

"I'm well aware. But you need to be patient. I have to earn the Space Force's trust first. That might take some time. Figuring out this lizardmen agenda is a good start. Are you sure it's only one race? There were at least three distinctly different creatures down there."

"I am sure. What will you do now?"

"Head home and fill Stella in. Which, depending on how it goes, may lead me to telling her about the plan and that could be a problem."

"What are you talking about?"

"I think she's really digging being back in the military. Second bite at the apple after what happened. Getting screwed over and kicked out always left a sour taste in her mouth. This is like a fresh start."

"I understand but considering what she did, I believe she got off lightly."

"What? You think *don't ask, don't tell* was okay?" I heard metal whining and realized I was gripping the steering wheel too hard.

"No, That policy would make no sense to my people. But Stella Johansen knew the rules and joined anyways, so she knew the risks. That is what I am talking about."

"What do you mean?"

"She swore an oath to obey orders, rules, and regulations. Adultery is illegal in your military. She knew that and she slept with a married woman anyway. Knowing her, we both know it was unlikely an isolated case. It is most likely she had been involved with multiple married women. Under the rules of your country's military, any such incident would have been Conduct Unbecoming."

"But... I mean it's Stella..." I said lamely.

"You excuse her bad behavior because she is your friend. But how many marriages has she destroyed? Yes, I know human relationships are complicated, but we both know her. Two minutes of whispering in a married woman's ear and suddenly, the woman's underwear is hanging off Stella Johansen's chandelier. Meanwhile her husband and children are waiting for her at home."

"Stella never had a chandelier." I replied absently. I'd never thought that of it that way. Her stories were always funny, but was that because I never thought of the people in it as real?

"You understand what I mean."

"That's some pretty deep thinking. I didn't think this was an issue with the Sarli."

"We are not talking about my people. We are talking about yours and marriage is currently a standard in your culture. I believe Stella Johansen is possibly self-sabotaging herself with such actions."

"Okay, there is some merit to what you say, but you'll never convince me someone shouldn't serve in the military simply because they're gay."

"I was not trying to."

"Do you think I should tell her about the plan?"

There was no immediate answer, and I was beginning to think we got disconnected when KayCee finally answered.

"I will leave that up to you. Stella Johansen has a lot of faults, but loyalty is not one of them. I do not believe she would ever betray you, but the question you have to ask is should we put her in that position in the first place? Is that fair to her?"

"I don't know. That's why I was asking."

"Where is Jeopardy Jones in all this? You have not mentioned her at all."

"Ex-girlfriend." I reminded her.

"Yes, that was a rather cold way to end a relationship."

"Jay-sus! I didn't want to break up with her. It was for her own safety! It's not like I could just pop by and see her."

"I appear to have hit a nerve."

"It's just that Stella said pretty much the same thing. Oh, and Stella said Jeopardy has a fiancé now."

"I see, That is unfortunate. Still, would you expect her to pine for you forever?"

"Of course not. It just feels like she's avoiding me. I haven't seen her at all. I don't blame her, but I'd like to apologize at least."

"You have said she is getting married."

"Well... I said she has a fiancé. There is a difference."

"Now you sound like Stella Johansen. Perhaps you should leave it alone."

"That's the plan. If for no other reason than not dragging her into our nonsense. And for the record, you brought it up."

"Do not stand outside her window with a boombox. I do not think that will work so well in real life. I believe the legal term is stalking."

"Lloyd Dobler? Really? All I said was I wanted to apologize. No more movies for you."

"It does not matter. I have been reading a lot of online magazines lately. Do you know what Nice Guy Syndrome is?"

"Listen, I already have one Stella in my life giving me undeserved crap. I don't need a second. I need you to be you."

"Fair enough. I have just been trying to keep you on the straight and narrow, as your people say."

"Pretty sure no one really uses that term."

I pulled in front of the apartment I was sharing with Stella. It was two stories tall, and the apartment doors opened to the outside. The second floor where we were had a long walkway/porch on the front. Its stairs were in the middle of the complex and led to the parking lot out front. I think it had been a motel at some point in its past. Stella's rental car was already out front. "I'm home, or what passes for it these days. Gotta go."

"Good luck."

Chapter 12 –
Pizza and a Thong

I walked into the apartment and sighed. I had cleaned it up the night before, but you'd never have known it. Clothes were strewn everywhere. Dishes were piled up on the counter and there was a smell of burnt food in the air.

"Stella! What the hell?"

She popped up from behind the kitchen island still wearing her uniform shirt. It was completely unbuttoned revealing the white T-shirt underneath. "Oh, hey. Yeah, I was cooking dinner and ran down to do a load of clothes in the laundry room. I started chatting with someone and lost track of time. Place damn near went up in flames."

I pushed some clothes aside on the couch and plunked myself down. "Considering our last house actually did burn to the ground, I don't think we'd ever be able to get insurance again if this one went up."

"Eh, it's a rental. Anyways. I think we're going to have to order out or go someplace." She started filling the sink with water and squirted some detergent into it. "You'd think the Space Force could spring for a better apartment. Something with its own washer and dryer."

"We're supposed to be a maintenance worker and a security guard, they got us an apartment within our supposed means."

"I know. Still, we could have come up with something. You just mentioned insurance. We could have claimed I got a nice settlement." She shoved all the dishes into the sink.

"You did, thanks to Tavish doing some shady internet stuff."

"You know what I mean."

"I'll keep that in mind the next time we pretend to be ourselves." I spotted a bottle of Irish whiskey on the coffee table and opened it. Not bothering with a glass, I took a deep gulp straight from the bottle.

She moved from behind the island, all thong and no pants. After years of living with her, I barely noticed. "Tough day?"

"You have no idea." I told her about going to the subbasement with Manny and discovering the aliens.

"Alien lizard people. Like V?"

"In the alien abduction circles, they're referred to as Reptilians. But, yeah, kind of. Just without the cheesy 1980s hairstyles."

"What? Those were works of art. I miss those days."

"I don't. You personally put that hole in the ozone with the amount of hair spray you used."

"It was worth it, Mullet Boy. Don't make me find our yearbook."

"Ouch!"

"Yeah, I went there." She sat down next to me and grabbed the bottle, chugging an amount that would have dropped a frat guy.

"Hey, what about the dishes?"

"They need to soak."

"You mean they're going to stay there until I get sick of it and clean up your mess."

"It's only fair. I cooked."

I made an exaggerated look around the apartment. "Really, 'cause I don't see any food."

"It's the thought that counts." She took another swig. "I'll report back to Brennan and fill him in. Let him know we think you've been made."

"Tell them I need KayCee. If they're already on to me, there is no point in separating us. I need her at the helm."

"So, you're a boat now?"

"Yeah, the *USS Shut Up*." I pulled the bottle away from her and took a much smaller sip than she did. "I wonder how they knew I was there."

"Brennan thinks they've infiltrated everywhere. They may have had access to records of our little adventure last year. Maybe using our real names wasn't such a great idea." She sighed and pulled out her phone and made a call. "I need the package. Oh, and bring three large pizzas. One pepperoni, one meatlovers and…"

"Hamburg and feta but have them put the feta on after it comes out of the oven, please. Also, two cheesesteaks and three large fries. Plus, an order of onion rings."

"You get all that?" Stella asked the person on the other end of the phone. She rolled her eyes at the response. "Just do it."

"Package?" I asked after she hung up.

"Secure communication device. Wasn't safe to leave it here, in case our apartment got searched."

"Oh, so that's what happened. I thought you were just a slob."

"Hey, it's laundry day, remember. She leaned to the side, squishing me into the cushions as she stuffed the phone back into her shirt pocket.

"Really? Couldn't have leaned the other way?"

"There's only one way I lean." She gave a cheesy grin. "And it's not toward guys."

"Har-har. I'd laugh but you just bruised my ribs." I pushed her back on her side of the couch. "Why do you even need to lean to put it in a shirt pocket?"

"Whiniest superspy ever." She propped her feet up on the coffee table. "Listen, can you make yourself scarce after work tomorrow? I'm having a friend over. She's a veterinarian."

"Perfect. Let me guess, it's whoever you were chatting with in the laundry room."

"No, I met her at the supermarket. Wait, what do you mean perfect?"

I waved my arms around the apartment. "Because now I don't need to pick up. You always clean up before a conquest."

"I... Shit!"

"Check and mate."

"That *is* the plan. You going to the movies?"

"Actually, the maintenance crew invited me out drinking."

"Wow, look at that. Lock Ferguson actually bonding with coworkers. Has hell frozen over?"

"I dunno. Have you stopped drinking?"

"Not in this lifetime. She grabbed the bottle back and proceeded to finish it off. She wiped her arm around her mouth and lobbed the bottle behind us.

"Hey, that could have broken!"

"Naw, there's a pile of clothes back there. So, listen. You really think your new pal Manny got neutralized, MIB style?"

"Oh, yeah! He didn't know where the hell he was."

"That's a bit scary. How do you know you weren't zapped?"

"Because if I was, they would not have left in the part about the aliens."

"Good point." She scratched somewhere that caused me to inch farther away on the couch. "So, tell me about your adventures on the road. Did you solve a new mystery each week?"

We swapped bullshit stories while we waited for the pizza. I mean the secure communication device.

Eventually there was a knock at the door. Stella hopped off the couch to answer it. One of the agents was holding four pizza boxes with the subs and fries on top. His eye's bugged out of his head when he saw Stella standing there in nothing but a shirt and thong. My mental image of Stella is the one I've known for years. A fifty years and change, large, overweight woman who's a drunken slob. In reality, since she rejuvenated in KayCee's medical pod, she was a six foot, stacked, athletic, blonde who was... a drunken slob.

Stella grinned at his shock. "Bet ya seen something like this in videos, huh?"

"Ah." The man forced his eyes up. "S... pizza...and stuff..."

"You know it's kind of boring here. You want to come in for a threesome?"

He looked around, probably for a hidden camera TV crew, but his eyes lit up with a hope that was about to get crushed. "I... I'm not sure I should. I need to get back to my partner. Orders..."

"No, it's good. You can have me anyway you want, but you should know." She hooked a thumb toward me. "He only does guys and since his transformation he got..." She picked up one of the large subs and bounced it in her hand a couple of times. "...big. Like *really* big."

Sweat literally formed on this guy's brow. "Um, no, thank you."

"Leave the guy alone, Stella." I came over and took the food. "She's messing with you. She's a lesbian and I'm not. I mean... I'm not gay, not a lesbian. Well, I mean I'm neither."

"Yeah... Sure. No problem pal." He started backing away.

"Just the tip?" asked Stella. "Sorry, I meant do you want a tip?"

He turned and hurried away toward the walkway stairs. I poked my head out the door and yelled after him. "No, seriously, I'm not gay!"

Turns out several of our neighbors were outside. Realizing the looks I was getting, I pulled my head in and slammed the door. "Son of a bitch!"

"Oh my God! That went so much better than I planned." Stella grabbed the food and put it on the coffee table.

"We have to move!"

"Why? Because our pretend neighbors think you're gay? So what?"

"I..." I scratched my chin, trying to figure out how to explain to my lesbian roommate that I didn't want people to think I'm gay without stepping onto a minefield. I finally sighed "Okay, you got me in a box here."

"Yes, I do. Burnt food aside. This has been a good day." She grinned and pulled a laptop out of one of the pizza boxes. I flipped open the rest. "Damn it!"

"What?"

"They cooked the feta!"

One heart attack amount of food later, Stella contacted Brennan through the laptop.

"We may have to wait until this weekend to reunite you with KayCee," Brennan told us after he had been filled in.

"Why?" I peered suspiciously at his image on the laptop. "What are you doing with her?"

"Nothing. She's working in the lab. I just don't want the bioform to leave here. It's too risky. You'll have to fly back on your days off and merge with her then."

"We just told you my cover is blown and possibly Stella's as well. We need her."

"I'm not disagreeing with you, but you'll need to wait. Besides spy craft is like chess. You move, then they move. They may accelerate their plans now that you are on to them, but it will be a war of shadows. You'll go back to work tomorrow, and both sides will pretend nothing is amiss until one of us is ready to make a move."

"You're assuming aliens know how to play chess," I groused. "How about using a volunteer?"

"To do what?" the colonel asked.

"To transport KayCee. Just have her hitch a ride inside a volunteer and then fly them out here. Once we meet up, KayCee can merge with me, and it's game on."

"Sounds good to me," Stella mumbled around a slice of pizza.

Brennan leaned back and rubbed his eyes. "Yeah, that might work. I'll just have to find someone willing to do it. I'm not going to order anyone to merge with her."

"I wouldn't ask you to, and KayCee would refuse to do it if the person wasn't willing. There *is* some danger to it."

"Give me time to figure it out. In the meantime, go do that night out with your coworkers. See if anything is off with your new buddy. Or any of the others for that matter." He drummed his fingers on his desk. "I'd love to get a scan of his brain. See what it shows."

I raised my eyebrows. "You're not serious?"

The big man shrugged. "Of course, I am. But there is just no way to do it without raising suspicion."

"Right, because you and your people would never abduct anyone off the street in broad daylight."

"One, you are now one of my people. Two, you were a special case."

Stella peered into the screen. "Why can't we just raid the place and send troops into the tunnel?"

"They'll be gone before our boots hit the tunnel floor. The Sleestaks have been avoiding us for years."

I shuddered at the name he used. Stella cocked her head. "Wait! How long have we been aware of them?"

"Fall of '81. Now, how long have they've been doing it is a much-debated question. They had infiltrated certain industries and our space program. That's why we created that miniseries that came out in '84."

"*V*?" I asked. "That was you guys? Why?"

"Before my time obviously, but yeah. Propaganda purposes. If they got discovered, we didn't want people feeding them Reese's Pieces, riding around on bicycles, and hiding them from the government."

"So, they don't really eat live mice?" Stella sounded disappointed. "Because that scene was awesome!"

"I don't know, maybe. It was before my time." Brennan leaned forward in his chair. "They have been very tough to pin down. They don't use a bioform like KayCee's people do. Instead, we think they use human lizard hybrids to infiltrate."

"What do you mean hybrids?" Stella sounded fascinated at the idea. "Like they're mating with humans?"

"Really?" I asked her. "The idea of having sex with a giant iguana excites you?"

"Hey, don't kink shame me!" She grinned. "I'm just saying the idea of sex with an alien is intriguing. What's wrong with that? You saw what KayCee really looks like. Are you saying you wouldn't sleep with her in her natural body?"

"KayCee looks very different than these things, and to answer your question, no, I wouldn't. She's been living in my head for a year, it would be weird."

"Okay I get that. But what about if it was one of her coworkers?"

"Ah. Well, maybe."

Brennan cleared his throat, bringing our attention back to his image on the laptop. "If we can put a pin on which one of you wants to play Captain Kirk, any chance you were able to search Doctor Kemp's office during your little adventure?"

"You know that's the second Kirk reference I got today." I shrugged at him. "Sorry, I couldn't. I was assigned a different building. I'll see what I can do tomorrow. If not, the next day for sure. Karen has meetings Wednesday mornings, and the maintenance crew allegedly slacks off while she's gone."

"Good luck and keep me posted," Brennan said as he signed off.

Chapter 13 –
Why Do These Things Happen to Me?

The next day found me in the locker room with the other maintenance workers. Karen threw around some snide remarks but didn't single me out this time. Apparently, I was no longer the new guy as HR had hired two more workers. A tall, lanky fellow with a shaved head in his fifties and a cute woman with shoulder-length raven black hair in her late twenties or early thirties. I was left on my own as Manny was assigned to show the woman around.

I didn't know the name of the guy who gave the briefing, but I was assigned to Building A, which housed Kemp's office.

After the briefing, I walked over to Manny, who was talking to his new trainee. "Hey buddy, you got a second?"

He gave me a blank look for enough seconds that it started to become uncomfortable before shaking his head. "Sorry, Lock, I didn't get a lot of sleep last night. I had the strangest dreams. This is one of our new hires. Itza Canul. She's originally from Belize. Itza, this is Lock Ferguson. He's from New Jersey and just started this week as well."

"Hello, Lock." She held out her hand. "It's a pleasure to meet you." My brain did a skip, unable to determine the origin of her accent. Well, more accurately, her lack of accent. It was so generic USA, it had stumped the analyzer Kreb installed in my head when he turned me into a superweapon. My brain switched gears and informed me that her facial features showed Mopan ancestry, a subethic group of the Maya people. My eyes simply told me she was beautiful and very short.

"Hi, Itza. Nice to meet you too. And I'm from New Hampshire, not New Jersey." Her hazel eyes were so light they almost looked golden. "Manny, I got Building A today, but I don't know the layout."

"Yeah, Karen likes to do that to the new people. She throws you in the deep end without a life preserver and then yells at you for drowning." He pulled a pack of papers out of his locker and handed it to me. "Here's a cheat sheet. Start with the top floor, empty the trash cans in all the offices and break rooms. Once you've done that, start at the top again and clean and stock all the bathrooms."

"No vacuuming or sweeping?" I flipped through the packet. It was photocopies of hand-drawn layouts of the floors of each of the buildings. It was a huge security breach and had probably been made by one of the maintenance people. It even listed whose offices were where.

"Only if someone asks you to. Otherwise, it's done during off hours. Each floor has its own utility closet, with supplies and equipment. Don't take anything to another floor unless you run out. There's a clipboard to mark supplies we're running low on."

"Sounds well thought out. What's with the stars penciled in next to some of these offices?"

He hesitated, glancing at Itza before continuing. "Those are people watch out for."

"Pain in the asses? Likes to order you to do stupid stuff that doesn't really need to be done?"

"Had them in your last job too?"

"Oh, yeah."

Manny grabbed my arm as I turned away. "One last thing. Keep those maps I gave you on the down low. We're not really supposed to have those."

"No problem, I get it. Thanks, buddy." I waved at both of them and headed to Building A.

I rode the elevator to the top floor, grabbed a utility cart out of the storage closet and got to work. The actual work was very similar to my old job as the municipal janitor in my hometown, but there was a big difference. In my former employment, the town hall and the other government building were in a state of decay, and I had to fight to get enough toilet paper for the bathrooms. Here, everything was gleaming and state of the art. The toilets not only flushed themselves, but there was also a cleaning cycle!

Another thing that was different was how I was treated. Everyone who worked in town hall had known me all my life, and while I had been the town laughingstock as the kid who claimed he had been abducted by aliens, there had at least been a familiarity with the people whose offices I cleaned. This was a very different situation. I may as well have been invisible as I knocked and entered offices to empty the waste barrels. The only ones who didn't treat me as a nonentity were the ones that had stars on Manny's maps. Even they had no idea I was new as they barked out their various orders. One guy claimed he had told me three times about the spots on his windows and if I didn't clean them this time, he would have me fired.

He, at least, will remember me. After inspecting the window, I plucked his glasses off his head, wiped down the lenses and placed them back on him. He blinked a couple of times, looked out the window and turned red. He mumbled something, sat down and furiously started typing on his computer, refusing to look up while I was still in the room.

Kemp's office was mid-level, and I timed it so I was on the floor when he left for lunch. His clothes were rumpled, and his hair hadn't seen a comb in a while. He stopped and smiled as he started to walk past me. "Sorry, have we met?"

"No sir," I replied. "I've only been here a few days. This is my first time assigned to this floor."

"Well then, welcome to the floor." He held out a hand. "Edward Kemp."

"Lock Ferguson." I shook his hand. He seemed nice enough but had one of those smiles reserved for talking to the very dim. The type that made it seem they were in on a joke you didn't know about.

"Nice to meet you." He gestured toward his office. "I am going to lunch right now. Perfect time to take care of my trash. That way I am not in the way."

Ah, one of those.

Some people don't know what to do with themselves when the janitor shows up. They prefer we take care of their offices when they aren't there. It's less awkward for them that way.

"Sure thing, Dr. Kemp. I'll take care of it right now."

"Excellent. Thank you." He paused. "You know what. I have a good feeling about you. I sense great things in your future."

"Umm, thanks." He nodded and walked away, whistling.

Strange dude.

Once the elevator doors closed on him, I entered his office, leaving the door open. My "how to be a spy in ten easy steps" trainers had told me that no one would pay attention to a janitor fussing around an open office as they walked by. But if someone walked in, they would want to know why I closed the door to empty the trash.

I increased my hearing and once I determined no one was near, I slipped a data retrieval device into his computer port. While it cracked his security and downloaded his info, I quickly looked through his desk drawers and filing cabinet. Aside from a stash of vanilla porn magazines, there was nothing even vaguely incriminating. Even his trash was boring.

Once it was done, I retrieved the device, emptied his trash barrel and moved on. My very first time as a spy, and it was boring as hell. So was the rest of my day. I completed all my assignments and returned to the locker room at the end of the shift to change out of my overalls.

As I walked into the break room, Itza was talking to several of the other maintenance workers. Seeing me, she waved. "Lock, are you going with the rest of us?"

"Yup. I just need to do something really quick, and I'll meet you all there. Where are we going?"

"Chicanery's Pub on Main Street," one of the others called over. "You can't miss it."

"Thanks." I gave a wave back and headed to my car. I zipped over to the gate guard to find out Stella had already left for the day. I called her, but she didn't pick up.

"Damn it, Stella." I wanted to hand the stolen data off to her, but she was making it difficult. I looked at my watch. I had no idea how long the crew hung out at the pub, but figured I had enough time to drop the device off at the apartment and head over to Main Street before everyone left.

I gunned the rental around some corners and eventually made it back to where Stella and I were currently staying. I jumped out of the car and took the stairs two at a time.

Going out with coworkers shouldn't have been a priority, but KayCee and I had been on the run for so long that I hadn't hung out with anyone but her in a year. Not that I had a choice with hanging out with KayCee since she had been forced to set up residence in my brain. The whole time she was renting out space in my skull, I had resented it. But now that she was gone, I was missing her presence.

I got to our apartment to find a pair of women's underwear hanging from the doorknob. The repeating pattern of cats and magnets told me they weren't Stella's. I was familiar enough with my slob of a roommate's taste in clothes to know she didn't wear anything that cutesy, regardless of the double meaning. "Damn it, Stella. It's supposed to be a sock!"

Grumbling to myself, I plucked the underwear from the knob to get at the lock and used my key. I moved up to the deadbolt and discovered my key didn't work on it.

Are you kidding me? She didn't give me keys to both locks?

I banged on the door. Stella had turned the music up to cover any noise she and her friend might be making, and unfortunately it was loud enough to drown out my pounding. There was a back door on the other side of the building. Maybe Stella hadn't locked the deadbolt on it. I zipped down the stairs and had just passed the laundry room when I heard a woman shriek. I turned to find an older woman pointing at me.

"Pervert!"

"Excuse me?"

"I caught you." People started poking their heads out of their doors. Not Stella though. Her attention was on somebody else at the moment. I shook my head in confusion. "Lady, what are you talking about?"

She waggled her finger at me. "You were stealing women's panties from the laundry room. In horror I realized I was still holding the underwear from the doorknob.

Oh, this is not good!

"N-No, that's not what happened." In a panic, I waved the underwear as I was talking, which from the look of people's faces, just made things worse. "I didn't steal these!"

"Well, whose are they then?" she demanded.

"They belong to a woman who is with my roommate."

"Do you always go around sniffing your roommate's girlfriend's panties?"

"What? No. She's not even her girlfriend."

"So, you just sniff stranger's panties then?"

"There was *no* sniffing! Can you stop saying panties, please?" My face felt hot in embarrassment, and beads of sweat formed on my forehead. This was a nightmare.

Her glare somehow deepened. "Why? Are you getting excited over the word?"

"There has been a misunderstanding here. Can I just explain?" As I spoke, a man stepped out of the small group that was gathering to watch the spectacle that was my life.

I groaned as I recognized him as one of the neighbors who had been present during the pizza debacle the other night. He was currently wearing a T-shirt commemorating the tenth anniversary of a local gay pride parade.

Oh, God. This is actually about to get worse. How is that possible?

He gestured at me while addressing those present. "Not only is he a pervert, but he's also a homophobe!"

"I am *not* a homophobe!"

"So, just a pervert then?" snarked my original accuser.

I ignored her. "My roommate is gay!"

"Jesus, that's like saying some of my friends are black." said a black guy who stepped through the crowd and started holding hands with Parade Guy. I was in full panic mode at this point, while a tiny part of my brain kept chanting, *Don't mention my black ex-girlfriend, Don't mention my black ex-girlfriend.*

"Look, I am not a pervert, nor a homophobe."

"So just a racist." The woman asked. She'd have fit right in at Salem in the 1690s.

"Where did that come from?" I asked, my exasperation clear in my voice.

"That dog whistle comment about black friends," she told me.

"I didn't say that!" I pointed at the black guy. "He said it."

"Why are you verbally attacking my boyfriend. Because he's black or because he's gay? Or both?" shouted Parade Guy.

"Because he said it!" I half shrieked. "And it was a correction, not a verbal attack!"

His boyfriend leaned on his shoulder. "Is this the one who shouted at the pizza guy last night?"

"Yeah, that's him."

The woman cocked her head at me. "What do you have against pizza? Who's anti-pizza?"

Oh, for the love of God.

"He's probably not a homophobe," said the boyfriend.

"Thank you!"

"I think he's closeted gay," he finished.

I started to raise my hand to pinch the bridge of my nose when I remembered I was still holding the underwear. I hastily stuffed them in my pants pocket.

"Self-hater." Parade Guy nodded. "That's the worst. So sad."

"I am not—" my brain kicked in at the last second—"staying here to listen to any more of this."

I stomped over to my rental car, the group following me with the crazy lady at the front of the pack.

"I saw you stuff those panties in your pocket. You're trying to get rid of the evidence."

I ignored her and tried to open the door. Unfortunately, without KayCee, my powers get a little wonky and sometimes respond to cues in my body, like an adrenaline spike. So, when I went to open the door, I ripped off the door handle.

As I stood there stupidly staring at it, someone in the crowd laughed and I snapped. Growling, I grasped the door and ripped it off the hinges, tossing it aside. There was stunned silence and I got in and started the car up.

I try very hard not to be a petty person, but sometimes I fail. As I drove away, I flipped them all off.

CHAPTER 14 –
WHY I SHOULDN'T DRINK WITH COWORKERS

"I hate my life." I continued to mutter to myself as I drove the rental car to the pub. I ignored the looks I got driving with a missing door and kept an eye out for cops. I didn't know if it was legal to drive the car like this, but the way my luck was going, I'd somehow end up getting arrested, and I didn't think Brennan would be thrilled if he had to send someone to bail me out of jail.

I pulled into Chicanery's Pub's parking lot. It was a large establishment and shared a parking lot with several restaurants. I found a spot in the back between two large pickup trucks. Hopefully no one would notice the lack of a door.

Entering the pub, I was assaulted with loud southern rock and a lot of hooting and hollering. Apparently, it was a very popular location for after-work drinking. There was an empty stage on my left and in front of it was a mechanical bull. It was currently being ridden by a bleach blond in daisy dukes and a tube top. She was more in danger of falling out of her top than off of the bull. It was spinning so slowly I had to check to see if it was even on.

I spotted a couple of my coworkers waving their hands at me. Itza, Manny, Karl, and about ten others were sitting at a large table in the corner. I made my way through the crowd of guys cheering on the blond. Itza looked good, having changed into a white cotton shirt and jeans. She patted an empty seat next to her and I slid into it.

"What's with the wannabe Pamela Anderson?" I asked.

Several of the other older workers laughed but Itza gave me a quizzical look. "Who?"

Guess they didn't have Baywatch in Belize. Or is she too young? God, I'm old. I might look in my thirties but if I had a lawn, I'd be yelling at kids to get off of it.

"The blonde." I jerked my thumb toward the bull rider. "Everyone here is dressed like they just got off work but her. She looks like she escaped from a music video from the '90s."

Karl, the guy who had originally invited me out, leaned over. "She works here. All the waitresses dress like that and take turns on the bull. Fair warning, service this time of day is slow."

I scanned the crowd and spotted various waitresses in similar attire. "Oh, I get it. It's a breastaurant!"

Itza snorted as she took a drink and wound up with the hiccups. "That's a good one."

"Not my joke. That's what they call these places." I waved at a waitress, who started making her way over. She was a brunette instead of a blonde, but she had the same tube top and shorts, and would never be endanger of drowning.

"Oh! I learned something new. We don't have them where I'm from." Itza seemed to be a few drinks ahead of me. So did Manny, who was staring off into space, letting the conversations flow around him.

"Breasts? Really?" That was weak. I always had weak game, but that was a new low.

She snorted again. "You're funny!"

I leaned over to Karl. "How many has she had?"

He pointed to her beer and held up two fingers. "Oh, and the last one of us here buys a round."

Wow, she must be a lightweight.

"You sir, are full of shit!" I gave Karl a grin. The waitress purposely leaned over me, giving me a good view of what Stella liked to refer as *guaranteed tip generators*. I forced myself not to look and instead gestured around the table. "A round for my friends, please."

"Is that a Massachusetts accent?" She smiled, recognizing my struggle for what it was.

"New Hampshire, actually."

"Close enough. What can I get for you?"

Karl said service was slow. Might as well plan ahead.

"Five shots of tequila please." That turned a few heads. The waitress raised an eyebrow but didn't say anything.

As she walked away, Itza put her head close enough to mine I could smell the beer on her breath. "I like them."

"What?" I turned back to her.

"Breasts!" She gave hers a squeeze. "I haven't had these for too long, but I like them. Very bouncy, they are."

"Oh, well, they look very real."

Oh boy, she must have pregamed before getting here. Then again, she's not slurring and isn't glassy eyed. I might just be judging based on hiccups and some awkward banter. Maybe this is just not-at-work Itza. I hate being sober around people who have already started drinking.

That thought reminded me of something. I closed my eyes and mentally disabled my ability to process alcohol. It was one of the few things I made sure I knew how to do without KayCee. Otherwise, I could drink forever and not get drunk and that was not how I wanted to go through life. Especially after what I had just gone through at the apartment complex.

I opened my eyes to see the waiter coming back with a helper. Their trays held our drinks. "I thought Karl said service was slow."

Itza shrugged. "I think your order piqued her interest."

The drinks got handed out. The waitress saved mine for last, lining up five shots of tequila in front of me. Each had a slice of lime perched on the edge of the shot glass. With a flourish, she placed a saltshaker in front of me before watching me expectantly.

"What?" I looked around. Not only was the whole table watching me, but a couple of other patrons had also walked over to watch. "Ah, I think you have the wrong idea. I was told service could be slow at this time of day, so I got these to space them out."

"No way, Lock." Itza waved her hand around the room. "You can't disappoint everyone."

"Oh no. Peer pressure! My only weakness."

"Wait." The waitress put her hand on my shoulder. "Your name is Lock? That's so funny."

"Well, it's a nickname." I suddenly had a bad feeling.

"That's the name of the founder of my religion."

Oh no! It's not possible.

She pointed to a charm on her necklace. Much like my hometown, it was deep in a valley surrounded by two mountains. I stared at the charm in shock. It was a mop made of gold. "I follow Lockism. You said you were from New Hampshire, right? That's where it was first formed. Is Lock a common name there?"

Oh. My. God.

I turned back to the table and poured salt on my hand, licked it, downed a shot, and sucked on the lime. I repeated it four more times in rapid succession and quickly had five shot glasses in front of me containing nothing more than lime rinds. "Again, please."

As my table erupted in cheers, the waitress shrugged, gathered the glasses and headed back to the bar.

"Is that something you do a lot?" Itza asked. "That seemed excessive."

"First time." My stomach rolled for a second but settled down. "It's been a bit of a day."

Things got a little blurry after that. When I came up for air, Manny and several others had left. I found five more empty shot glasses in front of me and that I had been carrying on a conversation with Itza. "Ah, sorry. Drank those quicker than I should have. What were we talking about?"

"You asked how long I'd been in the States."

"Right, that was it."

"I've only been here a month."

Only been here a month and she already passed the background check for the job? No wonder the aliens were able to sneak in.

"Really. Your English is flawless!"

"English is actually the main language of Belize."

"Oh, I didn't know that."

Still, I'd think there be some type of accent.

She took a sip of her drink. "It's very different than I thought it would be."

"TV and movies don't do us justice?"

"My family was very strict. I didn't see a lot of TV or movies. But my schoolteacher was from here and told me stories."

I guess that could explain the lack of an accent. Why am I even thinking about this? Brennan and Stella have turned me paranoid.

"So, what do you think so far?"

"I think I have a lot of catching up to do." She moved closer to me.

"Um." The changes to my body had left me with an athletic body and a rugged-looking face that did turn the occasional eye. However, my confidence still thinks I'm an old, overweight geek with a bad comb-over. It didn't help that I was a charter member of what Stella called the *2x4 club*. As in, I'd have to be hit over the head with a two-by-four to realize someone was hitting on me. I was forty before I knew being asked in for coffee didn't mean coffee. And since I didn't drink it back then, I missed more than a couple of opportunities over the years. Now, adding in the booze I had been putting into my system, I found myself struggling to come up with an appropriate reply.

I must have taken too long because she frowned. I ducked my head. "Sorry, the booze is slowing me down."

She ignored me, staring over my shoulder.

I turned to see two large guys standing in the doorway of the pub, scanning the room. The weather was warm, but both were wearing light coats. Always a great way to hide any weapons that you're carrying. One was bald, the other had a buzzcut. Both had muscles to spare. "Who are those guys?"

"Remember when I said my family was very strict? I think those men were sent to bring me back."

"What? Is your family in a cult?"

"Something like that."

I lowered my voice. "It's not Lockism, is it?"

"What's that?"

"Never mind." I stood up. "I'll take care of them. Do they have any weapons?"

"None that they would use in a public place like this. But they are very dangerous. You should not get involved."

Karl interrupted his conversation with another coworker when I stood up. "Problem?"

"Maybe." The two spotted Itza and started striding across the room, shoving anyone who got in there way. *Combat Mode Lock* started to take over, but I squished it down in my brain. My base abilities were so advanced, two guys in a bar should be nothing more than a chance to impress Itza. Besides, after the day I had, I thought punching a couple of idiots was just the therapy I needed. I'd like to have blamed those thoughts on the tequila, but in truth, I'm just an idiot.

Without thinking about it, my mind reached out to the bar's music system, mentally thumbing through its song selection. *Oh look. They have Country and Western!*

I smiled as I found one that I liked.

The two stopped in front of me. Their stances and demeanor screamed military training. I stepped into their view of Itza. "The lady doesn't want to go with you. To quote Manumana the Slender: 'Leave or you will anger me.'"

Baldy didn't bother to reply, throwing a punch at me instead. He had me by about four inches and sixty pounds. I should have gone flying. His eyes widened in surprise when I didn't budge. I grabbed his arm and took him to the ground in a modified arm bar takedown. Van Zant's *Takin' up Space* started playing across the bar's sound system.

Baldy's partner did a spinning back kick. Stella, who unlike me, is an actual martial arts practitioner, sneers at kicks above the waist. Claims it's flashy bullshit that will get you hurt in a real fight. Normally, I'd say she was right, but Buzzcut was unbelievable fast. His foot was a blur as it came at my head.

Well, a blur to everyone in the room but me, thanks to the alien modifications made to my body. I caught his ankle and shoved him back and to the floor. The two scrambled to their feet. Both men took fighting stances as they studied me.

Karl stepped up next to me. He raised his fists in a way that told me he probably hadn't been in a fight since second grade. "You heard him. Get out of here."

Baldy shot forward striking Karl on the chin who dropped like a puppet with its strings cut. Buzzcut launched a fury of blows at me, that I kept deflecting. Unlike the movies where the bad guys only attack the hero one at a time. Baldy also started swinging at me before Karl even hit the floor.

These guys had worked together before. They weren't getting in each other's way and their attacks were quick, hard, and efficient. All things I should have noticed. But I was stronger, faster, and very, very drunk. I planted my legs, ignoring kicks and attempted leg sweeps. Instead, I concentrated on blocking their hands.

I was actually enjoying myself. With all the changes wrought to my body, I barely qualified as human. As good as they were, it was the equivalent of being attacked by a couple of fourth graders. Keep blocking and try not to hurt their feeling by laughing.

Then a fist made it through, hitting me in the upper chest. And it hurt. *A lot.*

What the hell?

I upped my speed and after a few strikes so did they. At this point everyone but Itza had backed away from us. She was staying behind me. Someone had even dragged poor Karl away. The pub bouncers were close but not interfering. They looked a bit shellshocked at the flurry of swings.

I got hit again and then again. Each strike was painful. More than it should have been from a vanilla human.

Shit. They're not from Itza's family. They're here for me. Oh, crap! I still have the stolen data stick on me!

I cranked my speed up to eleven and threw a punch at Baldy. It got inside his guard and connected with the side of his jaw. At that level of strength and speed, it should have broken it. Instead, he staggered back, shaking his head as he collected himself. Buzzcut stepped up the intensity to cover for his stunned partner.

Okay. They can take a serious punch. That means the kid gloves can come off.

While still keeping it close to human range, I increased my speed and strength even more. I grabbed the back of Buzzcut's head, spinning him around, and slamming his face through the wall next to me. Said wall wasn't sheet rock, but rough-hewn wood boards with various bric-a-brac nailed to it. Buzzcut's head smashed through the wood, sending splinters everywhere. When I let go, his body went slack, held up only by his head being stuck in the wall.

Baldy snarled something I didn't catch and reached for his rear waistband. I closed the distance and throat-punched him before he could draw whatever he was going for.

He staggered back, grasping his throat and making a weird gurgling sound. He pulled a gun that my brain IDed as a Sig Sauer P220 Hunter, which means it was chambered in 10mm with eight rounds in the magazine and another in the pipe.

I pulled the pistol from his hand, ejecting the magazine and racking the single round out of the pipe. I field stripped it and dropped all the pieces except for the barrel which I stuck in my pocket. That done, I grabbed Itza by the hand and made for the door.

I expected her to be scared but instead saw a gleam of excitement in her eye and a wicked grin on her face. I frowned. "Do you know those guys?"

"I've never seen those two before, but I'm sure they were sent for me."

"They may not have been." I took us out a side door. "I have people after me as well."

I led her over to my rental.

Both her eyebrows rose at the sight of it. "Where's the door?"

"It fell off." I waved her to the other side. "Get in. Let's get out of here before the cops show up."

"Should you be operating this? You've had a lot to drink."
Good point.

I concentrated, reactivating the abilities that allowed me to process toxins and poisons. By the time I got in and started the car, I was completely sober again. "Yeah, I'm good. I have a high tolerance."

I pulled the car out of the parking lot. In the mirror, two motorcycles headed toward us at a high speed. "Crap. My luck isn't good enough for that to be a couple of joy riders."

I pushed down on the pedal and slowly watched the speedometer needle creep up. "Fucking cheap-ass government. No more economy models!"

"What was that?" Itza turned back from watching the bikes.

"I said you look like a model."

"Oh, you're so sweet." She tucked a loose wisp of hair behind her ear. "Do all Americans fight like that?"

"Umm, yeah, sure? All those action movies are totally true." I turned a sharp right and a hubcap rolled off a tire. "See!"

The bikes easily overtook the POS I was driving. One held back and the other was inching up on the driver's side. Their clothes told me these were different guys then back at the pub. The one closing on us drew a pistol. "Fuck this! Time for some hardball. Can you hold the steering wheel for a second?"

"I don't know how to drive."

"What? How do you get to work?"

"Carpool?"

"Well, just hold the wheel straight for a second."

As soon as she had a good grip on it. I let go and pulled out the gun barrel I stole earlier out of my pocket. As the biker started to line up a shot on me, I whipped it straight at his helmet visor. With the strength I put into the throw, the gun barrel punched through his helmet like a rifle round. He flipped backwards off his bike which crashed into a guard rail. "One down."

The back window shattered as bullets flew past us. Itza jumped in surprise, and I grabbed the wheel as she let go.

She hunched down in her seat. "Do you have a weapon?"

"I don't. Do you?" I watched as the remaining bike followed us. The driver wasn't making the same mistake as his buddy. Instead of coming along side of us, he stayed behind the car, carefully picking his shots.

"No, but I'm thinking I should after this."

"Yeah. Not a bad idea." The biker ran out of rounds. As I watched out the rear mirror, He ejected the magazine, trying to pull another out and load it. "You might want to hang tight for a second."

While the biker was distracted, I slammed on the brakes. Before he could recover, his bike struck the rear of our car, upending him off the motorcycle and onto the roof. Thanks to the lack of a door, I was able to reach up and grab his flailing arm, pulling him to the ground.

I hopped out of the stopped car and pulled him to his feet. My plan was to question him, but he had somehow held onto the gun and tried to point it at me. I pushed it aside as a round went off. I tore the gun out of his hand and threw it.

Grasping his jacket with both hands. I lifted him off his feet. "What the hell do you want?"

My head snapped back in surprise as the irises of his eyes turned to slits. "Fuck!"

He snapped his arms out, breaking my grip, and fell into a crouch. Before I could react, he did a spinning leg sweep, taking both my legs out. I actually saw my boots above me before hitting the ground.

I rolled to the side as he tried to pounce on me, and scrambled to my feet. The idea of getting into a ground game with a guy that might be part snake didn't appeal to me. As he came at me, I *moved*, slipping behind him and snapping his neck.

As his lifeless body crumbled to the ground, Itza poked her head out of the car. "Lock, are you all right?"

"Yeah, stay in the car for a minute." As I answered her, I saw steam coming out of the car's engine compartment with a stream of liquid pouring out of it.

Damn, they killed my car!

I pulled the guy's body into a nearby alley and pulled out my phone, calling Stella. It went to voicemail. "Seriously? You better not be ignoring my call because your still doing stuff with your latest. Contact! Contact! Contact! Watch your six!"

I hung up and pressed a predial.

A prerecording of a woman's voice answered. "Washington Circus. For a list of our shows, press one. For tickets, press two. For employment inquiries, press three."

I pressed three.

"Good morning," said a woman in a chipper voice. "This is the Washington Circus Human Resources Division. How may I help you?

"I'm replying to the ad online," I told her.

"I'm sorry, we have no openings at this time. Please feel free to try again later."

"That's too bad." I sighed before saying the rest of the code phrase through gritted teeth. "I'm an experienced geek. No one is geekier than me."

"Hello Geek, This is Ticketbooth. What can I do for you?"

I hate my freaking codename! Damn it, Brennan!

"I need to speak to Ringleader."

"He's in a meeting, Geek. Can I take a message?"

"I had a run-in with several of the competition's roustabouts. I have one with me now, but he won't be playing anymore local shows."

"Standby, I'll pull him out." There was a click, and elevator music started playing.

There has to be a level of hell where this type of music is played on a loop forever.

The music stopped. "Geek, this is Ringleader."

I gave a sigh of relief at Brennan's voice. "I had an encounter with about four roustabouts. They were a new type of employee I haven't encountered before."

"Is Cannonball with you?"

Yeah, give Stella the cool codename.

"No, I was out with coworkers at a local pub when this encounter happened. She's at the apartment and I need to find a new ride to get there."

"Not a problem. There is a clown car around the corner from the apartment with a couple of lion tamers. I'll have them backstop her. If the competition isn't there, they'll sit on it and see if anyone shows up for the late show."

"She's not alone. There's a ticketholder with her. A female."

"Of course, there is." His tone was more resigned then frustrated. Stella was Stella after all. "You said you have a roustabout with you, and they can't play shows anymore?"

"Correct."

"Do they look like ticketholders?"

"Yes."

"Oh, that's a good find! Ping is showing you in an alley. Leave them and I'll send a couple of lion tamers for a pick up. Do you need an extraction?"

"Well, I'm sort of on a date with a ticketholder, a coworker."

"You're as bad as Cannonball. Go to ground somewhere else until then. I'll have a message sent to you on Cannonball's status as well as when you can go back. Do you think it's safe for you to go to work tomorrow?"

"Depends on what happens the rest of the night. But yeah, I'll give it a shot."

"Okay. Listen, that package you asked for will be there tomorrow. Do you need anything else?"

"Yeah, My car didn't really survive this. Can someone handle getting it out of here?"

"It'll be taken care of, and we'll get you a replacement."

"Something fast this time. We got passed by a kid on a tricycle."

"You should be used to that. I know what you drove for the past couple decades. Anything else? Butler? A private cook perhaps?"

"Yeah, one last thing, I really hate the codename I was assigned."

"I know. Why do you think I picked it?" He chuckled.

"This is totally because I demanded to keep the beard."

"If that was true, your codename would have been Bearded Lady." The phone went dead.

"Bastard!" I stuffed my phone in my pocket, pulled a piece of cardboard over the dead guy and walked over to the car. After seeing the amount of fluid on the ground, I didn't bother to see if it still drove. "Itza, are you all right?"

The passenger door opened, and she popped out. "I'm fine. What happen to the other guy?"

"I knocked him out," I lied. "We should get out of here before more of his friends arrive, but the car's too damaged to drive."

She pointed to the bad guy's downed motorcycle. "What about that?"

"I dunno." I walked over and pulled it up. The front wheel miraculously remained undamaged from the impact. Aside from some dents and scrapes, it seemed functional. "The problem is, I don't really know how to ride a motorcycle. And these sports bike can be tricky."

"How hard can it be?"

"Well, I mean I know the basics of it. It's like driving a standard. Clutch, shift, gas. It's doing all that while balancing that has me concerned."

A wicked grin appeared on Itza's face. "I'm willing if you are."

"Yeah, that's cause you're still buzzed. Trust me, it's a bad idea."

She walked around the bike. "How does the passenger stay on?"

"Well, they'd have to hold onto the driver."

"*Rea-lly*? So, if you were driving it, I'd have to hold onto you? Tightly?"

"You're evil, you know that?"

She just smiled and patted the seat.

I sighed. "Fine, but if I die in a motorcycle accident after surviving everything that happened tonight, I'm going to haunt you!"

***

Thirty minutes and fifty miles later, I pulled into the parking lot of a bar. Itza was trembling as she climbed off the bike. "I'm sorry. I should have believed you. You are really bad at motorcycling."

"I know, I'm sorry." I climbed off the bike as well.

"I mean *really* bad!"

"Yeah, I get it."

She stretched, trying to work the kinks out of her back. I found it a welcome distraction. "Now what?"

"I'm not sure." I looked around. The bar whose parking lot we pulled into was a generic watering hole and the area was a cluster of strip malls and storefronts. "I guess I could call a rideshare."

I pulled out my phone to see I had a text message. Cannonball safe. Hunker down for a couple of hours and then you can return.

"Huh."

"What?"

I pointed at the bar. "Or we could kill some time and let things cool down before calling for a taxi."

That evil smile reappeared. "Are you offering to buy me a drink?"

Screw it.

Once again, I turned off my ability to shrug off alcohol. "You know what. Yes, yes, I am!"

Chapter 15 –
Repercussions and Hangovers

I woke up sweating with a pounding headache. Opening my eyes, I found myself in my own bed. Well, the one in the apartment Stella and I were currently staying in. There was movement on the other side of the bed, and I turned my head to find a very nude Itza sleeping beside me. Her side of the blankets had been flung on top of me.

Huh.

I vaguely remembered a lot of small talk and jokes between us at the bar. The type that only seem funny when you've had a few drinks. At some point thinks start to get fuzzy. Then details started drifting back into my brain. Intimate details.

A quick check revealed I was equally naked. I slowly slipped out of the bed, finding my clothes from last night crumpled on the floor. I scooped up what I could and scuttled out of the room, quietly closing the door behind me.

I dressed in the hallway. Pulling on my jeans and T-shirt before slipping into my sneakers. My socks and underwear apparently hadn't made it out of the room with me.

I turned to discover Stella at the end of the hall. Holding two coffee mugs and the biggest shitting grin I've ever seen on her face. Repressing a sigh, I held my index finger to my lips and followed her into the kitchen area.

Stella wordlessly handed me one of the mugs. I took a sip. It was hot chocolate, and it was delicious. "No coffee?"

"We're out. So! I'm not the only one to get lucky last night, huh? She must have taken an early flight." She paused. "Do you smell that? Oh God, the toast!"

"Yeah, let's talk about last night. To start, you freaking locked me out!" I called after her as she dashed over to the counter.

"Well, we wanted some privacy." Stella pulled out two burnt remains from the toaster oven. "Damn it. Nothing in this place works!"

"I got chased around last night by a bunch of disguised lizard people trying to retrieve the data I stole! You know, the data I was supposed to have given you? And by the way, it's supposed to be a sock on the knob. Not underwear!"

"That was my date's doing. I didn't know she turned the deadbolt." Stella emptied a box of cereal into a bowl. "By the way, do you have her underwear? She couldn't find them and wants them back."

"Do you have any idea what happened to me yesterday because of that?" My tirade got interrupted by the doorbell ringing. "Now what?"

"You were supposed to be out drinking with friends." Stella shrugged as she poured milk into the bowl. "The only person I was expecting was Fortune Teller, and she obviously came in late last night."

"Who's Fortune Teller?" I asked as I opened the door. Standing in the doorway was Jeopardy Jones. "Me, I'm Fortune Teller."

"Oh. Umm, hi?" My brain turned to mush at the site of my ex-girlfriend. Wearing a white summer dress, her trademark braids hung down her front. The tips were now dyed a sunset orange. She looked... good.

My brain glitched. My delight at seeing her, warring with uncertainty at what she would say, had combined with complete and downright terror with the fact that a very nude Itza was asleep in my bed.

Jeopardy's right hand swung around connecting with the side of my face. I blinked in surprise at the sting. She pushed me aside and stepped into the apartment, shutting the door. "A letter? You broke up with me in a letter? What the hell is wrong with you?"

"I was trying to keep you safe."

"Do you know how condescending and misogynistic that sounds?" I rose in the air as she utilized her telekinesis. "Do I seem like a fragile flower to you? Or did you forget how I handled myself during that galactic mess of yours last year?"

"Well, when you spell it out like that, yeah. I see your point." Even without her powers, Jeopardy was probably the most squared away out of all of us who had been involved in last year's fiasco.

During the whole thing, I had been a big mope, Stella had just smashed everything in sight, and my cousin Tavish had been, well,

Tavish. Jeopardy had been the one who had remained clearheaded and rational throughout the whole misadventure. I didn't count Brennan. He showed up toward the end.

"Put me down, please. We have nosy neighbors."

Her power snapped off and my feet hit the floor with a thunk.

"I'm sorry. Stella already chewed me out about it. Competence and gender had nothing to do with it. I'd have done everything I did even if you were a guy."

She arched an eyebrow at me. I held up my hands. "Well, not *everything*. It's just that what had happened with Tavish, I couldn't deal with losing anyone else."

Her face softened. "I *am* sorry about Tavish. I read your report on what happened. To lose him twice like that. I can't imagine it."

"Thank you, that means a lot. Not to sound ungrateful, but why are you here? And why am I the only one with a sucky codename?"

"I suggested *Asshole* for yours, but Colonel Brennan insisted this mission had to be circus-themed. As to why I'm here," She tapped her temple, "I brought KayCee."

"They sent you? I thought you were on some sort of secret mission."

"They pulled me off. They wanted to get her to you ASAP, and since I've previously had her in my head, it seemed the easiest way to do it." Golden motes of energy emerged from her skin and floated across to me. Panicked at the idea that Itza could walk in and see the transfer, I stepped directly into the cloud of motes. Motes that made up the energy form of the Sarli alien named KayserCeenarlos. Or as her human friends liked to call her, KayCee.

The motes of energy merged with me, and I heard her familiar voice in my head.

"Ah, that's better. As much as I care for Jeopardy, it is very cramped in her head compared to yours. Hello, Loughlin Ferguson. I have missed you."

"Yeah, I missed you too." I did a double take. "Wait a minute. Did you just say I'm emptyheaded?"

"I thought that was a given," Jeopardy said with acid in her voice. There was a snort from the kitchen area behind me.

"Shut up, Stella." I said.

"These are for you." Jeopardy handed me a set of keys. "It's the Mustang out front."

"Mustang! Cool."

She kept her hand out. "You have a data stick for me?"

"Oh, right." I dug into my pocket for it. "I missed you, Jeopardy. I know I bungled everything, but I did miss you."

"Even with your stupidity, I did miss you, Lock. It's just..." As I pulled the data stick out, the remaining contents of the pocket came out too, tumbling to the floor as I handed her the data stick. Jeopardy stared at the underwear Stella's conquest had left behind. "Apparently, you didn't miss me as much as I thought."

"It's not what you think. It's a whole misunderstanding."

"Lock." My roommate's voice had a tone of warning.

"Not now, Stella." I didn't look back at her.

"Lock, seriously."

"Can you stay out of this?" I whirled around to see Itza emerge from the hallway while buttoning up her shirt.

She looked at Jeopardy and then back at me. "Am I interrupting something?"

"No," Jeopardy said in a voice so cold I could feel frost forming on my shoulders. "It appears I am."

"Either way, I have to get to work. So let me get out of the way." Itza waved at my roommate. "You must be Stella. Nice to meet you."

"Hi." Stella's face was as blank as I had ever seen it as she waved back at Itza.

"I had a great time last night, Lock. We'll have to do it again. But no motorcycle next time." She kissed my cheek as she walked by, stopping in front of Jeopardy. "Hello. You would be Jeopardy. Lock told me so much about you."

"Really, he didn't mention you at all." Jeopardy bent over and hooked the underwear with her index finger. She straightened up and held it out to Itza. "Don't forget these."

Yeah, I'm a dead man.

"Ah, the infamous panties!" Itza smiled sweetly at Jeopardy. "Those aren't mine. I understand they belong to a lady veterinarian that lives in town. Lock told me the most delightful story about them last night."

Jeopardy's jaw dropped as Itza walked out of the apartment, leaving the door ajar. After what seemed like an eternity, her teeth snapped shut, invoking an image of a bear trap slamming closed.

"I swear to God I can explain."

"Don't bother."

"Wait a minute." I growled, frustration getting the better of me. "Why are you mad? You're the one that got engaged."

"What are you talking about? I'm not engaged. I'm not even seeing anyone."

Fucking Stella!

"But you're right. Why should I be mad? After all you already dumped me, right?" Jeopardy threw the underwear at my head. As I managed to catch it, she stormed away without another word.

As I stood there stunned, the woman from yesterday walked by the open door. She stopped, staring at me with the underwear still in my hand. "You are really sick, you know that? Damn pervert!"

"Hey, lady." Stella pointed a spoon at her, milk dripping from it. "Don't you kink shame him."

I gave the lady a quiet smile and swung the door shut. I turned, flinging the damning underwear at Stella.

"Thanks." She caught it. "Umm, about the fiancé thing."

"Seemed funny at the time? Maybe make me squirm a little?"

"Well, part of it was payback for dumping Jeopardy."

I started walking to the hall. "Not really your call, was it? Maybe should have let Jeopardy handle that part?"

"Well, in hindsight, yeah," she said sheepishly. "Where are you going?"

"To get ready for work, because even with a new body and superpowers, I'm still a lowly janitor incapable of having a normal relationship."

"That's not true at all," she called after me.

"Thanks."

"You're a maintenance worker now."

"I. Hate. My. Life."

Chapter 16 –
Pet Projects

The next morning, I walked around the Mustang. "What a hunk of junk!"

It was from the 1970s, and the panels were all mismatched colors with Bondo and rust warring across all of them.

"You are supposed to be keeping a low profile and need a car that would fit your alleged pay scale."

"KayCee, I asked for something fast. The only thing fast about this is how quickly it's going to the junkyard, and all these colors isn't what I would call low profile." I touched my side. "This thing feels weird."

"It is better there than in your pocket. What if you are searched? I still cannot believe you had been keeping it in your bedroom."

"Where else was I going to put it? It's a moot point now. Tell me about the car."

"Open the hood."

As I did, a gleaming engine with lots of chrome greeted me.

"This is a 1970 Ford Mustang Boss 302. A street legal version can do zero to sixty in 6.9 seconds with a top speed of 137mph. This one is considerably faster. Its appearance can give the lie that it's a pet project you have been slowly working on for years."

"Okay, I have to admit. This is actually pretty badass." I slammed the hood shut, got in and turned the key. I was rewarded with a deep throaty growl. "Oh, yeah. I could get used to this!"

"Don't. Because it really is someone's pet project that they have been working on for years."

My joy turned into a sense of impending doom. "Whose?"

Colonel Brennan's.

"I knew it. I just knew you were going to say that!"

"In order to keep the colonel's motor vehicle undamaged, I suggest we activate your enhanced driving skills."

"Sorry, my what?"

"It's one of the many skills Kreb installed you with."

"Are you kidding me, I almost killed myself in a car chase last night. Why am I hearing about this for the first time?"

"You are not. Remember earlier this year you said you were being overwhelmed by the abilities you were exhibiting?"

"Yeah, you were able to isolate and shut off the ones we didn't think were necessary... Oh! Well, shit. I don't even remember that one coming up on the list."

"To be fair, it was a large list, and you were a bit preoccupied with hiding from your government."

"Well, turn on the driver skills, I guess."

"Do you want all of it or just specific vehicles?"

"What's all of it?"

"It allows you to identify and expertly operate all land, air, and water vehicles of human design as well as many of the vehicles of my people."

"That... That seems a lot."

"Shall we start with automobiles and see how it goes?"

"Sounds like a plan. Oh, add in motorcycles if you can."

"Consider it done."

There was a fluttering in my brain that I had learned to recognize as KayCee mucking around with the programming Kreb had installed. KayCee insisted I imagined it, but it was a distinct feeling.

"That should do it."

New knowledge flooded my brain. It was disorienting but passed quickly. I grinned and threw the Mustang in reverse, whipping out of the parking spot. I took off onto the road, rapidly shifting and weaving in and out of cars.

"About Jeopardy Jones."

"Nope, not having this conversation." I downshifted, weaving in and out of traffic.

"Very well."

"How did it go at the base?"

"I was treated very well. But I am feeling bad about deceiving Colonel Brennan and the rest of his team. They have been very welcoming of me."

"Well, yeah. You have something they want." I slid through an intersection where the light may have been just past yellow.

"You have driven through a red light."

"It was pink!"

"Perhaps slow down. Getting stopped by the police could bring undue attention. Especially if they are looking for you concerning your adventures last night."

"Spoilsport." I slowed the car down to a reasonable speed. "Did you learn anything?"

"The base security system was impressive and should have been beyond human capabilities. It took some time, but I was finally able to remotely connect with their computer system. Once I had gained entry, I was able to confirm that they have somehow been able to access my starcraft."

"Crap!" I scratched my chin. "Which means they are playing nice with you in order to find the control orb."

"It is a logical conclusion. Without it they will be unable to operate Quiet Contemplation."

"I still say that is a stupid name for a spacecraft."

"I did not name it."

I pulled up to the front gate of Murtaugh Solutions Unlimited. Without Stella there, I was waved through after showing my badge. "Well, we did assume that they had recovered the crashed lander. You think they got it working without the orb? Somehow used it to get to the starcraft."

"That is the most logical theory at the moment."

"Okay, Spock." I pulled into my parking spot. The throaty growl of the Mustang came to an abrupt halt when I turned off the car. "So, they used the lander to get to *Quiet Contemplation* and somehow managed to get on board. Then what? Reverse engineer it?"

"After putting it in an orbit closer to Earth, yes."

"This is both bad and good." I made sure the car was locked before heading to the building. I'd never hear the end of it from Brennan if it got stolen. "Bad that they are poking around with your people's tech and good because it means we just need to find the lander. You think it's at Ducharme?"

"No. I believe it is here. Do not forget to use a Bluetooth receiver or you will start getting looks."

"Right. No one wants to be the crazy guy who talks to himself." I fished out an earbud and stuck it into my ear. "Right. Wait a minute, you think the lander is here? At MSU? Why?"

> *"This is a test faculty for Murtaugh Solutions Unlimited. Considering their contracts with the United States Space Force, it makes sense that they would receive the lander for study. This is where they do their test flights."*

"Yeah, I haven't got over to the airstrip section of the compound yet. Just two of the buildings." I entered the lobby and flashed my badge at the lobby guard. The *Get Smart* theme played in my head.

> *"Please don't do that. It's annoying."*

"Sorry." I pointed at the ear bud as the guard glanced at me in confusion. He nodded and waved me through. "Considering what's going on, why would they send it here?"

> *"It is all very fascinating. Colonel Brennan gave me a deeper brief before I left. It appears that the Detra Ka infiltrated the US space program at the very beginning. Which makes sense."*

"Wait, Ka? Who are the Detra Ka?" I rode the elevator to the floor the locker room was on.

> *"The Detra Ka is the name of the race of reptilian aliens you encountered."*

The elevator doors opened before I could ask more. Manny and Karl were talking in the hallway. Karl's face split into a big grin when he saw me. "Lock, buddy! You made it!"

"Manny, Karl. How are you?" I asked a bit confused.

"We're fine." Karl threw an arm over my shoulder as we walked to the locker room. "Hey, those were some awesome moves you had last night. You an MMA fighter or something?"

"Yeah, something like that. Sorry, things got a little chaotic last night."

Manny shook his head. "That was reckless. People could have gotten hurt. You should not have provoked those men."

As I opened my locker and took out my coveralls, Karl waved his hand dismissively at Manny. "Provoked. Those guys messed with us and got what was coming to them. It was great. I can't wait until next week."

"What about the cops? Are they looking for me?" I finished buttoning up my coveralls.

"Yeah, right!" Karl snorted as he stepped into his own coveralls. "There's fights at Chicanery's every other night. As long as no one's dead, the cops just kick everyone out."

"Dodged that bullet," I muttered after he stepped away.

"Indeed."

During the briefing, I looked around for Itza but didn't see her. The other new employee was missing as well. After Karen got done chastising us for both real and imagined infractions, we headed out to our assignments. I grabbed Manny on the way.

"Hey, Manny. Have you seen Itza?"

"She didn't come to work today. I suspect it had to do with the men who were after her."

"No, Manny. Those guys were after me. What about the guy that had started with her, the Ichabod Crane looking dude? He's not here either."

Manny's face went blank, and he just spaced out. I waved my hand in front of his face. "You okay?"

He blinked and nodded. "Yes, I'm fine. It is as you said. They were after you. I was mistaken. She must not be feeling well."

"Okay, sure. But what was that? You just zoned out for a second."

"I have... micro-seizures. Due to epilepsy. I'm fine now."

"Oh, sorry man. I didn't mean to pry."

"Not to worry, I'm used to it. But you should forget Itza. She's trouble. I can tell."

"That's the best kind, buddy." I gave him a light punch on the shoulder and headed to my assignment. It was the same building as the day before.

Grabbing the maintenance cart, I resumed my conversation with KayCee. "So, you know these people then?"

"There are a spacefaring race, like my people. Though we use different types of technology."

"Are they dangerous? Are they trying to take over the world? And more importantly, do they eat live mice?"

"They are like any race. Both good and bad. Yes, they do eat their food live. I do not believe they are trying to take over the world. In fact, I think I know who they are."

"Who's that?"

"I suspect they are the legendary Lost Colony."

Chapter 17 –
The Lost Colony

"What the hell is the Lost Colony?" I pushed the cart into an empty office and emptied the wastebasket.

"The Detra Ka have a hierarchy similar to some insects on your planet."

"Right. I ran into the warrior, worker, and creator castes."

"Those are the main three, but there are other castes. They are ruled by a queen. In fact, Detra Ka means the queen's people in one of their ancient languages."

"So, what does Detra Treyga mean?"

"Queen's worker. Detra Tal means queen's warrior and Detra Bel means queen's creator."

"Creator?"

"Scientists, engineers. Skill sets like that."

"No kings?"

"Never. Each colony is ruled by a single queen and the queens are the only females."

"So, the only female in your entire colony is either your mom or your sister?"

"Correct."

"That is both gross and really sad. They must have some pretty twisted porn."

"As I was saying. When the colony gets to a certain size, another queen is born and the colony splits, the new queen and her people move to an uninhabited area and establish a new colony. After they became a spacefaring race, they adapted and expanded. Now, a single colony generally inhabits a planet. Currently there are eight planets inhabited by the Detra Ka. The majority of their worlds are ruled by a single queen."

So, what's the Lost Colony?"

"While the Detra Ka generally has good relations with other races, their queens do not get along. This may be a biological

safeguard to make sure the colony splits. Whatever the reason, some queens try to kill others and absorb their colonies. That is why most planets are only ruled by a single queen.

"More than two thousand years ago, a new queen was born on a Detra Ka planet called Malum. Normally the senior queen sees to the upbringing of the junior queen. The squabbling does not begin until the junior queen reaches maturity. The Detra Malum is a particularly vicious and warlike queen and tried to kill the adolescent queen several times. This forced the immature queen and her followers to flee the planet before they were ready."

"And I take it they got lost? Hence the name?"

"They were headed to an uninhabited and sustainable planet called Virtus."

"If they are cold-blooded like the reptiles on Earth, I'm guessing that planet is significantly warmer than here."

"Correct. Whether the young queen and her people were lost in some unfortunate accident or the Detra Malum had them destroyed is up for debate. We do know that the Detra Malum later sent her people to Virtus to establish a feeder colony there and she is currently the only Detra to rule two planets. In fact, She is now called Detra Malum Virtus."

"She's still alive? How long does that race live?"

"It is a top-tier galactic civilization. Being their queen means she receives the very best of their medical advancements. Barring accident or assassination, she could live several thousand more years."

"Wow! That's insane. So, you said she's called Detra Malum Virtus. Does that mean Queen of Malum and Virtus?"

"Yes."

So, instead of going to Virtus, they somehow ended up here. Is Virtus close to Earth?

"Nothing is close to Earth. You are the galactic version of North Sentinel Island."

"Har, har." I tugged on my beard. "Then how did they get here?"

"I do not know. We could ask them. You do speak their primary language."

"Maybe. Do they jump bodies like your people?"

"First, do not call it that. Second, only my people have evolved the ability to move their consciousness through energy

transfer. That being said, the Detra Ka are more advanced in biotech than my people. I suppose it is possible they may have a technological work-around to accomplish the same thing."

What about making Lizardman-Human hybrids?

"I assume you mean a hybrid of human and Detra Ka. They are not lizardmen."

"You know what I mean."

"Yes, they could easily do that. It would make it easier to move among your people undetected."

"In order to take over the world!" I exited the office and pushed my cart into the next one. The woman at the desk looked up briefly and went back to tying on her computer.

"That does not make sense. Only small parts of your planet is inhabitable for them, and they would be forced to live underground."

"Isn't that what they are doing?" The woman looked up as I spoke. I smiled at her and tapped my ear bud. "Sorry, it's my grandmother."

Without bothering to reply, the woman resumed typing.

"Yes, but that cannot be sustainable. And where is their arkstar?"

I waited until I left the woman's office before answering. "Sorry, their what?"

"An arkstar. It's a colony craft maintained by a small crew while the rest of the colony is in suspended hibernation. It's how they move to new planets."

"If they crashed here, they may have disassembled it for parts."

"That does make sense. Especially if what I suspect is true."

"What's that." Rather than keep going into offices while talking, I pulled a feather duster out of my cart and started dusting the artwork on the hallway walls.

"While I am not diminishing your people's accomplishments, you have made some startling technological advancements in the last hundred years or so. Fifty-six years after your first powered flight, you landed on your moon."

"What are you saying? The lizardmen faked the moon landing?"

"Of course not. But I do think they have been nudging you along. I also think your government is aware of it."

"That explains why Brennan doesn't want to raid the tunnels. The government is probably letting the Detra Ka improve our tech while simultaneously trying to prevent them from taking over. That's some serious Cold War shit right there."

> "My thoughts as well. What's even more impressive is that both the Detra Ka and the humans were able to hide this from my people. Though, now that I think of it, the fault may lie with us. Just your recent advancements in biotech should have been a clue."

"What about climate change?"

> "Sorry? I do not follow."

"You said they prefer higher temperatures than what we have. Do you think they've been causing the climate change or is that us?"

> "I must say I have not been paying much attention to it. Most planets have cycles, they have hot periods, and they have cold periods. Whether the current climate is a natural cycle or the result of outside influences, I do not know. But I highly doubt that the Detra Ka would take actions."

"What do you mean it might be natural? The ice caps are melting, and water is receding. They keep finding towns that had been lost under water."

> "How did the towns get built there in the first place if this is due to unnatural events?"

"I... Huh." I scratched my chin. "I might need to research this further before we continue this discussion."

> "For the record, I am not denying climate change. I am just saying I do not know enough about the subject to render an opinion."

"Like I said. I'm going to do some online searches on the matter."

> "That is not a good idea."

"What? Why not?

> "Your track record for internet research is not the best. Remember you became convinced that the purple dinosaur on that children's show was really a demon after reading some blog."

"Hey, that made perfect sense. The children all chant around a summoning circle and 'puff', Barney the demon appears."

> "They stand in a circle singing, There is no chanting or summoning circle. And it is a dinosaur, not a demon."

"Really? It's purple. Name one dinosaur that's purple."

> "Dino."

"I... Okay, that was a good one." I fought to keep a grin off my face. "So, what's our next step?"

> *"Delta Black wants to stand by while they determine their next move. I believe this gives us a perfect opportunity to scout the airfield to see if the lander is there."*

I glanced down the halls at the offices I haven't gotten to yet. "What about my work? I still have most of the floors to do."

> *"Do I need to remind you that this job is just a cover?"*

"Right, sorry. Old work habits." I glanced around to make sure no one was watching. We need to figure out a way to get through security at the airfield. My job cover won't cut it."

> *"Are you sure? Who cleans the hangars?"*

"Huh. No idea."

> *"I am tapping into your cell phone in order to set up some arrangements through blind cutouts to provide a distraction."*

"Let me know how it turns out." I started wheeling the cart to the next office.

> *"Where are we going?"*

"I'm going to keep cleaning until you're ready."

> *"Once again, I remind you that you don't really work here."*

"Yeah, but Karen doesn't know that, and I don't need her yelling at me."

Chapter 18 –
Things that Tick

"Why does it always involve me getting naked?" I whispered as I studied the gatehouse leading to the airstrip.

"Your clothes can't blend with your surrounding like your powers allow you to do."

"You can literally buy camouflage clothes in the store."

"It is not the same and you know it."

I didn't want to admit it, but KayCee was right. One of the powers we had discovered over the past year scanned the area around me and then my skin duplicated the image. It wasn't invisibility but it was close to it. As long as I didn't move too fast. Not that I was moving very quickly barefoot while covering my junk with my hands.

"Finally." I watched the delivery truck make its way down the road toward the gatehouse. I turned up my hearing as the guard waved it to stop.

The delivery guy leaned out of his window. "I got a delivery for the airfield."

The guard checked his computer tablet. "I'm not showing anything. What is it?"

While he was distracted, I leaped the twenty-foot-high fence, clearing it without touching. As I hit the ground I froze, waiting to see if I got spotted. The guy in the van motioned toward the back of it. "I've got a dozen gallons of prop wash and several yards of flight line."

The guard double checked the tablet. "Nope. Whose it for?"

"Doctor Forth."

"Who? We don't have a Doctor Forth. What's the first name?"

I slowly started inching toward the hangars, while still following the conversation, partly to make sure I didn't get caught and partly because I wanted to see how it turned out. The driver checked a clipboard. "First name is Sally."

"Sally? Sally Forth? What are you? A smart-ass?"

"What? That's what it says."

"Get out of the van.' The guard opened the door and grabbed the driver by the arm. "Now!"

"Wow, seriously?"

"You did not find that humorous?"

"Gallons of prop wash and rolls of flight line? What if that guard didn't catch on?"

"He does work at an airfield. I felt it was an acceptable risk."

"That driver is going to be in a lot of trouble."

"I have little sympathy for him. He is a spousal abuser."

"Really?" I glanced back at the driver as he was spread over the hood of his own van. He seemed mousy.

"That was why I picked him. I would not send just anybody into the lion's den. The difficult part was hiring someone online last minute to make the packages."

Making it to the hangar, I hid in its shadow. "What's actually in the van?"

"Several five-gallon buckets filled with water and a few boxes containing garden hoses. As well as one box with a clock in it."

"A clock?"

"Yes, A very loud, ticking clock."

As she said it, an alarm sounded through the area.

"I have noticed your people get nervous around things that tick. Well, packages that tick, anyways."

"You could have just phoned in the bomb scare."

KayCee disagreed.

"No," that would have caused them to search every building and would have put us more in jeopardy of getting caught."

I mentally winced at her saying 'Jeopardy.' "This is somehow better?"

"Yes. Everyone is focusing on the van, and they will need to wait until a bomb squad gets there. This plan should give us plenty of time."

"You might be on to something," I agreed as people left the hangars and headed closer to the gate to watch. "Me, I'd have headed the other way and got as far away from a possible bomb as I could. People are weird."

I slipped around to the front of the hangar and looked in. There was some next-gen fighter jets in there, but no lander. The same for the next two hangars. For all three of those, there was a guard at the door I had to slowly maneuver around to get a look. I did spot a very familiar-looking drone. But that was a past adventure.

The fourth hangar had no visible guard, and the hangar door was closed. "Crap."

"Find some liquid."

"I know the drill, thanks."

What is the problem then?

"I hate going into liquid form. It feels weird and disorienting and I'm always naked when I reform."

You are already naked.

"Well, there is that." I moved over to where a couple of SUVs and a crotch rocket were parked. I peered into the windows of the vehicles. "Damn. Nothing to drink."

"What about that container on the back seat."

"That's a quart of motor oil."

And?

"And I'm not going to drink oil. What's wrong with you?"

"Fluids are fluids."

"Thank God Stella didn't hear you say that!" I shook my head. "It's oil. I'll get sick."

"A normal human, maybe. But not you."

"I mean from the taste. I still have taste buds and a gag reflex."

"Loughlin Ferguson, we have limited time. Just do it."

"God, I hate my life." I tried the door handle. Just my luck, it was unlocked. I grabbed the oil container and made my way over to the closed hangar. Anyone watching would have seen the container floating in some very blurry air.

"You would go faster if you were not covering your genitalia with one hand."

"Can you retrieve the lander's orb please?" The muscle and skin on the left side of my abdomen shifted and a small chrome orb emerged from the internal pouch we had created for it. I placed it in front of the large door.

"We need to speed this up."

"Just be quiet, please." I mentally steeled myself and took a big swig of the motor oil and immediately gagged. Before I could puke it back up, KayCee triggered my transformation and I changed into a large puddle of oil.

I pushed myself under the hangar door, forming a small wave to take the orb with me. I remained pooled on the inside of the hangar, listening for anyone inside. I have no idea why I could hear and not see when in liquid form, but that was how the power worked.

After a minute of silence, I took a chance and reformed, the orb getting swept back into my abdomen as I did so. A large, black curtain set ten feet back from the hangar door blocked my view. The curtain ran the entire width of the hangar.

"That's promising. Why have a privacy curtain in an already secure area?" I laid flat on the surprisingly cold floor and peered under the curtain. "Bingo!"

KayCee's lander sat on the other side.

"That is very good news. Get closer."

"In a second." I rolled under the curtain, stood up and looked around. "Turn off the camouflage mode, please. You see any clothes?"

"There is a set of lockers at the far wall. There may be something you can wear in one of them."

"Good eyes." I felt my skin return to normal as KayCee deactivated my camouflage ability.

"I will remind you, they are in fact, your eyes. I only see what you see. The difference is, I pay attention."

"Yeah, yeah." I paused at hearing a sound from inside the lander. Before I could react further, seven people exited the lander. I recognized the three in the middle. Manny, Itza, and the Ichabod Crane guy that got hired the same day as Itza. Ichabod and Itza had their hands bound in front of them. "Itza?"

"Lock? What are you doing here? And why are you naked?"

"I... spilled something caustic on my clothes." My hands moved to cover my nether region. "Why are you in handcuffs?"

The two men in front strode confidently toward me. They and the other nonmaintenance guys were all dressed in golf shirts and tactical khakis. They screamed either Feds or private military contractors. Either way, not much of a challenge for me.

"Detra Ka Human hybrids detected. Enhanced abilities, unknown capabilities. Use caution."

As the words came out of my mouth, I felt my body shift into combat mode. "KayCee?"

> "That was not me. It appears after your last battle, your warning system can now detect the hybrids and has automatically gone on the defensive."

Itza cocked her head on hearing my auto warning. "You can speak Sarli?"

"Oh shit, that's not good." The first guy took a swing at me. Nasty looking claws formed at the end of his hand. They dripped with a vile looking green liquid. My body reacted before I could, and it wasn't fooling around. I caught the hybrid's arm and spun, throwing him clear across the hangar and through the sheet-metal wall.

As I did so, the second hybrid scored, slashing across my back with his claws. I kicked out, snapping his knee. As he fell to the floor, I started to kick him in the head, but lost my balance. I staggered back, woozy. My vison blurred. "Wha-what's happening."

> "It appears the hybrid's claws secrete a fast-acting poison. Counter measures have been started."

"Great. Let me know if they start to work." I fell back, my head hitting the concrete floor. "I'm just going to lie here and try not to puke."

> "Loughlin Ferguson, there are other enemy combatants. You need to get up."

I tried to reply but my tongue felt swollen and heavy, and I had trouble concentrating. Several heads entered my vision peering down at me.

"Why isn't he dead?" asked the hybrid who clawed me.

"Our source states that he has enhanced healing abilities and that your venom would only have a limited effect," Manny told him.

"Manny? Oh no. You're with them?" I slurred. "I liked you."

"Let's see him heal this." The hybrid I had kneecapped pulled out a gun. The sci-fi geek part of me was disappointed that it was a Beretta 92sf. The rest of me was greatly relieved it wasn't a ray gun like the one Kreb had shot me with. It had vaporized a good chunk of my flesh, and I really didn't want to go through that again.

Manny pushed the hybrid's hand away. "No, we were told to bring him alive."

"Yes, sir." The hybrid tucked the gun in the back of his pants and hauled me up. "What do you want to do?"

"Put him in the trunk of your vehicle and take him down below. Do it quickly. I do not know how long the venom will keep him incapacitated."

"*You're* incapacitated... in your pants!" I slurred as I gave Manny the finger.

"*Loughlin Ferguson, antagonizing our captors is not wise.*"

As they pulled the hangar door open, Limpy the kneecapped hybrid clawed me again. This time in the right bicep. He smiled at me. Reptile eyes peeking through for just a second. "Here's another dose. Just in case."

Manny gestured toward the two hybrids guarding Itza and Ichabod. "Put them in the other motor vehicle and take them back."

"Pants!" As they were escorted out, I pulled away from Limpy and fell to the floor. "Solomon Grundy want pants."

"Nudity is the least of your problems, human."

"I swear, good quotes are wasted on you aliens." As Limpy started to pull me up, I licked the concrete floor and activated one of the few powers I could do on my own. Once Limpy brought me to my feet, I hit him with a fist made of concrete.

"*Oh, that was an excellent idea.*"

Limpy staggered back and swung at me. His poisonous claws scraping harmlessly across my concrete skin. I didn't bother getting fancy and grabbed his throat with both hands and squeezed, lifting him into the air.

Tiny chips of concrete flew off as he clawed, kicked, and pounded on me trying to get free. None of it worked. As soon as he lost consciousness, I let go. I knew I should finish him, but I couldn't let them get away with Itza.

I rushed toward the hangar intent on saving her.

"*Loughlin Ferguson. What are you doing?*"

"Rescuing Itza."

"*But we may never get another chance to retrieve the lander!*"

I skidded to a halt, hit by a dilemma as hard as my concrete skin. "Crap!"

Chapter 19 –
The Dilemma

"KayCee, they could kill her!"

"If they were going to do it, they would have done it here. They want those two as captives. After the bomb scare and the damage to this hangar, security will be doubled. This is our best chance at retrieving it. Your friend Itza is not the only one whose life hangs in the balance."

"I know that KayCee, but we can't trade one life for another."

"It's not that simple, Loughlin Ferguson. You know that."

I looked out the hangar door. An SUV was driving away at high speed along the taxiway. Whichever way they were leaving, it wasn't through the gate we entered. "Stop the SUV."

"One moment."

Just outside, an engine roared to life. "Is that the motorcycle?"

"The motor vehicle is shielded. I am unable to disable it."

"Damn it." I stepped out to see the hybrid I threw through the wall sitting on the crotch rocket. My brain identified it as a Kawasaki Ninja H2R. "These guys are tougher than I thought."

He gawked at me in surprise and drew a gun. Bullets pinged off my concrete skin as I marched toward him. "That still stings you know."

"Perhaps you should hurry up with this then. I would remind you we are on a timetable."

Seeing the rounds having no effect, the hybrid leaped at me, claws extended. He was fast but I was waiting for it. I stepped aside before he contacted, and he hit the ground. I turned as he rolled to his feet. "I'll only going to ask once. Where are you taking Itza?"

He snarled and leaped at me again.

"Okay, I tried." I caught him in midleap, my hands spreading across his face and swung him down, driving his skull into the tarmac. There was a satisfying crack, and he went limp.

I straightened up and stared at the departing SUV. "I'm not liking what I'm changing into."

"You mean the concrete? You should be able to revert now without the ill effects of the venom."

"Wasn't what I meant. I just enjoyed smashing his skull. That's not me, KayCee. Never has been. Not really." I swung my leg over the motorcycle as my body changed back to normal.

"Loughlin Ferguson, I know this is a difficult choice, but you need to think of the bigger picture."

"You know what?" I tossed the helmet aside and gunned the engine. "I choose not to have to make a choice."

The weird database in my brain hadn't just told me the make and model of the motorcycle. It had also informed me of its specs. Like the fact that it was the fastest production bike in the world and topped out at 249mph in the right conditions, and that a testing flightline in Nevada was about the most perfect condition you could get.

I cycled through the gears getting up to a speed that had the wind wanting to tear me off the bike. "I really wish I took the time to find clothes!"

"The good news is you no longer need be concerned about sunburns. I suspect that would hurt significantly in some of your more sensitive areas."

"Not funny. I'm more worried about dumping the bike and getting road rash in those areas you just mentioned."

"Humor must be different on this planet. My people would have found that hilarious. What is your plan?"

"Brute force. Pump up my strength levels please."

We caught up to the SUV shockingly quick. Itza and Ichabod were in the rear seat while the unknown hybrid was driving. Manny fired some rounds at me from the front passenger side. I swerved to the driver's side and came parallel with the rear door. I reached out and tore the door from the hinges and flung it behind me.

Avoiding an attempt to swerve into me, I closed, reached in and pulled Itza out. I swung her behind me on the bike. She slipped her bound hands over my neck and held on for dear life.

As soon as she was seated securely behind me, I slammed on the brakes. The bike dipped forward with the rear wheel coming off the ground and threatening to send us cartwheeling over the front of the bike. As Itza clung desperately to me, I balanced on the front wheel and pivoted the bike so that when the rear wheel came down, we were facing in the opposite direction of the SUV. I gunned the engine again and headed back to the hangar at flat-out speed.

Somebody must have finally looked up from the fake bomb because security cars were racing toward us. "KayCee, want to give us a little time?"

I felt a feather-like touch in my brain as she activated one of my abilities. The security cars' lights flickered and went out, and the cars slowly rolled to a stop.

"I have electronically disabled them."

"Excellent."

Itza leaned into my ear. "What about Bel Crat?"

"The scientist lizard guy? What about him?"

"You left him in the vehicle. Are we just leaving him with his captors?"

"What are you talking about?" It took me a second to realize what she meant. "Wait, Ichabod is Bel Crat?"

"Who's Ichabod?"

"Never mind. Look, we don't have time to get your friend. Once things calm down, you can fill me in on everything, and we'll see if we can rescue him later."

She was silent for a second. "I will trust you, Lock. You have no idea how much lies in the balance. Please don't betray me."

"Wasn't planning on it." I slowed my speed but didn't stop. Instead, I drove into the hangar and right up the lander's ramp, only stopping when we were inside the lander itself. The room was circular, not surprising considering it was a flying saucer. Instead of the empty chrome room I was expecting, the control chair was up, and a table with a control panel had been installed. I waited until Itza clambered off to park the bike. "KayCee, what's with the control panel?"

"I assume it is a work-around to fly the lander without a control orb. Analyzing."

"Stay here," I yelled to Itza. I sprinted down the ramp and over to the lockers lining the hangar wall. I rummaged through them until I found a flight suit that was a little baggy but fit. I scrambled into it and pulled on a pair of boots that were a size too big for me. "KayCee, how we looking?"

"It appears they dismantled the lander and then put it back together and repaired the damage."

"Is it flyable or did we just do this all for nothing?"

"I would not take it into space, but it should be fine for atmospheric flights."

"Good enough."

"Lock!"

I turned. Stella stood by the hangar door in her security guard uniform, breathing heavily. She held a walkie-talkie in one hand and her ax in the other. "Stella? What are you doing here?"

"Someone called in a bomb. Then a certain naked idiot was racing around on a motorcycle. I'd have been here sooner, but someone killed my cruiser. I had to run the rest of the way."

"Ah, sorry about that. Didn't know you were in one of the security cars. Quick, get in the lander."

"The lander? Lock, Delta Black sent it here for study. You don't have to steal it."

I zipped up the flight suit and headed toward the lander. "I'm not stealing it. I'm reclaiming it for KayCee."

She sighed. "Lock, don't do this. I like KayCee too and there is a place for both of you in Delta Black. Don't betray your country, your people, over a misguided attempt to get her home."

"You don't understand, and I don't have time to explain." I paused at the top of the ramp. "We kept you in the dark to keep you safe. Stay here and stay out of it. You don't need to get into trouble. Leave it to us."

"How long have you known me?" Her ax melted away reforming into the armor she wore under her uniform. Stella walked up the ramp, brushing past me. Her eyes widened in surprise at seeing Itza standing there, her hands still bound. "Kidnapping women is not really your style. What's going on?"

"Kaycee, close the ramp." I could hear vehicles pulling up. I waved at Itza. "Stella, I don't know what all this is yet. It has something to do with the lizard people."

"Well, tell me what you do know."

"We're on the clock here. You coming or not?"

She stared at me, a frown on her face. It seemed a lifetime passed before she finally nodded. "Okay but this better be good."

"Oh, it's real good!"

Chapter 20 –
Itza Complicated

The chrome walls of the lander changed to show our exterior as I sat in the command chair. Kaycee gave a mental order to the control orb, and additional chairs rose from the floor for Stella and Itza. I watched the screens as we passed out of the hangar and shot straight up. Thanks to the lander's inertia dampeners, we felt nothing. "I thought you wanted to stay out of space?"

"That is correct. I am just creating some distance."

Stella pursed her lips. "What's KayCee saying?"

"The lander needs some minor adjustments after Space Force poked and prodded it, but everything's fine."

"Time to explain."

"Let's deal with this situation first." I pointed at Itza.

"Isn't that the broad you took home?" Stella moved over and plopped down into the chair.

"Broad? What are you a 1920ss gangster?" I turned my attention to Itza. "Okay Itza, what's the deal? Why did those guys capture you?"

Her head swiveled from me to Stella and back again. "Are you Sarli?"

"No, but one of my closest friends is," I told her.

"Thank you. That was very sweet."

I ignored KayCee. "Itza, how did you get involved with the Detra Ka?"

"Before I answer that, why did you pull me out of the motor vehicle?" She held up her arms, jingling the handcuffs. "Am I your prisoner?"

"Once again, no. I saw you were held against your will, and I stopped it. I suppose I should have taken off the cuffs. Let me see them." I reached out to snap the restraints and stopped. They looked like nothing I'd ever seen in any cop movies or shows. "Stella, I know we have some advance equipment, but these cuffs don't belong to Delta Black, do they?"

Stella shook her head. "Never seen those type of restraints before. What's KayCee think?"

I suspect they are Detra Ka in origin.

"I was afraid you were going to say that." I studied the restraints. The bands surrounding her wrists were of an unknown metal and about two inches wide. Instead of a chain, there was a thick cable connecting them. They looked like they were designed to hold someone of advanced strength. Someone like me. I took a step back from Itza, a horrible suspicion running through my brain. "On second thought. Let's hold off on the cuffs for a minute."

Stella rolled her eyes. "Now what?"

"Itza, I'm going to ask you one more time." I was really hoping my suspicion was wrong. "How are you connected to the Detra Ka?"

"It's complicated."

Stella snorted.

"Something funny?" I asked, still watching Itza out of the side of my eye as I glanced at my roommate.

"Just, you know. Her name." Stella gestured with her hand out, fingers pinched together, and said in a really bad Mario Bros imitation, "Hey, Luigi. Itza complicated."

"Seriously?" I asked. Itza just looked confused.

"It was funny." Stella shrugged. "Okay, maybe not the best time."

"Ya think?" I turned back to Itza. "Truth time, Itza. Are you, in fact, Detra Ka?"

Itza sighed. "Yes."

"Oh, hell!"

"So, she's an alien?" Stella glanced between us. "Wait a minute! Duuude!"

"Don't say it," I warned her.

"Lock. Buddy. Way to go. You might be the first human to score some alien tail!"

"You have no idea," I muttered before raising my voice, angrily gesturing at Itza. "Stella, for crying out loud, she's right there. Show a little decorum."

"Yeah, all right. Still!" She raised her hand for a high five. "Put it there."

Before I could react, Itza snapped her restraints with minimal effort and raised her hand up. Stella and I both leaped back, going into fighting stances.

Itza looked around, confusion on her face as she continued to hold her hand up. "What? I thought we were celebrating the first sexual congress between our particular races?"

Stella looked over at me with a wry grin, leaned forward and high-fived Itza. "I think I like her."

"I hate my life," I muttered to myself. "First time since Jeopardy and it had to be an alien."

"Loughlin Ferguson. Very few races have the sexual hang-ups that you possess. In fact, there is an intergalactic saying that when spacefaring races meet for the first time, it either involves fighting or fu – "

"I get it," I said, trying to interrupt her before she could finish her sentence.

"Sometimes both."

"I said I get it."

"Get what?" Itza asked.

"Nothing, I was talking... to someone on my comm link." I pinched the bridge of my nose. "Future reference. Most humans like to know who and what they are getting into bed with."

"I do not see the problem. I was wearing this human form at the time. Admittedly significantly upgraded, but still human. You, yourself, did not tell me you are not typical of your species. From your friend's comment, I take it you are, in fact, a human. Yes?"

"Yes." I waved my hand. "We're getting off track. My understanding was that the only females are the queens. So that makes you a queen?"

"Partially correct."

"In what way?" I asked.

"Incorrect in that I am not a queen."

I found myself unable to speak. I felt my lips moving but nothing was coming out. Stella did not have that problem. She leaned forward. "You're a guy? Hey, that goes back to the whole 'tell a person before sex' speech."

"What? No! Though several of my people do call me their queen, until I secure a colony for my people, I am only a princess."

My legs weak, I staggered over and plopped down in the control chair. Stella watched me with a strange expression mixed with sympathy and amusement. "You okay, buddy?"

"I need a moment. That was a bit of a shock."

"Hey, I thought you were a staunch supporter of Team Alphabet?" Apparently, amusement won out.

"There are a lot of things I support that I don't want to personally experience. Bungee jumping, for example."

"Can we circle back?" Itza asked.

"Sure." I straightened up in my chair. "Are you trying to take over the world?"

"I meant circle back closer to the testing complex." She stared out the window. "But to answer your question, no, I'm not. I'm trying to get my people off your planet and headed to our original destination."

"Then why are you replacing humans with hybrids?"

"I'm ashamed to admit there is a rebellion going on among my people. It started while I was in stasis. There is a faction of my people that, instead of heading back to the stars, want to modify this planet to better fit our needs."

"Nailed it."

"It was a lucky guess."

Itza glanced back at me. "I really need you to turn around."

"Why?"

"Because I'm getting out of range of the –" Itza suddenly collapsed to the floor. I rushed over to her. Stella stayed back, ax at the ready in case it was a ploy.

I turned her over. Itza's eyes were wide open, but she didn't appear conscious. "KayCee. What's going on here?"

"As I said before, the Detra Ka cannot shift into energy form like my people. Instead, they must be transmitting their consciousness into their hybrid bioforms."

"So why did she just collapse and is she okay?"

"Based on her comments, I believe we flew out of range, and she lost the signal."

"If we head back to the base, will she regain consciousness?"

"She's not unconscious. She has simply returned to her actual body. If we enter range again, she should be able to reestablish the link."

Itza's body suddenly collapsed into a puddle of green goo. I jumped back. "Holy crap! What's going on?"

"It appears there is a disposal system built into the body, to avoid in-depth examinations."

The goo started hissing and vapors rose as it started to disintegrate.

"Now what?" I asked.

"You should both stand back. The lander's sensors are showing that the vapor is releasing chemicals that would leave a human who has inhaled it disoriented and with short-term memory loss. One moment. I will vent it out of the cabin."

I waved a very annoyed Stella back. "Kaycee says don't breathe the gas."

"Yeah, no kidding." Stella snorted as the lander's vents sucked the vapors out. In seconds, nothing remained of the goo or the gas. Except for the broken restraints, it was as if Itza had never been there.

"Very efficient."

"Not how I would describe it," I muttered.

"The Space Force has launched fighters, and they are heading toward us. I had wished to make some repairs first but having now run out of time, I think we should proceed to my starcraft."

"I thought you said going into space was a bad idea based on the condition of the lander?"

"Correct, but it will be in worse condition if the fighter jets shoot us down. Considering they are coming right at us, I suspect a tracker has been attached to the lander."

"Care to fill me in?" Stella asked impatiently.

I told her what KayCee had said.

"Which leads me back to my original questions. Why are you stealing the lander?" She held up her index finger. "And don't say it really belongs to KayCee."

"Well, it does. But that's not why we took it."

"Then why?"

"We need it to save Tavish's life."

Sadness filled her face. "Tavish is dead, Lock."

"Yeah, but only sort of."

Chapter 21 –
Sort of Dead

"What do you mean he's only sort of dead?" asked Stella. She blinked as the lights on the panel changed color. "And how are you doing that without a control orb?"

Her eyes narrowed. "You have the orb for *Quiet Contemplation* with you."

"Yup. I retrieved it from where we hid it after I was sworn in." I felt the lander shift. "KayCee, any issues?"

> "*Stella Johansen's fellow Space Force personnel are shooting at us from F-22 Raptors.*"

"The fighter jets?" I frowned. "Anything to worry about?"

> "*No. Their efforts are quite laughable. However, I am experiencing more trouble making orbit than usual. The hacks that put the lander together should be fired.*"

Stella pursed her lips. "What's KayCee saying?"

"The lander needs some minor adjustments after the Space Force poked and prodded it, but everything's fine. Well, that and there are some fighter jets shooting at us, but it's nothing to worry about."

"Whatever. Explain the Tavish comment or I swear, I'll turn this lander around right now!"

"Okay, Mom. You win." I laughed.

> "*You are aware she does not possess the ability to do that, correct? While that control panel may allow limited flight, it cannot override the orb.*"

"It was a joke, KayCee."

> *Just checking. We will be exceeding the ceiling for the F-22s in a moment.*

"Understood." I pointed to Stella. "Remember how Kreb sucked the oxygen out of Tavish's medical pod?"

"Of course."

"Well, Tavish used his ability to connect and control computers to transfer his consciousness online."

Stella gave me a flat stare. "Like Lawnmower Man or Transcendence?"

"Yeah, like that."

"You remember how both those movies ended right?"

"That's kind of my point." I held out my hand. "Let me see your cellphone."

She gave me a skeptical look but dug it out of her pocket. I took it and opened it and touched the orb to it. "You there?"

"I am." said the electronic voice of my dead cousin. "Hi, Stella. Good to talk to you again."

"Tavish?" Stella asked.

"Yes. I'd say in the flesh, but you know..." he answered.

"Prove it."

"I know what really happened to Mrs. Mulrooney's turtle in third grade."

Stella's eyes widened. "Holy crap. It is you!"

"Wait a minute," I interrupted. "You both know what happened to Mrs. Mulrooney's turtle? That was the biggest mystery of the school year. What did you two do?"

"Don't worry about it," they said in unison.

"I suspect the turtle did not fare well."

"Yeah," I mused.

Stella glared at me. "So, you played us? Let yourselves get caught."

"Well, yeah. The lander was the only way to get back to *Quiet Contemplation*, and the Space Force had it. We needed to made it look good or it would have been suspicious."

"Did you think that maybe it would be nice if you clued me in?"

"Well, it wasn't like we knew you were working with the Space Force."

"True." Stella refocused. "So, Tavish, does this mean you're Skynet now?"

"Definitely not," Tavish said in a firm tone. "That's why we're trying to put me back into my body."

"That makes no sense,"

"The longer I'm disincorporated, the more I'm losing my empathy," my cousin told her. "I'm significantly smarter but without all the squishy bits. I'm turning more Spock than Bones and that's not a good thing when I can do what I can do online."

"Like what?" Stella asked.

"Want to know the nuclear launch codes?"

"Oh, shit!" Stella leaned toward the phone. "Really?"

"Yup!" Tavish's electronic voice told her.

"That's why we need the lander," I said. "To retrieve his body from the med bay of *Quiet Contemplation*."

"That makes no sense." Stella repeated. "Not to be insensitive, but it's a decaying corpse."

"Not quite." I gestured to the phone. "KayCee, why don't you handle the explanation."

KayCee answered me both in my head and over the phone. "Very well." "KayCee?" Stella stared at the phone. "I thought you were in Lock's head."

"Once again, I am not actually in his head. That being said. I am currently within him. I was able to create a device that lets me speak through electronics like your phone. I based it on how Tavish does it."

"So, Bluetooth for disincorporated aliens?"

"That's what I said," I told my roommate. "Well, you said it better. But yeah."

"To answer your question, Stella, when Tavish was being suffocated by Kreb, he was able to transfer he consciousness to the computers aboard my starcraft. Then the lack of oxygen interrupted the blood supply to Tavish's brain and his life functions ceased.

"Once Kreb stopped interfering, the medical pod's functions should have reverted to normal which means it would have placed the body into stasis. Aside from possible damage to his brain, Tavish's body should be intact and revivable."

"Tavish was always a little dain bramaged," Stella said. "How bad is his head after what Kreb did to him?"

"*Dain bramaged?*"

"Also, a joke," I explained. "Move on."

"*The lack of oxygen may have caused irreversible damage to parts of his brain, or it may be something that can be repaired. We will not know until we have examined his body.*"

"And if it is?" Stella scratched an armpit. "What do we do then?"

"We've been building an artificial brain," Tavish told her. "We can insert it into my skull, and I can download into it. I'll be like robocop, except the reverse. A cybernetic brain in a human body."

"What?" Stella stopped midscratch. "You couldn't change spark plugs and you're telling me you built a robot brain? And how do you do that without hands?"

"Well, I have access to all the data on the internet all at once. I'm currently smarter than any human who has ever lived. I also have a lot more resources at my disposal. I've been tapping into different manufacturing plants to make what I need."

"What if your body is too decayed?"

"It shouldn't," my cousin told her. "But if for some reason it's not viable, I'll build an artificial body, that I can download into."

"So, you'd be what? An android?" Stella asked.

"Something like that," Tavish replied.

"So why don't you download into it now and then switch to your body later?"

"It's not a sure thing. I put in certain parameters, but I don't know if it will solve the empathy problem. Also, I don't know how many times I can do a transfer. It's not like how KayCee's people do it. I'm worried I could get stuck and won't be able to transfer out again."

"Why didn't you tell me?" Stella demanded.

"Tell who?" I asked. "Stella my best friend or Sergeant Johansen of the US Space Force?"

"I... Yeah, okay, fair enough." She rubbed her face. "Then what? What happens after you save Tavish."

"Originally, we thought we'd take *Quiet Contemplation* to see KayCee's people. Get her back in her body. Maybe get Tavish and I returned to normal."

"Really You'd go back to being the way you were?" my roommate asked.

"Beats getting shot at all the time." I shrugged. "But now with another alien race trying to take over Earth. Well, we simply can't abandon it."

"I'm glad to hear that."

"Loughlin Ferguson, we have a problem."

"Satellites with weapon platforms?" I guessed. "You said they wouldn't be an issue."

"No, it concerns *Quiet Contemplation*."

"What about it?"

"It's not there!"

Chapter 22 –
Dude, Where's our Starcraft?

"What do you mean it's not there?" I sputtered. "It's not in orbit around Earth?

"No."

"Maybe we were wrong," I guessed. "Maybe it's still set in orbit around the sun opposite Earth."

"Unlikely. I cannot detect it there either."

"How can you do that?" asked Stella.

I programmed it to launch a probe at a certain location in order to angle any communications."

"We did suspect that the Space Force moved it," I reminded her.

"I did check for that first. As I said, it is not in Earth's orbit either."

"So, maybe it's the probe that's missing?" Stella asked.

"Possibly. The probe should be signaling back, and it is not. If you are right and the probe is the problem, *Quiet Contemplation* could still be where it should be. We will continue on our course. However, that leaves the question of what happened to the probe?"

"Drift, maybe?" I suggested, knowing I was grasping at straws. "Maybe the thrusters went offline."

"No. that should have set off an alarm."

"Let me check all the feeds on the various satellites and craft we have in space," Tavish said.

Stella gestured at the phone. "How long before we lose Tavish's signal?"

"Don't worry about me," my cousin told her. "I've got it covered."

"Hijacked all the communication satellites, didn't you?" She smirked.

"Yup."

"How far to the sun?" Stella asked.

"This time of year. It would be about ninety-four million miles and change," Tavish told her.

"That seems like it will take a while," said Stella.

"In an Earth vehicle, it would take years," I told her. "And that's not addressing the fuel issue."

"You need to take the movement of the sun as well," Tavish added.

Stella gave the phone the middle finger. "Har, har, har. I am very aware the sun doesn't orbit the planet. Not my first space ride."

"No dummy." He sighed over the phone. "Everything in the universe moves. Including the sun. You have to adjust for that in your calculations."

"This is all a moot point," KayCee said. "We are using a Sarli Lander, which means we will be there in about eight hours."

"Well, that's not bad at all. Wake me when we get there." Stella lay down next to a wall and immediately started snoring.

"How does she do that?" I wondered. "I'd be a ball of anxiety. I *am* a ball of anxiety."

Unlike Stella, I stayed awake the whole trip, trying to figure out what Itza's people were up to and what we were going to do if *Quiet Contemplation* was missing. Tavish's transmissions started getting patchy toward the end, so he signed off.

Which is why it was just KayCee and me staring out the window when the far side of the sun finally came into view. "Oh, crap!"

"It is as I feared. The starcraft is missing."

"Well, who the hell has it!" I yelled.

Stella woke with a snort. "What? Are we there yet?"

"Yeah."

She clambered to her feet and stood next to me. "Dude, where's our starcraft?"

"Someone jacked it."

"Like space pirates?" my roommate asked. Is that a thing?"

"No."

"Yes," KayCee said.

I raised my eyebrows. "It is?"

"Yes, but that is not important right now. The most logical explanations are either the humans, who don't have the technology, my people, who I would like to think would have contacted me before taking the starcraft, and finally, the Detra Ka who are looking for a way off your planet."

"So, you're thinking it was the lizard people?" Stella yawned.

"Most likely. But how would they get to it?"

"The same way we did," I guessed. "They used the lander. Are there flight records on this thing?"

"No," KayCee said. "But there should be. I assumed it was erased during the dismantling of the lander but perhaps it was done on purpose."

"Sure. We know they've infiltrated both the government and its contractors. Humans might not have figured out how to use *Quiet Contemplation* without the control orb, but I wouldn't put it past the Detra Ka to figure out a way to hot-wire it." I scratched the side of my face. "But if that's true. Why are they still here? They should have piled onto the starcraft and took off."

"Your girlfriend said something about a rebellion. Maybe they are fighting over it," suggested Stella.

"If that's true, then where the hell is it?" I mused.

"And what are we going to do about it?" added Stella. "Obviously we can't let them take over the Earth."

"No, of course not," I said. "We'll let Brennan know. I suspect he knows a lot more about the various moving pieces then we do and can probably come up with a better plan then we can."

"Brennan?"

"Yeah."

"The guy who's a colonel in the Space Force?"

"What's your point?

"The same Space Force you basically just defected from and stole a priceless piece of equipment from?

"Oh, that?" I smiled. "I got that covered."

Chapter 23 –
A Mental Reset

Brennan stared at me from across his desk, drumming his fingers. On the desk rested a certain silver orb. The window in his office normally looked out over a courtyard. Today it looked over a flying saucer parked in said courtyard. "Explain again how you stole the lander from the US Space Force *for* the US Space Force?"

"To be clear, not stolen. We didn't steal it. We tracked the alien hybrids to a hangar that had the lander in it. After a fight with them, we took the lander to make sure they didn't abscond with it."

"And you went to space why?"

"Well, if they had the lander, we were afraid they might have used it to get *Quiet Contemplation,* so we went to check on it. And as it turns out. It actually is missing!"

"So, then you flew the lander here, to one of the most top secret bases we have."

"We wanted to tell you as soon as possible."

"Couldn't have made a phone call from the lander?"

"Not really, sir. Wasn't secure."

The colonel's gaze shifted over to Stella who stood at attention next to me. "Is that about right, Sergeant?"

"More or less sir," she replied crisply.

"What's the more part of it consist of?" he asked.

"The usual Lock stuff, sir. Him running around naked, making stuff up as he goes along. Stepping in it about half the time."

"Hmmm." His tone easily conveyed that we weren't fooling him. "Let's make sure *it* doesn't splatter on the rest of us. I am not happy you hid the control orb from us."

"You can't blame me for testing the waters first," I said. "Can we get back to the part where the giant starcraft capable of destroying Earth is missing?"

"It's not missing, Captain." Brennan stated. "It's just not where you parked it."

"Right." It clicked into place. "It wasn't the aliens that stole it. It was you!"

"The term you're looking for is *us*, Captain. And much like you, we didn't steal it."

"That what would you call it?" I raised my eyebrows. "That starcraft belongs to KayCee's people."

"We salvaged it. Completely different," Brennan calmly informed me.

"They should not have been able to make entry much less move it."

"KayCee wants to inspect it. Make sure you didn't do anything to damage it like you did with the lander."

"The lander isn't damaged and neither of you are in a position to make demands."

"Are you kidding me? It was put back together with baling wire and duct tape. Look, we get it," I argued. "You've been playing a cat and mouse game with the hybrids. Letting them advance our tech while trying to prevent them from infiltrating our government and military. But they were on the lander, and I think they have completely taken over MSU. We need to know if they did anything to the starcraft."

His finger stopped drumming. "That will require you being read into something the powers that be consider above your paygrade. I have to meet with Senator Blutarsky, head of our oversight committee. I'll run it up the flagpole after the meeting."

"Senator Blutarsky?" The name tickled something in my brain. "Where do I know that from?"

"As I said, he's on our oversight committee."

"That's not it." I scratched my face. "Wait, I remember him now. Isn't he like, over a hundred?"

"He's in his eighties and he's one of our strongest supporters."

"Speaking of the '80s." I snickered. "I'm starting to remember. There were allegations of a bunch of wild sex parties back in the 1980s, right?"

"Those were never proven."

"Too bad," said Stella. "I'd have voted for him just based on that."

I fought back a grin. "Wasn't there something about him destroying his first college?"

"It was a parade not the actual college. My understanding is that it was a fraternity prank gone wrong. Besides, we're talking sixty years ago, for crying out loud. The man is a decorated Vietnam War veteran." Brennan stood up. "Enough. Go file a report on this. I'll send for you when I'm ready."

We saluted and exited the room. I waited until we were far enough away not to be overheard by his aide. "I remember him being funnier."

"That's the problem with being the guy in charge. You can't smoke and joke with the rest of the rank-and-file," Stella said as we entered an empty break room. It had a mini kitchen on one side and a lounging area on the other.

"Yeah, I wouldn't have figured Brennan for a behind the desk type of guy." I plopped down on what turned out to be a rather uncomfortable couch.

"That's what happens with promotions. If you go up far enough, sooner or later you wind up riding the pine." Stella grabbed two sodas from the fridge, tossing me one before sitting in a chair.

"I'm surprised he took it."

"Sort of came with the medal." Stella gave me her *You're an idiot* look.

"Which one? He has so many ribbons, he could probably take a bullet and it wouldn't penetrate."

"The one on top with the stars." Stella said in an annoyed tone.

"What about it?" I opened the soda and jumped up as it started spraying all over me and the couch. "Damn it!"

"Good God, they gave you a commission? I love ya buddy, but the idea of you as a captain makes me throw up in my mouth a little."

"Fair enough, I kinda felt the same way. I only did it to stick it to the man." I grabbed some paper towels from the counter and wiped the soda off my clothes and the couch.

"Says the straight middle-aged white guy from New Hampshire." Stella placed her unopened soda on the table next to her.

"Yeah, yeah. So, what's the ribbon with the stars..." It took me a while, but I got there. "Oh my God. You don't mean the Medal of Honor?"

"Bingo! Once he was awarded it, the promotion was guaranteed."

I was suitably impressed. I had never met a medal of honor recipient before. "What did he get it for?"

"Seriously?" She shook her head as I tossed the towels in the trash before sitting in a chair opposite her.

"What? I wasn't really keeping up on the news while I was on the run from you jackbooted stormtroopers."

"It was the whole saving the planet thing, you idiot. And any jackboots I may have owned came with stiletto heels and burned up with the rest of my bedroom toys when the house burned down."

"Argh." I shuddered. "I remember that whole dominatrix phase you had. As the person sharing a bedroom wall with you, *I* should have been the one with a safe word."

"What do you mean phase?"

"Hold on a second, that was a group effort. Why don't you and I have Medal of Honors?"

"First of several reasons is because we were civilians."

"Yeah, but we're military now."

"Doesn't count." Deciding it had had time to settle down, Stella carefully opened her soda. When a repeat of what happened to me didn't occur, she took a sip.

"Oh, that's bullshit."

"No, what's bullshit is the whole thing is classified. The guy wins the Medal of Honor and no one outside of Delta Black knows."

"At least the world doesn't think he's a loser janitor."

"Okay aside from the fact that it's cover, let me ask you, does maintenance work pay the bills, put food on the table?"

"Depends, but this current gig is pretty good." I shifted in my seat trying to get comfortable. The chairs were as bad as the couch. Not surprising since they seemed part of a set.

"Most are union with bennies and retirement, right?"

"The municipal stuff, yeah."

"There isn't a lot about your job that people don't do themselves at home, right?"

"Like you know how to use a mop." I took a sip. A lot of my soda had wound up soaking me and the couch, but the can was still about a quarter full.

"Normal people then," Stella said.

"Yeah sure, I guess."

"So, what's your problem with the job? It's not like you're employed as a fluffer."

I choked on the soda. She had timed it perfectly.

"Part of it is you're invisible," I said after coughing up the soda from my lungs. "At least until someone needs something."

"So are a lot of other jobs. And that's a reflection on the douchebags ignoring you, not the job itself." She leaned forward. "I can only think that your problem with the profession is that you think you're too good for it."

"What? No! It's... I don't know." I sat there quietly, Stella wisely giving me the time to process. "I guess... Huh. I'd have to say it's kind of been the symbol of my life. Stuck in a rut whether it was self-made or by Kreb. Being the town laughingstock all those years."

Stella shook her head. "Yeah, you got picked on in school and some adults such as Dennis continued it into adulthood, but not everybody in town did."

"Stella, the whole town called me Probed."

"A sucky childhood nickname that stuck. I bet half the town doesn't even remember why you're called that. Tell me something, how did Sticky Reynolds get his nickname?"

I opened my mouth to tell her and abruptly shut it as I realized I either didn't know or didn't remember. "I'm not sure I want to know."

"Freshman year, his cousin lent him some nudie magazines. They came back in less than pristine condition."

"Oh, yuck! I did not need to know that."

"Yet how often did you call him Sticky?"

"All the time," I sighed. "In fact, I don't think I know his real first name."

"It's Lyle, but that goes to my point. Most of our hometown called you Probed because that's what everyone else called you. Think about it. You were invited to all the birthday parties, cookouts, and whatever other social functions there were."

Stella continued, "Your problem isn't what the town thought about you and whatever job you have. It's your self-perception. You see being a janitor as being a loser because you view yourself as a loser and that's the job you had, so it must be a job for losers." She downed the rest of her soda and crushed the can. "And while you can blame the programming Kreb installed in you for most of it, that programming is gone now, so whatever you do from this moment is on you. You saved the world, for crying out loud, and you still view yourself as a failure."

"She is not wrong, Loughlin Ferguson."

LOCK'S EARTHLY MAINTENANCE

"Oh, now you chime in." I leaned back in my chair. "So, what do I do about it?"

"Change your perception," Brennan said, leaning in the doorway.

"That was a short meeting," I said.

"The senator doubled-booked. But don't change the subject." Brennan entered and sat down. "You were a janitor. Your mind has a twisted perception of what that means. So, change your perception. Own it."

"What do you mean?" I glanced over to Stella, who was nodding.

"You think a janitor is someone who cleans up someone else's mess," the colonel stated as he tapped on his phone.

"Yeah," I nodded.

"Well, isn't that what we do here? Clean up one alien mess after another."

"I guess." I wondered where he was going with this.

"Here's the definition of janitor." Brennan held up his phone and read from it. "One who tends to a premises and makes minor repairs. A caretaker, a custodian."

"Huh." I rubbed the back of my neck. "I never thought of it that way.

Brennan continued. "Janitor is derived from the Latin word *janus*. It means arch or gateway and refers to one who keeps guard at the entry gate."

Stella smiled. "The Earth could use some maintenance these days and it sure as hell needs a guard at the gate."

"*A protector.*"

Brennan lowered his phone. "We change codenames with every assignment but there has been a push lately to have permanent codenames. Tell me, Lock. What do you want for yours?"

"Janitor." I whispered.

"Done!" He smiled. "Now, I've been cleared to take the three of you up to *Quiet Contemplation*. But I do have one question first."

"What's that, Sir?" asked Stella.

"Why the hell is the couch I'm sitting on all wet?"

Chapter 24 –
Behind the Dark

"Why are you grinning like an idiot?" asked Stella as we rode in the back of a golf cart headed to a nondescript hangar on the far side of Ducharme Station.

"Because we're wearing flight suits." Instead of the sage green or desert tan used by military pilots or the blue of US astronauts, ours were black. A black Delta patch outlined in a subdued silver was on our right chests and our rank insignia on our shoulders.

"So?"

"It's cool."

"You are such a nerd."

"The correct term is geek, thank you very much," I said as we pulled up to where Colonel Brennan waited for us in front of the hangar.

"Ready?" He was dressed the same as us except he had a leather patch on his left side with the words *shot glass*. Over them were two winged insignia. I pointed at them. "What are those?"

"Aviator and Astronaut badges," he said.

"And Shot Glass?" I asked. "I thought your name was supposed to go there."

"Can't really be a secret organization if we walk around with our names plastered across our chests. Shot Glass was my call sign."

"I thought it was Knight One."

"That's the armor," he said.

"There a story behind that call sign?" Stella asked.

"Yup. But you're not going to hear it." He smiled. "You ready to go for a ride."

"You're coming? Don't you have meetings and paperwork?"

"Yes, and this is a hell of an excuse to skip them." He hesitated. "Listen, I expect all of you to be professionals. That goes double for you, Lock. Jeopardy is at the location we're heading to, and I know things are weird between you two right now. Is this going to be a problem?"

"No, sir."

"Good." He gestured to the hangar. "Let's go take a space ride."

Stella and I stopped short after walking through the hangar door. Inside was a flying saucer, but while KayCee's lander was weaponless, this one had various weapons platforms mounted on it. Its skin looked like burnished steel instead of the chrome-like metal that KayCee's people used for their crafts.

"I am in so much trouble when I get home."

I stepped up and ran my hand over the surface. "What metal is this?"

"It's a classified alloy," Brennan said. "We were unable to duplicate the original covering of the lander."

"That is because the ore needed is not native to your planet."

Stella walked around it. "This is a fantastic copy."

"It's a hybrid," Brennan admitted. "We reproduced what we could and got creative with what we couldn't. Want to go inside?"

"Hell yeah," Stella shouted. "Hey!"

While she had been busy hooting and hollering, I strode up the ramp and looked around inside. KayCee's lander had a very minimal look to it. All chrome with one chair in the middle. This craft had an airlock built around the landing ramp. Once inside, I saw screens mounted along all the walls. It appeared they were unable to duplicated the lander's ability to make the walls translucent during flight. There was seating for six. Two of the chairs were obviously for a pilot and copilot. In front of both chairs was a more finished version of the control panel that had been installed onto the lander. There were fighter jet style joysticks as well. Everything else was dedicated for storage.

Brennan stepped next to me, nodding at the joysticks. "Made it a little more familiar for our current pilots."

"I guess that makes sense." I looked around. "Who's piloting?"

"I am. At least on the way up. Think you can figure out how to pilot it in enough time to fly back?"

"I think KayCee can fly it no matter what modifications you do."

"Not KayCee, you."

"Seriously? You want me to fly it?"

"You, Stella, and Jeopardy. The other two will have to qualify the more traditional route, but with your abilities, we figured you can just download how to fly it."

"That should not be a problem. Setting it up now."

"Oh, that's awesome!" I felt a slight flicker in my mind as KayCee activated one of my abilities.

Brennan settled into the pilot seat. "Lock, take the copilot chair. Stella, you have your pick of whatever is left."

I jumped into my seat. As I looked over the control panel, my brain identified what each button and switch was for and explained how to use them.

I tore my eyes away from the controls as Brennan tapped me on the shoulder. "Sorry?"

He pointed to the restraint harness attached to my chair. "Buckle up."

I felt myself frowning. "You couldn't duplicate the inertia dampeners?"

"We did, but it's regulations to be buckled in in case of failure."

"Oh, right." I struggled into it.

Brennan flipped a series of switches. There was a hum as the craft powered up. The wall screens came to life showing the hangar we currently sat in. Another switch retracted the hangar roof. "Control, this is the *Alan Shepard*. Are we cleared for liftoff?"

"*Shepard*, this is Control. You are cleared for launch."

"Roger that. Launching now."

"Safe travels, *Shepard*." At those words, the craft lifted up and shot into the sky. A large grin spreading across Brennan's face.

"You're enjoying this, aren't you?" I accused.

"Of course! This is the best part of the job."

Stella leaned in. "You named it after the first American in space. Nice!"

"Normally I fly the *Gus Grissom*, but since Admiral Shepard was from New Hampshire like you two, I thought we'd use this one, even if he *was* Navy." Brennan's grin widened.

"How many landers..." A thought hit me. "Do you still call these landers?"

"Orbital fighters."

"But it can leave orbit."

"Depends on which orbit you're talking about."

"What?" I asked confused.

"How many orbital fighters do we have?" Stella asked before Brennan could explain further.

"The exact number is classified. There were seven in the first-generation including *Shepard*. Each one was named after the Mercury Seven astronauts. We like to think of them as the ancestors of the Space Force."

"Acceleration on this is great," Stella pointed out as we broke orbit. "Where are we headed?"

"Hope you're a Pink Floyd fan because we're going to the dark side of the moon."

"Meh," KayCee said over the radio. "It's slightly slower than my lander."

"Seriously? It's not a competition," I told her.

Brennan shrugged. "I'm trying not to waste fuel, so it'd take us a bit longer to get to the moon than we could at a high speed But yeah. We weren't able to match the top speed of the lander."

"See," KayCee said.

"But our shields are significantly better."

"That is not possible."

"Well, we might have had help." Brennan smirked.

"How do the shields work? "I asked.

"Once activated, they deflect energy weapons and hard impacts," he explained.

"What do you mean hard impacts?" I cocked my head.

"Bullets, missiles, space debris, that sort of thing," Brennan hit a couple of buttons and pictures of the orbital fighter appeared on a small screen mounted on the control panel. "KayCee, this is everything we have on the orbital fighter. If you and Lock can do your thing, we can get him rated on it."

"Colonel Brennan, are you not afraid that you are revealing secrets to me?"

"Not really. It's all based on your lander's designs except what we couldn't replicate. Aside from some control differences, there is not much for you to discover."

"Very good then. Loughlin Ferguson, are you ready?"

"Hit it," I told the little alien.

Words and pictures scrolled across the screen at an incredible rate, and I felt the information pouring into my brain. Within a minute, it was done. It was significantly more of a download than I needed for the motorcycle, and I felt like my ears needed to pop. I opened my jaws a couple of time.

"What are you doing?"

"Trying to relieve the pressure in my head from all the info added."

"There is no pressure," she said. "You are imagining it."

"So, you're saying it's all in my head."

"Has anyone told you that you are not as funny as you think you are?" KayCee added.

"Really?" Brennan raised his eyebrows. You're done already?"

I shrugged. "It's not like I have to memorize it. Once it's in my brain, I'm good."

"Okay then. Let's find out." Brennan motioned to one of the lockers. "KayCee, I packed your bioform in there if you want to use it."

"Excellent." Golden motes exited my body as KayCee's energy form left me and floated over to the locker in question. The motes slipped through into the locker and a few seconds later its door popped open, and KayCee in her bioform stepped out.

As she buckled into a seat, Brennan gestured at the control panel. "Lock, you ready?"

I placed my hand on the joystick. "Ready."

"You have flight controls?"

"I have flight controls."

"Roger that, you have flight controls."

My powers didn't just allow me to know everything about the fighter. It transferred over to muscle memory as well. When my hand gripped the joystick, it was as if it had a million times before. Brennan gave a series of instructions, and I put the craft through its paces.

After a few minutes of this, the colonel visible relaxed. "Most of the pilots we've trained had some issues dealing with the difference between this and a fighter jet. G-forces being the biggest difference. You need a much lighter touch up here."

"That makes sense," I agreed.

"Ready for some weapons testing?" he asked.

"Not a lot to shoot up here." I told him.

"It's all simulated."

"Sure." Without being told. I turned the weapons simulator on and rapidly went through several scenarios without a scratch.

"Jesus!" Brennan breathed. "If we had twenty more of you, we'd never have to worry about a dogfight again."

"One of me is enough, thanks."

"Okay shut it down." He turned around in his chair. "KayCee, you ready?"

"I am sorry. Ready for what?"

"I know you can operate a lander using an orb, but let's get you use to flying an orbital fighter." Brennan pointed at the panel. "The flying is the same, but the controls are different. Should be too hard to get the hang of it."

"If you insist," KayCee said.

"I do, in fact." He grinned.

"Very well." Kaycee moved into my seat after I exited.

It took KayCee some time to get used to not using the orb. She struggled a little bit but got there in the end. Brennan then had Stella move into the seat to practice using the weapons system.

KayCee leaned in to watch Stella blow up imaginary bad guys. "You have a serious flaw in your system. Your firing control computer will not work against starfighters."

Brennan turned to her. "What do you mean?"

"You are relying on technology to target your enemies. However, in most spacefaring civilizations, military starcraft use communication counter measures to prevent that. Because of this, their pilots fight using line of sight." KayCee pointed to the screens. "I apologize for not thinking of this earlier, but by using cameras and screens to operate by, you have effectively blinded yourself to enemy fighters."

"Oh, that's not good," Stella said.

Brennan frowned. "Your lander didn't have any such tech on it."

"The lander is not a military craft," the little alien informed him. "There is no need for it."

"But *Quiet Contemplation* was," the colonel pointed out. "Why didn't we find such tech on it?"

"Such equipment is expensive and kept out of the hands of civilians," KayCee explained. "It was removed as *Quiet Contemplation* was being decommissioned."

Brennan swore. "That's bad, that's really bad. Does it jam communications as well?"

"Everything but a craft-to-craft tight beam."

Stella stared at the screens. "How hard would it be to retrofit some windows in this thing?"

Brennan flipped a switch and the monitors slid down below the wall revealing windows with metal hatches over them. He flipped another switch and the hatches lowered allowing us to look out into space. "The material for the windows is not as strong as the rest of the fighter. It was determined using the screens was a better option and only to use the windows if the system went down."

"So, your people fly by sight? Like the old dog fights in the world wars?" I asked KayCee.

"During combat use. If you get close enough, you can pierce the jammers enough to get a targeting lock, but other than that, yes. It's why we have windows around the entirety of our crafts."

"Good thing we're not at war at the moment," Stella added.

"Yeah," Brennan pulled up a keyboard from the control panel and started typing. "Give me a minute. I need to relay this back to Delta Black."

After he received a reply, he leaned back. "Well, fixing that problem is up to the eggheads now. Who wants to fly next?"

It was a long flight. Eventually Stella went to sleep and KayCee went into some sort of standby mode. She explained this allowed her to fix some software issues remaining in her bioform. That just left Brennan and me awake and flying the craft.

My mind drifted and, in an effort to stay awake, I asked Brennan a question that had been nagging me for some time. "You mind explaining the whole Cold War with the Detra Ka thing. You seemed to have skimped on some of the info."

"Yeah, Fair enough." He nodded and his fingers ran across the panel. "Let me just fire up George."

"George?"

"Nickname for the remote control," he said.

"Ah."

"To answer your question, I argued against compartmentalizing the intel, but there were still concerns regarding you and KayCee. There was also an argument of what fresh and unbiased eyes could uncover."

"Well, we seemed to uncover a hornets' nest."

"As far as we can tell, the Detra Ka have been guiding humanity for a very long time, advancing our technology much quicker then we think it would have advanced on its own. As I said, we didn't catch on until the 1980s, but once we did, we were able to see their fingerprints going back much further."

"The atomic bomb?"

"Yeah, they had a hand in it," the colonel replied.

"So, who was the alien?" I asked. "Einstein or Oppenheimer? Or was it both of them?"

"Neither actually. The Sleestaks work hard to remain in the shadows, always staying out of the limelight. Einstein and Oppenheimer were human, but several of their assistants weren't. They would insert themselves into society, moving behind the scenes."

"And then taking over someone's identity."

"No, that's actually a very new development. We grew concerned when bona fide humans started acting strangely. We needed to find out if they were turned, brainwashed, or replaced. And more importantly, what caused the Sleestaks to change their way of doing things? They had to know it would raise flags."

"Especially if they always lurked in the shadows. Something must have happened. You sure they've never done anything like this before?

"Not that we know. The taking over people thing is definitely new. As to the staying in the shadows." He hesitated. "Well, there may have been one exception or possibly even the reason for the rule."

"So, who are we talking about?"

"Guess."

"Modern day or in the past?" I asked.

"Past."

I thought about it for a second. "Nikola Tesla?"

"Got it in one." Brennan confirmed. "His inventions and theories were so advanced that our resident eggheads think he might have been a Sleestak."

"Sleestak?" asked Stella, waking up. She nudged KayCee who came out of sleep mode or whatever it was called she had been doing.

"We didn't know the name of their race until you three told us. In fact, we've never seen a full-blooded Detra Ka, Only the hybrids. Officially, they was referred to as Reptilians, but unofficially we just called them Sleestaks. You know, from the show *Land of the Lost*."

I shuddered. "Well, you nailed it. The Detra Treyga are dead ringers for Sleestaks. So close, I think Sid and Marty may have seen one."

"Oh, God," Stella chortled. "How were you not curled up into a ball sucking on your thumb?"

"I never did that," I groused.

Brennan raised his eyebrows. "Explain, please."

"We'd watch that show every Saturday when we were little, and every Saturday night Lock would have nightmares about being chased by Sleestaks." Stella ratted me out.

"It was the hissing," I admitted.

"That is amusing," KayCee said, "because the Detra Ka's version of a boogeyman is a larger hairy version of humans with sharp teeth and claws. Boogeyman is a very silly name by the way."

"You mean like a werewolf?" asked Stella.

"No, it's based off an ancient enemy of theirs." KayCee cocked her head at an angle not possible for humans. "Question. If the creatures on the show frightened you so much, why did you not simply stop watching?"

"That just proves you know nothing about humans," Stella told her.

"Being scared was the best part," I added as Brennan nodded in agreement.

"You humans are such a strange race. Fun, but strange!"

Chapter 25 –
Many Small Steps

As we neared the moon, I sighed. Brennan looked over at Stella, who had resumed napping and then back at me.

"What?" Brennan asked.

"I was just thinking how cool it would be to see Tranquility Base."

"Oh, you should have said something. The hangar Stanley Kubrick filmed it at is on Ducharme Station. The set is still there, I can show you when we get back."

"I... It... The moon landing was really faked?"

He snorted.

"That's just not funny!"

"Yeah, it is." He made a course adjustment. "I can do a flyby, but we can't land near any of the sites. Not just the manned landing but the unmanned ones as well, both the hard and the soft."

"What do you mean hard and soft?"

He pointed out the window where I was able to make out some debris on the surface of the moon. "A hard landing is when we intentionally crash an unmanned spacecraft into the moon. The Soviets did it first in 1959, we followed up in 1962. Soft is when the unmanned craft lands undamaged. A bunch of countries have done it since. Last one was India."

"I had no idea."

"Most people don't. It's getting pretty crowded up here these days. Hell, China actually landed on the far side of the moon back in 2019." He pointed at the window again. "Look."

I held my breath as Tranquility Base came into view. "Stella, Look."

Stella opened her eyes. "I've seen this episode."

My mouth dropped as her eyes closed and she started to snore. Brennan just grinned.

I watched in wonder as Brennan drifted by the other landing sites, flags still planted in the ground. "What must it have been like to actually walk on it?"

"It's a little weird," Brennan said nonchalantly. "You have to do this little hop-skip thing. Easier to just ride in the buggy.".

"You... You walked on the moon?"

"A couple of times. It's all classified though. Too bad, too. No way my siblings could top that one at Christmas." He looked at his watch. "We made good time and can spare a few minutes. You want to take a stroll?"

"Seriously?"

"Yeah, why not? We'll chalk it up as training." He glanced back at KayCee. "You'd think he'd never been to space before."

"To be fair, we spent most of the time trying to stop Kreb from murdering us all," KayCee reminded the colonel.

"Excellent point." He grinned. "Let's just get to the no-fly area. Don't want any of the other countries spotting KayCee's footprints."

As I continued to stare out at the screens, he activated the window. "*Alan Shepard* to *Diana*."

The was some crackling over the air. "This is *Diana*, Go ahead *Shepard*."

I leaned over to KayCee. "This *Diana* lady sounds a lot like Major Quinones."

KayCee nodded. "I do believe that was in fact Major Quinones and not a female."

Brennan rolled his eyes at both of us. "*Diana*, we'll be diverting for a quick training mission at usual. Set the arrival time back sixty please."

"Roger that, *Shepard*. Tell them I said try not to trip." Quinones signed off.

After a few minutes, Brennan set the craft down on the surface. There was a small thud as we landed, and Stella came awake with a grunt. "We there yet?"

"We're going for a quick stroll on the moon." Brennan told her. "Want to come?"

"Hell yeah!" Stella started struggling out of her harness.

Brennan helped us into our EVA suits. Once he was sure they were on properly he put on his. Stella hooked a thumb at KayCee. What about her?

"My bioform is all I need," the little alien told her.

"Cool." My roommate patted her EVA suit. "Beats the hell out of this bulky thing."

"Do you want to walk on the moon or not?" Brennan asked, gesturing for us to enter the airlock. Once we were all in, the door shut, the air was pulled from the room, and the artificial gravity disengaged. The colonel lowered the ramp and we slowly exited. Brennan went first with me right behind him. As the ground crunched beneath my foot, I could hear Neil Armstrong's famous quote in my head.

I took an additional step and felt myself floating up. Brennan grabbed me and settled me down. His voice came across my radio. "There's a trick to it. Wait until everyone is out, and I'll show you."

As I waited for Stella and KayCee to come down the ramp, I took in the view. The surface was desolate but had a strange beauty to it. That beauty paled in comparison to the Earth. It was huge, it loomed over us, seeming much closer than the moon ever did when we were on Earth. It was blue and green and white and was utterly fantastic looking.

I'd seen the Earth from orbit before. Hell, I plummeted from orbit and landed on Earth wearing nothing more than a space blanket. But the view from the moon was just so much more magnificent than from orbit. I felt overwhelmed by emotions I couldn't put into words.

Stella stepped next to me. "Wow."

I smiled, not taking my eyes off our home planet. "It's great, right?"

'Huh? No, I mean what a rip-off."

"Excuse me?"

"I was always told you could see the Great Wall of China from the moon, and I can't see crap." She told me.

"That... That's what you take away from this experience?"

Brennan interjected before Stella could reply. "You can't see anything on Earth that's man made from this location. Under the right conditions and knowing what you're looking for, you can sort of see the Great Wall of China, as well as some of the Egyptian pyramids. But it's a lot clearer using photos."

"Hey, Lock," Stella said. "You know what else you can see from here?"

"Your mother's butt?" I beat her to the punch.

"Damn it!"

"All right children, gather 'round." Brennan's voice went into teacher mode. "The gravity here is about one-sixth of Earth. So, you weigh about 16 percent of what you would back home. This means, among other things, that you can jump about six times higher than normal."

"Cool," Stella whispered. Unseen in my helmet, I nodded in agreement with her.

"That, plus the cumbersome EVA suits means you can't simply walk around up here like nor..." Brennan stared as KayCee walked by. Her bioform somehow compensating for the gravity difference. He cleared his throat and recovered. "Unless you're an alien showoff from a more technologically advanced society. I'm going to show you the best way to move around in your EVA suit without using up your energy."

We watched as he demonstrated a sort of lope and hop system of moving around. It was familiar to both Stella and I from having watched footage of the moon landing many times over the years. But once Brennan had us attempt it, we quickly found watching and doing were two very different things.

Stella repeatedly would go face first into the surface but in a slow-motion pratfall sort of way. Not that I was much better. Every time I stumbled, I seem to float ten or fifteen feet away before doing a sideways belly flop.

After some practice, Stella and I started to become, if not proficient, then at least at the level where we didn't seem like we were staggering home from the moon pub. Brennan was a surprisingly patient teacher and even let us take pictures with the cameras attached to the EVA suits. I was a bit surprised by that. "Really? Aren't you afraid it will out the whole secret operation you have here?"

"It's really not that secret anymore," he said. "My guess is this whole thing will be public knowledge in five years. In the meantime, don't show the pictures to anyone. Besides, even if it got out, people would just say it's a deep fake anyways. We've had more than a couple of leaks handled that way."

I thought back at all the UFO footage I dismissed over the years and wondered how much of it had been real. I gave a mental shrug and promised myself I wouldn't be one of the leaks. I screw up enough as it is, I didn't need to add leaker to the resume. Too bad though, Stella got a really good one of me and KayCee with the Earth in the background, with KayCee's long fingers throwing up a peace sign.

"Okay, boys and girls, time to wrap it up," Brennan stated just as I was feeling tired, something that didn't happen a lot these days with my new abilities. Stella must have been feeling wiped out as well because she didn't bother to argue.

I waited at the bottom of the ramp as KayCee and Stella went up. I wanted to be the last in for reasons I couldn't articulate. As Brennan turned toward me, I tried to explain. "I... Go ahead. I just need a minute."

"Take five, Lock. I get it. I felt the same way my first time here." He loped up the ramp.

I turned and stared toward the Earth. Watching it loom over me, I knew without a doubt that the big blue planet and the people on it were worth fighting for.

Chapter 26 –
Dog Fight

As I gave a last look around, I spotted a series of specks on the horizon. I upped my vision, zooming in to spot five orbital fighters heading our way. "Why do I have a bad feeling about this? Hey, Colonel!"

"Colonel? Brennan?" Realizing no one could hear me, I loped up the ramp and hit the button to restore gravity and air. As soon as the airlock opened, I staggered inside, lifting off my helmet. "Couldn't you guys hear me? We have multiple orbital fighters coming inbound."

"What?" Brennan stuffed his EVA suit into a locker and rushed over to the controls as Stella continued to struggle out of hers. "I'm not showing anything."

"I tried you on the EVA suit's radio." I said.

"That sounds like communication counter measures have been activated." KayCee stated. "Do the approaching orbital fighters belong to the Space Force?"

"We're supposed to be the only ones with them. But I'm not taking any chances." Brennan raised the ramp and began lifting off. "Lock, get in the copilot seat and see if you can raise them. Maybe your suit radio conked out."

I shoved my helmet and gloves into Stella's arms and rushed to do what he said. "Anyone actually think that's what happened?"

"No, but do it anyways." Brennan told me. "How many fighters and where did you see them?"

"Five. Coming from there." I pointed out the window to where the specks were getting larger.

Suit secured, Stella plopped down in the seat behind me and leaned forward. While not up to my level, her eyes were better than any normal humans. "I see them."

"This is the *Alan Shepard* to approaching craft. Please identify." I waited for a response before repeating my message. Again, I was met with silence. "*Shepard* to *Diana*, please respond. *Shepard* to *Diana*."

"I believe we now know why the Detra Ka did not install communication countermeasures in your orbital fighters," KayCee said, buckling into her seat.

"Yeah," Stella agreed, doing the same. "They planned on using them on us."

"Well," Brennan pointed us at the approaching craft. "Let's go say hi."

"Are you crazy?" I said. "Head to where you have KayCee's starcraft hidden. I doubt any of their weapons can damage it."

"There's a problem with that plan." Brennan grimaced, flicking another switch as the other crafts closed on us. "That's where they came from."

"Crap!" I twisted my head as music flooded the cabin. "'Fortunate Son'?"

"I like a little CCR when I'm gaming," Brennan said. "Five's too many. We need to even the odds. Lock, you need to take the controls.

"I have flight controls." I gripped the joystick tightly.

"You have flight controls," Brennan acknowledged.

"Wait, what are you doing?" I asked.

"Something stupid." Brennan placed his fingers on the small screen in the control panel and then punched in a code. His chair flattened back and lowered into the floor. Sealing up after him.

"What the Bruce Wayne was that?" Stella asked.

"No idea," I replied. I studied the formation of the approaching craft. Part of my download involved battle tactics. There was a thunk from down below. "Now what?"

"I am not sure," KayCee replied. "They have not fired on us yet."

"Knight One has entered the game!" a deep announcer voice crackled over the radio as an armored suit roared up from under us. The pilot seat rose from the floor, now empty.

"Oh, I'm totally stealing that line," I muttered before raising my voice. "Two against five. That's a little better."

"Not by much," Stella grumbled. The enemy craft fired on us as they flew by.

"Yeah, about that." I scanned the controls. No damage, our shields had held. "KayCee, get in the pilot seat."

As she did so, the craft flew by again. This time I fired on them, my shots raking over a fighter. Its shield flared blue. "Well, that didn't do much. KayCee, you have flight controls."

"I do not, Loughlin Ferguson, you do."

"Oh, for crying out loud. It means, I'm transferring control to you.

"Then why did you not just say so."

"Just take control."

"It is done."

I stood up. "Stella, sit here and take over weapons."

"Roger that." As Stella slid into my vacant seat, I headed to the lockers. "Lock, what are you doing?"

I pulled the locker open and donned my helmet and gloves as the music switched to 'Run Through The Jungle.' "Stupid is *my* thing. I can't let Brennan take that away from me. KayCee, try to get over to one of those fighters."

"Understood. This is a very bad idea, Loughlin Ferguson."

"I know." As the cool calm signaling combat mode swept over me, I cycled the airlock and lowered the ramp. Holding tight, I watched the battle. The *Shepard* rumbled as we took another hit. My brain fiddled with the communication system of my EVA suit. As I watched an enemy craft approach below us, I launched myself toward it. My brain triggered the announcer voice. "Janitor has entered the game!"

'Ace of Spades' started playing just as the craft banked, causing me to miss it. I shot past it, drifting away from the fight. "Fuck that noise. This is not my first rodeo."

I reached down under my air tank, the skin, muscles, and bone of my hand becoming dense and strong. With my index finger I punched a hole into the tank. It propelled me back into the fight.

The suit was too bulky and limiting my movement. I grabbed my left shoulder and tore the arm off my suit. As my skin adjusted to the vacuum of space, I did the same to the right arm. One of these days, I need to learn how to use my powers when not in a life-or-death situation.

The fight wasn't going great. No one had managed to do any serious damage, but I couldn't see our shields holding on forever. I angled into the path of an approaching fighter. As it flew by, my arm shot out like a snapped rubber band and connected to its side. The palm of my hand shifted into a super-sucker that clung to the side of the fighter. Even in stretch arm-strong mode, my shoulder was ripped from its socket as the fighter pulled me along.

Gritting my teeth, I retracted my arm, reeling myself to the side of the fighter. A pair of hybrids peered out the window in surprise. With both of my hands in super-sucker mode, I spider crawled to the entrance. At the same time, my mind hacked the flying saucer's computer, forcing the ramp down. Once I was in, I retracted it and cycled the air and gravity.

I relished the shock on the faces of the hybrids as the airlock opened to the strains of 'Shipping Up To Boston.' "Avast, ye scallywags. Taking your ship, I be. Arrr!"

Chapter 27 –
Space Booty

I dropped the lifeless body of the second hybrid onto the deck of the orbital fighter. A fighter that was now mine for the taking.

"Arrr. Space booty!"

His companion was already turning to green goo. Knowing that the hybrids were just a type of bioform, and their essences would be shunted back to their real bodies allowed me to cut loose in a very brutal fashion.

"Three against four. The odds are getting better." I sat in the pilot's seat and moved up behind an enemy fighter. It ignored me, thinking I was on its side. This gave me all the time in the world to target one of the windows. Once I was ready to fire. I sent a tight beam transmission. Using the skills I'd copied from my cousin Tavish, my mind hitched a ride on the tight beam, entering and seizing the computer systems of the enemy craft. "Bye-bye, fuckers!"

I turned off their shield and shot out the windows. Two bodies were quickly sucked out into space. Still mentally controlling their craft, I powered down the now empty fighter and headed toward the other fighter. "Make that three against three."

Having seen what I did to their friends, they went into evasive maneuvers. Brennan flew up near me, painting me with a tight beam transmission. "Lock, is that you?"

"Roger that, Boss!"

"How did you do that?"

"Hacked the system Tavish-style and shut off the shields." We banked in opposite directions to avoid being strafed by enemy fighters. Brennan circled back, firing mini missiles from arm launchers. "That's brilliant. But maybe just open the landing ramp instead of damaging the fighters. I'd like to add them to the collection if I could."

"Greedy, greedy," I said. "Set up a distraction for me, please."

"Right. Follow my lead. But make it quick—I'm almost bingo fuel." He swept by KayCee's fighter, pointing at a craft. Brennan and KayCee boxed it in, concentrating fire on it. As it fended off their attacks, I snuck up behind it and repeated the tight beam trick, this time depressurizing the cabin. Turns out hybrids need oxygen.

As we moved toward the next target, the two remaining craft split up. One headed out while the other attacked us with everything it had. As I hacked into the remaining fighter, Brennan shot after the fleeing one. The extra speed must have spent his fuel even quicker because his thrusters stopped firing.

As I finished disabling the last fighter, KayCee tight beamed me. "Loughlin Ferguson, go after the other enemy craft. I believe it is trying to get out of range of the communication countermeasures in order to alert others. We will pick up the colonel and follow you."

"Crap! Okay, heading out." I pushed the orbital fighter for everything it had. It quickly became obvious I couldn't overtake the enemy craft. He skipped around the circumference of the moon, staying close to the surface. In a short time, I could no longer see the Earth as we came around to the far side of the moon.

I checked communications but I was still being jammed. I needed to alert *Quiet Contemplation* that an attack was happening. Jeopardy was on it with the other Space Force personnel, and I couldn't let anything happen to her. I mean... them.

"Jeopardy. That's it." I did have a way to reach her, and for once it didn't involve the powers the mad alien scientist foisted onto me through forced experimentation.

When Kreb came back for me a year ago, KayCee was able to train Jeopardy in both telekinesis and telepathy. Skills apparently all humans have the potential to use. Jeopardy used those abilities to great effect and helped win the battle against Kreb.

As a die-hard *Star Wars* geek, I'd be a liar if I said I wasn't jealous. Who wouldn't want the powers of a Jedi? So, while KayCee and I were on the run, I pestered her to train me in them. And she did. The problem is, I wasn't good at the mental stuff. KayCee insisted I'd get better with enough practice. However, since we were on the run from government agents and were trying to stay inconspicuous, I didn't get a lot of chance to practice. Both telepathy and telekinesis needed subtlety, something I did not have a lot of. I was a complete no-go with telekinesis and I wasn't much better with telepathy. I was unable to read minds and it was all caps when mentally communicating. Just a big mental shout, really.

I switched out of combat mode and calmed my mind, reaching out trying to find her. After a minute or so, I sensed her. "Jeopardy."

"*Lock? Stop shouting and how the hell are you doing this?*"

"No time to explain. We were just attacked by hybrids using orbital fighters. I think you might be next."

"*You were attacked? So, this is different from Colonel Brennan's message about the flaws with the orbital fighters?*"

"Yes!" I paused. "Actually, that might have been what triggered the attack. So, go on alert."

"*Okay. Hold on a second.*" She broke the link, only to reestablish it a moment later. "*Okay, I told Quinones, and he sounded the alarm. What— Oh shit!*"

I felt the link break again. "Jeopardy! Jeopardy!"

"Oh God, was I too late?" I continued to follow the enemy fighter skimming across the surface of the moon. As I did so, a tight beam transmission came through. "*Shepard to Janitor.*"

On hearing Brennan's voice, I looked back, seeing a speck in the distance. I zoomed in to see the *Shepard* following after me in a straight line. I was shocked they were able to connect at this distance. "I read you, *Shepard*."

"*What's your status?*"

"I can't catch the fighter and communications are blocked. I don't know if it's on our end or theirs, but I was able to reach out to Jeopardy using telepathy. She was about to warn Quinones before we lost contact."

"*Telepathy? That's a new one. Why did you lose contact?*"

"I think they were attacked. Or it could be that I just suck..."

I forgot what I was saying as *Quiet Contemplation* came into view. Floating in space, it was attached to a type of space station. The station had four construction slips. KayCee's starcraft was in one, wrapped in scaffolding. What was surprising was the three additional slips. One appeared to have an asteroid attached to it that was currently being drilled into. The other two slips contained starcrafts that appeared to be carved out of asteroids. Mounted weapons and hangar entrances dotted the surfaces of each. Thrusters that looked suspiciously like those of *Quiet Contemplation* jutted out of the rear sections. "Son of a bitch! You guys are making starcrafts out asteroids!"

"Yup," Brennan confirmed. "Welcome to the *Diana*. Earth's first space yard. Do you see anything?"

I zoomed my vision in again. "I can see orbital fighters dog fighting each other over one of them."

"Which one?" he asked.

"The one closest to *Quiet Contemplation*. They don't seem to be firing on it though, just our fighters."

"That makes sense. It's the *Armstrong*, which is now finished. Just needs to pass testing. They're trying to steal it!"

"What's the plan?" I asked.

"The *Aldrin* and the *Collins* aren't operational yet. The *Armstrong* is the priority. Get on it and stop them from leaving. Major Quinones is the Delta Black representative on *Diana*. Get a hold of him or Colonel Blackwell, *Diana*'s commanding officer, get a sitrep and see what they want to do. I'm guessing it's getting on the *Armstrong*."

"Roger that." Time seemed to inch by until I was close enough to tight beam the Diana. "What about the fighters?"

"I gave KayCee the control orb," Brennan said. "She's confident she can duplicate your trick."

I smiled. More likely she planned on using Tavish's consciousness to do it, but he didn't need to know that yet. "Good luck. I'm going to try *Diana* again."

"Roger that. Be safe and see you there."

I aimed a tight beam at the space yard but couldn't make a connection for another two minutes. "Janitor to *Diana*, please come in."

"Go for *Diana*," a man answered.

"I'm currently chasing an orbital fighter controlled by bad guys inbound to your location. The *Shepard* is following but is a little farther out. Is the CO available?"

"Standby one, Janitor."

A woman's voice came on. "This is Blackwell."

"What's your status, Colonel? Where do you need me?"

"Do you not see the battle taking place around the *Armstrong*, Janitor?" she snapped.

"Yes, ma'am, I do. What I need to know is what I can't see. Where will I do the most good?"

"Sorry, that was uncalled for." I could hear her take a deep breath and let it out. "The enemy infiltrated some of my staff. They are being backed up by additional forces. Where they came from, I don't know. Aside from the orbital fighters, they have combat teams on the *Armstrong*. I had a skeleton crew on there and they're currently fighting a rear-guard action with the enemy troops. Daytime and Risk have taken a team over to reinforce them, but we lost communications. Considering your skill set, you would be best used by backing up your fellow Delta Black members on the *Armstrong*. We can't let them take that starcraft!"

"Roger that, Colonel." I switched the beam back to the *Shepard* and filled Brennan and the others in.

"Yeah," Brennan said. "That's about what I figured."

"I assume Daytime and Risk are who I think they are."

"Yup."

"Daytime?"

"Any downtime in flight school found Quinones watching soap operas and talk shows."

"Ouch!" I winced. "And what did you give your two traveling companions?"

"You mean Barfight and Gazoo?" Brennan asked.

"And once again the roommate gets a cool nickname," I grumbled.

"Head in the game," he cautioned. "You're getting close."

He was righter than he probably figured. The fighter I'd been chasing did a loop and headed back toward me, several of his friends in tow.

"Oh, crap!" I went into a series of evasive maneuvers, but against that many and without back up, I started taking hits. I was too busy ducking and dodging to use my trick with their shields. In fact, the only shields I was paying attention to were mine because they were getting weaker and weaker.

This was a game of attrition I couldn't win. Figuring I had enough air in the cabin to pull it off, I diverted all power to the thrusters and shields and pulled a Rickon Stark, heading toward the *Armstrong* in a straight line.

Once I shot past them, I poured on the speed. They followed after, pounding my craft with everything they had. We entered the dogfight and additional fighters targeted me. My shields failed, and pieces were being shot off my orbital fighter.

I aimed at an open landing bay just before I had a rupture. My remaining air was quickly sucked out into the vacuum of space. Since

I'd already punctured my EVA suit's oxygen supply to get to the fighter, this left me with only the breath in my lungs.

Been there, done that. Got the T-shirt.

Once the next couple of shots disabled my thrusters, the enemy fighters broke off. With no propulsion and venting atmosphere, they no longer considered me a threat.

As long as I didn't get knocked off course, that was fine by me. My momentum should carry me into the hangar. Given my powers, I was mostly confident I'd survive the crash. Mostly...

At the last second, a fighter trying to evade being shot at clipped me, sending me into a spin. I struggled to see if I was knocked off course, but everything was topsy-turvy. I raised the hatches that covered the windows just as my fighter impacted something huge, the metal tearing open down one side and everything went black.

Chapter 28 –
Boarding Party

With the power gone and the hatches up, I couldn't see a thing. I altered my vision, allowing me to see faint light trickling into the large tear along the craft's side. The impact knocked half the breath out of my lungs, and even with my adaptive abilities, I was struggling not to take a deep breath.

Not bothering with the airlock, I clambered out of the tear along the body of the lander and found that I was in the *Armstrong's* depressurized landing bay. From the scrape marks, it looked like I clipped the edge of the entrance coming in and then slammed into the far wall.

I climbed off the wreckage of my craft and jogged across the bay to its nearest airlock. I punched the button next to the door and waited impatiently. Then waited a little longer.

Oh, Come on!

My mind reached into the door's electronics. It had been locked remotely. I countermanded the order, and the door slid open, allowing me to slip into the airlock. The door resealed and blessed air pumped in. I took a series of deep, ragged breaths. Canned air never felt so good.

Once the airlock was fully pressurized, the air door opened, and I entered a small room. Open lockers lined the walls, EVA suits hanging in them.

The sight of them made me realize the stolen fighter must have had some EVA suits on board. If I had figured that out in time, I wouldn't have had to do the whole starve for oxygen thing.

"Speaking of." My EVA suit had gotten shredded in the crash. I grabbed the collar and tore off the remains. "That's better."

The coldness of the floor quickly reminded me I didn't bring shoes. I looked around but didn't see any. More importantly, I didn't see any weapons either. "Ugh, I hate my life!"

The room opened into a corridor, and I slipped into it. The walls of both the room and the corridor was smooth metal. The rooms were hollowed directly out of the asteroid that the *Armstrong* was created from. A series of LED lights hung from the ceiling allowed me to see.

Even counting on the fact that we had aliens secretly helping us build it, this was a momentous achievement for mankind. Within a year's time, the Space Force had captured several asteroids, towed them to this location and hollowed them out, not only making them habitable but turning them into NexGen starcraft.

From what I saw of the hangar entrance, they had left a lot of meat on the bone. In fact, I would bet hollow was the wrong word. More like they had carved a series of interconnecting tunnels, leaving a lot of the asteroid still surrounding them from the vacuum of space.

That much iron nickel had to make these things pretty impervious to the weapons of both the Sarli and the Detra Ka. And that didn't include the improved shielding Brennan had been bragging about. Even without the special alloy that the Sarli used on their spacecraft, I bet they would be hard pressed to match the *Armstrong's* defenses.

I shook my head. "Quit geeking out, you idiot. Get in the game."

Remembering the direction of the *Armstrong* and what side I had crashed into, I figured the front of the starcraft was on my right. That was probably where the command center was. I padded down the corridor and took a left turn directly into a Detra Ka boarding party. Two Detra Tal, a Detra Bel, and a couple of Detra Treyga.

"Crap!" As warriors, the Detra Tal were the most dangerous of the group, but it was the Detra Treyga that freaked me out. The whole hissing Sleestak thing was still completely unnerving.

I licked the wall and went into combat mode, all my worries washing away as I launched myself at the closest warrior. As I did, my body changed into the iron nickel the *Armstrong* was made of. My thumbs slammed into a Detra Tal's eyes. They might have tough skin, but as it turns out their eyeballs pop just fine.

He screamed, falling back, his tail whipping out of control. I leaped out of range and turned toward the next one, surprised he hadn't attacked me already. I was even more surprised to see the Detra Bel waving his arms at me and speaking in English. "Stop, Lock Ferguson. Please stop!"

I stepped back, arms up in case it was a trick and studied this member of the creator caste. "Bel Crat? Is that you?"

"You remember me. Excellent. Please stop fighting."

"Okay." I lowered my arms. "I'm listening."

"Help Gicklie." Bel Crat motioned to the Detra Tal currently rolling on the floor, clutching where his eyes had been. Two of the Detra Treyga rushed over to help him.

"Are you here to steal this spacecraft?"

Bel Crat made a strange hissing sound that I took to be his species equivalent of a sigh. "The Detra Terra explained the schism among our people, yes?"

"You mean Itza?"

He made another hissing sound, this one sort of stuttered.

Is he laughing?

"Itza was the name of the Detra Terra's favorite handmaiden," he explained. "She likes to use her likeness and name when appearing in a human form."

"Handmaiden? Are you are taking human slaves?"

"No. That is not our way. However, the Mayans believed us gods and at the time, it was just easier than explaining the truth."

"Mayans? You've been here that long?"

"Unfortunately, we have. But we are drifting downstream. Let us return to the matter at hand. Yes?" He looked up and down the corridor.

"Fine."

"The traitors know that we did indeed plan on taking one of your starcraft in order to leave your planet once and for all," Bel Crat explained. "They decided to take it for themselves. We are attempting to stop them. But we underestimated how many they were. They also seem to have human allies. We are currently at a stalemate. They have the control deck, and we have the engineering section. Last I heard, each side was trying to convince the other to leave."

Slipping out of combat mode, I glanced down at the Detra Tal I'd injured. "Ah, really sorry about that."

"Fog of war, as you humans say. We can repair his eyes once we get him to the medical station. The Detra Terra is meeting me there along with your former sex partner."

"The term is girlfriend. Not sex partner. You should know that if you... Wait. Jeopardy is with Itza?"

"Yes, we were on our way to assist them when we ran into you."

"How far are we?" I should have asked Brennan to give me the schematics of the *Armstrong, Aldrin* and *Diana*. "I'll go with you and speak to Itza and Jeopardy. Is Quinones with them?"

"He is, and we are close." He motioned down the corridor and gave me a series of directions showing that his idea of close was very different to mine. It sounded like a twenty-minute walk. In a battle, a lot can happen in twenty minutes.

Okay." I flinched as a Sleestak—I mean Detra Treyga—walked by me. "Let me lead and I'll get us there."

"As you say." Bel Crat dipped his head.

Cranking up my senses in an attempt to detect any of the bad guys, I moved to the front of the group and headed toward where Bel Crat said med bay was. It was surprisingly anti-climactic. Well, for me anyway. I'm sure poor Gicklie would disagree.

I may have gotten a little complacent by the time I rounded the last turn. Two Space Force Guardians were waiting, armed and ready. Finally relaxing, I waved at them. My relief turned to shock as both fired at me. Several rounds struck me in the chest. I'm not going to lie, those hurt. Well, they did for the few seconds before the next round hit me. I took that one in the center of my forehead.

Fun fact. The average human skull is about 0.25 inches in thickness. Stella, I'm sure, would argue that mine is significantly thicker and not because of my superpowers. And while she might be correct, it didn't stop the .227 fury round from punching through my skull, tearing through my nice and squishy brain and bursting out the back of my skull, leaving a much bigger hole then the one it created on entry.

In other words. Lights out for Lock.

Chapter 29 –
The Answers to Some of my Questions

"He's a lot more formidable than you think," I heard Itza say.

"You'd be surprised at what I think," Jeopardy replied.

I groaned and opened my eyes. I was lying on a bed in sick bay. A curtain blocked my view of the rest of the room except for Gicklie on the bed next to me, his eyes covered in bandages. I winced more at the sight of that than the pounding in my head. I tried to sit up only to discover that was a bad idea, as everything went spinning. Groaning, I lay back down. I heard the curtain draw back, and Jeopardy's and Itza's heads appeared. I gave a slight grin. "Talking about me?"

Jeopardy rolled her eyes. "Really, you idiot? What? You think we were comparing notes?"

"Ah." That thought hadn't occurred to me, but my stomach dropped as she brought it up. "No?"

"Besides, you think I'm going to fail the Bechdel-Wallace test?"

"Wallace?" I frowned. "I thought it was just called the Bechdel test."

"Well, you thought wrong, again." Jeopardy didn't quite snap at me, but her tone was close to it. "We were assessing one of the enemy combatants. He's formidable."

"He?" I tried sitting up again. This time successfully. "Well then, you failed your test."

"Excuse me?" Jeopardy arched an eyebrow at me.

"The parameters I read just said a man, it doesn't say anything about the man needing to be a love interest or ex or whatever..." I trailed off on seeing the murderous look in her eyes. "Just saying."

"How is your head?" asked Itza, who currently appeared human.

"Pounding, and I'd like to get out of here." I swung my legs off the side of the bed. "Printed out a new body I see."

"That's not really how it works, but yes." She stepped back as I tried to stand.

Finding myself remaining upright, I looked at both of them. "So why exactly was I shot?"

"Yeah, about that." Jeopardy pulled on one of her braids, something she did as a stalling tactic. "They were actually aiming as Itza's people. Lucky, they missed and hit you."

"Lucky?" I didn't quite yell. "How is that lucky?"

"Because her people don't instantly heal and shrug off bullets like they're gnats."

I pointed to the bed I just got out of. "Does it look like I just got hit with a gnat?"

She frowned. "What happened there anyway? You normally go all Super Lock and shrug the rounds off. You've been hit with bigger ones and didn't even limp away."

"Okay. First off, healing fast doesn't dull the pain. Getting shot is just as painful for me as it is for you."

That set her back. "Really? I didn't know that."

"Yeah." I gingerly touched the back of my head, wondering if I had lost any memories from being shot and if I had, how would I know. "Secondly, KayCee and I have been working on control, trying to get my body to stop reacting without conscious effort. It, uh... might have bled over to areas I didn't want it to."

As I stepped out into the main area of the med bay where Bel Crat waited, Itza placed her hand on my shoulder. From the fire in Jeopardy's eyes, that didn't go over well. I carefully stepped away, letting her hand fall off.

"Normally, my abilities automatically adapt to a threat. With bullets, it usually means changing my body's composition so the rounds pass through me harmlessly."

Itza glanced over at Bel Crat who nodded. Ignoring them, I turned my gaze back to Jeopardy. "So, about the not-so-friendly-fire incident. How did trained military personnel all miss their targets and hit me?"

"I can answer that." A short Hispanic man in a black flight suit like mine walked into the room, flanked by two guys who by their similar attire were members of Delta Black.

I nodded. "Major Quinones."

"Ferguson. Glad you're all right." He pointed to a side room separate from the med bay, and Jeopardy, Itza, Bel Crat, and I followed him in. The Delta Black members stayed outside, posted at the door.

From the table and chairs, the room appeared to be some sort of conference room for the medical personnel.

As the rest of us sat down, Quinones shut the door and turned toward Itza. "Any luck?"

She shook her head. "They said they would consider your offer, and I'm waiting to hear back from them."

He nodded to her before answering my earlier question. "Not including members of Delta Black, the personnel on this starcraft are not front-line combatants. They are here for their expertise in installing and maintaining the equipment that will be used on the *Armstrong* once it's fully operational. We only had a minimum-security force here, and most of them didn't survive the initial attack."

Now that I thought about it, the personnel I saw did seem on the geekier side.

"I thought it already was operational," I said. "I thought all you had to do was some final tests."

"Those tests determine if the *Armstrong* is fully operational or not," he said.

"Whatever." I never really liked Quinones. Back home, when Delta Black was investigating us, he kept coming down hard on me.

My tone must have betrayed my feelings. His posture became less rigid. "Lock, you know back in your hometown, I was just playing bad cop to the colonel's good cop, right? It was never personal. I definitely respect everything you did in stopping Kreb."

That... made sense. "Fair enough. Where are we?"

"Colonel Brennan was able to clear the airspace and then secure the *Aldren*. Colonel Blackwell has secured the *Diana*. For whatever reason, the rebels left *Quiet Contemplation* alone."

"The metal alloy the Sarli use in the construction of their starcraft is toxic to our people if exposed for large amounts of time," Itza explained. "A quick jaunt in a lander to the moon and back is fine, but if we tried to use *Quiet Contemplation* to travel to a different star system, only corpses would arrive at the final destination."

"Heh!" I grew uncomfortable as everyone in the room turned to stare at me. Itza's eyes narrowed. "The death of all of my people amuses you?"

"What? *Absolutely not!* Just, you know. *Final Destination*. The movie franchise? No?" I was met with a blank stare. "And... you have no idea what I'm talking about, do you?"

"I do not," replied the ruler of the Detra Ka with a grim look.

"It was a reference thing." I dipped my head. "No disrespect to your people was meant."

"Anyways," the major stirred in his seat. "Regarding the *Armstrong*, we have this level and the one below it. They have the level above, which includes the command deck. When the fighting started, it was a three-way free for all. Itza reached out to me to explain her side, and we formed an alliance against the others." He sat down across from me. "We only have about twenty armed personnel, most who have never held a gun outside of yearly qualifications. I have four Delta Black left and your friend Itza has about half of the thirty people that came with her."

"Ouch." I rubbed my jaw. "How many people do the bad guys have?"

"We think the rebel Detra Ka have about fifty left on board. Most are hybrids. Some are humans that are being controlled. But there's a bigger problem."

"What's that?" I asked.

"At least two of the humans don't seem to be controlled and they have advanced abilities. We think they may have been experimented on by Kreb."

I continued to rub my jaw as I mulled that over. The alien mad scientist known as Kreb the Incorrigible had abducted human children, experimenting on them for years, in order to turn them into living weapons to fight his enemies. He had always referred to me as Human Weapon System 12 which meant there had to be at least eleven others. Six had been a woman named Mary, 10 was my cousin Tavish and 11 had turned out to be my childhood bully Dennis McKeene. All three were now dead, though I hoped Tavish's condition would only be temporary.

That left at least eight people out there that Kreb had turned into living weapons. It wasn't inconceivable that the rebel Detra Ka had reached out to a couple of them and turned them to their side. "Do we know what they can do?"

"Only one." Quinones said in a grim tone.

"Well, what is it?"

"Force lightning," answered Jeopardy.

"What? They're Sith?" Possessing the soul of a true geek, I was both horrified and intrigued at the same time.

"Let's keep it real, please." Quinones said. "He has some sort of energy projection ability. It's a... powerful skill. It's been described as blasting out from him in a radius."

"So, not force lightning at all." I said. "And the other one?"

"Female. That's all we know. Anyone that's gone up against her hasn't come back.'

"That can't be good. Do we know if they're being controlled?"

Itza shook her head. "This is not a process known to our people."

There was a knock at the door, and one of the Detra Treyga entered slowly with a tray of drinks, doing the whole Sleestak hissing thing. I couldn't stop myself from shying away from it when it placed a drink in front of me.

"I have a question." I waved my arms around. "How did you build all this without being detected?"

"We've had a platform in orbit for a few years now," Quinones said. "Officially, it's a weather satellite. In reality, it launches stealth craft. But we had nothing like this. We did have plans to eventually build an orbital station for building starcraft, but that was years off. That changed when we retrieved KayCee's refueler. As a former military starcraft, it had the equipment to dismantle smaller asteroids into raw materials and print new parts out of it."

"*Quiet Contemplation* has that capability?" I raised my eyebrows.

"Yeah." The major leaned back in his chair. "It goes through them horrifyingly fast too. We built *Diana Station* using it and then reprogrammed it to hollow out some larger asteroids to create our own starcraft."

"You did this all in a year?" I asked.

Quinones shrugged. "Well, as it turns out, we had some help."

Bel Crat bared his teeth, or maybe it was a smile. "The hardest part was breaking the starcraft's encryptions."

"Perhaps we should discuss the rebellion," Itza said.

"Sure, how did this rebellion start anyways?" I asked.

"The females of my people do not get along. There can never be two queens." Itza took a sip of her drink. Once she did so, Bel Crat had a taste of his. I noticed Jeopardy and the major left theirs alone. Temporary alliances only go so far after all. Itza placed her cup down. "Once our population grows to a certain size, another female, a future queen is born. When a queen has a female offspring, the queen generally tolerates her until the future queen has aged to maturity and has attracted followers."

"Sorry," I held up a hand. "What do you mean followers?"

"When there are two queens, a male instinctively picks a queen to obey. When the new queen has enough followers, they depart to form a new society."

"That sounds like bees," said Jeopardy.

Itza shrugged. "It is a repeating hierarchy in a variety of different species in the universe."

"Why does the old queen allow the new queen to take followers?"

"There is a biological need in my people to perpetuate the species." Itza took another drink. "That being said, if a new queen stays too long, then the two queens will war on each other."

"And you stayed too long," I guessed.

"Quite the opposite. The Detra Malum, what you would call my mother, is a particularly vicious queen and wouldn't or couldn't let me fully mature. Fearing war, I fled her world before I had gathered enough followers."

"So, you *are* the Lost Colony," I mused.

"The Lost Colony?" Itza cocked her head. Unlike when KayCee does it, it seemed very humanlike. "Explain, please."

"A Sarli friend of mine had heard about your story. You're known as the Lost Colony."

"Colorful, but lost isn't quite an accurate description." Itza stared into her cup. "Due to the devastations of war with the ancient enemy, the technology of the Detra Ka is not what it used to be. Many generations before my birth, we lost the secret of jump-drive technology. Instead, we relied on arkstars, manned by a small crew while the rest of us slept in hibernation chambers.

"The Detra Malum had ordered several of her loyal followers to pretend to follow me. When their rotation for crew came up, they tried to disable the arkstar and kill us all. They managed to sabotage the arkstar before the crew found out. The loyal crewmembers bravely fought and defeated the assassins, but the sabotage was irreversible, and the vessel was slowly going critical. The ranking officer plotted a course to the closest habitable planet and jettisoned the hibernation section with what equipment they could scrounge. Thanks to the bravery of that crew, we were able to safely make it to that planet."

"Earth." Jeopardy breathed. Long before all the craziness, she had been a blogger specializing on the existence of aliens. She might be in the Space Force now, but she had lost none of her interest in the subject.

"Yes, Earth." Itza nodded. "We landed in the Mediterranean, near Rome to be exact, and quickly discovered the planet had a native sentient species."

"Humans," I said.

"The issue of queens is a biological matter. That aside, we do not go to war with other species lightly. Our ancient battle had been too costly for us to ever consider that idea unless there was no other options available."

"It didn't help that there was a lot more of us then you and we have already developed weapons that could easily kill your kind," added Quinones.

"That was also a factor, yes." Itza agreed. "Even still, there were suggestions for us to subjugate your people and become the ruling race. I overruled that. I found the idea of it abhorrent. In addition, the planet is not ideal for my people. The air may be breathable, but it's uncomfortable and far too cold for our liking.

"There was still the problem of how to get off the planet. Outside of the hibernation section that landed on Earth, we had very little of the needed technology to get us off of this planet, nor did we have the right type of scientists to make such technology.

"The Romans did not react well to our arrival, so we moved our people far away to a more comfortable climate and introduced ourselves to the locals. The plan was to hibernate while a revolving team would work together with our new neighbors to advance their technology and after a century or two be able to get off this planet."

"Who were the locals?" Jeopardy asked.

"The Mayans," I told her.

"Correct," Itza stated. "It did not go as well as I had hoped. The divide was too great and no matter how much we tried to stop them, they started worshipping us as gods. This was particularly disturbing due to some of their preexisting habits. You have no idea how upsetting it is to wake up from hibernation to find out that hundreds of sentient people had been murdered as sacrifices in your name."

"I'm freaking out just hearing about it," Jeopardy said. "So, then what happened?"

"The Spanish and their quest for gold is what happened. They did not react well to meeting our kind." Itza took another sip, gathering her thoughts. "We went into deep hibernation, allowed the world to forget us. While we had no Detra Bel who could build me a starcraft, we did have several bio engineers. So, when we awoke again, we created humanlike forms we could mentally link to and control with our minds. What you have been calling hybrids. We then infiltrated your scientific communities, offering a suggestion here, a hint there. Speeding up the already incredible pace of your technological breakthroughs."

"That brings up a question," I said as she took a breath. "You lost your connection when we flew too far away on the lander. How can you maintain a connection this far from Earth?"

"My people are heavily involved in Project Ironsides. More so than any other time before. We planted a linking device up here in order to work this far out in human form."

"So, what went wrong?" I asked.

"Tal Bavra, the caste leader of the Detra Tal, never believed the plan could work. He always argued that we should try to change this planet to suit our needs and to push humans aside." She started to take another drink before realizing the cup was empty. "The only way for my people to survive is for me to be able to breed more of us on our new planet. For that to happen, I needed to remain in a certain physical age range. Therefore, I hibernated significantly more than the others, which meant I was relying heavily on those I assigned to carry out my wishes. Tal Bavra never directly disobeyed me but apparently, he had created a backup plan, planting certain of his followers in professions that were unhealthy for the planet, hoping it would cause a rise in temperature. I had some inkling of what he had been doing but let it go, hoping he would come around."

"Your people caused global warming?" Jeopardy shrieked. "Oh, my God I can't wait... Damn it, I can't report this at all, can I?"

"Nope," answered Quinones. "Sorry, Still top secret."

"This sucks," she grumbled.

The major leaned toward Itza. "Why didn't you call him to task?"

"Because he was the crew leader who saved us all those years ago, and I owed him that much."

"When did he go full Apocalypse Now?" I asked.

I sighed at the blank look she gave me. "When did he go into full rebellion?"

"About ten months ago. Somehow he learned how to control humans."

"Not from the Detra Bel, he didn't," broke in Bel Crat. "Where he learned this is a complete mystery."

"I know." Itza patted his hand. "Tell the rest, please."

Bel Crat stirred uneasily in his seat now that all eyes were on him. "As the Detra Terra said—"

"Hey Gamera, wait a minute," I said. "I just put something together."

"Sorry?" Bel Crat gave me a confused look.

"Terra, that's Latin for Earth," I said. "I guess you probably picked that up during your Roman Holiday."

"Lock, what's your point?" Jeopardy asked.

"Detra means queen," I explained. "This whole time he's been calling her the Queen of Earth."

Bel Crat grew even more confused. "I do not see the issue."

"The issue," growled Quinones, "is that she is not the queen of our planet. No one is, or ever will be."

"He only meant to show respect to me." Itza held up a hand. Her bearing regal, very different than the girl I had drinks at the bar with. "He never meant to show you any disrespect. My people have never been in a situation like this before, and as the only adult female of my people on this world, the term would not be inappropriate among my people."

"He needs to find another way to describe you," Quinones told her in no uncertain terms.

"He will do so." She turned to the Detra Bel. "Is that understood, Bel Crat?"

"Yes... my queen."

"Please continue," she commanded.

Bel Crat nervously rubbed the front of his shell. "As I was saying, Tal Bavra started acting strangely about ten months ago. His posture, his way of speaking changed. He started posting guards where none had ever been. But as head of the Detra Tal, that was his right. But then he cut both me and the head of the Detra Treyga out of more and more of the planning. Then he refused to awaken the... my queen, at the appointed time, letting her slumber longer."

I frowned. "Why did you let him?"

"They are warriors, we are not. Each caste has their role. Fighting is not our way. It is theirs. The only time one not of the Detra Tal was allowed to see my queen was during required inspections of her hibernation pod, and I was under guard when I did those. Fortunately, you appeared in the lab and thanks to you, I was able to free my queen."

"Thank you, Bel Crat," Itza said. "Once I was awake, I discovered that several of the Detra Tal and the Detra Treyga would not obey my commands. Something that should not be physically possible in my presence."

"How does that work?" asked Jeopardy.

"Parts of the brains of our males are hardwired to obey the commands of the queen," Bel Crat explained. "They are triggered by the timbre of her voice."

"That sounds like mind-controlled slavery," I said.

"Other species, including the Sarli, have made similar comments." Bel Crat shrugged, something I would not have thought possible from someone with a turtle shell. "It is how we evolved and who we are. We no more concern ourselves with it than you humans do about the fact that you only breathe oxygen."

"Really?" Jeopardy said excitedly. "What else can you breathe?"

"Let's stay on target," Quinones ordered. "What happened next?"

"After Bel Crat explained things, I confronted Tal Bavra who ordered a few of the Detra Tal to confine me. Having found several Detra Tal still loyal to me, Bel Crat was able to free me. Based on what he told me of your encounter, I thought you might be a potential ally while I figured out what was going on. After securing a base of operations, Bel Crat created bioforms for us and placed false profiles of us as new hires into the database of Murtaugh Solutions Unlimited. We were going to observe you for a few days to see if it was worth pursuing an alliance, but things went a bit askew when Tal Bavra sent warriors after us."

One of the Delta Black stuck his head in and asked to speak with Major Quinones.

He nodded and stood. "Excuse me a minute."

While we waited for him to return, Bel Crat leaned over to me. "May I ask you a question?"

"Sure."

"You seem very uncomfortable with our worker caste, the Detra Treyga. May I inquire why?"

"Damn. That obvious?" I chuckled. "They resemble creatures from a show that frightened me as a child. It's a bit hard to shake it."

"I see." He nodded. "Many of our people experienced the same thing with the creatures on this planet. It's the fur. Our ancient enemy was large with much hair. Over the centuries, outlandish versions of the enemy found their way into our folktales and scary stories."

"Really?" I leaned back in my chair. "You might not want to watch any werewolf movies then."

"In fact, I have seen some. Similar, but not quite the same. The ancient enemy actually resemble your—"

Quinones burst through the door interrupting him. "It was a delaying tactic. They attacked the engineering section. Jammed communications so no one could get word out."

I stood up. "How bad?"

"They took engineering and are pressing this way."

"Okay." I rolled my neck, trying to crack it. "Time to go to work. Any particular orders or just let me do my thing?"

"Thing?" asked Itza.

"Organized chaos," Jeopardy explained. "He's a human wrecking ball."

Quinones checked his sidearm and smiled at me. "Do what you best and we'll hold it from here. Watch out for those two humans."

I returned his smile. Mine was much eviler. "Oh, I have a plan for one of them. I'll just wing it with the other."

Chapter 30 –
Bad Moon Rising

With a rifle strapped to my back, I headed for engineering as another idea came to me. I chuckled and concentrated on shifting my body. While in combat mode, I seemed to use my abilities instinctively. Not so much when I wasn't.

I finally got my body to comply, my bones shifting and muscles growing. My flight suit ripped in several places. For once that was all right because it went with the look I was going for. I glanced at my reflection in a bulkhead door as the final part of the shift burst out of my skin.

"Heh-heh." I opened the door to hear fighting. I ran around the corner where two guardians were shooting at a pack of advancing Detra Tal. Shifting into combat mode, I *moved*, bursting past the guardians and growling. "Stand down, I have this."

As I did one of them let out a shriek. "Is that... is that a werewolf?"

Cue music.

With that thought, "Bad Moon Rising" started playing over the intercom. I tore into the Detra Tal, several of which wore expressions strangely similar to the shrieking guardian.

Five Detra Tal, warrior caste. Based on last analysis, threat level moderate to weapon system's current configuration.

My transformation had given me claws capable of rending steel. It had also given me speed and strength beyond my normal combat mode. Adding in the surprise my appearance caused, all of this allowed me to engage the enemy in close quarters combat with a significant advantage.

In fights like these, my body mostly works on auto pilot. This allowed me to follow the conversation the two guardians were having.

"Todd, is the werewolf on our side?" asked the one who had shrieked.

"I think so, Kyle," replied Todd. "He's fighting the enemy, after all."

"Should we help it?" Kyle asked.

"They're all over the place. I couldn't get a clean shot off on my best day, and you shoot worse than me. Besides, he told us to stand down."

"Yeah, but why should we listen to him?"

Todd pointed at me. "He's wearing captain bars."

"He is?" Kyle squinted at me. "When did we start recruiting werewolves? I didn't even know they were real!"

"Don't be racist, Kyle."

"I... what?" Kyle sputtered. "I'm not racist."

"Sounds like something a racist would say."

"Shut up, Todd."

I tossed the limp body of the last Detra Tal aside and stared at the pair of them. They both straightened up, Kyle firing off a half-ass salute. "Uh, thank you, sir."

"I'm pushing forward." I growled at them. "Maintain the perimeter."

Todd gulped. "Roger that, sir."

I bounded away, trying not to laugh. When I finally got to the corridor before engineering, I had to duck back to avoid a barrage of plasma fire. Crates had been stacked in the hallway. Several hybrids and Detra Tal had set up behind them, creating a kill box for anyone dumb enough to go down the corridor.

Up to now, the Detra Ka had pretty much been using human weaponry. From the looks of the weapons they now used, they must have raided *Quiet Contemplation's* armory. An armory KayCee swore didn't exist.

I had been hit by one of those weapons before and barely survived it. I wasn't in a hurry to get shot by one again. I peered around the corner, getting a quick glimpse before superheated plasma peppered the wall next to my head.

I reached out with my mind trying to find something useful. I had hoped the corridor might have an airlock I could override, but there wasn't any. Nothing jumped out at me as I skipped through the computer system. "Huh."

I had been thinking in a box. While nothing in the systems by themselves was helpful, that didn't mean I couldn't use the various routines to cobble together something to give me an edge.

With a few mental commands, the temperature started dropping dramatically in the corridor. In seconds, I could see my breath. I then killed the lights and the gravity at the same time. As my opponents started to drift off the deck, I crawled around the corner, my claws digging into the metal wall.

Dodging some wild firing, I made short work of the bad guys. I reinstalled the gravity, lights and temperature. As gravity kicked back in, I ducked to avoid getting hit with some goop that had been a hybrid a few minutes earlier. Holding my breath to avoid the *forget me* vapors the goop gave off, I scooped up one of their ray guns. It was made of a chrome-like metal with a tank of green liquid on the top of it.

Yup. This is definitely a Sarli design. Damnit KayCee. What else haven't you told me?

I tucked the ray gun in my flight suit and made my way to the next airlock. As it opened, a burst of explosive energy hit me, and I fell to the deck injured. As I waited for my body to speed heal, a black man in his fifties walked toward me. He was skinny and on the short side. His hair more salt than pepper.

"Human Weapon System 7 identified. Threat level unknown. Analyzing."

He crouched down to look me in the face. "Lock, my dude. Are you cosplaying a werewolf or something?"

He stood up and back, and I slowly rolled into a sitting position. I shook my head. "I don't know you."

"Don't you? Kind of, sort of? Human Weapon System 7 at your service. But you can call me Calvin." He gave a mock bow.

"Where's Hobbes?" I smirked.

"I was told I could take you dead or alive, but I don't want to drag your heavy ass all the way back. So how about you behave, and I don't have to turn up the juice."

"That wasn't full power?" I asked as I stood up, dusting myself off.

"Nah, man. That was just level one.

"Analysis incomplete. Human Weapon System 7 has the ability to project a destructive energy burst. Threat level minimal. Duplication of projection ability in process."

Calvin raised his hands. "What's all that nonsense? What do you mean minimal? I just lit you up like a light bulb and that was the easy setting."

"You understand Sarli," I said calmly, making sure not showing any emotion in my face.

"Helps to know the code your system runs on, doesn't it? Besides, I think that's built into all of us."

I cocked my head. "You seem well informed. The Detra Ka fill you in or did you have a run-in with Kreb?"

"How about you stop with the questions and start with the walking?" He pointed back the way he came. The walls on the others side of the door showed damage from his blast.

"Why would I do that? You're the worst weapons system they could have sent against me."

"I must have zapped you harder than I thought." Calvin scowled. "You forget the part when I knocked you for a loop a few seconds ago."

"Oh that?" I smiled. "That was nothing."

"Hard way then." He disappeared, reappearing directly in front of me in a burst of white energy emanating in all directions. This time I was ready with my absorption ability. As the concussive blast washed over me, I channeled it into my energy reserves.

I dusted imaginary lint off of my flight suit while maintaining my smile. "See, I already learned how to absorb various types of energy. In fact, I can probably absorb the fire from those ray guns your friends were using. But I was hit with one last year before I learned this party trick and it hurt a lot. I mean a real lot. Enough that I'd rather not try it if I don't have to. But your little party trick? That's nothing."

He disappeared again, this time reappearing in a bigger blast of energy farther down the hall. The crackling and popping was so loud that I had to shout the last bit to him. "All you're doing is topping off my batteries."

He disappeared before reappearing in front of me again. The blast was definitely bigger than the first time, but I absorbed it easily.

Crestfallen, Calvin lowered his hands. "Then why didn't you say that at the beginning?"

"I needed time to study your power. I want it for myself."

"Analysis complete. Subject has ability to teleport distances. Secondary ability of energy dispersal on completion of teleportation. Duplication of ability complete."

"And you just gave it to me." I continued as if I didn't just spout some jargon in Sarli. "What's with the blast effect when you arrive?"

"The theory is that I fold space when I jump. When I do so, extradimensional energy is dragged along with me as I travel. It disperses away from me in the form of an explosion as I arrive."

"The farther you teleport, the bigger the bang?"

"Pretty much."

"Is there a limit to how far?"

"Not yet. I do have to either see or have been to the place I'm teleporting."

"That's an awesome power."

"It was until I met you. You really just absorbed all that energy?"

"Yup."

"Well, that sucks," complained Calvin. "But have you met Rory?"

"Who?" I asked.

"Me." A nude redheaded woman phased through the wall next to me. I did a doubletake. Nude was maybe not the right word. I could see right through her, but her, ah... more private areas were blurred.

"Human Weapon System 9 identified. Human Weapon System 9 using unknown ability. Analyzing."

Before I could do anything, she reached out to my head. Too surprised to stop her, her fingers slipped into my skull without resistance.

She smiled. "Nighty night."

Every color on the spectrum lit up in my head until merciful blackness took me.

Chapter 31 –
They're Coming to Take Me Away

"We need to get clear. If a couple of those orbital fighters get on our tail, we're screwed."

Those words from Calvin were the first sounds I heard on gaining consciousness. The second was gunfire and ray gun blasts. I didn't care, I had woken up pissed. This was the second time in a day I got knocked out. Third time in the past three months if you count that bullshit with Stella.

I opened my eyes to find I hadn't reverted to normal while I was unconscious and still looked like Lon Chaney Jr. on the night of a full moon.

Starting to second guess that idea. The bad guys weren't exactly shrieking in fear at the sight of me.

I was also strapped to a gurney inside an orbital fighter. Calvin and the redhead were standing on either side of me.

Rory. Calvin said her name was Rory.

Apparently, she had found a jumpsuit along the way, it's zipper dangerously low. I craned my head to look at her. She appeared to be in her late twenties. Pretty with green eyes. Based on the time of Kreb's experiments, she would have been roughly my age regardless of her looks. "Powers don't work on your clothes?"

She glanced down at me. "No."

"Yeah, I have the same problem with some of my abilities." I flexed, expecting to snap the straps holding me. "What the hell? What did you guys do to me?"

"We gave you a shot. Something to prevent you from accessing your powers. We're taking you to him now."

Geez, all they had to do was wait until I fell out of combat mode. Without KayCee, I can't do much in normal mode. Wait a minute...

"He? He who?" I asked. I didn't bother getting mad or threatening. That was Stella's standard go-to when we were growing up. I always tried to get along. It's harder to beat someone up if they're being friendly. Or in this case, kill.

"You know who," she said.

"I really don't."

An explosion rocked us.

"What the hell was that?"

Calvin checked the straps holding me down. "That's your friends. While we diverted forces to deal with you laying waste to our people in engineering, Black Carrie and the Lizard Queen led troops to take the control deck."

"Black Carrie?" I snorted on hearing his name for Jeopardy. The orbital banked as something sizzled by us. "Okay, that's pretty funny. But don't let her hear you say that. We have this whole thing going on about black superheroes with the word black in their names."

"Superhero?" He stared at me as we dodged more fire from other orbital fighters. "She's a demon, that's what she is. Throwing shit around with her mind. Then wannabe Ironman and the blond space Viking showed up and everything went to shit. Thanks to you decimating our forces, we didn't have the personnel to hold our ground and we're being forced to retreat."

"So just surrender already." Try as I might, I couldn't access my abilities.

"Nah. No way. I have no interest in being dissected in a lab again." Calvin grimaced. "Hard pass."

Again?

"Besides," Rory said, "you might be our ticket to surviving this. He wants you really bad. You screwed up a lot of his plans. Not that it matters. We'll do what he says regardless."

"Yeah? Well, Tal Bavra can go piss up a rope!"

They glanced at each other. Calvin gave a half-shrug. "Sure, whatever man. You keep telling yourself that."

I glanced out the window. The hybrid piloting the orbital wasn't sparing the horses. He had it pushed up to eleven and the engine whined from the abuse. "We aren't going anywhere if he blows the engine."

Calvin gave that half-shrug again. "Not our department."

The pilot glanced back toward us. "We're clear. They just looped back toward the starcraft. With so many others to fight, they don't think it's worth chasing one orbital fleeing the battle.

I changed direction. "So, Rory, which Human Weapon System are you?"

"Lucky number nine." She answered.

"Nine? My cousin was ten. We're practically related." For no other reason than my hands were bound by my sides, an itch developed on my nose. "What was that neat trick you did? Phasing?"

"Why, want to add it to the collection? I heard you can copy the powers of the other weapon systems. Something Calvin should have remembered."

"As a matter of fact, yes, I would like to copy it," I told her honestly. "It's pretty damn cool. Who told you I could copy abilities?"

She crossed her arms and gave a small smile that had no humor in it. "You'll see soon enough."

"Well, that's not cryptic at all." I wiggled my nose, trying to get rid of the itch. "So, how exactly do your abilities work?"

"I can diffuse my molecules enough to slip through solid objects." She leaned over and scratched my nose. "Better?"

"So much. Thank you. So, what did you do to me back on the *Armstrong*?"

When I use my phasing abilities on a brain, it disrupts the electrical impulses."

"Yeah, a lot of that going around these days," I mused. "What if you do it to a computer?"

"Usually fries it." She leaned against one of the many storage lockers lining the wall of the orbital. "What was with the wolfman get up?"

"The Detra Ka have a mythological boogeyman that is similar looking. Thought it would give me a psychological advantage."

Calvin looked over his shoulder at the hybrid piloting the craft. "That true?"

"Sort of, not really," the alien answered. "Too short and the face is all wrong."

"Hear that, Lock?" Calvin chuckled. "You're short and your face is all wrong."

"I've been hearing that since junior high," I said. "Story of my life."

"Yeah, you and me both." He grinned. "So, when did the government team up with the queen's forces? Is that new or did we miss something?"

"No idea. I'm just the janitor. They tell me where the mess is, and I go clean it up."

His grin widened. "You going to clean this up, are you?"

"It'll be spic and span when I'm done, Calvin. You'll be able to eat off of it."

"Off of what?" His grin faltered. "I think I lost the metaphor."

I paused. "Yeah, me too."

Rory moved to the pilot and leaned down. "How much longer?"

"Not too long. I have to start shedding velocity soon. Once we enter orbit it will be quick."

"We don't want to keep him waiting."

"I understand," the pilot responded.

"That's pretty good English for an illegal alien," I called over.

"I've been on this planet longer than you, pal," he shot back.

"Wow." I looked back at Calvin and bobbed my head in acknowledgment. "No wonder they could pass unnoticed. He has the mannerisms down cold."

"Yeah," Calvin acknowledged. "It's freaky."

"Hey," I called over to the hybrid. "What are you in your real body? Detra Tal, Bel, or Treyga?"

"Detra Treyga and proud of it," he answered without looking back.

"Great. Another Sleestak."

"Okay, Cha-Ka," he said over his shoulder.

"Ow! He called you Cha-Ka! That had to hurt." Rory pulled at the fur on my arm. "You sure that wasn't what you were going for?"

"Damn it," I grumbled. "Can't believe I just got burned by a talking lizard."

Calvin moved over to the pilot leaning on the back of the chair as he looked out the window. We were in the outer atmosphere. "How are we doing? I don't want to tell you your job, but this thing isn't sounding right."

"It's not." The pilot shrugged. "But it will get us to him."

And when we do, I'm going to find some way to get free and tear off Tal Bavra's head and punt it down a hallway. Let's see how well the rebellion holds together when their leader's been reduced to a soccer ball.

"As long as we get to him without crashing." Calvin glanced down at him. "Not all of us are using fake bodies."

While they talked, I tried concentrating on my powers. Still nothing. Switching gears, I tried to revert back to normal. After a few tense seconds, I breathed a sigh of relief as my body shifted back to my usual form. My beard even grew back.

Rory watched me closely as I did it. "That looks a lot better."

"Thanks."

"But..." She reached into a pocket on her jumpsuit and pulled out some sort of high-tech hypo-spray. "That means you'll be able to access your powers again."

"Wait a minute." I struggled against my straps. "You don't have to do that."

She pressed the hypo against my neck. There was a faint hiss, and I felt a sharp pinch.

"Nighty night, Lock."

As the blackness took me, I had one final thought.

I hate my life!

Chapter 32 –
Dirt Nap

I thought I had been buried alive when I woke up. I couldn't see and was lying down. My head hit dirt when I tried to sit up. A quick check with my hands revealed I was surrounded by earth. The pocket of air I was in was slightly bigger than me.

That can't be right. I'd be out of oxygen.

I'm not claustrophobic by nature but I was starting to feel it before my hand hit metal. The right side of the hole I lay in appeared to be some type of metal hatch. It moved with a quick push revealing a dim light.

I shoved it open and peered around. I was in a cave similar to the ones I had first found the Detra Ka in. I was on a type of earthy shelf. Other hatches dotted the cave walls, their length making me think I was either in sleeping quarters or a morgue.

I rolled out to my feet. The only thing in the room was a series of tables holding various electronic equipment. Thick black electric lines ran from a door-size opening in one wall to the equipment on the tables. Aside from some computers, I couldn't tell what the equipment was.

I tapped the skin over my embedded comm spike. "Hello, KayCee? You there? Crap!"

Running a hand through my beard, I tried to think of what to do next. My eyes fell on the hatches.

"Just what are you used for, anyways? Is this really a type of mausoleum?"

Morbidly curious, I opened one of the hatches. Behind it was another small, earthen alcove like the one I'd been in. This one was occupied with the body of a human in a security guard uniform. Raised by countless sci-fi movies, my first thought was he was a snack for the Detra Ka. I check for a pulse. Finding one, I relaxed for 1.2 seconds before remembering that they might eat their food alive.

I gave him a nudge. "Hey. Hey, buddy."

He rocked slightly, which allowed me to see a cable underneath him. I rolled him to the side. The cable came up from the dirt and connected to the back of his head. "What in the Matrix is this? Shit, I think this is an unoccupied hybrid."

The idea of it gave me the willies. I looked around at all the hatches. They weren't alcoves, they were pods for the pod people. I moved to the computers. They were regular computers. Top of the line next-gen but built by humans none the less. "Then again, I'm literally judging them by their covers. There could be all sort of alien crystals and circuits and who knows what in there."

I turned one on, waiting for it to boot up. My ability to infiltrate electronic devices should allow me to overcome any security features it might have. Hopefully I could find something useful on it.

A voice from the other side of the opening called out in Sarli, the language of KayCee's people.

"I'm in here, Weapon System 12."

"Well, this can't be good." I slowly walked through the opening into another cave. Like the one I was just in, this one was about twenty-by-twenty feet and held a series of computers. There was a table along the back wall. Whatever was on it was covered by a sheet. There was also a lone Detra Tal in this new cave. The bad feeling I was having got worse on seeing him.

Detra Tal are huge. But this one made the others small. His muscles had muscles and he bristled with so many weapons he looked like a walking cutlery store. Scars crisscrossed his hide. I knew the Detra Ka stranded on Earth didn't have the tech of the rest of their race, and while that might have applied to their medical capabilities as well, I guessed those scars were left as a point of pride for this warrior.

"Tal Bavra, I presume?" I said in English.

"Yes," he replied in the same language. "And no."

"Well, that's cryptic."

"We'll get back to that." His lower arms rested on the hilts of a pair of swords. Not in a threatening way, more of out of old habit. His upper arms tapped away at the computer he was in front of. "Where is the control orb for *Quiet Contemplation*?"

"Why? Your people can't use it. The materials it's constructed from is toxic to your people." I stalled, trying to give myself some time.

"You know nothing of my people. No matter what you may have heard from Protector KayserCeenarlos."

"Yeah? Well, your queen filled me in on some stuff as well. Including on how you betrayed her."

"Betrayal? Are you aware of how the hierarchy of the Detra Ka works?"

"The queen is in charge, and the rest of you do what she says."

"No, Weapon System 12, it is much more than that. A male of the species is immediately enthralled by the voice of a queen. The mere sound of her voice triggers impulses in the brain. Her pheromones have the same effect. So does recognition of her facial features. Everything in the male is programmed to obey the female, to do anything to please her."

"Yeah, described like that, it sounds like a raw deal. But that's evolution, right?" I paused as something occurred to me. "Wait, you found a work-around, didn't you? That's why you and your people can defy your queen."

He finally looked up from his computer. He stayed silent, letting me work through it.

"Okay. I get it. No one wants to be enslaved. But did you try peacefully approaching her about it? She seems reasonable. I mean it's not her fault this was how your people evolved." That sounded weak even as I said it.

Wait. Am I trying to justify her willingness to enslave an entire gender just because she slept with me? What is wrong with me?

"Okay, that didn't come out right. Obviously, what you're describing is a bad thing. I need a minute to think this over."

Tal Bavra smiled. Well, I assumed that was his version of a smile. "Whoever said it was evolution?"

"W-what?"

"The Detra Ka are more advanced in bio science, in genetic manipulation, than the Sarli. They are a fallen civilization, having lost much of their technological knowledge after their great war. How do we know a small group didn't seize power by manipulating the genetic structure of future generations?"

"You know from the tone of your voice, one would think you're more impressed with the idea than disgusted."

He had that creepy smile again. "Oh, I am, Weapon System 12. Using their research, I've made great strides in my own work."

"You reprogrammed your troops. That's why they follow you instead of the queen." I frowned. "Or did you boost your own pheromones and stuff?"

"Very good, Weapon System 12. I told you I sensed great things in your future."

"In my future? I've heard that before... Doctor Kemp. You're Kemp! Or you were in him, I should say." I rubbed my beard. "Or are you Kemp inside Tal Bavra? You do keep referring to the Detra Ka as if they are a different race than you."

"I am not Kemp. I subjugated and possessed him so I could speed up the building of the humans' starcraft. And while we did meet while I was in control of him, I am not he."

"How? I thought the whole point of using hybrids was because the Detra Ka can't possess someone like the Sarli can."

"That was true. At least until *I* got here." He moved from the computer he had been tinkering with to the table in the back.

I shook my head. "I don't understand. What do you mean 'got here'? You've been here for generations."

"Since I fell from the sky." He pulled the sheet off the table revealing the head and upper torso of a Sarli bioform with only one arm. It was blackened and seared as if it had been in a furnace. Or in the heat of reentry.

"Oh crap!"

Chapter 33 –
Out of the Frying Pan

"Kreb! How? I watched you hit with a missile and then burn up on reentry. How did you survive?"

He gestured to the charred and melted wreck on the table. "Enough of the bioform remained for me to survive in it. The Detra Ka had tracked my fall and retrieved the remains of the bioform to study. They thought to learn from me, but it was I who learned from them."

I frowned. "You're different. Kreb was colder. Dispassionate. You're more..."

"Alive." He gave a predatory smile.

"I was going to say maniacal. Though, maybe addled might be just as good to describe you." I didn't know what he was up to and needed to stall because I was up to something as well.

"Yes, I didn't survive unscathed. Parts of my energy form were destroyed. I had to absorbed the life force of the scientist studying me in order to restore my essence. Emotionally there was some bleed through." His smile grew wider. "I have to say. I enjoy it. It is a much more vibrant way to experience life."

"You ate a guy's life energy? That's a whole new level of wrongness!"

"True. Absorbing another's life energy is forbidden. Even by my country. But I had no choice, or I would not have survived." He licked his lips with a snake-like tongue. A hungry look came across his face. "Words cannot describe the exquisite feeling."

A sick feeling washed over me. "It wasn't that one time, was it? You've developed a taste for it."

"Oh yes, taste is an excellent way to describe it. Each caste of the Detra Ka has a distinct flavor to their life energy. The Detra Tal are the best. So primal!"

He must have taken the revelation on my face as fear. "You have nothing to worry about in that regard. Human life energy is... unappetizing."

"So, what? You just ate your way through the Detra Ka until you landed into Tal Bavra?"

"First, I learned what I could about the sciences of their race. Once I learned how the queen controls them, I experimented on various workers until I was able to duplicate the queen's abilities. After drugging Tal Bavra, I gave him the control abilities of their queen and took him over."

"Then you started turning other Detra Ka?" I almost smiled as my brain informed me of the success of something I had been trying to achieve while he rambled.

"Exactly. I wanted to use my pawns to speed up the creation of new starcraft in order to return home." He started typing on the computer again.

"So why start abducting and brainwashing humans?"

"The Detra Ka's way of doing things was too slow. Using hybrids to play the part of the humble assistant to human scientists, suggesting a course of action here, nudging an experiment there, was too slow. After my years of experimenting on you humans, it was child's play to turn the needed people in the program into my slaves. I did alter my technique though. Can you tell the difference?"

"You used the same process to control Detra Ka on humans? And it worked?"

"Of course not." His voice dripped with scorn.

There's the arrogant prick I remember.

"I refined my previous techniques with humans to achieve similar results. Different process, same end goal. Completely subservient, but still able to function without oversight."

I remembered what he had done to Dennis McKeene's brothers. He had basically lobotomized normal humans into mindless drones. Another weapon system experiment, a woman named Mary, he had used like a rental car, with no care for her well-being. He had possessed Mary the longest, and when I met her, she had been dirty, underfed and completely neglected. Initially I had thought she had been a meth addict. "You're giving them more free will now?"

"Not quite. They still have no choice but to carry out all my orders, but they are more self-aware and receive pleasure impulses when serving me. One of the things I learned from the Detra Ka."

"A happy slave is a productive slave?"

"Exactly."

"So, Rory and Calvin? They are their normal selves with the exception they are compelled to carry out your orders."

"Yes. In a way, I have you to thank for it."

"The fuck you say?" I took a step toward him without realizing it.

"I saw how effective you were compared to Human Weapon System 6. The one you called Mary. Even allowing for the difference in your abilities, you were much more effective, because of your free will and your need to survive. While I originally planned to use you all as a form of sentient weaponized bioforms, this is so much better. My country can send you in as combat troops to fight without ever having to endanger our people."

"I'd ask about the human lives, but we both know your view on my race."

"Indeed."

"Why are you telling me all this?"

"I admit I feel a small need to show off my accomplishments. But in truth there is a much darker reason to why I brought you back to the Detra Ka caves under your government's research facility." He gestured toward the cave I awoke in. "This was originally a storage area for hybrid bodies that were not being used. I've since turned this series of caves into my laboratory. There are no cracks for you to slide through in your liquid form." He waved his arms, gesturing to the walls. "It's where I do my best work. And it is where I shall alter you to become one of my sentient slaves. You caused me much pain and trouble and I want you to suffer. To be aware of what was done to you and be able to do nothing about it even as you beg and scrape to please me."

"Jesus, you're even more messed up than before. You've gone full Lex Luthor."

"I waited until you were awake to do the process. It's extremely painful."

"Of course, it is." I was putting on a brave face, but I was terrified of what he was planning. My other encounters with him had left me a PTSD gibbering wreck with frequent nightmares. KayCee had been a big help putting me back together as a functioning adult, but what he was planning might just shatter my mind forever.

"You think I'm just going to let you?"

He flexed his four arms, the tip of his tail whipping wildly behind him. "I do hope not. This body is the peak example of the Detra Tal. I wish to compare it to the advances I made in you. That's why I have unblocked your abilities. Once I have my answers, then, and only then, will I subject you to the new process. Battered, awake, and screaming for your own death."

"Lock."

Jeopardy's thoughts entered my mind.

"We got your message and are on the way. Earthside troops are already entering the caves."

The whole time I had been letting Kreb monologue, I had been using my electronic warfare abilities to hack into his computer and sent out a message to Delta Black. I projected my thoughts back to her, only able to do it because of the established link.

"Watch out," I thought to Jeopardy. *There are two others like me here. Black male in his fifties named Calvin and a redheaded woman in her twenties named Rory. He can teleport with explosive results, and she can phase."*

"Rory Donnelly and Calvin Anders. Both were on my list."

"List? What list?"

"Never mind, not important right now. Are you safe? Where are you exactly?"

"Oh, you're going to love this. I'm with a very not-dead Kreb."

"What! You said he burned up on reentry."

"Well, enough of him survived to start eating the life forces of the Detra Ka. He's behind the rebellion and the infiltration of the space program. He's controlling a bunch of the Detra Ka and some of the humans."

The telepathic link Jeopardy established broke as pain erupted across the left side of my face. I staggered back, holding the side of my head that Kreb had struck. The calming feeling flooding through me signaled that I had gone into combat mode.

"You seemed distracted. Was I boring you?" He hadn't drawn any weapons, instead flexing his claws as he stalked toward me. His tail arced over his head like a scorpion, the stinger on it glistening with venom.

"I'm not going to lie." I backed away, circling around to keep a table between us. "It was a bit of a snoozefest."

"Perhaps, this will be more interesting."

"Why? Because you have claws?" I stopped behind the table, my feet straddling the large power cable along the floor. Holding up an arm, I willed my fingernails to lengthen and harden, forming sharp and pointy claws. I lifted the middle one up. "Look, I can do that trick too."

"I am well aware of your abilities, Number 12. It was I who gave them to you."

"Just Number 12, now? Are we using informal names now? We friends?" I took a fighting stance. "If you know all about me, then tell me how I survived reentry?"

He stopped. "I will admit, I *am* curious how you did that."

"Like this." My claw swept down, severing the power cable. With my right hand, I grabbed the live end, absorbing the electricity and redirecting it at Kreb with my left hand.

When I said this power cable was thick, I didn't mean like an outside extension cord. This cable was thicker than my thigh, and while I didn't know how many volts and whatnot coursed through it, it was a lot. A stream of electricity arced across the table from my hand into Kreb's chest. His body convulsed and blue fingers of electricity crawled across his hide.

A circuit breaker must have popped because the cable went dead. As the last of the electricity petered out of my fingers, Kreb slumped to the cave floor, black smoke rising from his chest. "You're not the only one with new tricks."

I stalked around the table. My claws reverting to normal fingers. I reached down to pull one of his swords out of its sheath. At this point I didn't know what it took to kill Kreb, but I figured cutting off his head was a good start.

As I reached for the sword, one of his hands beat me to the handle, his eyes popping open as it did. "A good effort, Number 12. But futile."

I shuffled back and pulled my next trick out of my sleeve.

I ran.

CHAPTER 34 –
AN UNFORTUNATE POSITION

"*Lock!*"

Jeopardy's mental projection rang through my mind, startling me so much I almost careened off a tunnel wall as I fled. Lying in my wake were two Detra Tal who had been guarding the entrance to Kreb's lab. I had taken advantage of their surprise as I fled, pausing only to get in some vicious headshots.

"Cripes, Don't do that, you about gave me a heart attack!"

The tunnel came to a T. I picked left and kept moving. "I just sucker punched Kreb and I'm on the move."

"*Cripes? You've been reading too many comic books. What are you? Wolverine?*"

"Just trying it out. What's your status?" I ran into a group of Detra Bel. With Kreb having spent the last year taking control of the minds of various Detra Ka, I didn't know who to trust and didn't want to hurt anyone more than I had to. I pushed through them, plucking a beaker filled with a green liquid out of the hand of one of them as I went. "What's your status?"

"*Entering orbit now. The troops in the tunnel are not making much progress. We made an agreement with your lizard girlfriend not to harm her people. Problem is, we don't know who's controlled and who's not. And it's not like we have a lot of less lethal that works on them.*"

"Okay, not my girlfriend. It was a very drunken one-night stand. My first ever, I might add."

"*Whatever. Not a conversation I want to have. The point I was trying to make is it's slow going until we can get there with their queen. Even the loyal ones aren't sure it it's a trick or not and won't stop resisting until they can see her in person.*"

"That's annoying. I get it. But it's annoying." I slid to a stop as a squad of Detra Tal blocked my path. The image was a bit jarring. This super advanced alien race that looked like the offspring of a three-way between a crocodile, a turtle, and a snake were armed with M-4 rifles. Part of my mind rebelled at the image, thinking they should be wielding ray guns like Kreb. The rest of my brain was busy thanking various deities that they weren't.

I lifted my arms as they opened fire. I didn't need to bother. My body shifted, allowing the bullets to pass through me like going through Jell-O. This was one of my older tricks, but the sensation of projectiles rippling through my flesh always felt odd.

More of the warrior caste came up the tunnel behind me, blocking my escape. As they prepared to open fire as well, I scanned the walls and floor of the tunnel.

"Bingo! Jeopardy, we might lose contact again. I have to change shape."

"I need to conserve energy for when we touch down anyways. Just... stay safe."

I felt her break the mental connection.

"That was promising," I told the Detra Tal that were firing on me. "I think she's starting to forgive me."

They didn't seem to want to continue the conversation, so I downed some of the contents of the flask. My mouth lit up like it was on fire. "Oh God, I think that was acid!"

My body shifted again, turning into the contents of the flask. Which apparently was in fact, actually acid. Now in liquid form, I hissed and bubbled, burning through the jumpsuit I had been wearing. I rolled toward the cracks in the earth closest to me and slipped into it.

I traveled along the tiny crevices in the rock and dirt. After traveling some distance, I stopped and rested. This deep, Kreb couldn't get to me without machinery, if he could even detect me. Time was on my side, so I waited, giving Stella, Jeopardy, and the rest of the Space Force troops time to get here.

Deciding I had waited long enough, I made my way up, trying to make it to the uppermost tunnels. Once I figured I was high enough, I searched around for a way out, finally dropping out of a tunnel ceiling. I fell about ten feet onto a tunnel floor and slowly reformed into my natural shape again.

The toughest part of being in liquid form was being unable to see. I can sense my surroundings but can't describe why or how it works. While it is a very handy skill, I was always happy to have my vision return. I was less thrilled about being naked again.

The tunnel I was in was vacant, but I could hear noises farther along. I padded toward the sound, which slowly formed into words. I recognized Calvin's voice, telling someone to find another way. I approached a curve in the tunnel and carefully crept forward, spotting Calvin and Rory with some Detra Ka. Rory was actively using her power and was once again nude with her private areas fuzzed out like a movie nude scene that had been censored.

"Human Weapon Systems 7 and 9 identified. Resuming analyzing Human Weapon System 9."

Everyone's heads whipped around to look at me on hearing those words being uttered my own betraying lips.

"Uh, hi?"

Calvin smiled. "Lock, my man! Good to see you. Any chance you'll give up without a fight?"

"I was just going to ask you that." I scanned the area. Not counting Calvin and Rory, there were two hybrids and two massive Detra Tal.

Calvin's smile faltered. "I'd love to, to be honest. But we don't really have that option."

"Yeah, Kreb filled me in on the whammy he put on you guys. Any pointers you can give me?"

Rory started to say something but jerked up short. Pain filled her face. She took a deep breath and blew it out. "Wish we could, but the blocks he put in prevents us from doing it. Even when we know it's in our best interest."

I nodded as I wondered how she did the whole breathing thing while out of phase. "I'll take it into account, but I can't promise what will happen."

"I can!" shouted a familiar voice from behind them. The Detra Ka whirled around as Stella stepped into view. She looked magnificent in her alien chrome armor; it was as if she had stepped out of the cover of a classic sci-fi book.

I pointed at her battle-ax, which dripped with the blue blood of the Detra Ka. "What happened to less lethal?"

She shrugged, spinning the ax handle in her hand, the blood flicking off the blade and spattering the tunnel walls. "Less lethal is not the same as nonlethal. This is me being less than my normal lethal self. Got yourself abducted again, huh? No probing, I hope."

"First off, fuck you. Second, these guys," I pointed at Calvin and Rory who were listening to our exchange with baffled looks on their faces. "Are being mind-controlled, so go easy."

Stella studied them for a moment and then leered at Rory. "Nice boobs. How come they're all fuzzed out. Show 'em off, sister!"

"Stella." I sighed. "Stop sexually harassing the enemy."

"You say harass, I say compliment," she countered. "I see you and her both shop at the less is more clothing store."

"Look—" I suddenly lost control of my vocal cords and spoke in the alien tongue of Kreb's people.

"Human Weapon System 9's primary ability identified. Altering molecules to move through solid matter. Duplication of ability in process."

Stella slung her ax over her shoulder. "Are we doing this or what?"

"Fine. You take the Detra Ka, I'll take these two." I pointed at Calvin and Rory. "Where's everybody else?"

"Taking their sweet-ass time, trying to minimize casualties," she grumbled. "I got bored and sort of chopped my way through."

"You fought through our troops by yourself?" Calvin choked out.

"What? You thought Lock was the big gun?" My roommate laughed. "He's just the warm-up act."

"Hey now, not in front of the bad guys," I called out.

"Bad guys?" Stella snorted. Bunch of lizards, an old man, and Boobarella. Not exactly the Brotherhood of Evil Mutants."

"Duplication of Human Weapon System 9's primary ability complete."

Stella grinned. "Did you just say what I hope you did?"

"Yup."

Rory frowned. "Duplication? That can't be good."

"It means it's time to fight!" Stella launched herself at the Detra Ka.

Following her lead, I closed in on Calvin and Rory. I ducked a mini teleport blast from Calvin. Rory used the distraction and swooped toward me, gliding through the air, fingers outreached.

"Very spooky looking," I said. "You must kill it on Halloween." I let her get close, trusting my body to do its thing while in combat mode. I grabbed at her wrists. Instead of my hands passing through her, I locked onto her. Her eyes widened in surprise. I took advantage of her shock and flipped her over me and toward the floor. A normal person would have slammed into the ground, bruised and battered at the very least. She, on the other hand, when right through it.

Hoping she couldn't float back up, I turned toward Calvin, just in time to take a blast of energy. I staggered back before my body adjusted and used it to top off my energy reserves. I hadn't dared do it when I was zapping Kreb, in case the electricity wasn't enough to stop him. Which as it turns out, it wasn't.

As I absorbed the energy, I strode toward Calvin, whose eyes widened. I stopped in front of him. He raised his fists and smiled at me. "Nothing personal?"

"Sure." I dodged his first swing and blocked the second. He was faster than normal humans but nowhere near my level of speed, or even Stella's. He also had no form, just swinging away. "You, um, don't seem to have a lot of combat skills."

"I get it, you're a more advanced model. You don't have to rub it in." A look of desperation formed in his eyes. "You know my programming won't let me quit, right? I'll keep doing this forever if I'm not stopped. Preferably not permanently, please."

"Oh, right, sorry." I *moved*, putting significant effort into the blow. My punch slid past his defenses in a blur. With the strength I put into it, he was flung backwards, tumbling over into the dirt.

I looked around. No sign of Rory. Stella had decapitated both hybrids, shunting the Detra Ka possessing them back into their real bodies. However, the two warriors were pressing on her. There was a lot of sparks at the clashing of blades and the Detra Tal shouted various battle cries at her. Stella on the other hand, was dropping f-bombs like she was flying over Berlin in 1945.

Before I could assist her. Calvin rolled over and slowly picked himself up. I winced as he looked up. That whole left section of his face was a mess. At a minimum, I had shattered his left orbital bone.

"G-got to do better that that," he slurred.

"Calvin, if I hit you any harder, you're going to have brain damage. I get that Kreb programmed you to obey at all costs, but don't make me kill you."

"Not m-my choice." His sad smile showed he had lost a tooth as well. Must have been when he hit the ground.

"Just maim him already and get over here." Stella grunted, pushing off a Detra Tal that had been trying to crowd her so she couldn't use her ax.

"He's being controlled," I yelled at her. "It's not his fault."

"What isn't? My death? No, it'll be because you couldn't man up and make a tactical decision." She ducked the swing of a nasty serrated sword. "It's called acceptable losses."

"Well, I don't accept them," I informed her.

"Yeah, me either!" Calvin yelled as he tried to take a swing at me. "We didn't kill Lock when we had the chance. Least he could do is return the favor."

"Nice try," I said. "I'm sure Kreb gave orders to take me alive which is why Rory... Huh!"

"What? When she what?" Calvin asked, still trying to attack me. It was the equivalent of holding the head of a small child to prevent them from reaching you and just watching them swing away at the air.

"When she did this." My body sensing what I wanted, shifted into phase. Once again, I wished it would be this receptive when I wasn't in combat mode. I didn't bother blocking Calvin's next swing and his arm swiped through me. It was an odd sensation. Kind of like when your arm or leg goes to sleep. But in this case, it was my torso.

I reached over and plunged my fingers into his temple just like Rory had done to me. Calvin cried out in pain, his eyes rolling back in his head before dropping like a sack of potatoes. "Fuck! I hope I didn't just lobotomize him."

"Hey, Lock, remember me, your lifelong best friend? Little help?" Stella's back was to the wall as she deflected stinger jabs from the two warriors. "These guys actually have some skills."

"Right!" I ran toward one, reaching for his head, my fingers flexing. He reared back, swinging his swords at me. The blades didn't fare any better than Calvin's fists and all ten of my fingers reached into his brain. "Squishy! Squishy!"

The Detra Tal reacted the same as Calvin. Stella pushed off the wall, forcing the remaining warrior back. "Squishy! Squishy! What the fuck was that?"

"I dunno, seemed appropriate at the time."

"Dude, you ran toward him buck naked, arms outstretched, wiggling your fingers and shrieking 'Squishy! Squishy!' You looked demented."

"I was going for scary."

Stella used her ax to block the Detra Tal who tried to bolt past her and back up the tunnel. "If you mean scary like a creepy guy in a white van offering kids candy sort of way? Then, yeah! You nailed it. Pretty freaking scary."

"Wow! Really?" I walked over to the warrior. His attacks on me were just as ineffectual as the others and I did the whole phase stun thing on him. "I just saved your life, and you compared me to a pedophile? No gratitude, that's what that is. Didn't even thank me."

"I would, but..." She stepped over the body of the Detra Tal. "There was this whole 'you saved me so you could wear my skin as a housecoat' vibe going on."

"The only one demented here is you." I started laughing and was completely unprepared when Rory rushed out of the wall and tackled me. Whether it was an unconscious effort on my part or a conscious one on hers, we didn't phase through the floor.

Stella rushed over to help and quickly discovered she couldn't touch either of us. While Calvin couldn't fight his way out of a wet paper bag, it turned out Rory had skills. Specifically ground fighting ones. She kept applying holds and using leverage to negate my strength advantage. Only my speed allowed me to escape the submission holds.

"Crap! You know judo?"

"Some," Rory grunted as she tried to put me in a guillotine choke. "Mostly Brazilian jujitsu and sambo. Ten years of MMA when I was younger. My parents owned a dojo."

"Not fair. We're phased! I don't even know how this is working." I rolled away and out of the hold she was trying to put me in. "Stella, little help here."

"Lock, quit screwing around and end it," Stella ordered. "You've ground fought before."

"This is different," I shouted as Rory launched another attack.

"Why? Because she's a woman? You've fought me before. What's the problem?"

"Well, for starters," I grunted as I fought off Rory's latest grapple move, "we're naked."

"So what? You're starkers most of the time you're in a fight."

"Yeah, but thankfully my opponents aren't usually naked as well."

"You're saying you forgot how to fight because your rubbing up against her flotation devices?"

"Rubbing? I scrambled away and started to stand before a well-aimed kick took out my knee, sending me back to the floor. "She practically smothered me in them."

"Death by boobies. I could think of worse ways to go." Stella leaned down, resting her hands on her knees as she watched us grapple. "On closer inspection, I have to say they are, in fact, spectacular boobies."

"Thank you," Rory said, trying to bend my arm in a way it wasn't supposed to go.

"Are they real?" asked my very unhelpful roommate.

"As a matter of fact, yes," answered Rory.

"Can confirm," I added. "That being said. Maybe find a way to help me instead of leering at my opponent. Whose side are you on anyways?"

"Boobies," Stella replied. "I'm always on the side of boobies."

"Great!" I grumbled. "You wrestle her then."

"Would that I could, buddy." Stella sighed. "But I can't do the whole vision thing you two are doing."

"Sorry, lady, straight as an arrow," Rory said as she went for an eye gouge.

"Hey! That's not allowed in MMA," I yelled.

Completely ignoring my narrow miss with blindness, Stella gave a predatory grin at Rory. "I've talked a lot of straight women into switching teams for a night or two. Never say never until you tried it."

"I went to Wellesley. Trust me, I know. All about the D. Speaking of which..." Rory fired a punch right between the goal posts. "Cock shot, Lock!"

She actually landed the hit a little lower. My eyes crossed and I went limp. I mean, my body went limp... I mean, I fell down!

Rory rolled me over, trying for the guillotine choke again. Groaning in pain, I pulled my arm free and tried to crawl over and away from her. She switched to another move and was able to successfully put me into a submission hold called the triangle choke.

To perform the triangle choke, you use your legs to put pressure on your opponent's carotid arteries in order to stop the flow of blood to the brain. Before Rory could fully execute it, I was able to slip my arm out. My skin hardened in response to her attack preventing her from applying enough pressure to render me unconscious. Unfortunately, due to the nature of this particular submission hold, my head ended up in a location that allowed me to verify that Rory was, in fact, a natural redhead.

"Lock?" said a new voice.

Straining my eyes, I looked up at the person speaking. It wasn't good.

A familiar face looked down at me. "What the hell do you think you're doing?"

"Oh, ah... hey there, Jeopardy. How are you?"

Chapter 35 –
Combat Interruptus

"Isn't it obvious?" asked Itza, who stood next to Jeopardy, KayCee in her bioform, and several Space Force personnel of varying gender. "We interrupted them having sex."

KayCee nodded. "Yes, and apparently Stella Johansen is watching. I have heard this is a thing some humans like to do."

"Little help here," I asked in a faint voice. Though my skin had hardened enough to prevent Rory from rendering me unconscious, it was far from comfortable. "She's trying to kill me."

KayCee tilted her head. "On second thought, I believe that is the submission hold known as the triangle choke."

She shrugged as Jeopardy arched an eyebrow at her. "I watch a lot of your television."

KayCee reached down and tried to pull Rory off me. She straightened up as her hand passed through us. "Oh, that *is* interesting. They both appear to be in phase. Lock, have you duplicated her ability?"

"Yes," I squeaked out.

"And she now has you in a submission hold you are unable to break out of?" the little alien asked.

I gave her a thumbs up.

"Have you tried to stop phasing?"

"What?" I croaked out. The red flush creeping onto my face had nothing to do with the thighs tightly wrapped around my neck.

"Just stop phasing," KayCee repeated.

"Crap!" Rory muttered as I solidified, passing through her.

I stood up, catching the poncho one of the guardians tossed at me and pulled it over my head. As long as there wasn't a slight breeze, my nether regions were once again covered. "Rory, just give up. We have Calvin and soon we'll have Kreb too."

"Love too but as you know, I can't do that." She gave a little wave and sunk through the floor.

"You going after her?" asked Stella.

"The only thing I'm doing right now is looking for pants." I told her.

Itza approached the downed Detra Tal. "You didn't kill them?"

"No, I scrambled their brains a little bit, but they'll recover. Can you deprogram them?"

"I'm not sure but we will do our best." She motioned with her hand, and several hybrids pushed through the guardians and shackled the defeated warriors. "Jeopardy has told me of this Kreb person. He sounds formidable."

"I said he was an insane genocidal genius," corrected Jeopardy. "Though I will admit he is very cunning, in a Hannibal Lecter sort of way."

"How's the battle going?" I asked as a female sergeant who couldn't be taller than four foot eleven handed me a pair of OCP pants. She stood there smirking as I struggled into them. "You know I'm a captain, right?"

"If you say so, sir," she replied.

I decided to just ignore her. "Can *anyone* here tell me the current situation?"

"It's been slow going since we were trying not to kill anyone." replied the sergeant. "We pushed them back slowly until Agent Jones arrived with their queen. Since her arrival, the majority of Detra Ka we've encountered immediately surrendered. The few that didn't seem to have some sort of internal crisis whenever their queen arrived would flee rather than attack her."

"Really?" I scratched my beard. "So, Kreb's programming of the Detra Ka isn't infallible. How come this wasn't discovered before?"

Itza shrugged. Unlike when KayCee does it, it seemed perfectly normal. Not alien at all. "I think he was aware of it and made sure that the ones he had subjugated were not in a position to have conflicting orders or be in my presence for too long, if at all."

I nodded. "Yeah, that makes sense."

"Once we were on scene, we pushed forward, trying to reach you," Jeopardy explained. "Stella got impatient and struck off on her own. Basically, hewing a path through the Detra Ka on her way to you."

I winced at the idea she just killed a bunch of mind-controlled people to get to me. "A lot of casualties?"

"Shockingly, no," Jeopardy said. "She went all roggie protocols and started lopping off limbs."

"This is acceptable." Itza placed a hand on my shoulder. "Limbs we can replace. Your people have done a remarkable job trying to preserve the lives of my people, often at their own risk. I am proud to call you allies."

Jeopardy's face was studiously blank at Itza touching me. "The colonel is back at *Diana*, overseeing the mop-up of the remaining combatants. Our job here is to secure the Detra Ka tunnel system."

"Fine, what's next?" I asked.

"That's up to you, sir," replied the sergeant. "What are your orders?"

"Me?" I looked at Jeopardy. "I thought you were in charge."

"My position is... unusual. I'm not in the chain of command," she explained. "You're the highest-ranking officer here."

I looked over my troops. The same ones who mere moments ago saw me completely naked, getting beat up by a woman half my size. "Well, shit."

Stella sighed, stepping up beside me and rolling her head. She scanned the group, her eyes settling on the short sergeant. When she spoke, her voice was low and dangerous. "Something funny, Sergeant Vasquez?"

The sergeant snapped to attention, the smirk instantly disappearing. "No, Master Sergeant."

"Then get your head in the game. You can daydream about the captain's ding-a-ling when we're back at the base."

"Yes, Master Sergeant." She turned red. "I mean, no, Master Sergeant."

"Step back, Sergeant."

"Stepping back, Master Sergeant." Vasquez disappeared into the group of her fellow guardians.

"Snap to and listen up," Stella bellowed before turning to me and switching to a more normal voice. "What's the plan, Captain?"

I owed Stella a case of booze when we got back. Her Sergeant Hulka routine to my Captain Stillman gave me the time to get my thoughts together. "I'm a little turned around. Itza, how do we get to where the dormant hybrids are kept? Kreb was basing his lab there."

"It's not far. My people and I can show you the way."

"Good. Stel—Master Sergeant Johansen, how many guardians do we have?"

"We have Alpha Flight with us here—"

"Cool! The original team or the lame one with Major Mapleleaf?"

She ignored me and continued. "Bravo and Charlie are maintaining the areas we've already secured. With the losses we took, we currently have twenty-four guardians and one Sarli with us, not counting the Detra Ka loyal to Itza."

The rest of the Alpha Flight jokes I was going to make died at the mention of losses. I cleared my throat. "Three-person fire teams?"

"Yes."

"Have a medic dope up Calvin. I have no idea how long the whammy I gave him will last. Assign two fire teams to bring him back to the area we secured. They are not to let him wake up."

Stella pointed at several people. "Washington, sedate the prisoner. McCord, Levi, take Washington and the prisoner back to Tech Sergeant Chang and fill him in. Understand?"

"Understood, Master Sergeant."

They did as they were ordered.

"The rest of us will proceed double time to the lab and try to secure Kreb and all his equipment," I said. "Any resistance, I'm the tip of the spear. Only if I'm in trouble or the flight is being attacked do they engage."

"Loc—I mean, Captain." Stella grimaced. "That's not the standard way of doing things."

"Neither is what you did back there. I'm incredibly hard to kill. Providing we don't encounter any more phasing MMA fighters, there isn't a lot that can stop me."

"And if we do encounter such a being?"

"Fubar their ass."

"Roger that." Stella's smile was practically primeval.

Chapter 36 –
Lab Results

We did encounter resistance. The few that didn't falter at the sight of Itza quickly fell at my hands. While the warrior caste of the Detra Ka were formidable, once I added Rory's and Calvin's special abilities to my list of powers, taking them on became child's play. They couldn't touch me in phase mode, but I could drop them easily. Whatever humor the troops had felt at first encountering me and Rory was lost at seeing what I could do in combat mode with a full mad on. I was determined not to let Kreb get away again and buzz-sawed my way through in a way that even made Stella wince.

It was all for naught. Kreb had fled before our arrival. He did take the time to blow his lab though. Most of its contents were a smoking pile of ash by the time we got there. We set up camp, sifting through the wreckage of his lab.

Itza approached me as I conferred with Stella on a guard rotation. "Lock, do you have a second?"

Stella nodded at me and withdrew without a word. Military Stella was very different than Best Buddy Stella. It was taking some time to get used to the difference.

I smiled at Itza. "We've gone down a very strange path since a couple of drinks with coworkers."

She gave a self-conscious smile back. "I hope you will forgive me for deceiving you about who I am."

"Yeah, I get it. 'Hey, by the way, I'm an alien' is a bit hard to work into a casual conversation."

"Exactly. But that wasn't the reason I wanted to talk to you. The guidelines for this new alliance between your people and mine are still a bit unclear, so I wanted to let you know that I sent some of my warriors to check on the sleepers."

"I'm sorry." I moved some debris off a scorched table and leaned against it. "What exactly are these sleepers?"

"The majority of my people that still remain in hibernation since we came to this planet. The hibernation chamber is the most guarded area here, but since Kreb possessed my head warrior, I need to make sure they are safe."

"Um, how many are we talking here? Both awake and asleep?"

"Roughly seven hundred of my people are awake with approximately six hundred thousand in hibernation."

I whistled. "That's a lot of people."

"It's actually under the amount we normally have to start a new colony. However, with the way my mother was acting, I feared waiting any longer to embark on our journey to my new world. This planet isn't suitable for us. Long-term exposure can have debilitating effects on our health, and we don't have the resources to treat that many people."

"This impromptu alliance you forged with us. My bosses know how many of your people are here?" I asked.

"Yes. I was very upfront. We've dwelled in secret too long. If we had approached your people before, maybe none of this would have happened."

"Or you would have wound up at Area 51 being tested on..."

She nodded. "Such reactions by your people was one of the main concerns that I had."

I shifted uneasily. "I have to ask you something. Kreb made... certain allegations about you and the other females of your species."

Her face shifted at my words. It was hard to read. Not worry, but maybe concern. "What type of allegations?"

"The control you and the other females have on males. It negates their free will."

"They are happy to serve their queens."

"A happy slave is still a slave."

"It is the way it has always been. In all of our recorded history."

"Has it though? Your people are supposed to be highly advanced in the bio sciences." I paused, gathering my thoughts. I didn't want to all-out accuse her but needed to get my concerns across. "Kreb alluded to me that maybe this... matriarchy... isn't the work of evolution but genetic manipulation."

She stayed silent for a long time. More than enough that I worried I may have damaged this new fragile alliance between our people.

Well, between her and my government. She finally raised her head, looking me square in the eyes. "It may be a possibility that in the far distant past certain changes were done to our people. Certain... markers could be read either way. Because of that, there have been rumors and conjecture over the years. Rumors that have not reached the ears of any other female." She broke eye contact, turning her head away. "Or, if they had, then those queens dealt with the rumormongers swiftly and harshly."

"That's not exactly comforting to hear," I said.

She continued to look away. "To my knowledge, no real testing has ever been performed. We don't know what was done, by who, or why. We aren't even sure anything was done or if it has anything to do with the gender relations of my people."

I stepped around her, placing myself back into her view. "But these markers show enough that you're concerned about it?"

She didn't look away again, meeting me head on. "Yes. But stranded on a planet not suited for our people, populated by a sentient race that shows a propensity for violence... Ordering a study into it would have weakened my people's chances of relocating. I needed everyone striving to achieve the same goal. Get to our new home."

"You have to understand that I have a problem with this. That most of my people would have a problem with this."

"Yes." She nodded. "But get us to our correct planet and it will no longer be a concern for your people. We will not bother you further."

Now it was my time to look away. She repeated my trick, stepping into my view. "What? What is it you're not telling me?"

"KayCee had heard something about you."

"The Sarli?" Itza frowned. "What did she say?"

"You have to understand, you've been gone a long time."

"I, more than anyone, am aware of that."

"Well, according to KayCee, after you were declared lost, your mother took over your planet."

Her eyes crinkled in confusion. Her people in hybrid form had our reactions down pat. So much more that KayCee has been able to do. It made me wonder how many of our mannerisms were introduced to us by her people. The tone of her next words brought me back to the conversation. She spoke low, almost in a hiss. "You mean she gave another female my world?"

"Ah." I was suddenly less sure of myself. I towered over her but didn't doubt for a second her hybrid form was, at the very least, a match for me, and I didn't wish to be the target of her ire. Historically, at least on Earth, royalty were not known for their cool heads. "My understanding. And bear in mind, KayCee has no first-hand knowledge of this..."

"Whatever it is, just say it."

"You mother expanded her colony and now rules over both planets."

Itza's head snapped up and back. Confusion ruled her face. She started to speak and stopped, her mouth moving as she silently repeated to herself what I had just said.

"You okay?"

"That's... That's not how it's done. Ever! Not in the known history of our people."

I shrugged. "Well, it appears it has now."

"How long has she been on the planet? How entrenched are her forces? And how in the five rings of Orsk is she controlling a colony on a separate world?"

I raised both my hands in mock surrender. "Whoa, whoa. You're asking questions I don't know the answers to. I literally just told you everything I know about it."

She took a deep breath and exhaled. "I'm sorry. I did not mean to unload all that on you. This development is shocking. Would... Would KayCee be willing to talk to me about it? Perhaps answer some of my questions?"

"You'll have to ask her, but I don't see why not." I turned to look for KayCee when Bel Crat approached but stopped about ten feet away. "Your majesty. One of the scouts has returned from the hibernation chamber."

Itza motioned him forward. "What does he have to report?'

"It is not good Detra Ter..." Bel Crat looked at me and started again. "It does not look good, my queen. Kreb and his forces are entrenched on that level. He has walled off the chamber and is holding our people hostage!"

"Damn him," she snarled. "What are his demands?"

"To start with?" Bel Crat pointed at me. "He wants him!"

Chapter 37 –
A Bad T-Shirt and a Horrible Plan

I pulled my head from around the corner and looked at Stella. "What do you think?"

She peered around me, looking at the hybrids guarding the entrance to the hibernation chamber and shook her head. "Kreb's got it fortified with heavy machine guns and Claymores. From the disturbed dirt on the tunnel floors, I'd say he's buried mines as well. We go in that way, we take heavy casualties."

"Itza says it's the only way in. Heavy steel plates line the walls, doors, and floors of the chamber."

"Geez," Stella grumbled. "You'd think it was their bank vault."

"It's much more important than that." I scratched my beard. "I guess I could phase in. Can't help but think Kreb would have prepared for that though. KayCee? What are your thoughts?"

"I think phasing would be most unwise," she said. "Do you hear that faint humming?"

"You guys hear that too?" Stella tilted her head to the side. "I actually thought my tinnitus had come back."

"What is it?" I asked, ignoring my roommate.

"I believe it is a phase harmonic shield," KayCee said. "They are used to block phase missiles."

"What the hell are phase missiles? And why have you not mentioned them before?"

"They are an obsolete weapon of war and until now, I have had no reason to speak of them. They were developed on both sides during the war between my country and Kreb's. They were initially extremely successful as our starcraft do not have as much armor as the ones you are building. Phase missiles could bypass basic shields and several feet of armor before reverting to normal space and detonating. Phase harmonic shielding was integrated into our normal shield system. Once that happened, they were unable to penetrate our starcraft and bases. At that point, use of them ceased."

"So, they were phased out?" Stella asked with a grin.

I gave an obligatory groan before continuing. "They may be obsolete where you're from, but such things could have a devastating effect on my people."

"Your people duplicated our shielding technology, so your starcraft are fine. Even without the shielding, the thickness of the armor would prevent a missile from penetrating inside. The missiles can only phase for a few seconds. While the idea of boring out asteroids to create your starcraft is crude, it is also incredibly effective. The sheer mass of them can shrug off many advanced weaponries."

"Fine, so what do we do about this?" I jerked a thumb toward the hibernation chamber. "I'm guessing you think this phase harmonic shield will prevent me from phasing in?"

"That is correct, I am afraid," KayCee responded.

"Crap. He's always got some dirty trick up his sleeve." I rubbed my eyes, trying to rid myself of the tension headache that was forming. "Stella, leave what you think is the appropriate amount of troops guarding this tunnel. We'll regroup back at the lab and figure out our next move."

Once we returned to the lab, I contacted Brennan via a secure transmitter Jeopardy had brought. When I finally got a hold of him, he didn't sound happy.

"What is it, Captain?"

"We have a problem," I told him bluntly.

"Oh, we have much more than one. What's this particular issue?"

"Turns out the majority of the Detra Ka are in hibernation pods, and Kreb has secured the chamber they're in, holding them all hostage. He fortified the area and has taken precautions to prevent me from using any of my abilities to get in."

The colonel swore. "Has he given demands yet?"

"Sure, me in a box and a quick ride to his solar system."

Brennan frowned. "He still wants one of our starcraft?"

"Yeah." I narrowed my eyes. "Why do you think he no longer would want one?"

"I'm sending in additional troops with a major to take over the scene. I want you and your Baker Street Irregulars to catch the next flight back to Delta Black. There's been a development."

"That can't be good," I muttered.

"It's not. See you there." The screen went black.

"That was rude," I said. "Isn't he supposed to say over and out?"

"Maybe in 1945." Stella snorted. "What do you think this new development is?"

"I dunno. The way things are going, Kreb cloned me into an army and they're marching on Washington to demand Firefly be renewed."

She grinned. "I could get behind that."

Evidently backup arrived under the command of a major I hadn't met before. After warning him that Rory was still on the loose, Jeopardy, Stella, KayCee, Itza, Calvin, and I were sent back to Delta Black headquarters at Ducharme Station. Itza was allowed an honor guard and assurances were made that she was not a prisoner. She took it in stride and seemed less perturbed about it than I was.

It took two days to debrief us all. Turns out Calvin was a dental hygienist before Kreb tracked him down and reprogrammed him. Unlike me, he had successfully dealt with his childhood trauma of being abducted by aliens and had moved on with his life. He had a wife and two kids in college. Once it was determined he was a victim, and not a willing lackey of Kreb's, he was medicated and placed in a very comfortable detention area until it could be figured out how to deprogram him. While he kept trying to escape, he apologized each time.

The rest of us didn't see Itza the entire time, and I was getting more and more worried about it. I knew that many in our, or any government of Earth, wouldn't be too happy to discover she and her people had been secretly manipulating us for generations.

I was pacing in my quarters when Stella knocked. "Brennan wants to see us both plus Jeopardy."

"What about KayCee."

"Not right now, I guess."

"Any idea what it's about?"

"Probably not the lunch menu."

When we got to his office, his receptionist ushered us in. Brennan was on the phone but waved away our salutes and pointed to the seats in front of his desk. As much as I wanted to, I made a point not to listen to the other side. On hearing his next words, I regretted not doing so.

"I understand, Mr. President. Thank you." Brennan hung up.

Stella blinked. "You were just speaking to the president?"

"Yeah. First time. Normally I deal with a general or a member of our oversight committee. And to be honest, I prefer it that way."

"Where's Itza and why haven't we seen her?" I blurted out. "And what are we doing about Kreb?"

Brennan leaned back in his chair. "Geez, Lock, stop beating around the bush and just ask me what you really want to know."

"Sorry. It's just been two days of not knowing anything."

"Welcome to the military," Stella said. "Hurry up and wait is a way of life here."

"She's not wrong," Brennan admitted. "To answer your questions, Itza is in a separate area in the building, she's being treated like the head of a foreign government but kept in seclusion until we can figure certain things out. She understands the complexity of the situation and is being very gracious about it. Probably a lot more than any of the three of us would be."

"Oh." I deflated into my chair. "Good. I was worried."

"What? You thought I would send her to a lab for dissection?" Brennan asked with a grin.

"Well, no, not you personally..." I stammered. "But you have bosses. People that you answer to." I pointed to the phone he had just hung up. "And I don't know what they are capable of."

"I'm not saying you're right." He sighed. "But fair enough."

There was a knock at the door, and Jeopardy came in. She smiled. "Sorry, got tied up on a follow-up."

Unlike Stella and I who wore uniforms, she was in civilian clothes. While carefully keeping my eyes away from how well her jeans fit, my eyes landed on her T-shirt. It had a picture of the Marshall family from the *Land of the Lost* TV series. It was the scene with the rubber raft, except Giorgio Tsoukalos was also on the raft with his crazy hair. A speech bubble above him said, 'What if the Sleestaks are... Aliens.'

I pointed to her shirt. "Really? We're trying to maintain a fragile alliance with the Detra Ka, and you're wearing that?"

She shrugged. "I ran the idea by Itza while we were in the tunnels. She thought it was hilarious, so I made it."

"You have the equipment here to make custom T-shirts?"

"Well, my former job is now my cover story, so yeah, still need to sell merch."

Brennan motioned to the last available chair. "Not really the time for this, Agent Jones."

"I have a question, sir," stated Stella. "Lock and I are military, but you keep referring to Jeopardy as an agent. What's up with that?"

Jeopardy grinned at Stella's comments but didn't say anything. Brennan, however, raised his eyebrows. "What's up with that? Really?"

"What's up with that, *sir*?" Stella shrugged.

"You and Lock chose your particular paths," Brennan explained. "However, Jeopardy felt, and I agreed, that based on her skills, abilities, and experience, a less visible role would be better suited for her."

"And what role is that exactly?" I asked.

"Not something you need to worry about right now," Brennan said in a tone that signaled the end of the conversation. "We have something more pressing to discuss."

He turned his computer screen toward us. Jeopardy bent forward to see better. With our superior eyesight, Stella and I didn't need to. Not that my abilities made what I was looking at any easier to figure out. I threw up my hands in surrender. "I give up. Is that... A weather pattern?"

"Long range sensors spotted something headed toward Earth. At the speed it's going, it will be here in a few days."

Jeopardy leaned back. "I guessing no one thinks it's an asteroid?"

Brennan swung the screen back in his direction. "Not unless asteroids suddenly gained the ability to change direction."

"Another starcraft," I said. "This can't be a coincidence."

"Not likely." Brennan frowned. "Considering how long the Detra Ka have been on Earth, it's doubtful that it's more of their people."

"And considering what Mommy dearest did to Itza, it's probably a good thing if it's not," Stella mused.

"So that leaves us with it mostly likely being either KayCee's people..." Brennan held up a finger.

"Which considering we stole one of their ships, will make a meeting with them extremely awkward," I interjected.

"Or Kreb's pals." Brennan finished, raising a second finger as he did so.

"Great. A whole starcraft full of alien space Nazis," Stella muttered. "We're having enough trouble with just one."

"What has KayCee and Itza said about this?" asked Jeopardy before suddenly groaning. "Wait! You haven't told them, have you? That's why we're meeting without them."

Brennan nodded, leaning back in his chair. "I'm afraid so. The higher-ups wanted to hash out a plan before filling either of them in."

"And if whatever they have to say doesn't work for this plan, what then?" I asked.

"Then we get a new plan," Brennan answered.

"Seems like that's a bit of a waste of time," I pointed out.

"Not as much as this conversation. Let's get back on track," he ordered. "Lock, you were with KayCee when she tried to contact her people. Anything we need to worry about?"

"Not really. It was pretty much all about Kreb. She threw herself on her sword a couple of times, so if it's her people, she may be in more trouble than us. That was about a year ago. We're not even sure the message got through."

"Nothing else we should know." I paused. KayCee hod told me there were more of her people on the planet. Anthropology types. We had searched for them but were unable to locate any of them. At the time, she made me promise not to tell anyone. But now the fate of Earth was on the line. I debated on telling Brennan and finally decided that I needed to speak to KayCee first. If for no other reason than to tell her I couldn't keep my promise.

"Nothing?" Brennan reached into a drawer and pulled out the control orb. "How about the fact that you hid this from us."

"I explained that."

"Yeah, but you're still holding something back, aren't you?"

My head whipped around to glare at Jeopardy who recoiled at what must have been the anger in my face. She shook her head. "I did not read your mind and I wouldn't, even if they asked me to, which they didn't."

"I don't need a mind reader to know when someone is holding back or lying," Brennan said. "Or did you forget what I did for a living before getting chained to this desk?"

"Fuck." I breathed. "I'm sorry, Jeopardy."

"Yeah, maybe you shouldn't play poker," she said, crossing her arms.

I winced as Brennan rolled the ball back and forth between his hands. "Maybe... maybe not do that."

He stopped, twirling it instead. "Give, Lock. What's the deal?"

I sighed. "Tavish's consciousness is downloaded into the orb."

Brennan's hand came down, stopping the spinning. "What?"

"As Kreb was killing him, he jumped into *Quite Contemplation's* systems. He then jumped onto a spy satellite to save KayCee from me and Kreb. When the satellite was about to be destroyed, he jumped into the only place possible at the time. The orb."

Jeopardy and Brennan stared at me in disbelief while Stella very carefully studied the decorations on the wall in front of her. Brennan dropped his head into his hands for a moment before looking up to glare at me. "Are you fucking kidding me? You don't think this is something I should have known?"

"It got complicated. KayCee thought the starcraft's systems would have revived Tavish and keep his body alive. We were just trying to get him back to *Quiet Contemplation* in order to put him back in his body." I refused to meet his eyes.

"Did it ever dawn on you that I could have helped?" Brennan placed the orb gently back into the drawer.

The speakerphone on Brennan's desk crackled to life.

"We didn't want to put you in that position. I was worried the government might try to use me as a weapon. I'm much more powerful in the orb than I would ever be back in my body."

"Tavish?" Brennan eyed the phone like it was going to explode. "How long have you been listening in?"

"About the time you started rolling me around. I spend most of the time on the internet these days but I'm aware of any movement of the control orb. I've been surfing the web since you placed me in the drawer earlier. I appreciate that by the way. I couldn't access the outside while I was in that vault. Once you brought me into your office, I was back online, and I got to say, I missed it."

Brennan glared at me. "You let me bring a security risk like this into my office? I was on the phone with the president of the United States!"

"To be fair, I didn't know you were going to bring it into your office."

"How about the base then?" the colonel snarled.

Jeopardy reached over and grabbed my hand. "Colonel. We're talking about his cousin. You have to understand the pressure he must have been under. Let's face it. Their fears are not out of the realm of possibility."

I nodded gratefully, not trusting myself to speak.

"Lock, Tavish." Brennan reset into a calm voice. "Did you two ever wonder what we did when we discovered Tavish's body on the starcraft?"

"Wait? Am I'm dead?" my cousin asked. His fear was evident even through the robotic sounding voice he used.

"I..." I felt suddenly lightheaded. How did I miss that? "Oh God. He would have shown as brain-dead. You... Did you disconnect him?"

"After much discussion, we finally decided against it. But it was close, Lock. We very nearly transferred him to a hospital on Earth. Only because we didn't fully understand the medical equipment or what happened to him stopped us."

I fought back tears in relief. My cousin was a pain in the ass, but he was the only close family I had left. Plus, there was the whole saved my life thing, which I was sure he would never let me live down.

Jeopardy squeezed my hand. "It was the colonel who fought to keep Tavish there. Almost everyone else thought it would be better to move him to Earth."

I finally met Brennan's eyes. "Thank you for that."

"That goes double for me, Colonel," Tavish added. "I'd really like to get back to my body. Among many things, I really miss eating."

"Just stop keeping me in the dark. It's my job to protect you guys, not the other way around." Seeing me struggle with my composure, Brennan reached into another drawer and handed me a bottle of water. "In the end, this might just work out. If we can revive Tavish and he can use his abilities, this will greatly help the chances of our plan working."

"And what exactly is this plan?" Stella asked as I took a sip.

"We're going to turn Lock over to Kreb and give him *Quite Contemplation*."

I choked on my water. "That's a horrible plan!"

Chapter 38 –
Itza Complicated Too

I nodded to the two guards flanking the door to Itza's quarters. Leaning past them, I knocked on the door. After a moment, the door was opened by a hybrid assistant of hers. "Yes?"

"Lock Ferguson to see Itza. I mean to see your queen."

He nodded. "One moment, please."

It was closer to fifteen minutes, but he eventually returned and bowed, opening the door wider to let me in. As I stepped through, Itza jumped up from a chair. She was barefoot and wearing a white summer dress with some sort of geometric patterns in black thread. "Lock!"

"Hey, Itza." Before the door was shut, she plowed into me, giving me a bone-breaking hug. I gave a nervous smile. "Um, hi there."

She released me and stepped back, examining my face. "Is everything all right?"

"Yeah, I was just checking in with you." I rubbed the back of my head, trying to figure out what to say next. Itza motioned me to the couch. Her quarters were very nice, as military black sites went. There was a living room and a kitchen, as well as several closed doors. There was soft music playing in the background, and the room was lit with candles. "Are your lights not working? I can talk to someone."

"No, no. Everyone was very nice, all things considered. I just prefer candlelight." She pointed to the ceiling. "These lights are too bright for us."

Her assistant or butler, or whatever he was, quickly exited through one of the doors, closing it behind him.

Itza sat next to me, close enough that I could smell her perfume. "I'm glad you visited. I've missed you."

"I wasn't sure how they were treating you, Itza. Or should I call you by your title?"

"Itza is fine. I'm quite fond of it." Shifting on the couch, she folded her legs under her, causing her to lean into me. "I've been meaning to apologize, for not telling you about the... How do I say this?"

"Secretly an alien thing?"

"Yes, That. But you have to admit, it's a bit hard to bring up."

"Yeah..." I scratched my beard. "That brings up a question I've been wondering about."

"Only one?" She smiled. "I'm the queen of an extraterrestrial race that has been manipulating your people for generations in order to recapture the ability of space flight and you only have one question?"

"Good point. I reserve the right to have other questions later." I grinned.

"Fair enough. What's your question?"

"Umm, why did you sleep with me?"

"Wow." She shifted again. This time away from me. "That's a bit blunt."

"I know, I'm sorry, but I really need an answer."

"Well, why did you sleep with me?"

I blinked at her return volley. "Let's see. You were funny, interesting, and hot. I was drunk, still reeling from a breakup, attracted to you and... wait for it... a guy."

"You were attracted to me?"

"Yes."

"Me too."

"Too what?"

"I was attracted to you, you dummy."

"That's the thing I wondered about. Why were you attracted to me? In your real form, your species is very different from mine. I don't understand how you would be attracted to someone so different."

"You didn't find my real form attractive?" she said with mock outrage.

"Well, I only saw it once, and while you were very feminine for..."

"A lizard snake lady?"

"Well... yeah!" I winced as soon as the words left my mouth. "I'm so sorry. That's not what I meant."

She laughed. It was a pretty laugh, light and airy. "Relax, Lock. I'm aware of how different our people are. But you have to remember, I've been around humans for hundreds of years." Her smile widened. "Some of which, I was even awake for."

"So, what are you saying? Familiarity breeds attraction?"

"Maybe. I don't know. Part of it is that. Part of it is that, in hybrid form, we're more inclined toward humans."

"Really?"

"It's a biology thing. Part of the creation of hybrids."

"Oh, I didn't know that."

"Besides, did you ever wonder about trying something different, to be daring, maybe a little naughty?"

"You're a queen. What's naughty?" I asked. "You can do what you want."

"That's not even true for human rulers."

"I suppose," I admitted.

"Once a colony is established, a queen has to choose a mate from among those sent by other queens who has all the qualities and attributes you want to be passed down to the next generations. I don't get to pick him for love or because I'm attracted to him, but for the good of the colony. Until then I'm not allowed, I mean I can't..." She started blushing. "A hybrid form doesn't count. After all, it can't get pregnant. After I met you, and you were nice, and you were funny, and I might have been a bit tipsy... So, I thought, what the hell?"

"Did a little dance on the wild side?" I grinned.

"Maybe." She smiled back. "I mean your superpower pheromones didn't hurt either."

"Sorry, my what?"

"Your pheromones. The amount and strength of the pheromones you were pumping out that night was how I knew you were interested in me."

"You can detect pheromones?"

"I was always surprised humans can't."

"And you called them superpowered?"

"Did I not use that right? I meant that they were very strong for a human."

I sat there trying to process what she'd told me. How many women had I influenced? There was that Delta Black Guardian. The waitress at the bar. Maybe Rory hadn't been playing mind games with me and was actually hitting on me. My mind reeled at what I may have been doing. "Oh, my God. I am so sorry!"

She gave me a bemused look. "For what?"

"I swear I didn't know I was influencing you. I'm sorry I took advantage of you."

"What are you talking about?" She leaned forward. "Wait, do you think I mean your pheromones are some sort of mind control?"

"Well... I mean... you said they were superpowered."

She laughed. This time I didn't find it quite so endearing. "Lock, it's not hypnosis. It's nothing more than a biological edge. A way to get noticed. The rest is up to you."

"That's cheating though."

"How is that any different than being born with a beautiful face, or large muscles or..." She inhaled deeply, distracting me completely. "Having other things."

"Yeah, but that's a matter of preference. Also, those are visible things. Pheromones kind of sneak up on you."

"What about perfume or cologne?"

"I'm allergic. Well, I was allergic."

"I feel we're straying from the point."

"But you smell perfume and cologne. You can't smell pheromones."

"People wear pleasant scents and dress up to be noticed. They do artificially what you do naturally. Do you like the smell of baked cookies?"

"Sure, I think everyone does."

"Well, if there is two plates of cookies and one set is from the store and the other is freshly baked, which one will attract your attention?"

"The fresh-baked ones."

"But are you going to be unable to resist these cookies, even if they're the type you normally like."

"No."

"That's you. You're a plate of freshly baked cookies. You're not Rohypnol."

I let out a breath I didn't know I was holding. "So, I haven't Starfoxed anyone."

"I don't know that reference."

"But yet, somehow you know what Rohypnol is."

"Head of the secret alien race that's been advancing your sciences, remember?"

"Good point."

"Good." She climbed onto my lap, facing me. "Because I want a plate of cookies."

I stopped her as she leaned into me. "Wait."

"It's the whole lizard snake thing, isn't it?" She leaned back and since she had been kneeling on either side of me, that shifted her weight onto... it didn't help matters.

"No. I... Can you move?"

"Like this?"

I lifted her off and placed her next to me on the couch because the moving she was doing was very much *not* what I had meant. "Look. This is complicated."

"It was just a joke. I was led to believe you and friends make fun of each other."

"Wait. What's a joke?"

"The pheromones. I was just teasing you."

"Really?"

"Really. You do not have any more pheromones levels than the other humans. It was funny to watch you squirm though. I can see why you and your friends indulge in this type of humor."

I gave a large sigh of relief. "Okay, you totally got me."

"Good." She tried to climb back onto my lap.

I held out a hand to stop her. "When I said it was complicated, I was talking about the whole sex thing."

"I swear you humans make sex so much more complicated than it needs to be. Did you not like it before?"

"To be honest, some parts are hazy, but yes, I did enjoy it. That's not the point. My ex-girlfriend is back in the picture."

"Oh." She leaned back into the couch cushions, placing her feet up onto a hassock. "My understanding is that you and Jeopardy are no longer together."

"Well, we're not. But I would like us to be."

"I understand."

"You do?" I raised my eyebrows. "I have to say, I thought this would be more difficult."

"There is no reason it has to be. Besides, with your government's help, my people and I will hopefully be able to leave this planet soon. This was always going to have to be a short-time thing."

"I'm glad we have an understanding."

"So, we should decide on a number."

"Number for what?"

"How many more times we have sex. How long are you free today?"

"What? No. I just told you about Jeopardy!"

"Yes, and I wish you both all the luck in the universe, but that doesn't mean you and I need to stop having sex until you get back together."

"Yes, it means exactly that." I stood up.

She followed suit. "Fine, what about one last time, right now."

"Even if I agreed to that, which I wouldn't, there are guards out front and you have at least one of your people in the other room!"

"So?"

"So, they'll hear!" I hissed.

"Good." She giggled. "That will add to the fun.

"Not for me." I replied horrified. "Listen, I get that you don't have much more time in the hybrid body. Why don't you just find someone else you like?"

"No, it has to be you." She started chewing on her bottom lip. A trait I would have found endearing before she started giving *Fatal Attraction* vibes. I began to wonder if it actually *was* pheromones. "What if we invited Jeopardy to join us? Would that work for you?"

"I honestly can't think of a better way to permanently screw up with Jeopardy more. That would make my letter look like a bouquet of flowers."

She started pacing. "You don't understand. I'm not sure one night was enough."

"Enough what?" I asked completely confused.

She stopped pacing. The worried look on her face slid away into an expression I couldn't identify. "Nothing. It's complicated. Don't worry about it. I shouldn't have pushed. I'm sorry."

"Okay. They have me heading out on a mission soon. What exactly is your status?"

"I've been meeting with officials from your government for days. We struck a deal that will transport all my people to another world in return for all our advanced knowledge."

"And you are okay with this?"

"Aside from one detail, yes. It benefits both our peoples and will make us strong allies on equal footing." She started walking me to the door. Apparently, my visit was over.

"What's the sticking point?"

"The world. Thanks to star charts found in *Quiet Contemplation*, we have a current idea of what's out there. The problem is I want the world that was promised to me."

"That's a big sticking point."

"Yes, it is," she agreed. "Lock, is this mission dangerous?"

"No more then my usual adventures."

"Well, please be safe and please forgive my tantrum. I am used to getting my own way. Someone saying no to me is still a novel experience."

"Already forgotten."

"Will you see me when you get back?"

"Of course, our two peoples have a lot of work to do."

"I meant on a personal level." She looked up into my eyes.

I forced myself not to look away. "I don't think that's a good idea."

"I understand. Goodbye, Lock."

"Goodbye, Itza."

Chapter 39 –
Geek Cred

"Kreb!" I yelled down the hall for the third time before ducking around the corner. Just because shooting me won't kill me doesn't mean it didn't hurt. And the two Detra Ka guards posted at the entrance to Kreb's territory had already proven themselves trigger happy.

"Anything?" Stella asked.

"Absolutely," I told her.

"Really?"

"No! Your standing right next to me. Anything changes, you'd know as soon as me." I snapped at her.

"Someone needs a drink!"

"Sorry, I'm not happy with the whole 'Let's give up, Lock' plan."

"Well, I meant me, but sure, I can see why that would suck."

"Lock!" Rory's voice came from the entrance to the hibernation chamber. I poked my head out. Rory stood in front of the guards, wearing another set of coveralls. She motioned me forward.

"About time," I said as I edged out. "I've been waiting out here for half an hour What the hell took so long?"

She threw a thumb over her shoulder at the two guards. "Little bit of a slip up. Kreb delegated the guard duty and the guy who assigned these two didn't bother to see if they knew our language."

"Really?" I wondered if Kreb not being used to having free-thinking subordinates was something that could be used against him.

"Yeah, Kreb sent me down here to find out why you hadn't made contact yet. That major said you'd be here half an hour ago."

"Well, I'm here now. What does Kreb want and why does he only want to talk to me?"

She walked closer to me. "Do we have to do this by shouting down the tunnel or can we have a normal conversation?"

I met her halfway. "Forgive me for being paranoid, but last time we met you punched me in the balls. The time before that, you scrambled my brains."

She smiled. "I'm sure your brains were scrambled long before you met me."

I pointed to myself. "This is me walking away."

"Okay, okay. I'm being forced to do things against my will and being made to feel happy about it. Forgive me for enjoying true levity when I can find it." She sighed. "About that. Is Calvin all right? I know you captured him, but did anything bad happened to him?"

"No, he's fine. He's currently in a cell while they figure out how to deprogram him." I studied her face. "Why, what are you worried about?"

"Oh, I don't know." She pointed at her temples with both hands them made an exploding gesture. "Ka-blewie! I wouldn't put it past Kreb to be able to remote detonate us."

"Sure, I get it. He has threatened to do that in the past. Scans showed no devices that could do that to Calvin though."

"Good, good. Look, Kreb is holding a trump card. He has most of the Detra Ka on this planet held hostage. Unless the US government wants to be responsible for mass genocide, they are going to have to play ball with him."

"What's he want?" I asked, as if I didn't know.

"Same as before. You, me, and him on a starcraft out of here. Specifically, he wanted the one call *Quiet Contemplation*." She cocked her head. "You know, that's a horrible name."

"Yeah, I may have heard that before."

"Conjures up images of alien Buddhas on hippy spaceships," she continued.

"So how exactly does he want to do this?"

"Well, I assume he'll change its name to something like *Death to All who Oppose Me*. That seems about his speed."

"While you're not wrong, I meant about the exchange. Me and the starcraft in return for the hostages."

"We'll meet you on the ship—"

"Craft," I corrected.

"Whatever. Once he and I are onboard and have scanned the *ship*, he'll release the hostages and we go on our merry way."

That worked out better for us than I had hoped. I pretended to think it over. "We get to finish de-arming the starcraft first. Last time he had control of it, he came very close to destroying the world because it was easier than coming back to enslave us all later."

"Jesus!" Rory grew pale at the thought. Well, paler. "I had no idea."

"So, yeah. As long as it doesn't have any weapons, then he can have the starcraft. Earth will be lucky to be rid of him. Let his own people deal with him."

"What about you? You're willing to come quietly, even though you know you'll be tortured and enslaved?"

I shrugged. "How do I justify saying no at the expense of so many lives."

She stared at me silently.

"What?"

"I don't know. You actually seem sincere."

"You don't believe me?" After just being yelled at about my poker face, I was nervous I was giving something away.

"It's not that... I just wouldn't do it. For family, sure, but strangers? Maybe, maybe not. Definitely not for aliens that have been lying and using humans for hundreds of years."

"You're entitled to your opinion. I'm entitled to mine." I looked over her shoulder at the guards, then back at her. "So, do we have a deal or not?"

"How much time do you need?"

"Forty-eight hours should do it."

"Give me a minute." She walked away, pulling some sort of alien transmitter out of a pocket as she did so. As she turned it on, a humming noise filled my ears, preventing me from overhearing what she and Kreb talked about.

After a few minutes she shut the transmitter off and walked back. "He's accepted that provision. He gave me a bunch of dire threats for you. Do I really need to pass them on?"

"No."

She looked me up and down and sighed.

"What?"

"Nothing, it's just, you're not my type. That's all."

"I don't follow. What's that got to do with anything?"

"We're going to spend the rest of our lives on an alien planet doing Kreb's bidding in a life of indentured servitude. We'll be the only two humans there."

"So?" I asked.

"So much like most of the people behind bars, I'm not thrilled at the choice of either not having sex or having it to someone I'm not physically attracted to."

"Ouch! I'll try not to be offended by that. Have to say though, this seems to be an odd subject to bring up."

"That's because you're just starting out as Kreb's plaything. I've been at it for months now and have had plenty of time to think of all the ways being stranded on an alien planet will affect me. Freedom notwithstanding, food and sex top the list for me. So yeah, being the only two humans means at some point we'll probably consider bumping uglies."

"Based on your particular phrasing, we practically already did that." I grinned. "And it wasn't much fun for either of us."

"I don't know, I enjoyed that punch I landed."

"Well, I didn't." I paused. "You know it's more likely we're probably going to be kept in cages and then dissected, right? But should you be correct in what waits us, we're not stuck with each other. You could always date a Sarli. They're not human but they are pretty similar."

"I've seen your friend KayCee. While they might have the same set of limbs, I would not call that similar." She shuddered. "I heard you banged the lizard chick, so you might be okay with weird alien sex, but I'm not. Bleh!"

"First off, Itza was in a hybrid, and I thought she was human," I sputtered. "Second, you know KayCee's currently in a bioform, right? That's not her real body."

"A bioform? What's that?"

"It's the artificial body that they inhabit."

"Like the hybrids?"

"Sort of. Their actual bodies only have superficial differences than us. KayCee is quite cute in her real body."

"Really? Do you have any pictures?"

"No."

"Damn."

"Wait, what *is* your type?"

"Full-on geek," she said proudly.

"The fuck do you think I am?"

"Goofy jock is not geek. There is a big difference."

I waved at her, sarcasm dripping from my words. "You always looked like this then."

"I mean, I got older before I got younger, but, pretty much, yeah."

"Wow." I failed to keep the surprise out of my voice. "Okay."

"Why, you looked different?"

"If they drew him with less hair, I could have sued the creators of *The Simpsons* over Comic Book Guy," I admitted. "Hell, if my town could have supported a store like his, I would've *been* Comic Book Guy."

"Bullshit. Marvel or DC?"

"Comics, both. Movies, Marvel. Cartoons, DC. That being said, there are a lot of great independent stuff out there right now."

"Online gaming?"

"Not my thing, but I dabbled in WOW and Diablo."

"DnD?"

"I started back when it got delivered in a cardboard box and you had to color the dice with a tiny white crayon. Worked my way up to second and stayed there until fifth came out. And I don't care what the kids say today, it's D&D."

"I stand corrected. Still, wrong geek type. I prefer the long-haired, so skinny they could be an elf type." She frowned as she studied the doubt in my face. "What?"

"Online gaming, D&D, Marvel vs. DC. These are all basic. Something a nongeek would know. You never got specific."

"What are you saying?"

"Calvin explained that you were a psychologist before Kreb plucked you out of your normal life and into this crazy shitshow."

"So?"

"So, I'm not buying whatever — " I gestured between the two of us. " — this is."

"So, you think I'm playing mind games with you?"

"Yes, no... Not quite. I watched enough shows and read enough books to know experts say that a kidnapping victim needs to work at making sure the kidnapper grows to view them as a person instead of an object. It makes it harder to try and kill them later. Is that what you're doing here? Trying to form a bond? You have to know if Kreb's plan goes even slightly south, I'm pouncing on both of you."

"It may have occurred to me."

"I'm not a cold-blooded killer. I know you're being forced to do Kreb's bidding. I'm not going to simply kill you."

"I know. You seem like an actually good guy, Lock."

"So, the whole flirty, not flirting thing, just a way to get me off balance? Hesitate at the wrong moment?"

"Good guy or not, there may come a moment where you have no choice when fighting me. And yeah, while I'd like to not have to be in such a situation, I'm not above trying to get a psychological edge."

"Sorry, to wreck your plan. I already hit my quota of people messing with me this month."

"It was worth a shot. I should have known better. Kreb said you were smarter then you let on."

"So not really into geeks then."

"Musicians actually."

"Meaning guitarists."

"Of course. You play?"

"Not even the triangle."

"Too bad. I can only guess what passes for music on his planet. Something like funeral dirges, I suspect." She turned and walked back toward the hibernation chamber. "I doubt there are any gaming stores where we're going, so bring your books and dice anyway. You can teach me how to play. At least it will give us something to do in between serving Kreb's every whim.

Chapter 40 –
Plot Theory

I stared down at my only remaining family member. The relief of seeing Tavish's body in the med pod was indescribable. I was never comfortable in the med bay of KayCee's starcraft. Too many of the machines were also in the lab where Kreb experimented on me as a child. While I only remember fragments, some of those machines played heavily into my nightmares.

"How do I look?" asked Tavish from my phone.

Stella shouldered me out of the way and looked through the window of the pod. "Homeless."

"What?" my cousin asked. "What do you mean?"

"Your hair has got about a year's worth of growth," Stella said, "and there's some patchy clumps of hair sprouting from various parts of your face. I don't know what you would call those, but it's definitely not a beard."

KayCee moved past her and placed the control orb on a round disk at the top of one of the machines.

"Well, that's got to go," Tavish said. "I can't have a beard hiding my handsome face."

"Handsome?" Stella laughed. "Don't believe everything your mother tells you."

"How long is it going to take?" I asked KayCee.

"Long enough that you do not need to stay here," the alien replied.

"We don't mind," Jeopardy told her, standing in the doorway.

"I do." KayCee made shooing gestures with the long arms of her bioform. "I know you are excited to see Tavish Ferguson back in his own body, but all three of you will be underfoot during the process. Go prepare for Kreb. I will tell you when Tavish is ready."

"You make me sound like I'm the Thanksgiving dinner," Tavish complained.

"Well, you *are* a birdbrain," Stella said, as KayCee pushed us out of the room.

"Kicked you out already, huh?" Brennan waited for us in the hall of the starcraft. He was in the latest version of his battle armor, and there was no way he would have fit in the med bay with the rest of us. This one was practically a mech.

"Yeah," I admitted. "What's next?"

"Next, you go contact Kreb while the rest of us do our thing."

"Already? Aren't we going to wait and see what happens to Tavish?"

"Tick, tock, Lock," he said. "Either Tavish makes it out in time or he doesn't. We don't have time to wait around. I know that sounds cold, be you need to compartmentalize for this to work. To be frank, having a task on hand is better than pacing around for an hour watching the clock."

"I guess." I nodded to the others and headed for the control room. Jeopardy gave me an odd look. I wanted to think it was wistful, but I was sure I was just projecting.

"Lock! Wait up." Jeopardy hurried toward me.

"Hey." I stopped and waited for her to catch up. "What's up?"

"I had been hoping we'd have time for a talk on the way up to *Quiet Contemplation*, but there isn't a whole lot of privacy in a lander."

"If this is trying to talk me out of the plan, don't bother. Not unless you've come up with a better one."

"I wish I had," she said. "But you have to admit this is a longshot."

"Yeah, and let's face it, I've been playing the odds so long that at some point Lady Luck is going to side against me."

"That's sort of what I wanted to talk to you now. In case..."

I gave her a slight smile. "In case we can't later?"

"Right."

I leaned against a hallway wall. "Okay, I'm all ears."

"While I still think you were wrong for staying away from me and Stella, it's been about a year now, and I need to let that go. I thought I had. Well, up until I saw you again, that is. But that resurgence of wrath has been short-lived."

"Resurgence of wrath? Who talks like that? What are you, a supervillain?"

"Shut up and let me finish." She took a deep breath and started again. "I understand why you did what you did. It was stupid, but I get it. I just need you to understand that I'm no wilting flower. No damsel in distress."

"I get that. I've always got that. Don't forget," I reminded her, "it was you that saved Stella and me at the water tower. It you hadn't been there we'd have all been roggie chow. It wasn't a girlfriend thing. I'd have done it for any of the others, including Brennan."

"That's just it, Lock. You don't need to keep being a martyr. All of us are part of a team now, and we all share in the danger. You constantly sacrificing yourself is what made me angry more than anything."

"To be angry is to be human," I said.

"Really? Padme isn't the best person to quote. Especially that line."

"Well, you know. Strong female character and all that."

Jeopardy shook her head. "Her daughter Leila was a strong female character. Padme was a mess, if not an actual Sith!"

"Sith?" I threw up my hands. "Okay. I have to hear this."

"She had a decoy take her place and got her killed That's some Gaddafi type shit! She then nominates Palpatine as Supreme Chancellor? And what type of queen has lockpicks"

"A pretty cool one?" I smirked.

"She forces Anakin to disobey orders by going to Geonosis. When Anakin commits genocide, she explains it away with your little quote about anger and being human and not only never tells anyone, she marries him, causing Anakin betrayed his order and leaving him compromised." Jeopardy took a deep breath and continued. "She then put Jar Jar in charge which allows Palpatine to getting the emergency powers but still leaves her hands clean. How about popping out of Obi-Wan's ship just in time to send Anakin back over the edge?"

"But he killed her." I argued. "That couldn't have been part of any plan."

"Did he though? She lives long enough to have two Force-talented kids and then dies of... Sadness?" She snorted. "More liked she jumped out of the body now that the Republic was overthrown and Palpatine and his apprentice were both crippled of their full potential. She body-hops for a couple of decades and waits for the Empire to implode, planning to come back and rule with her Force-talented offspring. I say it again. Sith!"

"Damn, why are you not in Hollywood?" I said. I would totally watch that version.

"I'll make sure to get you and Itza tickets when I make it big." Her comment blew the wind out of my sails.

"Yeah, okay." I shifted uncomfortably against the wall. "Listen, about Itza..."

Jeopardy held up a hand. "I will admit that I didn't like seeing you with her. But it's been a year since we broke up. Well, since you broke up with me. You have a right to date who you want. That doesn't mean we can't still be friends."

Her proclamation that we could all be friends hit me like a punch to the stomach. Itza and I were never going to be a thing. It had been a drunken one-night stand because I thought Jeopardy was engaged. Besides, I was in the military now and she was... an alien queen who really looked like a lizard snake thing.

But none of that really mattered. Jeopardy was the one I had thought about nonstop over for a year. I had hoped once she had gotten past the anger, Jeopardy and I could have gotten back together. But I now found myself squarely in the friend zone. At least it was familiar. I spent a lot of time in that zone growing up. Why should my adult life be any different? Besides, I was probably going to wind up dead or enslaved later.

It's probably for the best. Which goes to show she's right as usual.

I smiled as I thought about it. Out of all of us, she was the smartest and the most emotionally well-adjusted. I didn't count Brennan or KayCee. He was our boss and kept what he was thinking close to the vest, while KayCee was an alien, and who knows how they process things. KayCee may have lived in my head for over a year, but she still caught me by surprise by some of the things she said or did.

"What are you smiling about?" Jeopardy asked, studying my face. Her own was inscrutable.

"Nothing. I was just thinking how you might be the smartest one out of all of us."

"Might? Trust me, there is no might." She might have said more but her comm chirped. She activated it. "Yes?"

"Where are you?" Brennan asked. "You said you'd just be a moment. I don't have to remind you that we're on a timetable?"

"Nope. Sorry, Colonel, I'm on my way now." She deactivated the comm and stretched up to kiss me on the cheek. "Good luck, Lock."

"Thanks." I watched her hurry off. I touched my cheek where she had kissed me. To say I was in emotional turmoil was an understatement. My actions over the next few hours would determine the fate of the free world, and all I could do was think about the girl I let get away.

"I'm such an idiot!"

Chapter 41 –
Meeting the Enemy

I stood in the control center of *Quiet Contemplation* watching the orbital fighter Kreb was on approach. I had an overwhelming urge to blow up his craft. Admittedly, I had no idea how to fire the one missile launcher KayCee's starcraft had, but even if I did, I had to make sure Itza's people were safe before I tried taking out Kreb. Well, that and the fact that we disabled the launcher.

I snorted as I thought about how far we had come so quickly. It wasn't that long ago I was trying to investigate Itza's people because they were suspected of sabotaging the human race. Now I was doing my best to save them.

I watched on the monitors as Kreb and Rory disembarked along with two Detra Tal. "What the hell?"

I pressed the comm button on the control panel. "Kreb! Why do you have Detra Tal with you?"

"They are my honor guard, Number 12," he coolly stated, looking out at where the Sarli version of a security camera was mounted. "Why are you not here to greet me?"

"I'm in the control room. The guards can't stay. The metal of this craft is toxic to them. You know that."

He gestured to the Detra Tal body he still inhabited. "I am very aware of that. However, it is not instantaneous, and they may survive on this craft for a short while without sustaining too much damage to their bodies."

"Why are they here Kreb?" I asked again.

"You have double-crossed me in the past. It seemed prudent to have a backup plan. We shall meet you in the control room and proceed to the next stage of our agreement."

I punched in a code to quickly secure the airlock doors that led out of the landing hangar. "No, we can do it from here."

"That is not acceptable. If I give you access to my hostages from here, you can simply vent the air from the hangar, blowing me out into space. A maneuver you have done before, I might add."

"Oh, you mean that time we both almost died in the coldness of space last year? Yeah, totally forgot about that." I drummed my fingers on the control panel as I thought. "I'm not just letting you on the craft while you still have control of the hostages. You are absolutely petty enough to kill them out of spite."

"What do you propose?"

"Release the hostages, and I'll let you into the starcraft."

"I will no longer have a bargaining chip, as your people say. How do I know you do not have troops on board ready to attack me?"

"Can you scan for life signs?"

"Not from here. I would need to be in the control room."

"What about Rory? Does she know how to scan for life signs?"

"I can instruct her. You wish to have her come up to the control center while I wait here?"

"Yes."

"How do I know this is not a ploy to try to free her."

I ground my teeth in frustration. He wasn't making it easy. "Wait in the damn orbital, and if you think I'm up to something, just blast the freaking airlock door and climb in."

"I had already considered that, but do not want to damage this starcraft any more than it already is." He paused. "However, I believe this may be the most acceptable plan for both of us. I will send her up. Stand by."

I watched as they all entered the orbital again. The fact that he did not want me hearing what he told Rory was extremely suspicious, but there wasn't a lot I could do about it. After a few minutes, I hit the comm. "Kreb! What's the hold up?"

The silence was deafening. I looked over the control panel, hoping I could figure out how to scan the orbital. I really should have had KayCee program me to know how to use the entire control panel instead of just what we thought I needed.

As I studied the panel, a ghostly hand rose through it, the index finger spearing me right between the eyes. "Boo!"

Chapter 42 –
Ride the Lightning

"You need to hurry, he's waking up." I opened my eyes on hearing Rory's voice. She had opened the door to the control room and Kreb and the two Detra Tal were racing down the hall toward it.

I groaned at my splitting headache and slowly got to my feet, making no move to stop them. Kreb shot me a suspicious glare as he slithered into the room. And I mean that literally as he was still in the body of the war leader of the Detra Tal. "You awoke early. Why did you not try to prevent us from taking control of the starcraft?"

I rolled my head, trying to relieve a crick in my neck. I had a youthful, highly evolved super body with accelerated healing, you think I wouldn't have to deal with such things anymore. I frowned at Kreb. "That would defeat the purpose. The deal was you get the starcraft if you free your hostages. Here's the starcraft. Now, release the hostages."

He lifted a device he was holding in one of his four arms. "I do not trust you. Do anything suspicious and I will detonate the devices I planted around the hibernation chamber."

I raised my eyebrows. "That's how you're doing it? A detonator?"

"Sometimes the old ways are still the best."

"What if I just removed your arm before you had a chance to press the button?"

Kreb gave me a condescending look. I had to admit his facial expressions in the body of the Detra Tal were much easier to read then when he was in a bioform. "You think I am I fool? This is emitting a constant signal. If it stops, that is when the explosive device goes off. And it will stop if my finger comes off the button."

"Yes."

The mad alien blinked at me. "Yes? Yes what?"

"Yes, I think you're a fool."

He tensed for a second as if he was going to charge at me, then visibly relaxed. I could see the effort it took to smooth his face of any emotion. "You are trying to bait me. It will not work. Surrender yourself and this craft, or I will kill all Detra Ka within the hibernation chamber."

"You don't want to know why I think you're a fool?" As I spoke, Rory gave me a WTF look but remained silent.

He moved toward the control panel. I slid to the side away from him and the others. My brain receiving the electronic message I was waiting for. "You still need the control orb."

"I do not." He started punching buttons with his free hand. "Remember, I was secretly controlling the Detra Ka when this was installed. It is of my design and allows one to bypass the control orb."

"And while you were secretly controlling the Detra Ka, the Detra Ka were secretly influencing the humans that were secretly building this control panel. I'm getting dizzy just thinking about it." I pulled a gum packet out of my pocket, offering it to Rory who just shook her head. Shrugging, I unwrapped a piece and popped it in my mouth. "But while you were secretly watching the Detra Ka secretly watching the humans, the Space Force was secretly watching the Detra Ka. And we were secretly watching the Space Force. See? Dizzy, isn't it?"

His finger stopped, hovering over the control panel. "We?"

"Yeah, Me... KayCee... and my cousin Tavish..."

Kreb straightened and turned toward me. "Tavish Ferguson. You are referring to Weapon System Number 10?"

"I'm referring to my cousin Tavish."

"The one I killed to punish you for your insolence? A lesson you obviously did not learn."

"Yeah, that one. I mean it would have to be that one. He's the only cousin of mine you've met. Which is probably a good thing since you have a tendency of killing my relatives. Just ask my parents. Oh, that's right. You can't because you already murdered them."

Rory's head recoiled in surprise. Guess she didn't know that part. Kreb ignored her reaction. "You speak in riddles. How can Number 10 assist you when he is dead."

"You mean when you turned the oxygen off in his medical pod and caused him to suffocate to death?"

"Yes."

"I... Wow, just never caught on to sarcasm, did you?"

"No."

"O...kay. Anyways, after you killed him, Tavish got better." I gave him the most gleeful smirk I could muster. "Who do you think shoved that missile up your ass when we were floating in space? Wasn't me, as much as I wished it had been."

Kreb was many things: insane, xenophobic, genocidal, but first and foremost he was a genius. It took him a split second to figure it out. "He used his abilities to upload his consciousness before he died."

"Yes, he did. Totally lawn-mowered himself." I waved a hand at his confused look. "Never mind. Movie reference, it would take too long to explain."

"Then this is now useless." He took his finger off the button of the device he had been holding the whole time. Horror filled Rory's face. As far as she knew, he just killed all the hostages.

"Yup." I leaned against the wall. "Tavish, you want to explain the rest?"

"Sure." Tavish's electronic voice filled the room. "Thanks to your monologuing... By the way, nice job on that, Lock."

"Thank you."

"As I was saying, Kreb. While you were monologuing, I identified the signal you were emitting back to Earth. I originally planned on duplicating it but after having a quick peek inside your device I realized I could use it to remotely disable your bombs. Which, of course, I did.

"Lock's friend Itza and her people have already removed the devices. And just to be on the safe side, moved the stasis pods to a different location. Let's see, I feel like I'm forgetting something. Oh yeah, Fuck you!"

"Next time I return to your pitiful planet. I will make sure to capture you for study. Goodbye, Number 10." Kreb's stabbed a finger on a button, and Tavish's transmission abruptly cut off. "Annoying, but trivial. I have what I need."

"The starcraft, sure," I said. "But if you think I'm going willingly with you, you have another thing coming." I sure as hell was not going to correct Kreb's assumption that Tavish was on the planet.

Without warning his tail stabbed out at me. I admit I had underestimated how far that damn tail could stretch. His venomous stinger plunged into my face... and back out the other side. I managed to phase myself just before he hit. My clothes dropping to the deck as I phased. "Hey now. That was rude to do while Tavish was getting his brag on. Too bad the only one of you that can touch me in this form is your ginger friend over there, and she might find that this time, things will go differently."

Kreb gave a shrug that rippled down his entire body and across his tail. "It matters not. I have control of the starcraft, and you are trapped on it with us. You can surrender now and remain in a peaceful cell or be hunted the entire time it takes to get back to my planet."

"Or I take your orbital back to *Diana* Station and help the Space Force track you down."

He turned back to the control panel. A few buttons later, a view of the hangar came on the main screen. "You are referring to this lander?"

"Yeah..."

His finger stabbed down again. The magnetic locks on the orbital disengaged as the hangar bay opened. A couple more jabs and an energy ray enveloped the orbital, pulling it across the floor and forcing it out into space, where it floated away."

"You guys have a tractor beam?"

"An odd name for a cargo hauler, but yes." A few more buttons and the hangar door closed. "Now, you will not be going anywhere."

"You really suck, you know that?"

Kreb pointed at Rory. "Get him. And do not fail this time."

Rory went into phase, her jumpsuit falling to the ground as she did. Unlike the rest of her, her private areas were fuzzed out.

"You really need to teach me that trick. I'm getting really tired at flashing my junk at everybody."

"Trust me, it's worse for us," she told me.

"Well, in that case, let me relieve you of that burden." I gave Kreb the finger and phased through the floor.

Rory followed. I phased through three decks, landing into a mostly empty storage room. I backed up against a wall and waited for Rory. She floated down from the ceiling, turning solid as she looked around. "Why did you stop running? What's the trick?"

"This," I said as Tavish sent an electric charge through the room, striking us before Rory had a chance to phase. Ready for it, I absorbed it easily. Rory, on the other hand, was neither prepared for it nor possessed my energy absorption ability. It was the equivalent of a giant taser. As she rode the lightning, I pulled out a syringe we'd hidden in the room earlier and injected her with the contents.

Tavish cut the power, and Rory fell to her knees.

I held out a hand to her. "Hurts like a bitch, doesn't it?"

"What did you do?" she growled as she slapped my hand away and slowly stood up.

"Our Detra Ka friends are really good with the bio sciences. They duplicated Kreb's power-neutralization serum. You remember, the one you shot me up with before? Well, it's currently coursing through your veins." I stepped back and phased through the locked door. "You might as well get comfortable. You won't be phasing for a while."

She pounded on the door. "You can't keep me here."

"Actually, I can." I told her through the window in the door. "It's going to be your cell for a little while. But don't worry. There's food and water in one of the cabinets. Another has some clothes for you. Figured you wouldn't want to be walking around in the buff the whole time. Some bedding as well."

"It's a good plan, but—" She rushed the door, trying to phase through it. She hit it hard, bouncing off and landing on her posterior.

"But nothing, you're going nowhere."

She picked herself off the deck. "No, you don't understand. I don't have a choice. Thanks to Kreb's orders, I'm compelled to complete my orders or die trying."

Crap!

"Yeah, I was afraid of that." I sighed. "Which is why we planned for it. Tavish, put her to bed."

The room was quickly flooded with a gas that the Detra Bel swore was harmless to humans other than rendering them unconscious. Rory hit the deck one final time.

"I know what Bel Crat's people said, but are we sure there's no side effects?"

"It's harmless," Tavish said through my comm. "Well, at least according to the medical geeks back at Delta Black who looked it over."

"That's slightly reassuring, I guess." I went back to the room I had phased into and dug my flight suit out of a locker. "That's better. Running around in the buff will never be in my comfort zone. Being naked as a jaybird isn't much of a confidence booster when you're facing down evil megalomaniacs bent on world domination."

"What's next?"

"I'll show my face upstairs, see if I can get his two guards to chase me around for a little bit." I slipped on my socks and boots. "Has he caught on that you're here yet? Or any other part of the plan for that matter?"

"No, he still thinks *Quiet Contemplation* is headed back to his home world. As long as he doesn't realize I'm sending him false data and images on the monitors, he'll have no idea that we're heading toward the unidentified starcraft."

"You do realize this is an incredibly stupid idea, right?" I asked my cousin.

"Yeah, but look at it this way, if it's KayCee's people, we just delivered their worst enemy to them gift wrapped. If it turns out to be Itza's people, they can't be too unhappy with us considering we just save thousands of their people."

"And if it's allies of Kreb?"

"Ramming speed and jump out the nearest airlock."

"What about if it's an alien race that's not even on the board."

"We defer to Brennan and hope they are more ET and less Xenomorph."

"Yeah, great plan." I poked my head out of the room. "Do you have eyes on Kreb and company?"

"Yes, you really don't need to tiptoe through the halls."

"Any issues being put back in your body?"

He was silent for a moment. "We didn't do it yet."

I stopped. "What? Why not? Is something wrong?"

There was a long pause before he answered. "No, everything's fine."

"Then what's the problem?"

"I... decided to wait. My abilities will drop significantly once I'm back in my body. Right now, I'm controlling the entire spaceship with ease."

"Starcraft, not spaceship."

"Whatever. My point is that I'm overseeing a lot of moving parts right now. I wouldn't be able to handle all of this if I was in my body, so I'm holding off until this is done."

"That's stupid. You don't need to control the entire starcraft, just the control room. KayCee can operate the rest using the control orb in the secondary control area. You know, the whole plan we came up with?"

"Secondary control can be overridden by the primary control room. And Kreb is perfectly capable of having installed something I could have missed. Why take that chance?"

"I don't know, because every moment you hold off is a chance something could prevent you from returning to your body."

"Trust me."

"Tavish, every time you've ever said that it was followed by a complete shitstorm. I just spent the last couple of months going through hell to get you back in your body, and now you're dilly-dallying?"

"Dilly-dallying? Who says that?"

"Our grandmother did, for one," I said.

"Yeah, I mean, our age."

"We're not exactly young. A lot's happened since being abducted thirty years ago."

"It wasn't thirty years ago," Tavish said.

"Yes, it was."

"Lock, we were abducted when we were fifteen."

"Right, thirty years ago."

"And how old are you now?"

"I dunno." I scratched the side of my face. "I think about thirty-five. It's hard to tell with this body."

"Not physically, chronologically."

"Same as you fifty-one.... Oh, shit."

"Yeah, more like thirty-six years ago." Tavish said smugly.

"What the hell?"

"Relax, you're not going senile. It's more common than you think. Especially with our generation. You'd be shocked how many think you're talking about the '80s when you say twenty years ago."

I suddenly felt old. "Why?"

"I don't know. Denial of aging maybe. Fear of growing old? Maybe it has something to do with people living longer, or it could just be Generation X's obsession with their childhoods. Either way, stop saying it was thirty years ago. You sound like an idiot that can't count."

"Fuck you. And get back in your body!"

"In a little bit. First, I... Huh."

"What?"

"Kreb got bored of waiting. He just sent the two Detra Tal to go find you."

"Good. That should simplify things. Lead me to them."

"Don't get cocky. The warrior caste is tough."

"Trust me, I fought enough of them to know. But the new phasing ability makes it a lot easier. Exploding teleports doesn't hurt either."

"Yeah, I get it, you leveled up. But don't forget, every time we think we have Kreb trapped, he has something up his sleeve."

"I'm the last person you need to tell that to."

"Really?" my cousin asked. "How many times has he killed *you*?"

"Point."

"Thank you."

"All the more reason to get back to your body." I reminded him.

"Will you get your head in the game?" Tavish demanded.

"Fine, lead me to them." I followed Tavish's directions until I was around the corner from them. They were doing a room-by-room search, so I ducked into a room to wait. The light flickered on as sensors detected my presence.

Quiet Contemplation was originally a very sparce starcraft. A lot of empty chrome rooms had the ability to change and adapt as directed by the control orb. Humans being humans, the Space Force had filled it up with a lot of stuff. The room I was in must have been meant for quarters. There was two beds, lockers, a desk and a kitchenette. I felt like I was in a hotel room. "Oh, look, they did leave the light on for me."

"Huh? Was that some sort of reference? You know I can't actually see in the room, right?"

"The motel commer— you know what? Never mind. Good material was always wasted on you." From the sounds they were making, the Detra Tal were still a ways away. "What do you think? Take them out now or have them chase me around for a while? How much longer do we have until contact?"

"About a half hour. I suggest having them chase you. If you take them out, Kreb may get inventive."

"What's he doing now?"

"Watching these two on the monitor."

"Goose chase it is." I popped out of the room, just as the two warriors rounded the corner.

"Meep-meep." I gave my best Road Runner impression and ducked into another room and then phased through the wall. Remember the Scooby-Doo cartoons where the monsters would chase them into one room and then come out of a different room? We did a one-way version of that. Every time they chased me into one room, I'd pop out of another. By the end of the half hour, both Detra Tal looked very frustrated. I'm sure my constant laughter wasn't helping.

Tavish keyed up on my comm. "Lock, time to finish these guys."

"Roger that."

After ducking into a room for what seemed like the millionth time, I spun around. As the two of them barreled in after me, I did the *phased fingers to the brains* routine.

"Now what?"

One of the walls lit up into a monitor, showing a cube-shaped starcraft moving toward us. "Oh crap! It's the Borg!"

Chapter 43 –
Lacutus, Is That You?

I stared at the cube-shaped starcraft. "How big is that?"

"Not borg sized, so stop thinking you're going to get assimilated by fictional characters," Tavish said. "Tonnage-wise, it's a little smaller that *Quiet Contemplation*."

"From what KayCee told me, *Quiet Contemplation* is on the large size."

"That's troubling. What's more worrying is it's definitely bristling with weapons."

"Run a comparison with Sarli and Detra Ka tech. Also, check with KayCee and see what she thinks."

"Already on it," Tavish said.

"Meanwhile, I'm heading closer to the control room."

"Roger that."

Before I could do anything the starcraft shuddered. "What the hell was that?"

"The other craft just fired at us. No real damage but... Oh boy. It was enough for Kreb to get suspicious. He's checking the monitor feeds."

One of the limitations of phasing was going up. I could go through walls and the floor but the ability to phase through ceiling was just out of my reach, literally. I ran to the nearest elevator. KayCee called them lifts, which make Stella suspect her of being Space British.

Once I got to the correct level, I raced to the control room. Unlike the spacecraft from science fiction, the control room is not at the top with windows looking out. It was in fact in the safest area of the starcraft — the middle.

I keyed the door with my mind and rushed in. Kreb stood in front of the monitor staring at the cube-shaped starcraft. At that magnification, it wasn't very borg-like aside from the shape. It was covered in the same chrome-like material as KayCee's starcraft. Each side had a multitude of gunports and missile launchers that screamed "weapon of war," not a starcraft of exploration.

Kreb turned to me. "False images and readings so I did not know where we were headed. I am impressed."

"Thanks."

Kreb turned back to the monitor which switched to an image of three Sarli bioforms. The bioforms were green, which according to KayCee meant they were part of the military for Kreb's country. That did not bode well for Earth. The bioforms I had seen before wore no clothing other than utility belts when needed. These wore chrome-like armor that seemed to be made of the same alien armor that KayCee had made for Stella.

That can't be good.

"Unidentified Kemtaran Alliance starcraft, stand down," a voice told us in Kreb's language. "This is the Volan Supremacy warcraft *A Glorious Reckoning*. Stand down or be destroyed."

"*A Glorious Reckoning*?" I chuckled. "And you gave KayCee crap for *Quiet Contemplation*?"

"Be quiet," Kreb ordered as he transmitted our image back to them.

The lead bioform's eyes widened at the sight of us. Various symbols were painted on his and his companions' armor. I guessed it was their version of medals or ribbons. "Detra Ka, how have you come to be in possession of a starcraft of the Kemtaran Alliance?"

"War Master Tigrafrentop, is that you?" Kreb asked in an imperious tone.

The eyes narrowed. "Who are you to know my name?"

"Dire Lord Krebdanturnvat, Science Master of the Volan Supremacy. My bioform was destroyed and I was forced to inhabit this Detra Ka to survive."

"That *is* interesting. If this is true, it is very good news indeed. Tell me, if you are in fact, Dire Lord Krebdanturnvat, where did we first meet?"

"At the Scourge of Teplees. The field was so littered with dead that we had to walk over them. Dominar Bubatopento made the introductions. You were drinking a purple-colored beverage of some kind."

"Pelga. It was a local concoction." Tigrafrentop inclined his head. "Very well, then. Well met, Dire Lord."

"Thank you."

"We intercepted a message that was transmitted over a cycle ago from the vessel you are in. It stated you were sighted on a planet in this solar system."

"Earth, yes. I was trapped there for some time until I could arrange transportation off the planet. Tell me, Tigrafrentop, how goes the fight?"

"Poorly, I am afraid. Remnants of our forces remain scattered after our defeat. We have been slowly rebuilding."

"It cannot be too bad. It appears you are able to build *Reckoning*-class starcraft. The plans for those were still being finished when I was stranded."

"Yes, unfortunately this is the first and only one we have been able to create. You and your pet need to come aboard. I must tell you, Dire Lord Krebdanturnvat, we have much to discuss."

Pet? Fuck you too.

"You will need to send a lander or use a docking tunnel," Kreb told him.

"We will use a docking tunnel. I wish to have this Alliance starcraft inspected. We may have use for it. You remember Battle Master Ronintorbo?"

"He was a Trooper Leader when I last met him, but yes," Kreb replied.

"Excellent. He will head the force coming to meet you."

"This is good. He will be able to confirm my identity in person."

"Exactly." The screen went blank.

"Chatty fellow, isn't he?" I asked. "Got to say, love the name of your various ranks. Very macho. Are they assigned based on levels of douchebaggery?"

Kreb gave me a cold smile. "Your fight is over now, Number 12. *A Glorious Reckoning* can vaporize a relic like this starcraft without depleting its primary battery. You have nowhere to go and no way to escape."

"Yeah, all right." I shrugged. "You've got me in a box right now. No sense fighting when I can't win. But any attempts to crawl inside my head, and all bets are off."

"Actually, with the equipment that should be aboard *A Glorious Reckoning*, I will no longer have a need to dissect you. A simple scan and I will be able to replicate your abilities in others." So much more elegant than the primitive tools of your people that I have been forced to use all these years."

My stomach did a flip flop at the word dissect. "Wow, you must really like being in that body. Usually, you can't wait to try and possess me."

"I have discovered that the Detra Ka, especially the Detra Tal, are surprisingly suitable for molding into weapons. Being an advanced race, I had never had an opportunity to study one before now. I suspect hybrids laced with your DNA will be nigh unstoppable."

"Study? You mean experiment on."

"Yes." He gave a single stiff nod. "As it turns out, due to the various centuries of genetic manipulation that they have done to themselves, they are ideal for my needs. In fact, after I scan what I need from you, I will no longer need to deal with your race."

I saw an opportunity there. "Wait. You'd let me go?"

"Of course not. I am very much looking forward to torturing you because of all the trouble you put me through."

"What if I was able to deliver to you all of the Detra Ka on Earth?"

"What do you mean?"

"My government doesn't want the Detra Ka on our planet. We've been forced into an alliance, but we know it won't last. They've been manipulating us for centuries. This is the first time we know where they all are, and most of them are in stasis pods. If you and your people agree to leave Earth and humanity alone, I'm sure I can convince them to give you all the Detra Ka residing on Earth."

"You would do this?"

"In return for not torturing and killing me? Sure, that's a no-brainer."

"That is... a more enlightened response than I have grown to expect from you."

"What's enlightened? I get to stay on Earth, The aliens that have been secretly manipulating my people are gone, *and* we'll never have to see you or your kind again. We get to live peacefully on our little planet while you run amok fighting your own people."

"At last, you have managed to see reason."

"Then we have a deal?"

"Yes, if you can get your people to agree to it."

"Not a problem. Ever heard the phrase 'illegal alien'? That's a term we use for humans who sneak into our country. Imagine how even less enthused my government is over the idea of real extraterrestrials sneaking in." I hooked a thumb toward the monitoring screen. "What about your people?"

"Once I have been properly identified, it will not be an issue."

"Then it's agreed."

"Yes. Now, where is Number 10?"

"What do you want her for. I thought you just needed to scan me?"

"She needs to be scanned as well. Her abilities have turned out to be very effective as you, yourself, quickly learned. She may be released along with you afterwards, as long as your government agrees to the deal. Now, I ask again, where is she? I have not seen her since you fought."

"Ah... That didn't work out so well. As Rory was turning solid, I pushed her through a wall. She wasn't able to recover in time. It... wasn't pretty."

"A minor inconvenience."

"Caring as always, I see." I scowled. "On the other hand, I phase-stunned your guards."

"Are you sure about that?" Kreb asked as the door opened and his two guards slithered in.

"What the hell? I fried their brains. They should be down for a bit longer than that."

"You think you are the only creature I've ever experimented on? I have had months to upgrade these two."

"Then why... Of course, you were using them to figure out what I was up to."

"Yes. But as it turns out, it was not necessary." He motion to the two of them. "Seize him."

Each warrior grabbed a bicep and wedged me between them, their claws piercing my flesh. "Ow, easy there, you Slytherin rejects."

"Our deal is still in place, Number 12," Kreb said. "But you have a way of irritating the ibuto while harvesting."

"That's not fair! I have never even seen an ibuto much less irritated it. If you're going to use sayings from your home planet, you could at least explain them."

Kreb walked out the door, the two Detra Ka forcing me along behind him. I shook my head. "Screw this."

As the three continued to ignore me, I activated my phasing ability, but nothing happened. "Shit! What did you do?"

"Their claws release the same neutralizing agent you were given before. None of your powers will work until it wears off." Kreb didn't even glance back at me.

"Well, that's just cheating, you kumquat!"

This time I earned a look back from Kreb. "Is that not some sort of vegetable?"

"It's a fruit, not a vegetable," I corrected before hesitating. "Well, I think it's a fruit."

"I fail to see how that is any sort of an insult."

"It was the first word to come to mind. It's tough always being this funny."

Chapter 44 –
Illegal Aliens

I continued to throw insults at Kreb until we made it to the chosen airlock. The giant space cube was much closer then I was comfortable with. It actually worked better for the plan, but if someone wasn't steady on the joystick, we were going to wreck more than just the starcraft paintjobs. I watched in fascination as a large, flexible tube extended out of the cube toward us. It clunked as it connected with *Quiet Contemplation*. Once it pressurized, the Detra Tal on my left let go of me and opened the door.

Fifty-one bioforms marched across the tube, all but one armed to the teeth and holding weapons that looked like '50s era ray guns. I winced when I saw them. I had almost died after getting shot with one of those weapons. They were nothing to fool around with.

They spread out, securing the area. The one bioform not brandishing a weapon, stepped up in front of Kreb. After a long moment, it gave a single nod. "It *is* you! Welcome back, Dire Lord Krebdanturnvat."

"Thank you, Battle Master Ronintorbo. What of my natural body?"

"I regretfully inform you that it was destroyed by the Alliance."

"Tell me, do you still have genetic samples of me?"

"Of course."

"Then no matter. I'll grow a new body when the time is right."

"We have spare bioforms, if you wish to get out of that." The Battle Master gestured at the body of the Detra Tal that Kreb currently inhabited. He somehow managed to convey his disgust at the idea with the gesture.

"It is not as horrible as you think," Kreb informed him. "But yes, I would like to be back in a fully functioning bioform."

I waggled a finger back and forth at the two of them. "So, you can just tell each other apart, when you're not in your real bodies? That's convenient. Especially when you're out at the local nightclub in someone else's body. Don't want to accidentally sleep with your sister. Is it still incest if you're both possessing other people? Oh wait, you guys normally stick to bioforms, and those don't have sex organs. Hey, does that make you all eunuchs?"

The battle master stepped closer, studying me. "What race is this?"

"Human," Kreb replied.

"Why have you let it keep its tongue?"

"I was just wondering that myself." Kreb gestured down the hall. "Do you still want to tour this craft? It is quite obsolete."

"Yes, I recognize that. However, we have few crafts at our disposal these days. If we can utilize it in our fight with the enemy, it may yet find a purpose."

Kreb pointed to my two guards. "Stay here with him. If he tries anything, cripple him but do not kill him. I have plans for him."

Ain't gonna lie. The way he said those last five words just sent a chill down my spine.

The black orbs of the battle master's bioform narrowed. "Why?"

"He is an experiment. This human may not look like much—"

"Hey!"

"But I have crafted him into a formidable weapon."

"If you say so, Dire Lord." The battle master glared at five of his troops. "Stay here."

The remaining guards did a cursory search of the room, even going so far to open the storage units lining the wall. After determining all the units contained EVA suits, they shut them up and commenced goofing off. If it had been me, I'd have checked the suits too. Someone the size of, oh I don't know, Jeopardy or KayCee could easily hide in the larger suits.

Which is why I wasn't surprised when all five of the Sarli troops suddenly stopped moving. My two Detra Tal guards went into alert mode. One held onto me, while the other carefully approached a storage unit whose door was slowly creaking open. Various edged weapons appeared in each of the hands of the Detra Tal closing in on the storage unit.

Jeopardy hopped out of the storage unit in an EVA suit sized for someone significantly larger. She looked like a small child in her parents' clothes. "I still can't believe you chose kumquat as your safe word."

"Code word! Safe word's something else."

"Even still, that's pretty stupid." She gestured up and the single Detra Tal moving toward her was flung upward, slamming into the ceiling and then back to the floor with even greater force.

I palmed an EpiPen from my pocket. "You're supposed to pick something you wouldn't actually use in normal conversation."

As I spoke, the Detra Tal still guarding me wrapped a large hand around my neck, its clawed fingers stretching to rest on my trachea. I resisted the urge to clear my throat, and instead dropped my arm down by my side, hiding the EpiPen. "Not supposed to kill me, remember?"

The warrior spoke for the first time. "Accidents happen."

"Crap." I looked over at Jeopardy. "A little help?"

"I'm currently brain-freezing five bioforms. Bioforms, I might add, who have very advanced programs that keep trying to find ways around my telepathic control. While doing that, I am also using telekinesis to pin down a very strong warrior of the Detra Ka. I have my hands full, mentally speaking…"

"Perhaps I can help." One of the other storage units doors had opened and KayCee, clambered out from behind one of the EVA suits.

"You hid behind the suit," Jeopardy said. "Damn, wished I had thought of that." Strain showing on her face at the mental effort she was putting out. "Ah, this is a lot tougher than I thought. In fact, I could use some backup."

KayCee approached the frozen Sarli. "I will assist. But I would point out you were late getting here, Jeopardy Jones. I had already secured myself by the time you arrived. I assumed you had hidden in the same manner."

"Yeah, past that subject now." Jeopardy gasped. "I'm losing them. If you're going to do something, do it quick."

KayCee took one of the ray guns from a frozen Sarli. "You need to understand every one of the Supremacy soldiers here is in fact a war criminal that has been sentenced to death by my people."

"Yeah, we get that," I said.

"Excellent." KayCee fired the ray gun at the head of one of the bioforms. The beam completely vaporized the head and upper shoulders.

"Jesus, KayCee," I shrieked. Even the Detra Tal seemed surprised at her actions. I used the moment to plunge the needle of the EpiPen into my thigh. Its contents burned as it spread throughout my system.

KayCee blew the head off another of the pinned bioforms. "I did just explain they have been sentenced to death. I would be remiss in my duty to my country if I do not carry this out. Trust me when I say I take no pleasure in it."

"I can't..." Jeopardy wobbled for a second and then slumped to the deck.

"Jeopardy!" I yelled, starting toward her. The grip on my neck tightened as the Detra Tal jerked me back. I had no choice but to stand there, hoping the magic cocktail I had just injected myself with would actually work.

KayCee continued lining up a shot on another target as the Sarli. "I too find myself in need of help."

The door slid open, and Brennan and Stella came in firing, Stella with a captured ray gun, Brennan launching mini rockets off wrist-mounted launchers. His suit must have had a guidance system because none of them missed, and no Sarli hit with them remained in enough pieces to be a threat. It was very Mandalorian.

Between Brennan, Stella, and KayCee, the enemy Sarli were destroyed in seconds. As Stella rushed to assist Jeopardy, Brennan looked at me. "Sit Rep?"

"Well," I pointed up at the Detra Tal holding my neck. "He's threatening to kill me. KayCee has gone all Punisher on the enemy soldiers here, and Jeopardy and I kind of have a problem with that."

"Why?" Brennan moved further into the airlock, ignoring the Detra Tal.

"She said they were already sentenced to death, and that she has an obligation to her people."

"Yeah, that part I get. Why do you two have an issue with it?"

"Well..." I looked at Jeopardy, as Stella helped her to her feet. The podcaster turned agent's hands were shaking. "Um."

Jeopardy pointed at the bioforms on the ground. "They're defenseless. That's murder."

Brennan's visor flipped open, and he started to move his hand up to his face before remembering it was currently encased in a big metal gauntlet. He extended one finger and carefully scratched between his eyes. "They are not helpless and they haven't surrendered. They moved to attack us when we fired. We're not cops, we're in the military and this is a current military engagement to save the entire frigging planet."

"But..." Jeopardy's face twisted in anguish.

"Yeah, it sucks." Brennan nodded. "But that's war."

"Enough talking!" growled the Detra Tal with his hand still wrapped around my neck. "Surrender or I will tear the head off of Number 12."

"We'll get to you in a minute," Brennan told him. "One alien species at a time."

Stella twirled her ax menacingly at the Detra Tal but remained silent.

Brennan shifted his attention back to Jeopardy. "We don't have a way to capture and imprison them at the moment. If we did, I'd use it, but we don't. If we had left them behind, they would have regrouped with the others and given them intel. They will then use it to kill all of us."

I cleared my throat but said nothing. Hearing my cue, Brennan turned back to face me and the Detra warrior. "You ready? We're behind schedule."

The Detra Tal snarled at him. "I said—"

"He was talking to me, not you." I phased through his grip and stepped to the side. Before the big warrior could react, Stella leaped forward, her razor-sharp ax slicing down. Made of an alien metal, one sweep was all it took for the Detra Tal to hit the floor, his head rolling away from the body.

I phased back and started scrambling back into my clothes. Jeopardy slumped against the wall. Sweat visible on her brow. I hopped toward her, pulling on my last shoe. "You okay?"

"Yeah, that took a lot out of me." She wiped her forehead.

"Quick thinking with the whole 'we don't need to kill them' routine," I said.

She glared up at me. "I was serious. We didn't need to kill them."

I stepped back in surprise. "Sorry, I misread it. I thought we were doing a bit to stall for time until the antidote kicked in. But everything the colonel said was correct. I thought you knew that. They were evil."

"I know, it's just..."

"No, I get it. No one here is happy having to take a life whether it's human *or* alien. I do really feel bad about the Detra Tal, though. Unlike the others, he was under Kreb's mind control."

"Lock." Brennan called over. "Any issues with the antidote Itza's scientists whipped up?"

"Aside from the time it took to go into effect, it was great. I mean it wasn't comfortable but anything that can break the lock Kreb's potion had on my abilities, I'm happy to take, burning sensation and all."

"Burning sensation, huh?" Stella grinned as she collected the enemy's weapons. "You might want to see a doctor about that."

"Har-har." I snatched a ray gun out of her hand. "I'm just glad Calvin had a sample of Kreb's potion on him when he got captured. Itza said without it, there is no way they could have created an antidote so fast."

"Any hiccups to the plan?" Brennan asked me.

"Not really. I mean I sold out Itza's people for my freedom but other than that, we're good."

"Excellent, stone cold, but excellent. I'm sure Itza would approve of your treachery in this particular case." He looked up toward the ceiling. "Tavish, you there?"

"Of course," my cousin's voice came through the hidden intercoms.

"Any luck accessing the other starcraft?"

"No. But then we didn't think it was going to be that easy."

"One could hope," Brennan said. "Okay, disable *Quite Contemplation's* flight controls then download into the control orb."

"Already disabled them. Downloading now."

Brennan motioned to each of us. "Stella, Jeopardy, you're with me. Lock, KayCee, once Tavish is downloaded, get him on the craft. I want to add it to my collection. Stella, Jeopardy, and I will contain the enemy troops on this side. Any last questions?"

KayCee raised her hand. "Colonel Brennan, I feel the need to point out that why you are all formidable in your fields, Kreb's allies are all in military-grade bioforms. They are not like the bioform I previously used, and I am not sure you are prepared for them."

Brennan smiled and pointed at KayCee. "That's a military bioform you're currently in, correct?"

"Yes."

"In fact, it's actually from Kreb's Military?"

"Also, correct, Colonel Brennan."

"Has there been a lot of defensive advancements to bioforms since 1947."

"Not really. They are used for long-term space travel, and the war was mostly fought on our home planet. Most of the research and development went into protective armor for our actual bodies as well as planetary vehicles. What few battles took place in space was between starcraft. There are some specialized versions but that is more the exception to the rule."

Brennan nodded. "Well, we've been studying that very bioform you're wearing for over seventy-five years, all while assuming there were more advanced models being made every year. Every countermeasure ever conceived is built into the suit I'm wearing. You yourself have said that Jeopardy's telekinesis and telepathy skills are far beyond your own people's."

"Yes, she adapted to it very quickly."

"Lock has been turned into a weapon so powerful, Kreb wants to replicate him to create an army capable of conquering worlds. And Stella... well, you've met Stella, right?"

"Those are very valid points, Colonel Brennan."

"Good. All right, people, let's go be space pirates. Arrrgh!"

CHAPTER 45 –
ARRRGH!

With KayCee holding the control orb that contained my cousin, she and I started across the tunnel. I had on a mask and air supply that Delta Black had rigged up for me. I didn't need an EVA suit as my body could adjust itself to the rigors of space. I could have survived without the air too, but that was uncomfortable and left me unable to speak.

My comm crackled to life with Brennan's voice. "Tavish, time to black out their communications. Hit it."

An evil laugh cackled throughout *Quiet Contemplation* as the Prince of Darkness himself welcomed all aboard. While the music played over the craft's comms, an announcer voice came over our secure frequency. "Knight One has entered the game. Barfight has entered the game. Risk has entered the game."

"Risk?" asked KayCee.

I shrugged. "Not bad. It doesn't give away her powers. On the other hand, it's a synonym of Jeopardy which, while cute, isn't really a good code name. That's like calling Stella Star or calling me Latch."

"Do I have a code name?"

"I dunno. Did the colonel give you one?"

"No." KayCee tilted her head. "Tavish Ferguson, do you have one?"

"No, but I'm thinking of going with Skynet," he replied.

I sighed as we crossed the bridge. "You are not using that. Your very existence is scary enough as it is. Besides, you're not an AI."

"How about Lawn Mower Man?"

"You really want them thinking you're going to try and destroy the world?"

"So, W.O.P.R. is out?" asked Tavish. "Shall we play a game?"

"How about Nerd but as an acronym. N.E.R.D.?"

"I could own that. What's it stand for?"

"I'll get back to you one that." I stopped and studied the enemy craft's airlock. There was an electronic pad that looked suspiciously like some kind of lock. "Tavish, can you open this can?"

"One can opener, coming up."

I waited. Nothing happened. "Tavish?"

"Umm, one moment. This is military-grade alien tech. It's a little harder than I thought."

I turned and looked at KayCee. "It appears we have a couple of minutes."

"Yes."

"How's the new bioform?"

"The left knee is somewhat stiff. Other than that, I cannot complain."

There was some faint explosions over our frequency. "They seem to have found Kreb and the others."

"I hope that Stella Johansen does not underestimate the Supremacy soldiers. They are fierce fighters."

"Brennan will keep her in check," I said.

Stella's voice came over the link. "Don't run! Why are you running? Get back here and fight. There's only two of us, you cowards."

"She seems to have it in hand," I said dryly.

"Indeed," KayCee agreed.

"By the way," Tavish said, "there are two guards on either side of the inner door. Neither one of them is paying the slightest bit of attention, but I jammed their communications, just in case." The airlock door slid open with an audible hiss. "Ta-da."

"About time. J.A.R.V.I.S. would have done it in about half that time." Both KayCee and I stepped in. "Okay, you can shut it now."

"Sorry, Dave," my cousin said. "I'm afraid I can't do that."

"Dave? Dave's not here, man." I answered as I drew my ray gun. "Now close the damn door and open the inner one."

"Nice one," he acknowledged as the first door sealed. There was a slight buzzing.

"What the hell is that?" I looked around trying to figure out what it was.

"You may relax, Loughlin Ferguson," KayCee said. "It is a scan in case of contamination."

The buzzing stopped before she had even finished speaking and the inner door slid open. Both guards whirled around in surprise. I shot one in the head, vaporizing it. KayCee got the other one the same way.

Tavish triggered the announcer voice. "Janitor has entered the game. Alien to be named later has entered the game."

"KayCee?" I asked, ignoring my cousin. "I was thinking..."

"Yes, Loughlin Ferguson."

"You've been telling me for a year that you're not in my head."

"Correct."

"But you told us to do headshots for the bioforms."

"It's not the same. My energy form is diffused and melded to you throughout your body. Unlike you, the bioforms are mechanisms and the head does in fact store the majority of our energy form. If you shoot the head with a Sarli weapon, enough energy is destroyed to kill the Sarli inhabiting the bioform."

"If you say so." I looked around. "Which way?"

"I am unsure," KayCee said. "As you are aware, I was a protector, not military. I do not know the setup of this starcraft."

"I was asking Tavish."

"Then please disregard my last statement."

"Disregarding." I told her. "Tavish, where are we headed?"

"Wait here for a moment. There is a security patrol passing through the route you need to go. I'll let you know when it's safe to proceed to the control room. Huh!"

"What?" I asked.

"We got lucky. Only about fifty Sarli on board."

"Fifty is a lot when they're shooting at you, Tavish," I reminded him.

"True, but it can man up to five thousand, so.... It could have been worse."

"Yup, very true," I agreed. "KayCee, why is there only another fifty?"

"Kreb's country was defeated in the war, The majority of his people were either killed, captured, or surrendered. Those who continue to fight are not plentiful in number. They also work in small groups to carry out various missions in order to not jeopardize the entire organization."

"You mean they operate in terrorist cells."

"Yes."

"So why make this craft so big?" I asked. "It has to be almost impossible for fifty people to operate it."

"Don't forget the ones on our starcraft," Tavish reminded me. "That being said, this craft can actually be operated by about five people. The majority of duties are done buy artificial stupids."

"What the hell is an artificial stupid?" I was getting antsy. I didn't like waiting.

"Computer programs that don't rise to the level of actual artificial intelligence."

"So that goes back to my original question."

"Why wouldn't Bobbi Sue go to the junior high dance with you?"

"I'm gonna smack you so hard as soon as you're back in your body. Scratch that, I'm going to have Stella smack you."

"Okay, okay. The reason they are so big is tonnage equals weapons and armor. The bigger the craft the more weapons and armor you can have on it."

"There is also the belief that when they strike at the Alliance, their people will rise up and join them," KayCee added. "So, there is space for additional troops."

"Is that a possibility?" I asked.

"Extremely unlikely. Their government had an iron grip on the people and many of their citizens were forced to fight us against their own will. The new government is peaceful and well-liked by its citizens."

"So, they're a bunch of Nazis living down in Brazil deluding themselves about the next Reich?" I asked.

KayCee tilted her head. "I know who the Nazis were, but I am not sure of the Brazil reference."

"Never mind," Tavish told her. "It's not a good analogy anyways. It's more like the Empire Remnants during the Mandalorian. These guys are itching for a comeback, building themselves up and are armed to the teeth."

"Now, that is a reference I understand," KayCee stated.

"Wait, you know Star Wars spinoff shows, but not that real life Nazis hid in Brazil after World War II?" I said.

"I like Grogu," the little alien informed me.

"Time to go," Tavish said before I could reply. "The way is clear now and I'm in most of the systems at this point. There are three in the control room, two in what I guess would best be called engineering, and the rest are in a barracks."

"Can you seal them in?" I asked.

"Yup, I— Crap!" my cousin said as an alert sound echoed through the craft. "That's a red alert."

"Did you set it off?" I asked. "Lock them in now!"

"Locked, but six of them slipped out of the barracks before I could. Counting the security patrols, that's ten on the loose. Everyone else is locked in. And no, I did not set that off. I'm trying to find out what did, but when the alert went off, I got booted from most of the systems."

"Janitor to Knight One," I called over the comm to Brennan.

"Go for Knight One."

"All hell just broke loose over here. Some sort of red alert. Did one of your bad guys get a warning through?"

"How the hell should I know?" Brennan replied, with gunfire in the background. "That's your cousin's department."

"How are you guys doing?"

"We're a little busy over here. Just secure the damn starcraft."

"Roger that," I said.

"Tavish, lead us to the control room," I instructed. KayCee and I followed his directions, which quickly led us to the hall to the control room.

"Tavish Ferguson, are any of the loose guards around?" KayCee asked, as I peered around the corner at the control room door.

"I'm not sure. I went blind in a lot of areas of this craft when the red alert went off." Tavish explained. "Two are trying to pry the barracks doors open. Most of the rest went to the landing bay hangars."

"Most? You don't know where they all are."

"No, but listen, there is some sort of fighter craft in there. A lot of them."

"A lot?" I needed to stop parroting him. I sounded like an idiot. "As in this thing is a carrier?"

"I was going to say Battlestar, but no, I think they are just being stored there. I'm guessing the ones we have locked in the barracks are pilots. I—" Tavish broke off.

"What?" I asked.

"It wasn't Kreb and the others getting a message through. War Master what's-his-name is trying to raise them to warn them."

"Warn them of what?" A feeling of cold dread started rising up my spine.

"Another craft has entered the system and is bearing toward us at a high rate of speed," Tavish told us. "We're going to have visitors."

Chapter 46 –
A Pirating We Will Go

Before I could ask further questions, two energy beams shot down the tunnel. One struck KayCee in the abdomen, or at least where an abdomen should be. Who knows what Sarli call it. The second beam creased the left side of my head. I screamed in pain as my body switched into combat mode.

"Two Volan Supremacy Bioforms armed with Dirgle Mark 5 firearms," Combat-Me told the rest of me. **"Threat level minimal."**

I phased and ran toward them. My mental state in combat mode definitely lacked emotions. I knew KayCee was shot. Maybe she was dying or dead, but my brain registered that simply as losing an asset. The horror of a close friend possibly dying wasn't there. But I knew it would happen after, that the pain and sorrow would come flooding in as soon as I slipped out of combat mode. Not for the first time, a little part of me buried deep in my brain wondered if everything wouldn't be better if I never came out of combat mode. Never have to suffer emotionally at losing anyone ever again. My parents, Tavish, even just breaking up with Jeopardy. All of it just washed away, leaving me as emotionless as Vulcans claim to be.

I phased through the enemy Sarli and whirled around. Turning solid, I slammed the one on the left into the wall before plucking the weapon from the one on the right and shooting them both with it. The energy beams completely destroyed their heads.

I was running back to KayCee before their decapitated bodies fell to the floor. I dropped combat mode as I knelt down, with a feeling of déjà vu. Memories of KayCee being shot by Kreb in an alley back in my hometown.

"KayCee, stay with me."

KayCee stared up at me. "Loughlin Ferguson, I was shot in my lower torso. I have no intention of going anywhere except somewhere to get my bioform repaired."

"I thought you were dead."

"No, but if I had been hit an inch higher up, I would have been in much more dire straits." She grabbed my arm. "Please help me upright."

I pulled her up. The beam hadn't gone right through her like the time Kreb had shot her, but it was leaking a lot of white fluid out of the entry wound. "How bad is it?"

"I will need to find another bioform shortly or we will have to merge again. This bioform will stop functioning soon."

"How long?" I asked as I pulled on my clothes.

"Within the hour is a reasonable estimate."

"Why don't we just merge now? I'm sure there has to be a spare bioform on this mammoth starcraft anyways."

"That would perhaps be for the best," she agreed.

"Hold on," Tavish broke in. "One of you needs to get to engineering while the other takes the bridge."

"Engineering?" I asked. "This thing has a warp core?"

"No, it does not," KayCee said. "That is a fictional device. Tavish Ferguson, are you referring to the main repair station?"

"Is that where you run all the bots that fix everything that goes wrong in this starcraft?" Tavish asked. "I didn't quite know what to call it."

"Damn Trekkie," I muttered.

"Hey, so I'm not up on the nomenclature of this particular alien starcraft. Bite me. I may no longer be connected to the entire internet, but I'm still smarter than you."

"Smart-ass maybe," I fired back at my cousin.

Before Tavish could respond, KayCee asked, "Could you explain why one of us needs to go there while the other tries to take over the control room?"

"Because we're probably going to need to fight off the starcraft headed our way," Tavish explained. "So, it would be nice if everything on this tub was actually working."

"What type of starcraft is it?" I asked.

"It's barely in sensor range," said Tavish. "It's just a blob at this point."

"Can it detect us?"

"If its sensors are more advanced than this craft, maybe," Tavish explained. "But if it's roughly the same then, no. In fact, it probably can't tell that we're a separate starcraft from *Quiet Contemplation*. They probably think we're just really big."

"That buys us a little time," I mused.

I can assist whoever is on the brid—I mean control room," Tavish offered. "But the repairs can only be controlled by the repair stations. It's a completely different system and we don't have time for me to try and take control of it."

I shook my head before I realized Tavish probably couldn't see it unless he was watching us through whatever passed for security cameras. "KayCee's bioform is damaged. I don't want to split up in case it fails completely. She needs to be able to jump into me."

KayCee palmed the wall next to us, steadying herself before standing on her own. "I will be fine."

"That must be Sarli for lying, because you have a big gaping hole in you," I said.

"I have survived worse," the alien reminded me.

"Yeah, by jumping into me. Or did you forget I was there?"

"No, but what other option do we have?" she asked.

"There have to be spare bioforms onboard," I said. "Where would they be kept?"

"I do not know." KayCee shook her head. "I am not familiar with this type of starcraft."

"Tavish? Any idea?"

"Standby," my cousin said. "Huh. Yeah, I found where they keep them, but you're not going to like it."

"The barracks?" I sighed.

"Yup," he confirmed. "Sorry, KayCee."

"There might still be a way," I said. "That's a lot of bad guys, but with the new phasing power..."

"There is not enough time." KayCee started walking down the hall. "And we are wasting it. Do what you need to do, Loughlin Ferguson, and I will do what I have to do."

"Damn it." I pulled at my beard as I watched her go. "Be careful!"

"You as well, Loughlin Ferguson." She rounded a corner and was gone.

I studied the control room door. "Tavish, any special security measures on this thing that may interfere with my phasing through it?"

Even though Tavish's essence was technically in the orb KayCee had, he still had control of the comms and was able to answer me. "You mean like what we did to Rory? Nothing that I can tell."

"Fuck it then." I ran toward it, phasing as I went. My clothes dropped to the floor seconds before I phased through the door.

The control room was designed very different from the one on *Quiet Contemplation*. There were five control stations. Four were arrayed in a semicircle facing the fifth, which was elevated slightly higher than the rest, I assumed the captain's chair. Each station had a single chair that was more like a race car seat with blank screens, blinking lights, and buttons. There was no large screen on a wall like you see in *Star Trek* or windows out into space like you see in *Star Wars*. Three of the stations had Sarli in them: the elevated one and two others. The door I came through was off to the side, so all three saw me as soon as I entered. While the control stations and seats were made from the same chrome-like matériel that was in KayCee's starcraft, the walls were a black material with blood red banners hanging from them, with alien symbols I didn't recognize.

I took all of this in with a glance. I targeted War Master Tigrafrentop in the captain's chair first. I dropped out of phase and into combat mode and licked the metal door, which triggered my body to transform into the same metal. While it was doing that, my left hand formed the shape of a blade, so when I vaulted over Tigrafrentop's control panels, a single swing of my arm decapitated his bioform.

Before his head bounced off the floor, I launched myself at the closest one and stabbed him through the temple. As I pulled my arm back an energy beam struck my chest dead center.

I staggered back. I looked down, expecting to see a large entry hole where my lungs used to be. My metal skin wasn't even scratched, which made sense when I thought about it. After all, what good was a security door to the control room of a warcraft if it couldn't stand up to weapon's fire?

Before the last Sarli had a chance to recover from its surprise and shoot me again, I leaped over and stabbed it through the head. I pulled my hand out, letting it return to normal as I scanned the room for any further threats.

I gasped in surprise as a red energy cloud rose from the decapitated bioform of War Master Tigrafrentop. "Shit. You're not dead! Should have stabbed you through the head instead of just lopping it off. Good to know for next time."

I backpedaled over to one of the corpses, grabbed its ray gun, and fired. I discovered it was effective on Sarli energy forms as well.

With all the enemies taken care of, I recovered my clothes and started dressing. "Tavish, you there?"

"Yeah. I registered some weapons fire. What happened?"

"Nothing I couldn't handle." I moved to the captain's chair and pulled Tigrafrentop's headless bioform out of it. "Where are we?"

"Is there another control orb?"

I spotted one in a hollowed area on the right armrest of the captain's chair. "Yeah, found it."

"Cool. Place my orb next to it. I'm going to jump over to it. It might take a minute."

I did as I was told before keying my comm. "KayCee, how are you doing?"

"I am almost at the repair station, Loughlin Ferguson," she answered. "How are you and your cousin doing?"

"I took the control room and now Tavish is trying to tap in. We are officially pirates."

"Actually, we're authorized by the government," Tavish said. "That makes us privateers. Well, me and KayCee anyways. You actually *are* the government. We'll have to get you a powdered wig and ruffles."

I sighed. "How long until you make it into the systems?"

"I just did."

"Very good, Tavish Ferguson. I will check in shortly." KayCee clicked off the comm.

"Tavish, KayCee could change the size of the seats on her starcraft. Can you do it with the captain's seat? It's a bit small for me."

"Here." The chair shifted and became larger. "Does that work?"

"Perfect." I slid into it and looked over the controls. "Well, I have no idea what I'm doing."

"Let's see..." Tavish sounded distracted. "You are in the war master's chair. From your left to right is the pilot station, the weapons station, navigation, and fighter control."

"So, what do I do next?"

"Nothing, I'll handle the craft's systems including weapons and flight. The fighters are grounded, and KayCee will be running repairs. You just be the talking head." The screens in front of me flickered to life, the Earth on one, and an approaching starcraft on another. It was a speck at this range.

I pocketed the control orb for *Quiet Contemplation* and studied the screen. "Are we in communications range?"

"There will be a lag, but yes. How you want to do this?"

"I was thinking Solo with a dash of Reynolds."

"Fly by the seat of your pants and make shit up as you go along?"

"It's fun and, quite frankly, pretty much what I've been doing for the past year, but I don't think so."

"How about a mix of Picard and Janeway?"

"I don't possess the poise for that."

"True. Sisko or Archer?"

"Do I get to punch Q?"

"What about Burnam?"

"I haven't watched that series yet," I said. "No spoilers. You know it has to be Kirk. I'll need to channel James Tiberius Kirk for this one. The one, the only, and the original."

"That would actually be Christopher Pike."

"I don't have the hair for Pike."

"Fine." He sighed. "Not so shockingly, it's got to be Kirk. You always played Kirk when we were little kids."

"Did you just sigh?"

"Yeah, so what?"

"You don't have a body. How can you sigh? You just did that solely for dramatic effect."

"You should talk. You're the king of sighers."

"No, I'm not!"

"You can't get through a day without sighing. Even that Robb guy said you sighed way too much."

"What Robb guy?"

The one from last year while we were on the run for the government. You know, the people you work for now?"

"What? We met a ton of people while we were on the lam."

"Lam, really?" His voice dripped with judgment. "It was what's-his-name, Robb something. You didn't hear him because you were too busy sighing all the time."

"Whatever. Having to deal with you and Stella all those years, I'm surprised my life isn't pretty much just one big sigh." I caught myself just before I sighed and instead, cleared my throat. "Let's get back on track. I role-play Kirk for this, agreed?"

"Agreed, but don't imitate Shatner," Tavish said. "I can't deal with the dramatic pauses."

"I... understand. I'll try... and keep it...brief..."

"You suck. Recording now."

"Wait, wait. Where am I supposed to be looking?"

"The main monitor."

"I don't see a camera."

"It's part of the monitor. Just look straight at it."

"Make sure none of those banners can be seen behind me." I leaned forward slightly. "Ready."

"Recording," Tavish told me.

"Unidentified starcraft. This is Captain Lock Ferguson of..." My mind flailed for a name for the starcraft. I sure as hell was not going to use *Glorious Reckoning*. "The *USS New Hampshire*. You are in Terran space. Please identify yourself and your intent."

"Okay, got it," Tavish said. "Not bad."

"Thanks." I leaned back in relief. "Can you trim out the pause?"

"No problem," he said. "Already done and sent. But... *USS New Hampshire*?"

"I blanked. I know USS means United States Ship, but I guess it could also stand for United States Starcraft. And why shouldn't this thing be renamed in favor of our home state? We don't have a lot going for us since the Old Man Of the Mountain crumbled."

"Yeah, it's just that there already is a *USS New Hampshire*."

"There is?" I raised my eyebrows. "I didn't know that."

"There's been a couple. The current is a Virginia-class nuclear-powered attack submarine commissioned in 2008."

"Crap! I didn't even know they named submarines. Do you think the Navy will be mad?"

"I'd worry more about Brennan, if I was you."

"Yeah, that's about right. But what the hell was I supposed to say. United States Space Force Starcraft is a bit of a mouthful, isn't it?"

"Lock, they've replied back."

I took a deep breath and let it out. "Play it."

Chapter 47 –
Visitors from Beyond

"Captain Lock Ferguson. Greetings. I am Star Commander SoCuasatine of the Kemtaran Alliance Starcraft *Call to Justice*. We are pursuing war criminals and did not realize we have entered into Dirtan space. In fact, we were unaware you had starcraft capability. We apologize for an offense we may have mistakenly given."

"Pause the message, please," I ordered. The picture froze on the main monitor. I groaned at the cheesy 3D rendering of Tavish that appeared in the monitor next to the main one. "You Max Headroomed yourself?"

"You keep getting nervous whenever I mention anything AI, so I went for this look. Seemed appropriate based on the origin story."

"Whatever. How about we get back to dealing with the alien starcraft currently heading our way?"

"Sure, but can I just say that *Call to Justice* is a badass name for a starcraft?" Tavish grinned at me.

"Yeah, it's a pretty cool name. But let's talk about their message."

"Yeah, about that, why did you have me stop it?"

"Dirtan?" I scowled. "You heard that, right? What the hell was that? Some kind of insult?"

"Earth, dirt, same thing. I'm guessing it's just a translator error."

"I took that into account though. That's why I said Terran."

"And where does Terran come from?" Tavish said in a tone that somehow conveyed I was being an idiot.

"It's the standard sci-fi term for someone from Earth."

"But what's its origin?"

"It's from Terra Firma. Which is Latin for… Crap!"

"Solid earth, or solid ground, or dry land." Tavish said gleefully. "Terra basically means dirt just like earth does."

"Damn it!" I took a breath and let it out. "Okay. Can you play the rest without the translator?"

"Sure, I'm the one who turned it into English. Are you going to be able to understand them?"

"I've got most of the languages from their planet programmed into my head." I tapped my temple. "So, I'll guess we'll see. But play it from the beginning though. Just so, I don't miss anything."

Tavish started it over and I understood it immediately, playing it through to where we had paused it. "We would like to meet with you, to see if you have knowledge of those we pursue. If this is acceptable, please give us the coordinates where you wish us to rendezvous."

I opened our secure link after the message ended. "Janitor to Knight One."

"Go for Knight One," Brennan replied. "I was just going to call you. We managed to take out the majority of those on this craft, but several enemy combatants made it over to your side and blew the connector tube."

"Tavish?" I asked.

"I'm not showin — damn it. They looped the system on me," Tavish snarled. "Yeah, looks like they jettisoned the tube. I can't see them either, so they've blinded the system to their location."

"Shouldn't you be able to prevent that from happening?" I asked, knowing what the answers would be."

"They shouldn't have been able to do that."

"It was Kreb," I stated. "He gave you your abilities. I'm sure he knows ways around them."

"Stella went after them," Brennan informed us. "Knight One to Bar Fight. Call in."

"I followed them over to the wannabe borg ship," Stella replied. "But I lost them once I got here. There's three of them floating around somewhere—"

"We have a launch," Tavish cut in. "Scratch that. We have multiple launches."

"Close the damn hangar," I yelled.

"What do you think I'm trying to do?" he yelled back.

"Knight One," I said over the comm. "Those are armed landers launching. You need to get to *Quiet Contemplation's* control room and get that missile launcher back online."

"Roger that," Brennan replied. "Risk and I are en route now. But remember, this craft was decommissioned. Even with the armament we added, it's still going to be technologically behind a newer warcraft. What's the status on closing the hangar and how many bogies are we looking at?"

"I've regained control of the systems and closed the hangar," Tavish reported. "Ten fighters got out. Wait, they're banking around toward this craft in attack formation. I'm raising shields."

"They're attacking us?" I asked in disbelief. "Don't you mean *Quiet Contemplation*?"

"Nope, they're going for the *USS New Hampshire*," Tavish stated firmly.

"Did you just say the *USS New Hampshire*?" Brennan asked. "I assume you're not talking about the attack sub."

"Um, we needed a name when we contacted the incoming starcraft," I answered sheepishly. "It's all I could think of at the time."

"No problem," the colonel said. "I'm sure the Secretary of the Air Force and the President of the United States won't mind you doing their job for them. Not to mention we already have a *USS New Hampshire*!"

"Guys?" Tavish broke in. "Can we get back to the whole getting attacked thing?"

"Can they even hurt it?" I asked. "This thing is a monster."

"Let's not find out," Brennan said. "Lock, take them out."

"Understood, Colonel," I replied. "Tavish, fire at will. And give Stella directions here."

"Will do," Tavish replied. "Lock, KayCee's repair station is in one of my current blind spots."

"KayCee, do you read that?" I asked over the comm. "KayCee?"

"Stella, head to the repair station, now!" I shouted.

"Roger that," she acknowledged. "Tavish, show me how to get there."

"What about the attack landers?" Tavish asked.

"It's a diversion," I told him. "They want to keep us busy. Nothing is ever straight forward with Kreb. He's up to something. You deal with the landers. Stella and I will head to the repair station."

"If you can, take him out," Brennan told us. "I've got *Armstrong* and *Aldrin* on the way here."

I faced the monitor. "Tavish, record another message, make sure the translator is off."

"Recording now," my cousin said.

I cleared my throat before starting. "Star Commander SoCuasatine, it might be easier if I just speak in your tongue. The translation program mangled some things. My people are referred to as humans, not Dirtans, and our planet is Terra which means *land* in an ancient language of ours.

"Anyways, I believe I know of which criminals you refer to, and we may be of some aid to you in that regard. Please proceed to the coordinates laid out and we will join you there shortly after we take care of some administrative matters." I took a deep breath and exhaled. "Tavish, please send that out."

"Sending now."

I vaulted out of the chair and toward the door. "We're getting attacked and you still had to take the time to bring up the whole dirt thing, didn't you?"

"Tavish."

"Yeah?"

"Shut it!"

Chapter 48 –
Repelling Boarders

I heard the sound of battle as I got closer to the repair station. At this point, the sound of clashing metal and Stella swearing pretty much signified combat. I rounded the corner just in time to see her cleave her ax deep into the skull of her last opponent. As he fell to the ground, Stella placed her foot on his chest and pulled her ax free. Four other bioforms littered the hall. "You okay?"

"Sure." She whirled her ax. "You know the best part of fighting bioforms?"

"What?"

"No blood and gore. I mean, there's the weird milky stuff in the torso, but that's it."

"What about that thing?" I pointed as an angry red blob rose up from the bioform."

Stella wrapped her helmet with her knuckles. "They can't get past my armor if I seal up my face. Not that I had to worry about it. I blasted the others with the ray gun, then this one was able to knock it out of my hand. After that I went medieval on his ass. You might want to watch out for that one though." She pointed to the angry red cloud moving toward me. "He's coming for you."

"Not an issue." I aimed the ray gun and pulled the trigger. No more cloud of red motes.

Stella nodded approvingly. "Nice."

"Thanks." I pointed to the remains of the bioforms. "I thought you said three?"

She shrugged. "They found friends."

"No kidding." I looked at the door to the repair station. "Did they make it inside?"

"I don't think so." She pointed to a device on the floor. Even though it looked alien, with strange glowing tubes, it still somehow managed to scream 'bomb'. "They were trying to blow the door when I found them."

I keyed my comm. "KayCee, come in."

Stella shook her head at me when we got no response. "They may have jammed her comm. You might want to slimer your way in there."

"Slimer?"

"I was going to say 'Casper your way in,' but you're too ugly to be Casper."

"Whatever." I phased, and as usual, my clothes didn't. I stepped through the door into a room full of alien computer banks. KayCee's bioform lay on the floor, her eyes closed. The milky liquid Stella mentioned leaked from KayCee's wound.

I unphased and crouched down next to her. "KayCee!"

"KayCee, are you there?" I shook her slightly, hoping that wouldn't hurt an injured bioform. "C'mon, don't do this to me."

Her eyelids opened, revealing the usual black orbs. "Loughlin Ferguson. You should not be here."

"Shut up and merge with me."

"Thank you." Her eyes closed and golden motes of energy emerged from the bioform, floating over and through my skin. Her thoughts entered my head.

"Ah, that is much better, Loughlin Ferguson. Thank you."

"What happened?"

"The damage to my bioform was greater than I thought, and I misjudged how much time I had before it would fail. I made it to the repair station, but the bioform failed shortly after I got here. I had to shut down almost all the systems in order to survive."

"Don't do that again, please." I stood up and keyed the door open. "I thought you were dead."

As the door slid open, Stella threw my clothes at me. "Cover up. I don't need to see your pasty ass. How's KayCee?"

"She's back in my head. Her bioform failed."

"She okay?"

"Perfectly fine now," KayCee said over the comm. "Thank you, Stella Johansen."

"Good." Stella looked around. "So where is Kreb?"

"Is he on the starcraft?" asked KayCee.

"Yeah, we thought he came here, but it looks like he sent some goons." I opened up the comm. "Tavish, we have KayCee, but there is no sign of Kreb. Is he headed to the control room?"

"Not that I can tell, but he could be messing with my systems."

"How did he get on board?" asked KayCee.

I quickly got the little alien up to date. "So, we need to get back to the control room."

"I do not think that is where he went. He would assume that it would be guarded."

"Sure," Stella said. "But where else would he go? He tried the barracks and the repair station. What's left?"

"He knows we took the starcraft," I said. "You know he's going to want it back. So, how does he do it?"

"There should be a secondary control room," KayCee told us.

"Sorry, what?" Stella sputtered.

"Most warcraft's have a secondary control room in case the first one is destroyed during battle. Do your people do not do this?"

Stella shrugged and muttered, "How would I know? I was Army."

I stared up at the ceiling, whether it was as a plea to God or an unconscious act because I was about to speak to Tavish, I didn't know. "Tavish, is there a secondary control room?"

"Not that I'm aware of."

"It should have one," KayCee disagreed. "It may be shielded from you, Tavish Ferguson."

"Well, I don't... Hold on a sec," Tavish said. "There's a blank spot the system keeps hiding from me. It's roughly the same size as the control room."

We followed his directions through the maze of a battlecraft. After several minutes, Stella keyed her comm. "Tavish, how are we doing with the assault landers?"

"I destroyed them all. This starcraft is a monster. There was some superficial damage to us but nothing serious. Which is good, because I can't access the repair programs. That was the whole point of sending KayCee to the repair station. Not to mention that's the only place that can lock Kreb completely out of the systems."

We entered a large room and skidded to a halt at all the bioforms waiting for us. Stella gave a snarl. "Hey, Tavish, I think the ones in the barracks got out."

"You're going to have to handle them," he said. "The large door at the end of the room leads to the area we think is the control room."

"Of course, it does,." she complained. "Any other great news you want to tell me?"

I didn't hear his reply as energy beams sizzled around us. We ducked around the corner. Stella gave me a crooked smile. "We're so fucked right now."

"Maybe, maybe not," I told her.

"Lock, there's close to fifty of them. I'm all for a good fight, but that's just asking for trouble."

"Yeah, but KayCee's back in my head now. And we work *so* much better together."

"Yeah?"

"KayCee, you've been roaming around my head for a while now, getting familiar with my new skills?" The little alien in my head replied.

"I have, Loughlin Fergusson."

"And?"

"There is a lot you've been missing. Unless, of course, you've been losing your clothes on purpose."

I blinked in surprise, ignoring the energy beams still being fired at us. "You know how to keep my clothes on when I phase?"

"Yes."

"That's great. But I'm talking about my ability to absorb energy. That should work for the beams from the ray guns, right?"

"Yes. There is no reason you should not be able to absorb them."

"Excellent. Think we can take them?"

"With the right theme music, yes."

"You hear that, Tavish?" Stella smiled. "Give us some tunes to kick ass by."

As I slipped into combat mode, my cousin's announcer voice came through the craft's audio system. "Janitor has entered the Game, Barfight has entered the Game."

A song mentioning machine guns that were ready to go blared through the air. I grinned like a madman. "KayCee, start absorbing those energy beams."

"I will, Loughlin Ferguson."

"Stella, stay behind me. We're moving in quick. I have lead and you have sweep up. Anyone we close in on is yours."

Stella whirled her ax. "Sounds good."

Once again, we rounded the corner. Stella hunched down behind me as energy beam after energy beam struck me. KayCee made sure I absorbed each of them. As I ran toward them, I flung the energy back at them. Some were able to duck. Those that didn't were torn apart by the energy I tossed at them like thunderbolts hurled from an angry Zeus. The ones I missed didn't survive much longer, as Stella whooped and hollered, her ax swinging back and forth. It was glorious and magnificent and a harsh warning not to fuck with humanity. And it lasted less than a couple of minutes.

One of them slung their rifle and threw an alien version of a concussion grenade over my head. Stella swung her ax at it, ready to knock it into the bleachers but it detonated just as she connected. Unprepared for it, the blast threw me forward onto my hands and knees.

With me temporarily out of the way, Stella became their target. Her armor was tough, the metal the Sarli used to protect their starcraft. But the enemy troops fired weapons of war at us. Weapons that had also been made by the Sarli. After so many hits in rapid succession, Stella's armor started to fail before I could get to my feet. Several of the shots pierced her armor and she fell with a grunt and a swear.

I screamed her name and things went red.

Chapter 49 –
Reckoning

"Loughlin Fergusson."
"Loughlin Fergusson."
"Lock. You need to focus."
"Wha...?" I shook my head. "What? Did you, KayCee, did you just call me Lock?"

I blinked and looked around. I was kneeling on the floor. No troops remained, but parts of bioforms littered the room. Some were half merged into the walls. "What happened?"

"You need to help Stella Johansen."

Everything came flooding back to me. Stella's body lay a few feet away. I scrambled over to her. Blood poured from gaping holes in her armor, her helmet had shifted back to reveal her face which was deathly pale.

I tried for a pulse but couldn't feel one through the armor. "KayCee, is she alive?"

"I do not know. You went into some sort of berserk state. I was not able to communicate with you or even access your abilities. I could not even leave your body. You had me completely trapped."

"Can you shift her armor back, so I can check her pulse?"

"No. Only Stella Johansen can control it now. I had to sever the link to the control orb when I made it for her, otherwise, anyone with an orb could have removed it from her."

"Can I teleport with her?"

"I do not know if you can take another person with you when you teleport. It might kill her."

"You need to enter her. Check her vitals. Stop the bleeding!"

"You know I cannot do that without permission."

"You don't think she'd give it? You know she would."

"That's not the same. That's not how my people do it."

"Fuck your people. She's human, an American. In our country, if a person is unconscious and can't expressly grant consent for medical aid, it's assumed the person has given implied consent to be treated medically. That's what this is. You'd be medically treating her."

"Loughlin Ferguson – "

"Do not let her die, KayCee!"

"I believe there might be a better way. You need to partially phase her."

"What? I can't phase anything other than myself."

"Not true, as I told you, there is a way to keep your clothes on by phasing them with you. Also, you managed to phase several of the enemy bioforms while you were fighting them. Look at the walls."

Sure enough, several of them had been combined with the walls. "Jesus!" I hadn't registered that when I first looked around.

"If you partially phase her, I believe she will be in a form of stasis. This should preserve her until you can get her to a medical pod."

I activated my comm as it was happening. "Tavish! Stella's down. Where's the med bay?"

"I've been listening," he said. "If you phase, the closest is two floors down and a short run down the hall."

I lifted Stella into my arms. "KayCee, phase us."

As soon as she did, we dropped two floors with Stella still in my arms and my clothes remaining on my back. KayCee did something and Stella suddenly got blurry, like what Rory did to her private areas when she was naked. "What was that?"

"She is partially phased. Caught between two forms of existence. Everything has slowed for her, including bleeding. But you need to move."

Not wasting any further time, I sprinted to the med bay at superspeed and laid Stella into the pod. "What about her armor? Will the pod be able to heal her while she has it on?"

"No. But I think I came up with a solution as you ran down here. This will be more complicated. We need to phase her armor but not her. I have to warn you, Loughlin Ferguson, I am not sure this will work."

"What do I need to do?"

"Lay your hands on the armor, I will do the rest."

I did as I was told and KayCee placed us into phase. The armor came with us.

"Now what?"

"*Pull it up and away from Stella Johansen. You need to remove it completely from her.*"

I grasped her breastplate and pulled. Everything but her helmet came off. I tossed the armor to the side. As soon as I let go of it, it unphased. Her wounds had chucks of meat and flesh missing. What was left was seared, scorched, or bleeding. I felt like my chest was going to burst and I couldn't breathe, the edges of my vision started going black. Suddenly everything snapped back. "KayCee. What just happened?"

"*You were going into a panic attack. I dialed your emotional levels down enough for you to be able to cope with the situation.*"

I nodded, feeling somewhat detached. Looking down at Stella, I no longer felt like I was going to vomit and pass out at the same time. I reached down and repeated the trick with Stella's helmet.

I closed up the pod, snorting as I realized something.

"What?"

"Nothing. Just... leave it to Stella to go commando during an actual commando raid."

"Sorry?"

"Don't worry about it." The lid slid shut with a sharp hiss and the lights on top started blinking rapidly. "Tavish?"

"There is a pulse and she's breathing on her own," Tavish said. "I'm not sure how. She has massive injuries."

"How good is this thing? Can it completely heal her?" Last time was only one shot. This time she was shredded with enemy fire. She looked worse than Anakin after his duel with Kenobi.

"*Flesh, bone, organs. These are things the medical pod can fix. It's her head injuries that we have to be concerned about.*"

"Brains are a little more complicated," Tavish added with a bitter tone.

I stopped. "What does that mean?"

"Nothing. Just complaining about what got me here," Tavish said. "I know you don't want to hear this right now, and please understand that I'm just as worried about Stella as you are, but you need to get moving. We need to take out Kreb and his bad guys before it's too late."

"Is Stella going to be all right here?" I asked.

"*Kreb and possibly a few stragglers should be all that is left. If we keep pressing them, they should not have any reason to come down here.*"

"Besides," Tavish added, "I'm going to seal the med bay after you leave. No one is getting in there without blowing a hole in this side of the starcraft first."

"That's the best we can do, I guess."

"Loughlin Ferguson. Now that you have had time to process Stella Johansen's injuries in a calm, logical manner, I am going to restore your normal emotional levels. It is not good to be this way too long."

"That makes sense. Do it." The flood of emotions staggered me for a moment, but knowing Stella was getting better medical care than anything on Earth allowed me some hope.

"Guys, you should hurry," Tavish said. "Kreb and his pals must be in the secondary control room, because they keep trying to override me and fire up the engines."

"Fine. Let's end this." Kaycee and I backtracked until we got to the area where Stella got hurt. I eyed the entrance. "Tavish, what can you tell me about that door?"

"Well, there is some type of energy reading around the door. He's definitely done something to it."

"How much you want to bet he's got an antiphasing field around that door?" I asked.

"That is not a wager I am prepared to make."

"Yeah, kind of figured that."

"Wait. Just the door?" I asked. "That doesn't sound like Kreb. Why wouldn't he do that to the entire room?"

"I don't know what to tell you," my cousin said. "The energy readings are just around the entranceway."

"He may not have the equipment for the whole room."

"Bullshit, that's a trap." I said. "He has to know we'd pick up on the energy signature. He wants me to phase through a wall or the floor and then he's going to zap me halfway through."

"That does sound like something he would do."

"Tavish, is that door airtight?"

"On a starcraft?" Tavish gave a sharp laugh. "Is there a door on this thing that isn't?"

I looked around. "What about an airshaft?"

"You going to John McClane it? Sorry, Lock. They're too small and currently sealed off."

"Well." I sighed. "I guess we try it Calvin's way."

"I would remind you that you cannot teleport where you have not been."

"According to Calvin, I can, if I've seen a picture of it."

"Which we do not have for you to view."

I ran my hand across the door. The metal was cold to touch. "Then we knock it down with the energy release by 'porting right in front of it."

"Did you say 'porting?"

"Saves time. Teleporting is such a long word. What about my plan, think it would work?"

"Possibly. The problem is wherever you teleport to before teleporting back will also suffer from a release of energy and you could damage the craft."

"I have a way around that." I gave a mirthless grin. "You forget, I'm a lot faster than Calvin."

"Accelerated speed. That might work."

"Let's find out." I *moved*, zipping down the hall at a speed no human could ever hope to match. Once I was far enough away, I 'ported. It was a weird feeling, like my entire universe stretched, then everything snapped back. I was in front of the door as concussive energy exploded out around me.

"Interesting."

"Did it work?" asked Tavish.

I studied the door. It still stood, but there was noticeable damage to it. The rest of the room was in worse shape. "It's a beginning."

It took me six more tries before the door was blown off its hinges. "That did it."

"Be careful."

Feeling winded, I stepped in a room similar to the main control room, except this one had odd devices on the walls, floor, and ceiling, as well as the door. The devices were linked with the weird tubing that the Sarli used instead of wires. "See. Told you it was a trap."

"I did not disagree."

Kreb was in the captain's seat. The Detra Ka body he inhabited was armored in the same metal that Stella used. "Crap. He stole a page from our book."

Kreb rose from the chair. Each of his four arms unsheathing swords made of the same metal as the armor. "Coming here was a mistake, human."

"Loughlin Ferguson. Based on the metal those blades are made from, they are capable of cutting your skin."

"Yeah, I kinda assumed that." I fired another energy beam, but Kreb deflected it with a blade. "Okay, the guy's an asshole, but I gotta give him credit. That was a cool move."

I shut my mouth and concentrated on the fight. Armed with four swords and a barbed tail, Kreb quickly had me on the defensive. Needing to create space I *moved*, my enhanced speed getting me to the other side of the room, only to find Kreb was right there with me, pressing the attack. He got me with two slashes before I phased.

"Okay, I need a breather. When did you get so fas— Arrgh!" Kreb's barbed tail punched through my shoulder. While it didn't physically wound me, it did somehow disrupt my phasing, causing an unbelievable amount of pain. "Crap, you modified yourself too, didn't you?"

As soon as he retracted the barb, I unphased and rolled away from him. "I have to admit, that hurt. You don't mind if I hurt you back, do you?"

Kreb didn't answer, instead he slithered toward me faster than I could respond, wrapping around me with his coils and pinning my arms by my sides. He was long enough that his head and torso still loomed in front of me. I tried to free myself from his coils. "Um, I'm not really a hugger."

Still quiet, he swung a sword aimed at decapitating me. Using all my strength, I managed to lurch to the side, causing him to connect with his own tail. Unfortunately for me, it connected with the armored side resulting in nothing more than some dramatic sparks. "You're awfully quiet. Normally you'd be boasting about how smart you are, and I'll rue the day or something like that."

"This is the time for action, not words." The coils tightened even more, and another sword swung at my neck. I phased at the last second and as the sword went through me, I also found myself free from the coils.

"Loughlin Ferguson, how did you know the phase disruption was localized to the barb?"

"I didn't." I grunted and grabbed Kreb's sword as it swung past. "Little help?"

Sensing what I wanted, KayCee used my abilities to place the sword into phase and I plunged it into his skull and let go. As soon as I did, it solidified and Kreb's entire head burst apart like a melon, splattering everything in the room but me.

Chapter 50 –
Finders Keepers

"Loughlin Ferguson. You have done it. The war criminal is finally dead!"

"Yeah, I... Nothing, never mind." I collected my clothes which managed to avoid getting splattered and got dressed outside of the room.

"Are you all right?"

"It's just... hard to process." I tied my shoes. "Tavish, how are we looking?"

"Good job on Kreb. But you still need to shut that control room down so I can have full command of the systems."

"You mean I have to go back in there?" I looked at the blood-covered room. "You suck, you know that?"

"Sorry."

"How's Stella doing?"

"Vitals are good. She's going to be pissed she missed the final boss fight!"

"Yeah." I cheated and phased my way back to the control room. KayCee walked me through shutting the panel down and then I pulled out what passed as wires.

I made my way back to the main control room and flopped down in the captain's chair with a sigh. "Tavish, what's our status?"

"I stopped to allow *Quiet Contemplation* and the *Aldrin* to catch up with us."

One of my screens blinked on, showing the two starcraft edging toward us. "ETA?"

"Five minutes," Tavish answered.

"Can you get them on the phone?"

"Actually, I have them on hold." A Hispanic woman wearing a flight suit appeared on one of my screens. "Janitor, This is Major Willa Chavez of the *Aldrin*. What's your status?"

"Major, I have command of the starcraft. Approximately fifty or more enemy dead. Sergeant Johansen sustained serious wounds and is in a med pod, and we have one combatant sedated."

The major raised her eyebrows. "You and the sergeant did all that?"

Another screen blinked on with Brennan taking up most of the picture. "There are four of them on board, Major. Do not discount the contributions of Protector KayserCeenarlos and Tavish Ferguson."

"Yes, Colonel," she replied.

"Where is the *Armstrong*?" I asked.

"I made the decision to keep *Armstrong* closer to Earth, just in case," Brennan explained. "How well can you fly that thing?"

"Well enough, sir."

"Then I think all three of our starcraft will go meet our new guests and show them a warm welcome. But Willa…"

"Colonel?"

"You're in my seat and I want it back."

"Sir?"

I'm coming over and taking command. If I'm going to meet the representatives of an alien civilization, I'm doing it on the *Aldrin*."

"Understood." She sighed. "It was fun while it lasted."

"Don't look so glum. I'm giving you *Quiet Contemplation* instead. Take the secondary command crew over in an orbital, and I'll zip over there in Knight One," he instructed.

"What about Risk?" I asked.

Brennan eyed me before answering. "She'll stay here. She's familiar with *Quiet Contemplation* and can be more of an asset for Major Chavez."

"If there is nothing further, I'll get started," Chavez stated.

"That's all, Major." Brennan waited for her to sign off. "How's Stella?"

"We almost lost her. She's in a med pod."

"Kreb?"

"I spattered his brains all over the room," I said grimly.

"He didn't leave the body in his energy form?" Brennan asked.

"I phased a sword through his head. He didn't have a chance."

"I can confirm that, Colonel Brennan," KayCee chimed in through the comm system.

"Outstanding work. All of you. That was a crazy plan, and you pulled it off. Kreb's dead, and we have a new addition to our collection of starcraft. The next round's on me."

"Don't let Stella hear that," Tavish chuckled.

"Are you having someone come over here and take command?" I asked Brennan.

"I'd like to, but we took off in such a hurry, I don't have anyone with the necessary experience," Brennan said.

"Wait," Tavish said. "We have an incoming transmission from *Call to Justice*. It's in real time."

"Lock, you handle it," Brennan ordered. "I'm heading over to the *Aldrin*. Try not to get us in a galactic war in the next ten minutes."

"Roger that." I sighed. "Tavish, put them on please."

Brennan was replaced by Star Commander SoCuasatine. "Captain Ferguson."

"Star Commander SoCuasatine, sorry for the delay. We will be heading toward your location momentarily."

"Captain, there appears to be two other crafts with you."

"Yes, there is. Due to your unexpected appearance in our territories, my supervisor thought it best that they accompany me to meet with you."

"Captain Ferguson, one of them appears to be the Alliance craft *Quiet Contemplation* and another is the very starcraft we've been hunting."

"You are not incorrect, Star Commander. Protector KayserCeenarlos and I fought the war criminal Krebdanturnvat, who I believe is also called Kreb the Incorrigible by your people."

"Kreb? You fought Kreb?"

"Yes. During the engagement, the Protector was forced to send *Quiet Contemplation* away to prevent Kreb from taking control. My people recovered it and now it's ours. We haven't got around to officially renaming it yet. But I think *USS Ferguson* has a nice ring to it."

"*I did not agree to your government taking over my starcraft.*"

"By what right do you think you can just take one of our starcraft?" sputtered the star commander.

"Finders, keepers?"

"Are you... Are you referring to the law of salvage?"

"*Say yes.*"

"Yes..."

SoCuasatine shifted in their seat. "We will have to investigate your claim further to see if there is merit. However, first I need an explanation as to why you are transmitting from *Glorious Reckoning*. A starcraft built and manned by escaped war criminals."

The transmission paused as Tavish spoke one name. "Kirk!"

I smiled as it resumed. "Star Commander, I am happy to answer your questions, but understand it's as a courtesy. I remind you: it is you who have intruded onto my people's territory uninvited. War Master Tigrafrentop did the same a short while ago and now he is dead, and my people have a new Battlestar called the *USS New Hampshire*. Though thinking back on it, the *USS Rubik* would be more fitting due to its shape."

"Battlestar? I am not familiar with that term."

"Too bad, great series. Though the ending on the reboot was meh."

"You are claiming to have killed Tigrafrentop the Terror and taken over *Glorious Reckoning*?"

"And most of his crew, yeah." I leaned back into my seat with a slight smirk. "Is now a bad time to talk about a reward? I was told there was one for Kreb."

"With just two starcraft? One an obsolete refueler and the other built by your people?"

"No, of course not."

Tension eased out of the shoulders of the alien on the screen. "I should expect not."

"My crew and I just used *Quiet Contemplation*."

"And defeated the most advanced warcraft ever produced by the Sarli? I do not think so."

"No." I shook my head. "We just hitched a ride on *Quiet Contemplation* to get there. And let me tell you, it was not very glorious."

"I don't understand."

"Me and three friends climbed into Tigrafrentop's warcraft and proceeded to fight them in hand-to-hand combat until they were all dead. I got the immense pleasure to pop Kreb's head like a water balloon."

The star commander's head snapped back in revulsion. "What *are* you people?"

The screen muted as Tavish's voice came out of the system. "I said be Captain Kirk, not Hannibal Lecter. What the hell is wrong with you? Brennan specifically said not to start a war."

"Unmute me," I ordered. Once it was done, I smiled into the screen. "Kreb committed atrocities on my world for decades before he was discovered. I will not apologize for doing what your people could not. I will tell you that humans are loyal to our friends and unrelenting to our enemies. Kreb and Tigrafrentop decided to be our enemies and were dealt with accordingly. Tell me, Star Commander SoCuasatine, do you plan on being our enemy?"

"No, Captain Ferguson. My mission was to capture Tigrafrentop and his fellow criminals," The Sarli Star Commander told me in a firm and unafraid voice.

"Then we shall meet and hopefully become good friends. I know Protector KayserCeenarlos is very much looking forward to reuniting with her people."

"The Protector is alive?"

"Alive and one of my good friends. She has been a great help and a credit to your people."

The screen froze, and Tavish made a hissing sound. "You did not just say that."

Even as the words left my mouth, I was cringing inside. I bobbed my head in embarrassment. "But, I mean, they're aliens. It's not the same context. It's not a skin color thing, they're a different species."

"Keep digging that hole, Mister middle-aged white guy."

"Oh God! Just don't tell anyone, okay. You know I didn't mean it like that."

"This is an official first contact between us and an alien race. The recording of this conversation is going to be historic and played for centuries. Generations of people of color are going to hear you say that."

"Recording?" All the bluff and bravado I had been doing leaked out of me like air from a balloon.

> *"I do not understand why you both are concerned about that phrase. I would be more worried about how you are portraying humans as bloodthirsty barbarians."*

"Thanks, KayCee. That definitely makes me feel better," I muttered and waved at the screen. "Put it back on."

The screen unfroze and the star commander tilted their head. "Captain, I would like to see Protector KayserCeenarlos."

"You will. We will be enroute to you momentarily."

"I mean now, on the screen."

I shifted uncomfortably. "Her bioform was damaged. KayCee is fine but is unable to come to the control room at this moment."

"Oh, no."

"You call her KayCee?"

"It's a nickname. KayserCeenarlos is a bit of a mouthful for my people."

The star commander frowned. "Very well. We await your arrival."

"Excellent. Ferguson out." I slumped in my seat after Tavish cut the feed. "Well, that was a disaster."

"It could have been worse," Tavish said. "But why did the commander seem upset about KayCee's nickname?"

"Yeah, that was weird."

"Tavish Ferguson. In my culture, abbreviating one's name is only done as a grave insult or by that of the closest of relationships."

"What?" I yelled. "Why did you tell us to call you KayCee?"

"At the time I was trying to gain your trust. And as you said, it is a bit cumbersome for your people to keep saying. It is not as if you knew our custom or meant any offense."

"Brennan's calling," Tavish said before I could say more. "He's calling from the *Aldrin*."

"Go ahead." I sighed.

"Captain Ferguson," the colonel said as he appeared on the screen. "Ready to go?"

"Yes, sir. But I think the star commander is a bit suspicious of us."

"That's understandable. It's first contact. Hell, I'm suspicious of them."

"If you say so." I shrugged. "Ready when you are."

"Then let's go. Oh, and Lock?"

"Yes, sir?"

"Choose your words more carefully in the future. Credit to your people? I know you're from the town of White People, New Hampshire, but I expect better." He signed off.

"Hey, we had an Indian mayor," protested Tavish a little too late. "I mean it was me, but still, he shouldn't blame your stupidity on the whole town. Besides, who's he to talk? He's from Massachusetts. They had forced busing for crying out loud."

"I hate my life."

Chapter 51 –
Contact

We neared the alien starcraft in a V formation. We were out front with the *Aldrin* behind us on our left and *Quiet Contemplation* behind us on our right. It wasn't like on TV, the distance between the starcraft was ridiculously far. I nervously leaned forward. "This should be interesting."

"Lock!" Tavish barked. "I just detected a tight beam transmission from the *Quiet Contemplation* to *Call to Justice*."

"What did it say?" I asked.

"You understand the concept of a tight beam, right?"

"Shut up. KayserCeenarlos, any idea?"

> "No and do not call me that. KayCee has been your name for me for a year now. Do not be concerned for the social norms of my people."

"Tavish, connect us with the colonel. I –" An explosion rocked the craft. "Tavish, what was that?"

"*Call to Justice* just fired on us," he explained. "Their range is much farther than we thought. We didn't have our shields up and they punched through our armor like it was tissue paper. Engines and weapons are both offline."

"Shields up!" I ordered.

"I did that ten seconds ago. Oh shit! *Quiet Contemplation* just hit *Aldrin* broadside with everything she had. *Aldrin* had shields up but has taken damage. Unknown how bad."

"Fuck! Raise *Call to Justice*!"

SoCuasatine appeared on one of my screens. The other screens each showed one of the other starcraft. "Star Commander, what is the meaning of this?"

"Your deception is over, Kreb. I -had my suspicions but didn't want to act until confirmation. Surrender now or be destroyed."

"Lock, a lander just launched from *Quiet Contemplation*," Tavish yelled.

I ignored him. "What confirmation are you talking about, Star Commander?"

"Protector KayserCeenarlos has escaped your capture and warned us before your ambush."

"Sorry, I did what?"

"Stand by, Star Commander," I said. "Tavish."

"We're muted."

"Kreb!" I growled. "It's him. I knew there was something off back in the secondary control room. He never calls me human. It's always Number 12 or Weapon System Number 12. Plus, he was suddenly a very skilled fighter, not to mention Kreb talks way more than that. He switched bodies with someone."

"Someone who is now on Quiet Contemplation."

"Shit! Jeopardy and my body are over there." Tavish moaned.

"Unmute us," I ordered. "Star Commander, you are being fooled. Let me guess, that lander supposedly has Protector KayserCeenarlos in it?"

"If you fire on it, we will obliterate you," SoCuasatine warned.

"You might find that harder than you think now that our shields up," I argued. "You need to listen. That's not Protector KayserCeenarlos in that lander. It has to be Kreb."

"You said you killed Kreb."

"I thought I had, but he's been known to fake his death before. Do not let that lander on to *Call to Justice*. I guarantee you he has some devious plan to take your starcraft."

"If that is not Protector KayserCeenarlos, then where is she?"

"Kreb destroyed her bioform, she had to take refuge inside me. That's where she is now, in my head."

"That is not how that works!"

"Geez, KayserCeenarlos keeps saying the same thing. Look, it's an expression among my people. It's not meant to be a literal description."

The star commander's head tilted. "I must admit. I do not see Kreb adapting to your people's way of speaking quite that well."

"That's a start. Hold off letting the lander...er, land, and let's talk this out."

"No, but I will take custody of whoever is inside the lander until I can find the truth of the matter."

I ran my fingers through my beard. "I don't like it, but I'll accept it."

"Lock, *Aldrin* is transmitting to both starcraft."

"Put it on."

Brennan appeared on a screen. "*Call to Justice,* this is Colonel Liam Brennan of the *USS Buzz Aldrin*. We were monitoring your current transmission, but our ability to transmit was down until now. Captain Ferguson is telling you the truth. I strongly suggest you do not allow that lander on your starcraft."

"Colonel, I do not know you or your people. I regret—"

I didn't hear the rest of the star commander's sentence as the transmission muted.

"Tavish?"

"We're receiving a tight beam transmission from *Quiet Contemplation,* Tavish said. "I'm putting it on now."

The screen showing *Quiet Contemplation* switched to Jeopardy. She had a nasty scalp wound. "Lock!"

"Oh my God, are you okay?"

"We missed some of the mind-controlled hybrids. Two of them were part of Major Chavez's team. Kreb was hiding on *Quiet Contemplation* in a bioform. The three of them caught us completely by surprise and killed Chavez and the rest of the crew. I was able to destroy the two hybrids but had to flee."

"Hunker down, we'll get you out," I told her.

"I'm not done. Kreb pretended to be KayCee and sent a message to the other starcraft claiming you were going to ambush them."

"We know."

"He then loaded some equipment on Chavez's lander and sent it toward *Call to Justice.*"

My blood ran cold. "He's not on the lander."

She shook her head and winced, a hand going up to her wound. "No, he's still on *Quiet Contemplation.*"

"Tavish keep her on the line and open it up to the others!"

"Done. But—"

I cut him off. "Star Commander, the lander's a bomb, don't let it on."

The image of SoCuasatine suddenly froze.

"Tavish?"

"I was trying to tell you. The lander has gone into their landing bay. I just registered an explosion there. Their shields and engines are down."

"*What about life support or weapons?*"

"I don't know," Tavish told her.

The image of SoCuasatine unfroze. "It appears I should have believed you. The lander has exploded, damaging my starcraft. But before it did so, it transmitted some sort of virus that crashed our systems."

"What's the status of your life support?" asked Brennan.

"It's completely failed," SoCuasatine replied. "Aside from communications, nothing else is working."

"How much air do you have left? And how many people do you have on board?" Brennan asked. "We can begin evacuating your people immediately."

"Colonel Liam Brennan, you misunderstand. We are all in bioforms. We do not need air to breathe. Just to speak and aid in the artificial gravity."

"Right. I should have remembered that."

"Colonel," I broke in. "We just spoke with Jeopardy. Kreb killed everybody but her, and is both on *and* in control, of *Quiet Contemplation*."

"Lock all your weapons on *Quiet Contemplation*," Brennan told me.

"Jeopardy is still on there," I argued. "So is Tavish's body."

"Do it, Lock," Jeopardy said softly.

"Tavish," I choked out. "I..."

"Doing it now," Tavish said. "*Quiet Contemplation* is firing up its engines."

I knew it was the correct thing to do, the tactical thing to do. But the idea of aiming *New Hampshire's* vast arsenal at *Quiet Contemplation* while it contained Jeopardy and Tavish broke my heart.

"Lock," Tavish yelled. "*Quiet Contemplation* is headed toward *Call to Justice* at full speed. Kreb's planning to ram her!"

"Lock!" barked Brennan.

"Tavish." I closed my eyes. "Fire all weapons."

Chapter 52 –
Bad Ideas

"Weapons are failing to fire," Tavish shrieked. "I'm locked out. There's a damn virus in the weapons system. It was dormant until we targeted weapons."

I snapped my eyes open. "Override it!"

"What do you think I'm trying to do?"

"Intercept that craft!" Brennan ordered his pilot. "Put us between *Quiet Contemplation* and *Call to Justice*."

"Colonel, they'll punch right through you," I told him.

"Don't underestimate *Aldrin*. In the meantime, unfuck yourself." His screen went blank.

"Did he mean you, or all of us?" Tavish asked. "Because I'm not having any luck with this virus. I also have to tell you that they aren't going to make it. At the speed *Quiet Contemplation* is going, Aldrin won't have enough time to get in between them and *Call to Justice*."

I stared at the screen showing *Quiet Contemplation*. "Jeopardy, can you get to the engine room and find a way to shut the power off, kill the thrusters?"

> "Loughlin Ferguson. That is not how space works. Even if you destroy the engine, the craft will maintain the same velocity."

"Yeah, KayCee. I've read enough sci-fi to know that."

"I'm already in the engine room." Jeopardy bit her lip. "But I don't know how to shut it down. KayCee, if I start crunching some of the machines in this room, am I going to blow myself up?"

KayCee projected her voice over the transmitter. "Destroying the tallest bank in the room should trigger safety protocols and shut down power to the engines. It will not blow you up, but I would not stand too close to it."

Jeopardy looked to her right and made a grasping gesture. The sound of rending metal came across the transmission. "That's about as destroyed as I can get it. It looks like a crushed soda can."

"Thrusters on *Quiet Contemplation* just stopped," Tavish told us. "However, velocity hasn't changed."

"Jeopardy, stay where you are. I'll contact you in a few minutes." I manually clicked off her screen, jumped out of the chair and walked over to the security door. I licked it.

"Dude, that's gross," Tavish said as my body transformed into the same type of metal.

"You have the bridge, Tavish."

"I thought we weren't calling it that. Wait, where are you going?"

"I'm taking a little trip."

> "Loughlin Ferguson. I know what you are thinking, but it is too far away, and if we did make it there, the energy buildup would be too great. If you try to teleport into Quiet Contemplation, you will tear a hole in the starcraft."

"That's not quite the plan." A year ago, Kreb had managed to trap me outside of *Quiet Contemplation,* forcing me to crawl along its hull until I could get back in. While I was out there, I had gotten a really good look at the entire length of the starcraft, all the way from the tip to the tail. "I'm not going to 'port inside the starcraft. I'm 'porting in front of it. I'm hoping the explosive energy discharge from a 'port that far will be enough to slow or stop *Quiet Contemplation,* preventing it from reaching *Call to Justice.*"

> "Loughlin Ferguson, that is suicide. We know very little about this power. We do not know if there is a limit to your range or the level of energy you will discharge after teleporting from that distance."

"Hopefully, a lot. Do you have a better idea?"

> "I do not. Proceed and may the stars guide us."

I took a deep breath and teleported.

Since Kreb reentered my life, I've traveled a road of pain and misery. Yet, none of it had prepared me to feel the pain I felt teleporting to *Quiet Contemplation*. I was stretched and twisted, and my skin seemed on fire and my organs smashed. My brain felt as if it was being electrocuted. It seemed to last a thousand years. In reality, it lasted about a second.

I appeared on the front end of *Quiet Contemplation*. The explosive energy that radiated out from my teleport crumpled its nose, but didn't stop the starcraft's forward motion. I slid along the side of it trying to grab something before I bounced away. My fingers gripped the side of a hatch, and I held on for dear life.

> "I am happy to report we are not dead, but it appears the starcraft was not stopped by the energy release. It is still headed

directly for Call For Justice."

"You know we see out the same eyes, right?" I subvocalized to KayCee. "Do you think it was enough to slow it down?" I felt sluggish. Not just my body, but my thoughts as well. The teleportation had taken a lot out of me.

"I do not know. I can tell you our energy levels are dangerously low."

"So's my oxygen level. Do we have enough juice to phase?"

"Barely."

"Well then we should— Jesus!" The nose of the *Aldrin* appeared in front of us, the starcraft cutting across our path seconds before *Quiet Contemplation* broadsided it. The impact threw me loose from the side of *Quiet Contemplation* and blowing precious air from my lungs.

"That's bad," I subvocalized. "That was a good chunk of our air supply. At least we slowed your starcraft down enough for Brennan to position between *Quiet Contemplation* and *Call to Justice*. Brennan wasn't kidding. That thing is tough."

"It is carved out of an asteroid. I can only imagine how thick its hull is."

"I think we just saved the lives of a lot of your people."

"I am very grateful for that. However, perhaps we should now be trying to find a way to save ourselves. Can you make your way back to the craft?"

"How? Doggy paddle?"

The collision had severely damaged both *Quiet Contemplation* and *Aldrin*. Pieces of both starcraft were torn loose from the impact and hurled into space. Several large and jagged pieces of metal from *Quiet Contemplation* headed our way. "Those look very sharp and we're out of options. We're going to have to 'port into *Quiet Contemplation*. At least it's close this time."

"You do not have enough energy to teleport."

"So, what's the worst that can happen? We don't go anywhere and get shredded by the metal storm headed our way?" My lungs felt like they were going to burst.

"You use up your life force and die instantly, while I am trapped in a lifeless body for the few remaining minutes it takes for that metal to reach us."

"Well, promise me you won't do anything weird with my dead body for the short time it's yours."

"I promise that you will never know if I do."

"Fair enough." I grinned. "Fuck it, I'm 'porting."

CHAPTER 53 –
WHERE THINGS GO HORRIBLY WRONG

There was the usual burning skin feeling, and I materialized in the main hangar of *Quiet Contemplation*. The explosive energy release that accompanied the teleport scorched the walls, but the jump was short enough and the hangar big enough that I only damaged the floor. I fell forward, a puppet with its strings cut as everything went black.

I woke to discover I had landed on my face. I tried to stand but my body was still not working. I was drained physically and mentally. My thoughts were in slow motion.

"KayCee." My words came out in a sort of mumble as my lips didn't want to form the words. As concerning as that was, I was more worried by the fact that the little alien that lived in my head didn't respond.

"KayCee," I subvocalized. Still nothing. This was bad. I had pushed my abilities while on empty and now I was paying for it. My powers were exhausted, and I had no control over my body. I didn't know why KayCee wasn't answering but I suspected it has something to do with 'porting on empty.

With nothing else working, I decided to try doing a mental shout. It wasn't supposed to be connected to my abilities. KayCee had always claimed any human had the potential for telepathy. Of course, my tremendous lack of skill kinda made that a lie, but I had no other tricks up my sleeve. Praying it would work, I gave the loudest mental shout I could, hoping Jeopardy would hear it. "HANGAR!"

I don't know how long I lay there before the door to the hangar opened. It had felt like eons. With tremendous effort, I was able to turn my head. Jeopardy dragged herself toward me. She looked horrible. Aside from the wound she already had during her transmission, she was pale and shaking. Her shirt was less clothing and more a mass of burn marks and blood.

"Lock!" She collapsed to her knees in front of me, coughing, her voice a wheezing shadow of how it normally sounded. "Are you okay? You look even worse than I do."

I tried to speak but failed, instead managing a blink. She cupped my face with a bloody hand. "I ran into Kreb. It was epic. I gave as well as I got, but the fucker had a ray gun.

"He got me good. I'm pretty screwed up right now. Down a lung and some other stuff. I'm telekinetically keeping my heart beating right now." She gave a ragged laugh and coughed up blood. "I'm literally keeping myself alive by sheer willpower. How badass is that?

"I think we might be screwed, Lock. Even if I had the ability, I can't even drag you to the med bay. The whole thing got destroyed in the collision. Tavish, his body. It's gone. I'm so sorry." Jeopardy suddenly stiffened, slumping over me. Her head landed next to mine, leaving us face to face. Her eyes were open, and I could see the bright light that had always been there had fled. She wasn't breathing.

I wanted to scream and rail against the injustice of it all. But I still couldn't move. In fact, if felt as if my heart was slowing down and the edges of vision was getting cloudy. I wasn't far from joining Jeopardy.

I wasn't religious by any means, but I prayed to whoever might be out there that it had all been worth it. That our deaths weren't in vain. The answer I got was like a slap in the face.

The sound wasn't very loud, but in the quietness of the hangar, it was as loud as a gunshot. I couldn't identify it at first. It repeated. There was a rhythm to it. A long, drawn-out sound, then a thump.

As I was puzzling it out, the hand of a bioform reached down and lifted Jeopardy up by the hair. The bioform studied her face for a moment and then looked down at me. "Hello, Number 12. You seemed to have really messed things up this time. I was hoping to destroy the Alliance starcraft, but you and your fellow humans have gotten in the way once more."

Kreb!

"Tell me, Number 12, why would you humans place your craft between mine and the Alliance craft? Why risk yourselves for a race you know nothing about?"

I snapped back to alertness and tried to leap up and attack him. All I accomplished was my body rocked slightly. Though, I may have just imagined that.

Kreb smiled and looked back at Jeopardy. "This one was impressive. Her telekinetic abilities far outstripped anything my people have ever been able to accomplish. If I had the time, I would have liked to have studied her brain, but you and your friends have disturbed my plans again. It really is a knack with you."

He casually tossed Jeopardy away like a discarded toy, revealing that she had gotten her licks in. His right arm had been torn out at the shoulder and the exterior of his bioform was covered in damage. Long tears in the skin seeped a white, milky liquid. His skull was deformed, and his right eye was gone. I had never been prouder of anyone then I was of Jeopardy at that moment. She had straight up fucked him up.

Kreb stared down at me again as he unhooked a device from his utility belt. "Yes, I can imagine what you are thinking. My bioform is severely damaged, again. But as usual, I do have a plan. One you will not like."

He waved the device over me and tilted his head as he studied the read out. "Well, this *is* interesting. You have managed to drain all but the last vestiges of energy within you. And according to this, you actually used the life force of Protector KayserCeenarlos to power your teleport. That is impressively ruthless. I must say I did not believe you had it within you."

Oh God! I killed KayCee!

"Though knowing the protector, this was more likely her sacrificing herself to save you." He reattached the device to his belt. "While it means I do not have to go through the trouble of extracting her from you before I take you over, I will admit I was looking forward to absorbing her life energy. I have developed such a taste for it over the past year."

The red motes, the energy force that made up Kreb, started to exit through the bioform's skin. But this wasn't the same angry red cloud of energy I had seen before. It was much more massive, and as it left, the damaged bioform fell to the floor, the one remaining arm draped over me.

The cloud continued to slowly exit. When it was finally free, it was three times Kreb's normal size and absolutely terrifying. A small shock from the bioform's arm jolted me from watching him. One of the open tears rested directly on me, and it obviously had the alien equivalent of a loose wire.

It wasn't much, about as painful as licking a battery. Still, it gave me a little bit of hope. I attempted to absorb it but couldn't even activate my power to do so.

Crap!

I tried again, straining with all my might. Something...tore... and I grew fainter, falling into darkness.

This is what it's like to die.

There was a pulse. A blip of energy. But it was enough to pull me back. I hungrily drank in the slender trickle of energy. My vision and the ability to think came back. I had used the last of my life force to trigger my energy absorption ability. What little energy I was able to gather from the bioform was enough to walk me back from the brink.

The angry red cloud hung over me for a second and then plunged down. I reached up as if I could stop it, my hand plunging into the motes of energy that made up the cloud.

Kreb's voice in my head was different then KayCee's. It had a cold vibration to it that was painful.

"After the collision, I did not think I would survive this, which is why I primed the engines to overload. After all, If I was finally going to die, I planned to take as many of you with me as I could. Neither this starcraft nor the human starcraft would have survived. I might have even taken out the Sarli as well.

"But thanks to you, things have changed. I will now power down the engines and pretend to be you, slipping away as always. I haven't decided if I will let you live on as my slave or — What? What are you doing?"

"Destroying you," I said as I sat up, my hand still extended. "It's your idea, really. You gloating about KayCee clued me in."

"Stop it."

"It never dawned on me, really." I was feeling stronger, my head clearing up. "Don't know how I missed it before. I mean, when you're in your energy form, you are just that... energy."

"No!"

"As you were quick to tell me, I have the ability to absorb energy." Kreb tried to pull away from me, but I wouldn't let him. "I almost couldn't have pulled this off. I was completely tapped out. But I was able to drawn enough power from your damaged bioform to activate my energy absorption ability."

"I will not die like this. You are a mere human. You will not be the one to kill me."

"Kill you?" I stood up, standing completely within his energy field. "This isn't me killing you. You're not worth killing. No, you're a fucking happy meal and the prize at the end is you'll be completely destroyed, and I'll be powered up by doing it."

I continued to absorb his energy, his cloud of angry red motes getting smaller and smaller as I ignored his mental wails of anguish and pain.

An explosion rocked the craft, knocking me off my feet. Another followed right behind it, and sections of the ceiling crashed down. Gaping holes opened in the floor decking.

Tossed about, I lost my grip on Kreb's remaining energy. What was left of him was roughly the size of a golf ball, which flitted through the wreckage before I could recapture it.

"Damn it."

As much as I wanted to go after him, it seemed we ran the clock out on the engines overloading. I went to retrieve Jeopardy's body, but I couldn't find it. I scrambled through the debris and smoke looking for her when an emergency alarm assaulted my senses.

"Knight One to Janitor, come in." I clicked on my comm as I sifted through pieces trying to find Jeopardy.

"Go ahead."

"Are you and Risk okay?" the colonel asked.

"She's dead. He fucking killed her." I threw a hunk of metal twice my size to the side, Jeopardy wasn't under it.

"Damn. I'm so sorry, Lock. But you need to get out of there. Readings are showing your starcraft is going critical, we have to pull away. Get out of there."

"I have to find her body first. I lost it in the explosion."

"I'm sorry about that, I really am. But you need to leave, now!" Brennan ordered.

"No, I owe it to her and her family."

"Have KayCee dampen your emotions-- you're in shock."

"She's gone too," I choked out.

"What? How? Never mind, tell me later. Lock, turn your emotions off."

"No, I have to find Jeopardy."

Tavish broke in. "Lock, Stella is in a lander headed your way."

"What? No! Wave her off," I yelled.

"If you don't leave now, she said she's going to land and drag you off by your beard."

"Tavish... your body..."

"It doesn't matter. Get out of there," my cousin begged. "If you stay, you'll end up killing both you and Stella."

"Fuck!" I picked up a small shard of metal and gave a final look around, hoping to spot Jeopardy. I didn't. "Jumping now, Get everyone clear."

I 'ported.

Chapter 54 –
Family Lies

"You lied to me." I stared down at the medical pod Stella was in.

"Yes," Tavish replied. A lot had happened since I had teleported back. This was the first time I had both the free time and the privacy to have this discussion with my cousin. This was a family matter.

The distance between the *New Hampshire* and *Quiet Contemplation* had widened after I had initially 'ported over there. If I had done a single jump back to the *New Hampshire,* the discharge of energy would have seriously damaged the interior of the starcraft, and I would not have survived it. Instead, using the shard I had picked up to transform my exterior to metal, I did a series of small teleports across the distance between the two starcraft. It had been like skimming a stone across a pond.

Since then, a lot had happened. At the last second, Tavish was able to use *Quiet Contemplation's* control orb to shut down the engines and prevent it from being completely destroyed. The starcraft was extremely damaged though, and would have to be towed back to *Diana* for a nuts-to-bolts examination to see if it was salvageable.

Brennan and SoCuasatine had a big powwow with Itza, who unbeknownst to me had been on the *Aldrin*. Our saving *Call to Justice* and her crew had lent us a lot of goodwill with SoCuasatine. Itza vouching for us was icing on the cake.

The Sarli ceded ownership of *Quiet Contemplation* and the *New Hampshire* to us in exchange for us forgiving her government for siphoning from our sun without permission. The fact that *Quiet Contemplation* was a wreck, and they couldn't take *New Hampshire* away from us with their own damaged starcraft probably had something to do with it. I wasn't sure the rest of the countries of Earth would be happy when this deal came out, but that was someone else's problem.

I hadn't realized I had lapsed into thought until Tavish roused me out of it. "It was the only way I could get you to leave the starcraft. No matter how upset you were, you wouldn't put Stella in harm's way."

"I understand the reasoning."

"You seem very calm about this, Lock. Did the med staff give you something?"

"No, nothing they have would probably work on me. I shut down my emotions."

"You can do that?"

"KayCee had showed me how. It just took some practice to finally be able to do it on my own. It's similar to combat mode, but without the autopilot aspect. Makes it a lot easier to control my abilities too. My issues with control may have just been down to nerves."

"That's weird and frankly doesn't sound healthy. What did SoCuasatine's people say about KayCee?"

"They believe she sacrificed herself in order to for me to make the jump. She's being honored by them as a hero who gave her life to save the crew of *Call to Justice*."

"You disagree?" Tavish's tone was mild, aimed at not setting me off. He might as well not have bothered. I was beyond feeling anything.

"I think I drained her dry making a jump to save Jeopardy. A task I failed miserably at."

"That's not true."

"You'd know about things not being true, wouldn't you," I said. "You and KayCee lied about how bad Stella's injuries are. The medical experts of three different races don't know if she'll recover."

"I'm sorry, but we needed your head in the game. You completely lost it when Stella went down. We couldn't risk that happening again during the mission."

"And what about the part where you lied about being able to be put back into your body?"

"That was on me. KayCee wanted to tell you, but I talked her out of it. Since it was my body, she agreed. We had spent the last year trying to get me back into it. For the exact same reasons I lied about Stella, I didn't tell you about KayCee being unsuccessful in placing me back in my body."

"What was the problem?"

"When I transferred my consciousness out of my body, the process fried my brain and nervous system. Me saving myself killed my body more effectively then Kreb ever did."

"I'm sorry, Tavish. That had to have been hard to hear."

"Little bit. But hey, we always knew it was a longshot. But don't worry about it. I have some out-of-the-box ideas on what to do next. Short term, the Sarli are going to help transfer me into a robot. I'm still trying to figure out a design. I'm leaning toward Johnny 5."

"They can't make it look human?"

"Probably, but that's boring. You know what's the weirdest thing about all this. I keep craving a bacon cheeseburger. I don't have taste buds, but I want a bacon cheeseburger so bad." He chuckled. "Don't tell my mom."

"Did you hear about what they're planning?" I turned away from Stella's med pod and stared out the window of the med bay. *Quiet Contemplation* floated in the distance. The fires had finally gone out due to all the oxygen being used up. A search for Kreb was scheduled, but the Sarli think he perished being outside a body for so long. I knew better. He was a cockroach. He always survived.

"No, what are they planning?"

"They want us to go to this Space United Nations thing."

"Oh, yeah. I did hear a little bit. It had a weird name, didn't it?"

"The Celestial Moot. Many of the spacefaring races belong to it. They meet every couple of years to hash out problems. The Detra Ka joined a few years ago, and SoCuasatine thinks Itza should go to the next one and try to settle her differences with her mother."

"The one who tried to kill her and steal her planet? Oh yeah, that should go great. Why do they want us there?"

"Both SoCuasatine and Itza think we should petition for membership," I told him.

"Isn't that jumping the gun? Very few people on the planet even know there are other life forms out there, much less be in consensus about joining them."

"Not the entire planet. They want the United States to join. Unlike on most sci-fi shows, turns out many alien worlds have more than one government. I was told it's actually rare for an entire planet to join as a whole. Even if the US doesn't want to join, they've asked for you and me to go."

"Why?" asked Tavish in a suspicious tone.

"A couple of reasons. SoCuasatine wants to honor all of us for what we did, and they also want you and me to tell of our experiences with Kreb. Plus, there's the whole reward thing."

"What good is space dollars?" Tavish asked. "Besides, what do I need any type of money for. Not like I have pockets."

"A lot of different races will be there. All different levels of technology. Maybe someone can fix your situation."

"Okay, That's a bit intriguing. When's the next Moot thing?"

"There's one coming up in a few weeks but obviously we couldn't make it in time. So, the powers that be are shooting for the next one. Which is good. I need to speak with Jeopardy's family and see to Stella. Plus, the Space Force needs time to prepare. Repair our current starcraft and expand our numbers. Brennan is already talking about reverse engineering *New Hampshire* and rolling out some Battlestars."

"They're keeping that term?" Tavish asked, surprised.

"I guess a couple of the generals were fans of the original series." I rubbed my eyes. "Anyways, Brennan has already been picked to lead the group going to the Celestial Moot."

"That was fast. The battle was less than forty-eight hours ago."

"He already has a working relationship with Itza and SoCuasatine, and both requested him. It makes sense." I shrugged. "Are you going to go?"

"I don't know." There was hesitation in Tavish's voice. "It depends."

"On what?"

"Brennan asked me to assume Jeopardy's mission. I'd like to finish it first."

I frowned. "Her mission? It has something to do with the people Kreb abducted, right?"

"How do you know that?"

"Something Jeopardy said when she found out Calvin and Rory's names. That she had been looking for them. What's the mission?"

"I'm not supposed to say."

"Tavish!"

"Fine, but you didn't hear it from me. We're trying to locate them and any of their adult children."

"To recruit?"

"Yeah," Tavish admitted. "They need to do it before other countries learn of us."

"We're the new arms race."

"Yeah, sorry."

"It is what it is."

"So, are you going to this Moot thing?" Tavish finally asked.

"Yes." Unbidden, my left hand curled into a fist. "I can't stay on Earth."

"Because you want to explore the stars?"

"Because Kreb finally escaped from Earth and he's out there." I nodded out the window. "My parents, Jeopardy, your body, and Stella. All of that is his fault. I'm going to track him down. He's not going to get away with everything he's done."

"Then what? Turn him over to the Moot thingy?"

My fist slammed into the wall, leaving an imprint of my knuckles deep into the metal.

"Lock?"

"Then I'm going to kill him."

THE END

Acknowledgements

I'd like to thank Megan Harris, who made the rough edges smoother. I'd also like to thank Lane Diamond (Publisher), Robb Grindstaff (Editor), and Kris Norris (Cover Artist) at Evolved Publishing.

And as always, this could not have been done without my beta readers:
Police Sergeant and Former Marine Corporal Jay Levasseur
Colonel Joseph R. Freitas (USAF Retired)
Former USAF Staff Sergeant Aaron Kinder
Keith "The Civilian" Berube
Author Extraordinaire Rachel Carr

About the Author

CIBA award winner Jack Cullen is a veteran, attorney, and police captain. An amateur barstool philosopher, he rarely tells his stories the same way twice.

Jack lives in New England with his family and a small horde of pets. His various adventures include waking up in the wrong country, being chased by jackals in Pakistan, floating through the Mayan underworld in an inner tube, and almost being run over by a supertanker while sailing across the Gulf of Mexico. When not writing, he can be found traveling around in a 1956 Willys Wagon called *The Professor*.

For more, please visit Jack Cullen online at:
Website: www.JackCullenWrites.com
Goodreads: Jack Cullen
Facebook: @JackCullenBooks
Instagram: @JackCullenBooks
Twitter: @JackCullenBooks

More from Evolved Publishing

We offer great books across multiple genres, featuring high-quality editing (which we believe is second-to-none) and fantastic covers.

As a hybrid small press, your support as loyal readers is so important to us, and we have strived, with tireless dedication and sheer determination, to deliver on the promise of our motto:

QUALITY IS PRIORITY #1!

Please check out all of our great books,
which you can find at this link:

www.EvolvedPub.com/Catalog/

Thank you!

Milton Keynes UK
Ingram Content Group UK Ltd.
UKHW042110131124
451149UK00006B/783